THE
SCORE

THE
SCORE

H. J. Golakai

Abuja – London

Hawa Jande Golakai is a German-born Liberian and a medical immunologist by training. She writes from her experiences as a refugee, scientist and contemporary nomad, a life that has fostered an intense passion for crime and twisted fiction. Hawa was listed by the Hay Festival in the Africa39 list of the most promising sub-Saharan African writers under the age of 40. She was the winner of the 2017 Brittle Paper Award for nonfiction and longlisted for the 2019 NOMMO Award for speculative fiction. Currently, she lives with her son between Monrovia and anywhere she finds herself.

First published in 2019 by Cassava Republic Press
Abuja – London
First published in the USA in 2020 by Cassava Republic Press

A CIP catalogue record for this book is available from the National Library
of Nigeria and the British Library.

Nigerian ISBN: 978-978-55979-8-7
UK ISBN: 978-1-911115-39-7
eISBN: 978-1-911115-40-3

Book design by AI's Fingers
Cover & Art Direction by Michael Salu

Printed and bound in Great Britain by Clays Ltd, Elcograf S.p.A.

Distributed in Nigeria by Yellow Danfo
Distributed in the UK by Central Books Ltd.
Distributed in the US by Consortium Book Sales & Distribution

Stay up to date with the latest books, special offers and
exclusive content with our monthly newsletter.

Sign up on our website:
www.cassavarepublic.biz

Twitter: @cassavarepublic
Instagram: @cassavarepublicpress
Facebook: facebook.com/CassavaRepublic
Hashtag: #TheScore #ReadCassava

To my Squad: family, friends, fans. Una insah, una know!

Prologue

Dawn sneaked up out of nowhere. Across the grass, patches of morning gold swelled and merged, inching over the dewy lawn. Blinking as rays striped across her face, Vee swallowed hard and picked up the pace.

She squatted and examined the dead man's feet. His shoes were relatively clean, except for discs of dried mud and grass caked to the back of the soles. Flecks of mud spattered the bottom inch of his trousers. She leaned closer and snapped a picture with her Samsung. Gingerly, the phone pinched between two fingers, she inched up the cuff and peered up his leg.

A flurry of gasps came from behind her, making her jump.

'Hhayi, wenza ntoni!' Zintle yelped.

'You flippin' crazy?' Chlöe said.

'Y'all got a better idea?' Vee hissed over her shoulder.

Huddled like lovers, Chlöe and Zintle shook their heads and wild-eyed her in silence, ample bosoms undulating in unison. Zintle tightened her grip on Chlöe's arm, chunky fingers digging trenches of red into Chlöe's milky skin.

'We're not supposed to touch anything. And you're touching things!'

'Dammit Bishop, I touched one thing! Can you shhh for a second and let me think!'

Vee wobbled getting to her feet and made a grab for a handhold. Her hand met nothing but air until it brushed against the dead man's leg. The body, strung by the neck to the coat hook, took up a gentle pendulous swing, the fabric of the man's jeans and leather of his shoes making a low, eerie rasp against the grainy concrete wall. Chlöe and Zintle shrieked and leapt

1

away. Vee toppled onto her butt, scrabbling in the gravel until she regained her footing and scurried over to them. Together, the circle heaved in harmony.

'I've never seen a dead person before,' Chlöe whispered. 'No, I mean I've seen a normal dead person before. At a couple of funerals, when they're clean and stuffed and made-up. But not like this.' Knuckles to her cheek, she moved her hand in frantic circles against her skin, a sure sign she was freaking out. 'Not, like, a brutal murder.'

'Mtshhhw,' Vee sucked her teeth derisively. 'Dah whetin you call *a brutal murder?* Is it anything like a very orange orange?'

'Ag, man.' Chlöe rolled her eyes. 'I mean... you know...'

'I've been to hundreds of funerals.' Zintle breathed with her mouth open. This was clearly a new one for her too.

'Exactly. Who's seen this kinda thing happen every day?'

Vee clenched her jaw, but held her tongue. In her lifetime, more recently than she cared to recall, she'd seen far too many abnormally dead people. Shot, hacked, diseased, starved... And once, bloated flesh piled high enough to darken the horizon of her young mind for months, years even. In comparison, this hapless soul had gone with reasonable dignity.

She averted her eyes, her heart reaching up her chest like a witch's claw, her throat squeezing shut. Now was not the time to indulge her acute phobia of dead bodies by losing her cool. The dangling man had her property. Every time she peeked, and she was really fighting not to, her eyes were drawn to his neck. His neck, a swollen, bruised pipe wrapped in the purple fabric of her silk scarf. Her flesh tingled and shrank, drawing her face tight. If there was ever a time to think clearly and quickly, this was it.

Neither was happening.

'Why isn't anyone coming? Why the hell is it taking so long?' Chlöe whined.

Zintle turned her back to the hanging man. 'They're coming.

We called them, so they should be here soon. But you're right, it's taking forever.' Eyes fixed to the gravel, she smoothed down the front of her maid's uniform and shuffled her feet. 'I want to leave this place.'

Chlöe's face softened. 'It's cool if you want to go back to reception. We can all wait there.' Vee whipped her a withering look. 'But you know what, let's all hang around a bit longer. Please. It'll look weird to the cops if we're left alone with him, when we're the ones...'

Vee launched another eye, sharper still. Chlöe fell silent, gnawing at her lips.

If Vee knew anything well, it was how the police worked. Their situation was bad enough already. Why escalate it from strange to outright damning, which sure as hell would happen when the police found out exactly which guests were present when the body was found? The less incriminating she looked, the better.

'I can't keep working here any more,' Zintle elaborated. 'Too much bad luck.'

Vee softened, too. The last 48 hours had been rough on all of them, but Zintle had borne the brunt. If she heard the phrase "excelling outside of one's job description" ever again, she would think of none other than the maid from The Grotto Lodge.

Zintle's face contorted. 'Ugghhnn, I feel sick.' She doubled over, clutching her stomach.

Chlöe's horror magnified. 'Sies man, don't throw up.' She rubbed a soothing hand over Zintle's back. 'If I see or even hear someone throw up, it makes me sick too.'

'I... uuggghhnn... won't vomit...' Zintle compelled herself, gulping in air.

'Oi! Can you not say "vomit" either? It's not helping.'

Vee edged closer. The man's eyes were shut, tiny slats of his whites just visible when she crouched. She'd always thought the

3

standard expression of a strangled person was one of bulging, terrified eyes, shot through with harried blood vessels. Rictus grimace, drooping tongue. Nothing like that here. Facial muscles slack, expression... not peaceful, or particularly anything for that matter. Just gone.

She sucked in a deep breath, clamped her airways and crept even closer. Once upon a time in a faraway lab somewhere, supernerds had taken time to deduce that the human soul allegedly weighed 21 grams. They probably hadn't bothered identifying its odour, or they'd have made notes on how different the human body smelled after death. Not decay, exactly; this man had been gone a matter of mere hours. Yet, there was that subtle yet unmistakable turn after the flesh and spirit parted ways, the most repulsive aspect of the thing. She stared at the noose of silk around the man's neck, throbbing alternately with regret and shame for feeling such regret.

'Don't even think about it.'

Vee whipped around. Eyes narrowed, Chlöe was staring her down over the head of a heaving Zintle, now snuggled against her chest.

'I wasn't,' Vee snapped. Maybe a tiny, foolish part of her was. But if she removed the scarf... hide it where? And explain the lack of a murder weapon how? Massive shitstorm potential. She flung Chlöe an equally fierce look in reply and turned back to scrutinise the body.

The scarf had been knotted twice, then twisted completely along the length of the man's windpipe. The noose closed in a third knot at the back of the head, where the loose material had been fashioned into a loop of sorts, easily slung over a worthy hook. Under the dead man's substantial weight, the craftsmanship of the coatrack was literally holding up. The tips of the man's shoes barely touched the ground. Breath held again, Vee zoomed her Samsung's camera and took a close-up of the garrotte. She stared at it for a long time.

A triangular tip of white poking out of his trousers caught the corner of her eye. She exhaled shakily. A furtive peep over her shoulder ran smack into Chlöe's glare, drilling a hole through the back of her head. Throwing a puppy-eyed plea, Vee deftly plucked the object from the man's pocket and stuck it in hers. She turned her back on Chlöe's widening eyes and frantic head-shaking.

'They're here,' she said.

Three older men who were clearly officers, flanked by two strapping groundsmen in blue jumpsuits, trudged across the lawn. The groundsmen looked as excited as they had two hours earlier, when they'd come across the florid-faced white man strung up outside their workroom door. They hung back with a couple of the officers, hands flying as they retold what Vee knew was a colourful extrapolation of a story they'd told several times already. The last of the group, hard-faced and decked in a trench coat that was absurd considering the growing morning heat, made a beeline for them.

A crowd of gawkers, guests and staff from the lodge was in full fluster by the time the officers were done with their preliminary questioning. A single crime scene technician, whom Vee had anticipated would be an entire team working with scientific flourish, simply clicked away at different angles on a basic Kodak and cut the body down. Another stab twisted under her ribs as the massive pair of scissors worked through her scarf.

Chlöe sighed. 'I feel cheated after all these years of watching *CSI*. We could've done that. Well, not take the body down *ourselves*, but…'

Vee tuned out. The best bit was kicking off. The cops formed a scrum of whispers for what felt like forever. They pulled Zintle, sobbing by now, aside. Head down with hands clamped under her armpits, she seemed to be speaking in fits and bursts. She shook her head and shrugged a lot. As the probing wore on, she stole guilty glances over her shoulder at Vee and Chlöe. One of the cops sneaked a comforting arm around her shoulder and leered down the front of her uniform. Finally, Hardface Trench, who was clearly the officer in charge, broke the huddle and set about creating another expert beeline. He had thrown off the coat, revealing a crisp blue shirt and pants of a brown so similar to his complexion that from afar he looked naked from the waist down.

"Ohhh Gooood, the main guy's coming…' Chlöe groaned. Vee steeled her spine and calibrated her facial expression to concerned but oblivious. In the pockets of her jeans, her fingers trembled as they stroked the rectangle of paper.

'What's your name, ma'am?' Hardface scowled in Vee's direction, not once glancing at Chlöe.

'Voinjama Johnson.' She let him blink, purse his lips, mouth the name soundlessly many times as he scribbled in a battered notebook, and offered no help. She wondered what highly revised version he wrote down. Probably just Johnson; most people went with Johnson.

'It's my understanding you know this man.'

'No, I don't.'

'Hhhmmph. He's one…' He squinted, flipping at leisure through the notebook.

'Gavin Berman,' Vee blurted.

Hardface stopped and raised his head very slowly. 'You just said you didn't know him.'

'You asked if I knew him, not if I knew his name.'

The policeman's head reared a barely perceptible inch as his eyes hardened. His body language computed a rapid adjustment from the easy way to the hard way, now clearly the only option on offer. 'Eh-hehhh. So you're being clever? Would you mind coming with me so long? So we can work out how everyone here knows everyone else, which you seem to know a lot about.'

He swung his arm out, as if to shepherd her along the path.

Neither Vee nor Chlöe – crowded to her back like a duckling to its mother – fell in step with him. The arm dropped. He flicked his head in the direction of the hotel's front entrance and abruptly strode off, a click of his tongue punching the air.

'Find Lovett Massaquoi *now*. Start with the room of that blonde he came with, then his,' Vee whispered to Chlöe. 'I doubt they've left yet. And call Nico.'

'I thought we weren't calling Nico!' Chlöe looked like she was about to cry.

'Change of plans,' Vee muttered. '*Go*.'

Shifting of Shape

1

Vee bit into the guava, spat out the brown bits and popped the rest in her mouth. A welcome breeze ruffled her hair. Lifting both arms, she made a disgusted face as the material of her blouse smeared against moist armpits.

'Wheh de hell dis child at?' she muttered, swinging the front gate back and forth. Waves of heat shimmered off the tarmac of the deserted street. Tiny lasers of sunshine drilled into her scalp and corneas. 'Twinkie!'

Nothing but another gust of air. 'Tristan Heaney! For God's sake, if I—'

'Right behind you.'

Vee jumped, closed her eyes and took a deep breath. Perhaps it wasn't such a bad idea that more African countries had laws protecting minors from corporal punishment. Because this lil' pekin was going the right way...

'Told you I was getting an ice lolly. Why you all yelling in the street and acting country?' Tristan grinned and brushed a wheat-blond fringe off his forehead as he tore the wrapper off the frozen treat.

Vee bit back a smile. 'If you're trying to imitate me, you sound like a moron. It's "ackin kuntry". And you shouldn't be shopping for goodies on your employer's time. Get to work.'

'I needed sugar for the trip.' He chomped into a lolly of the most unnatural green – she could only describe it as radioactive lime – and held it out. 'Want some?'

'No, keep your diseased ice cream. Didn't I tell you to stop buying from that nasty shop, before you go catchin' sum'n?' Tristan shrugged and carried on chomping. Vee shook her head. At his age, food from a sparkling supermarket or the creepy kiosk down the road was all the same. Another child headed down the highway to street-food hell. She was hardly one to judge.

'You sound like my mum. Only old people have to eat properly because it's good for their health.' He tipped his chin at the bulging bag looped over a slat of her picket fence. 'That's why I brought you those.'

'Very delicious, thank you.' Vee took another guava from the plastic shopper. 'Never seen the white ones before, though. And guava jam! That's sum'n else.'

'Mum makes it herself. Since Dad died...' Tristan averted his eyes and concentrated on the lolly, 'she does stuff like make jam.'

Vee nodded. All she knew about her young neighbour, she knew via her landlady Mrs Konstantinou, omniscient of all things concerning Leicester Street. Tristan's father had died of cancer a year ago, and the happy unit of four that occupied the cream-and-olive house on the corner had shrunk to three. More like two, since Tristan's elder brother, a UCT student, only dropped by on the odd weekend. The mother was an executive in something or other and hadn't returned to work. The woman barely opened the door to anyone, but seemed to trust Vee with her younger son.

'Well, thanks. I'll pass by later to thank your ma myself.'

'Cool. I like your thank yous. Will you bring that fried banana and ginger stuff you made last time?'

'It's called kili-wili, and it's plantain not banana. Now come on.' Vee prised the ice from his fingers and stuck her palm to his forehead to restrain him as he flailed for it. 'Una heah to run your mouf.'

Tristan backed out of reach, face souring. 'You're grumpy today.'

'Mssh. Move from heah.'

'Yes, you are. Your accent goes crazy when you're angry. And how come you're home in the middle of the day?'

'How come *you* home?'

'It's school holidays. Schoolkids are *supposed to be home* during school holidays.'

Vee opened her mouth and then shut it. Across the street, a silver Opel reversed into a space between two other cars. Her jaw clenched.

'Your friend's here. She looks pissed.'

'Yes, BBC Claremont. Thanks for the update.'

She flicked his ear, and he grinned and ducked into the yard. Vee watched, touched by the seriousness with which he readied himself for his task, retrieving a leash dangling from a mulberry branch, dusting off a raggedy ball and favourite chew toy from the lawn. He whistled and patted his thigh a few times. A large black Alaskan husky bounded through the back door, leapt over the veranda stairs and made towards him like a rocket.

'Uh-uh-uh,' Tristan chided, laughing and thumping his thighs some more. 'Sit.' He clicked his fingers and repeated the command. A little crushed but not thwarted, the dog obeyed, barking and wagging his tail ferociously.

She pursed her lips and folded her arms. Monro was trained to answer only to her commands. 'Since when you taught him that? Look, don't go teaching my dog all kinda kata-kata. That's outside the confines of your job description.'

'Huh?' Tristan frowned. 'Speak *English*.'

'Am I interrupting something?'

Vee tipped her chin at Chlöe, acknowledging her presence, and turned back to Tristan. 'Look, walk him, bring him home.

No extras today. Be back here by...' she glanced at her watch, 'one. Latest one thirty. And stay within the neighbourhood. What's rule number one?'

'Unaccompanied little boys are like candy for paedophiles,' Tristan droned.

'Exactly. You already a paedo lollipop with that blond hair and weird eyes. Don't be friendly to nobody. And rule number two?'

'Stay within our grid at all times. Ugh, why do I have to? No one kidnaps kids in this part of town, and I'm not a baby.' Tristan rolled his eyes.

'Baby or not. I spoke to your mother, we agreed, so that's how things stay.' Tristan was always pushing boundaries, in the vain hope she'd either trust him to roam the streets unmonitored or relax the perimeter they'd established. 'You're allowed to walk five blocks in any direction, and then turn around and bring your lil' narrow butt right back. If you go past Rosebank, you're too far out. If you reach Kenilworth Centre, you're too far—'

'Ag, that's not off the grid, it's only four from this direction!'

'Fineboy, I don't care. You want dis money heah or not?' Vee waved the cash, half his weekly wage.

'Fine. I'll just take him to the stupid park,' he grumbled. Like other small, clean and safe parks in the southern suburbs, Arderne Gardens off Main Road cramped Tristan's style, but it was a setting they agreed on. It was animal-friendly, green and boringly safe. The wildest he could get was letting Monro off his leash to harass the ducks while the lazy security guards turned a blind eye. 'That better be the full amount, with a tip for the extra weekend I came *and* walking him outside my usual working hours,' Tristan groused.

'Scram, you lil'—' Vee lunged to cuff him again and Tristan sprinted, Monro bounding through the gate after him. 'And you better get a haircut with that money! Mttsshw. Lookin' like a ghetto Justin Bieber.'

'How much time do you spend weekly arguing with an eight-year-old?' said Chlöe.

'Dah child gon send me grey.' Vee sank into a lawn chair and reached across the wicker table to refresh her mango juice, spiked with vodka. 'You know full well he's eleven. He's small for his age.' She avoided Chlöe's scowl and sipped. 'So what brings you to these parts?'

'Don't even. You barge out of the office in the middle of the day and come home, the next likely thing is I follow the first chance I get to find out what happened. Plus you broke every working woman's cardinal rule and cried at work.'

'*I damn well did not cry.*'

'Damn near. And I know you're gonna make Nico pay for that. The entire office is gossiping about it. Must you always butt heads with the powers that be? Didn't you have enough of that with Portia? You trying to get fired?' Chlöe took a breath. 'What happened?'

Fighting for you is what happened. Vee took another gulp of juice. Burped. Began...

———

'Ah, Johnson. Glad you could join me.'

Rifling through the filing cabinet opposite his desk, Nico van Wyk didn't turn or look up. 'Seat,' he pointed. Vee toyed with the idea of declining like a badass, thought better of it and sat. Nico towered almost two full heads over her and though his temperament was closer to a surly simmer than full-on belligerence, she'd seen him lose it a few times, *really* flip his shit, leaving underlings cowering on the brink of tears. Male underlings. Best not rock the boat.

He pulled a sheet from a folder and sank into his armchair. He vigorously massaged his face with both hands before dragging them over his head of dark blonde hair, buzzed short to downplay the balding dome on top. Deep-set, grey-green eyes that saved his face from being plain were rimmed faintly red.

He cupped his hands at the back of his neck and stared. Vee let him. Van Wyk was a consummate eyeballer; it seemed to temper his mind and mood. She waited it out, bouncing the tips of her heeled sandals against the floor.

'Okay, here's the thing,' he smacked a palm on the desk, 'and it's a lot of things. Saskia can't stand you. You're not madly in love with her either. She says you have authority issues and give way too much backchat. Her major gripe is you're mucking about with the online team, making it hard for her to do her job. Why can't you learn to stay out of her way? You've been here over a year. You should have the hang of it by now.'

Vee sighed. 'I'm not meddling. Not exactly. It's just .... Saskia's full of wahala. She's more concerned with running us and making sure everybody knows she's the office manager than quality output. Who cares if I help Darren and them? They're understaffed.'

'Februarie and the online guys were aces before you came, all things considered.'

'They're not. What things considered? We're a small newspaper with a tiny staff and if we all stuck strictly to our job descriptions, we'd sink within six months.'

'I know how badly you want to be part of the online team.'

'No, not particularly,' she lied reflexively. 'Okay yes, particularly. And that's part of my problem with Saskia. And working at *Urban*. You and Portia Kruger made a lot of promises to me and Chlöe, promises you're not keeping. Saskia's *style*, if I can call it that, is turning underlings into toilet paper. And Chlöe may be a junior but *that*, she is not. Hell, she even helps out on the Afrikaans editorial.'

'Does she now?'

'Yes! She's half Afrikaans but grew up mostly English. She learnt by pushing herself out of her comfort zone. Plus she studied languages at UCT. You know all this. Bishop is no typical boarie-missy.'

'Boeremeisie,' Nico corrected. He rubbed his eyes again. 'Listen, you're good, I can't argue with you there. Even with the liberties you take, like commandeering an office for yourself instead of sticking to the newsroom like everyone's supposed to.'

'I didn't commandeer, I borrowed an unused space.' She deeply missed having a real office, with a real desk, a sprawl of polished wood on which to dump assignments and empty mugs to her heart's content. And her old rooftop view, of downtown Cape Town and the Absa head-office building. *The Chronicle's* newsroom had an allure of the old guard, one she was over. 'I need a place to think,' she insisted.

'Use the inside of your skull. At work, unfortunately, one must learn to play with the other children. No self-respecting journalist hates a newsroom. And Chlöe…' He leaned in, raised both eyebrows and shook his head. The pink streaks under his eyes looked angrier up close. *You watch yourself there*, his look said. Vee clenched her teeth but said nothing. It was hard to argue Bishop's case when her performance barely spoke for itself.

'Is that all?'

'Oudtshoorn.'

'Hehn?'

'Oudtshoorn. You know where that is?'

Vee flicked through her mental archive. 'Mossel Bay?'

'Further. Out in the south-western Cape, Klein Karoo country. The Grotto Lodge is a two-star establishment out there, and they're gunning for their third this year. They put on their best face when we hosted the 2010 World Cup last year, and still didn't get it. They're not giving up this year, and that means all the stellar reviews they can get.'

He pushed over a thin manila folder, opened to a brightly

coloured pamphlet. 'Looks nice enough. Apparently it was a hotspot during the soccer, though why anyone would want to be marooned on any stretch of the Garden Route when it was pissing down at kick-off last June is beyond me. Bloody tourists…' Sighing, he rubbed his eyes hard enough to wrinkle his forehead. 'It's gone up in the revolving door ratings with the number of tourists and ministers' wives that have been passing through. If they need more positive spin, it can't hurt. They get publicity, we get advertising.'

She looked over the leaflet. Adorning the front was a hulking, rustic building of indeterminate architectural style squatting among some dusty boulders. "Quaint" was the first word that leapt off the blurb inside. She closed it. The look she shot him was a mixture of "I'm not following you" and "I am, but you can't be serious".

Van Wyk looked weary. 'Look, you know Lynne's on maternity leave. Again. She's all we've got on travel and tourism right now. The column can't marinate till she gets back. It needs wrapping up.'

'And who say I know about travel writing? Ahn know nuttin about it o, I beg you. I can't even whip up a dozen synonyms for "picturesque".'

He nearly smiled this time. 'It's a tad more involved than that.'

'I'm sure it is. Give it to someone who knows that.' She opened the folder, didn't know why she had, and slapped it closed. 'Why can't somebody from the arts and entertainment page handle it?'

'Because we're stretched that tight.' He paused. 'You're well aware how it's been finding capable free hands around here since we had to downsize, here and at *Urban*. You and Tinker Bell can step up for this.' He coughed. 'Sorry, that came out wrong. I'm confident you two can handle this.'

'So…' Vee blinked. '*This* you're volunteering me for. Yet you

17

bar me from the crime desk full-time. The job I was promised.'
She was whining but she couldn't help it. Khaya Simelane and
Andrew Barrow, autocrats of the crime page, had done a stellar
job pissing on their tree to keep her out. 'Even after all my
courses on web media and editing, which I put to good use
every day. Even though Darren needs and appreciates my help.
I still can't *join* the online team despite it being more popular
than print, or even contribute my two cents without issues.
Because of Saskia.' *Your top spy. Who you're sleeping with, on top
of your liquor problem. Hell, I wouldn't be surprised if your drinking
problem is because of her.* Vee ground her lips shut between her
teeth.

'It's complicated. Yes, I fully appreciate how empty that
sounds but—'

'I know. It's an emergency. Isn't it always.'

Van Wyk eyeballed her, no reply. She nodded, took the
folder and got up. 'Hang on.' He steepled his fingers and eyed
the ceiling, as if toying with an idea. 'I've been meaning to, and
I guess now's as good a time as any to ask. Did you take it?'

Vee frowned.

'Year before last, that case... with the private hospital...
and the crazy family...' He snapped his fingers. 'The missing
Paulsen girl,' he said. 'The pay-off. That the mother offered you
for your... diligent services. Did you take it?'

'*Excuse me?*'

'Johnson, come on,' he huffed. 'Look, you've got something.
You don't play silly buggers,' he clasped his hands in gratitude,
'which, between you and me, goes a long way to making
my life easier. Top reason I can't stand working with women.
Besides the melodrama and all the time off they take to pop
munchkins, of which I'm bloody gatvol.' He sat up straighter.
'What I'm driving at is: in a hive, know your bees. I need to
know my people. Now you *know* there have been whispers. And
I know that *you* know that *I've* heard, and if I've heard, then I've

speculated. I hate speculation. So…' he spread his palms. 'You'd hardly be the first or last journalist to take an incentive if they felt it was deserved.'

A nimbus of rage plumed between Vee's eyes. 'You joking me, right?'

Van Wyk shook his head.

'You *must* be joking me,' she said, surprised at the dangerous rasp in her voice. She stalked out of the office, slamming the door behind her.

———

'He said *what* to you?' Chlöe sputtered. 'He actually had the bloody nerve to go *there*?' Flushed and dewy with sweat and indignation, her freckles throbbed a deeper russet than usual.

'Oh, he went there.'

'But we didn't take that money from Adele Paulsen! I thought we cleared that up ages ago. Would we be broke if we had? Why would he have kept us on at *City Chronicle* all this time if he didn't trust us?'

'Exactly. Now that I've had time to think about it, who has sway with Nico and wants us out of the office, out of the way as much as possible? This has that fat, muppet-faced bitch written all over it.'

'Saskia? Are you sure? I don't like him either but I don't see him being this unprofessional about it. Maybe there's another reason he wants to get a rise out of you.' She scrunched her nose, unsure.

'Maybe.' *More likely he's testing how far he can push before I snap, giving him a reason to fire you.* She hadn't been forthcoming about every aspect of the meeting, omitting details of how Nico had looked particularly wolfish as he questioned Chlöe's exact role as her assistant. There was no easy way to break it to Chloe that their boss saw her as dead weight. 'Whatever it is, I'm thinking it can't be that bad to play along,' she hedged.

Chlöe's eyes popped. 'No. NO. Uh-uh, no way. Please get us out of this. Pleeaaase…'

'Calm down. I haven't said anything yet, and if we refuse he'll be forced to send someone else. It's not like I'm dying to be sent to some hairy buttcrack in the Karoo to write about mud huts. Not if I can help it.'

'Then please help it with all your might, because I *do not* do village.'

2

'Ugghh.' Vee pressed a hand over her eyes. 'I think I forgot it on the car seat.' She clicked her tongue, rustling through her handbag. 'No, I definitely left it…'

'You need your cell phone? Like, right now?' her male companion asked.

'Yes. I mean no. Well, not *no*-no, but maybe.' Vee looked up into hazel eyes, teasing her. 'It will be off, I swear. Because that's the unbreakable rule of quality time.' She tiptoed, snuggling a smile against his cheek. 'But it's on the seat, the glass could get smashed. And in case Chlöe calls? She's spinning all over the place right now. After today…'

'Oh right, 'cause it's Chlöe who's spinning right now.' He laughed and kissed her, and warmth buzzed through her. Vee struggled to remember her most important rule: start over, take it slow. Still, the thrill of familiar pleasures never ceased to amaze.

Titus Wreh dropped his arms. 'Go grab your phone, or I'll never hear the end of it. I'll get our table. The sooner we eat, the sooner we can leave, the sooner…' He winked and she punched his arm.

'Don't push it, mister man. It's been one helluva week.' She took him in, unable to quell the burn in the pit of her stomach; a tall stretch of warm brown skin clad in a casual olive-green shirt and dark slacks. He graced her with another suggestive

21

grin, dimple twitching and eyebrows waggling. 'You know you love the view, woman.'

She giggled. 'Hmm. After the wine, we shall see.'

She hustled away from Beluga's well-lit entrance, trying to de-fog her mental windscreen as the restaurant retreated from view. All she wanted tonight was a nice dinner with her ex-maybe-could-be-back-together-again fiancé. But this morning's fracas gnawed her open like pesky mice working on a forgotten toy at the back of a cupboard. Chlöe had taken her leave of Claremont and the sunny respite of Vee's veranda and gone back to the office. She left behind her agitation, which soured the rest of Vee's day.

A bribe. Vee shook her head as she walked. The word itself sounded fat with distaste, sour in her mouth. *A bribe!* Her current reality was a constant headwork of bills and taxes, not forgetting the ever-present tome at the back of her mind: should she bite the bullet and buy the house she'd rented for three years. She could just about afford it, if she ate only beans with palm oil and wiped her butt with leaves for another year. But nestled within that was an even deeper question: was she ready to call South Africa home? So much to chew on, yet somewhere in a parallel universe her more mercenary self was flush. Because she'd "taken dash", greased her mouth. She and Chlöe had escaped *Urban* on far from stellar terms. Vee knew of at least a couple of people who'd been running that kind of cheycheypolay, the most malevolent of gossip strains.

'We really should stop meeting like this.'

She jumped and stabbed air with her car keys. Peered ahead of her. Groaned and relaxed. 'Aaay my pipo.'

'What, you plan on mauling me with those? Come on, Cricket.' Joshua Allen grinned, sidling closer. 'Where's your enthusiasm? You're hurting my feelings.'

He had practically melted out of a brick wall onto the

sidewalk. Like some thug could've done, attacking her while her head was in the breeze. True, Green Point after dark was no Mitchells Plain, but still. Hand to throat, Vee scanned the semi-lit street. The only other presence was a car guard observing them with interest.

'Seriously? You think I'd jump you in a dark alley for ignoring my calls?' Joshua gave a short bark of laughter. 'Gimme a little credit. I'm way too lazy to carry grudges, you know that.'

'I give you credit all the time and you never deserve any of it, Joshua Allen.'

'*All the time? Never?* What cruel absolutes you wield against me, my lady.' He placed hand over heart in mock pain and fluttered his lashes. Vee battled to keep a straight face. 'All the better to heap the blame on me. While you, the biggest hypocrite alive, strings me along with sweet nothings. Forcing me to commit acts I've never done with any other woman...'

'Hehn! Don't dare blame your depravity on me.'

He nodded gravely. 'Alas, true. But with you it's *special*.'

'I don't have time for this...'

'Then you plunge the knife in my back and twist it by turning up here, looking hot with the very man you've been two-timing me with for months. The guy you dumped to be with me... the *same one* you dumped me *for*. After which you took me back... before dumping me again. Then you ignore me for weeks, and make this crazy list of rules to keep everybody at a distance...' He sighed and stroked her cheek. 'Highly punishing roller coaster. Can't we just agree that I lied and you shat all over my heart, and call it even?'

She smacked his hand away. 'How you know me and Ti here together?'

He leered at her from top to toe. "Of course. Who else would command all this sexiness, if not I?"

'And who would *all this*,' she gestured wildly over his physique, 'be for?'

23

His maroon shirt, sleeves rolled, complemented a toffee complexion and lifted shimmer in his dark eyes. As usual, his black curls were buzzed short but a new acquisition, a manicured beard, covered his jaw. He looked and smelled good. Off-guard-throwingly good, edible almost. Enough to make her forget, for a split second, that she hadn't come alone.

He murmured her name once, easing an arm around her waist. Vee stiffened and flinched at the first brush of his lips. Missing was the rush of heat and anticipation she'd felt in the same pose just minutes ago. With Joshua there were too many tacit promises, too much want and need, too much to lose. Too much of so much and not enough balance. With Ti it was simple; it made her blush how simple, how little she had to think. With Joshua… every fibre of her being literally hurt in trying to resolve their contact as either a step forward or one backward.

'Joshua, please… I can't.'

A bolt of hurt anyone else would've missed contorted his face. He dropped his arms and allowed her to step away, eyes darkening to black holes. 'I know. I'm sorry. It's just…' He brightened. 'Wow.'

She flushed. 'All right, I get it, I look hot. Stop your nonsense.'

'Forget you. I'm still blown away by this gorgeous lady right here.' Joshua brushed past her to caress the bonnet of her car. 'Sweet mother. How do you even own this again? I can't tell you enough how much I hate your guts.'

Vee puffed in relief and beamed. Gleaming gold with a chocolate-brown trim, the 1980 Chrysler CM Valiant GLX made every other car parked on the street look either washed up or too garishly modern. She still couldn't believe her luck. Its previous and only owner, once a senior manager at the Chrysler South Africa assembly plant until its closure, had kept it in stellar condition. He'd sold it very reasonably, to avoid his "grasping, pissant sons getting their paws on it", asking only that she cherish it and not drive it like a feeble female. Every time she eased behind the wheel of a piece of machinery as old as she was, she upheld her end of the bargain as much as the speed limit allowed.

'Technically, this baby's half mine. Like all your real babies are gonna be one day. Start getting used to it by letting me behind the wheel more often.'

'Pssh, half whetin? In what world can you can make that claim?'

'Excuse me, freeloader? The one where you've been exploiting my financial genius for personal gain, at no charge.' He cocked an eyebrow. 'Telling you how to work your money instead of just blowing it or sending it to all your hard-up relatives. Stocks, shares, where to invest, so you'd have some change to throw around. And build a house in Monrovia.'

She rolled her eyes. 'Okaaay, fine. Thank you, Mister Investment Banking Hotshot. Not like you made me millions.'

He cocked one shoulder and let it drop. 'I try. Come to think of it, you never okayed this purchase with me. Although as far as assets go, you did yourself a solid.' He caressed the bonnet again. 'You ought to be more careful, though. Major purchases like this, they raise eyebrows.'

'*Now* you tell me…' The Valiant was another fly in her ointment. *People are wondering, for instance, how you can afford a ride like that,* Chlöe's voice whispered in her ear. Her blood went up and her nose tingled with the start of tears. *I saved, that's how,* she said to imaginary Chlöe, imaginary Nico and a host of imaginary, petty colleagues. *I slaved and saved and slept with guys who know how to make money do fancy things. How's that for a how?* She snatched the cell off the driver's seat and slammed it locked. 'Don't follow me.'

'Whoa, what did I do? I'm making sure you're safe, nothing more,' said Joshua.

They moved at a lazy stroll; in tacit agreement their exchange deserved prolonging. He flanked her at a respectful but protective distance, never more than a step behind. A few times he forgot himself, raised an arm, then quickly lowered it with a regretful smile. Vee wished she didn't miss his usual proprietary hand snuggled in the small of her back as much as he clearly did.

They entered the steak, brown mushroom and fresh greens-perfumed atmosphere of Beluga. Titus's dimple lit the foyer when he spotted her, wobbled as he registered Joshua in step alongside, and Vee remembered why she'd devised the rules. So things wouldn't disintegrate from complicated to meltdown. Yet… a stubborn knot twisted beneath her ribs.

They hovered, waiting to be seated. Joshua didn't leave. The two men "what's upped" with sufficient graciousness, not quite like old buddies but enough to signal safe airspace. Vee tried not to pull at her collar, gulping and sweating like a choking cartoon. Why the hell wouldn't Joshua leave? Couldn't he just be polite – granted, perpetual jokes and assing around were more his style – but surely he still had manners? Only a moron would fail to read the room and notice how awkward she was around both her ex-lovers. Who used to be best friends.

'Oh, guess who I ran into. Small world!' Titus said. From behind his broad hulk stepped a well-toned length of caramel, topped with a sweep of cinnamon ringlets.

Vee's mouth soured. 'Aria?'

'Oh my God, Vee!' the ringlets spoke. 'Fantastic to see you. God, you look a-ma-zing. Haven't changed a bit.' Swept into a one-shouldered hug and a cloud of glorious-smelling shampoo, Vee blinked as a moist peck hit her cheek.

Aria Burke laughed. 'I know, craziness right? You run into my date, I run into yours…' She tucked a glossy spiral behind an ear, smearing her lips to reposition cherry gloss. She grinned.

It looked like a shark coming in for a bite. Vee tried to wrench Joshua's gaze, resolutely nailed to the crowd at the bar ahead, to hers. She could barely catch his profile, but his jaw was working like he was trying not to laugh.

Silence bounced around.

'Well.' Titus drew his coat closer as if shrugging on his usual diplomacy. He tried hiding his amusement with lousy success. 'Turns out we don't have a table. There's been a mix-up.'

'I'm sooo sorry, hey,' winced the blonde, waif-thin hostess on guard by the door, her expression Capetonian-horrified at the prospect of turning away two black couples against a cheery influx of white patrons. 'Like, I'm sure you *did* make a reservation, but it's not in our book. It's sooo hectic, sometimes things get muddled. If you're prepared to wait a bit...'

'Beluga on a Friday. What can you do?' Titus said kindly.

'We can share a table, that's what. Darling, I'm sure they can join us.' Aria linked her arm through Joshua's. 'It'll be like old times. We can catch up.'

'You know what, that's a fantastic idea.' Joshua stared Vee dead-on.

'Hey, I don't mind.' Titus rubbed his hands in agreement. 'Probably because I'm starving. Whatchu think, my jue, you game?'

The nucleus of rage in Vee's chest slowly began to weaponise. *No, she didn't. This bony-legged bitch did not just chunk a 'darling' in my face.* 'Why not?' she muttered.

As a waitron squeezed between them on the crammed floor space to take orders, Joshua offered up a toast.

'To friends,' he saluted solemnly, looking round the table.

Vee all but swallowed her tongue as she raised her glass to a very long evening.

———

Pack your bags, we're going to Oudtshoorn. No arguments. It'll be good for us.

Vee hit send, lowered her phone and waited.

Chlöe's first reply pinged in almost immediately, followed by a second ping... third... fourth...

After the eighth, the cell started to ring.

'Aay mehn, Bishop, get over it, we're going!' she shouted to the room, to herself, then put it on mute. They would leave tomorrow, before midday, if she could drag Chlöe and her mutinous pout out of bed and onto the N2 highway in time. They would use her car and bill the office for fuel... the Chrysler needed to stretch her treads.

Vee went back to the impressive dossier of spoils Lynne Hammond had indulged in and reviewed before taking leave, open on her lap. No wonder Hammond hadn't gone on maternity sooner. She hadn't wanted to pass the delights of the Arabella Sheraton and Twelve Apostles Hotel on to a lucky stand-in.

Instead, she left us this, she sagged, leafing through The Grotto Lodge's self-aggrandisement. 'Our rustic but quaint accommodation serves to create a wonderful lodge experience for the discerning, adventurous visitor. Situated just fifteen kilometres shy of Oudtshoorn, our location encompasses many colourful aspects of the Garden Route towns. Nestled near the famous Cango Caves, we offer rock-climbing excursions, guided hikes and sightseeing drives, as well as spa facilities, horseback riding and our unique military boot camp for the real outdoorsman. Perfect for family, group and corporate bookings. Call—'

Vee tossed the file. How the hell could anything be quaint and rustic at the same time? Chances were it was much closer to one than the other and, with their luck, it would be to the latter. Pastoral life had graduated from shameful to "an experience", and the hospitality industry's spin on the concept bordered on ridiculous. Poverty porn, wasn't that the catchphrase? She imagined bowls of sludgy rat soup in chipped tin cups, slurped down by a pack of enraptured fools with money to burn.

Chlöe was going to murder her.

She flicked off the bedside lamp, hit the highest setting on the fan and star-fished her limbs across the bed.

Retreat

3

The LG flatscreen made a tiny "zooop" as it went off, fading to black over the Harpo Studios emblem, trademark of Oprah Winfrey's empire. Heavy-hearted, Zintle Msengwana sighed to her feet. The queen of talk was serious: she was going off prime time television for good.

Zintle couldn't believe it. There wasn't much to make her days cleaning up other people's mess easier to stomach. If the halls were empty and the work hadn't piled up, relaxing in front of talk shows and soapies was the one treat she allowed herself before she started her routine. Management in some lodges was strict, and allowed only good clients to book rooms. At The Grotto, class and wallet size were one and the same and, judging from the nonsense Zintle had had to clean out of some of the rooms, that equation told a sad, disgusting story. At some establishments, management was more lenient, allowing longer breaks if the day was slow, or generous, handing out barely used or expired stock to staff who wanted it. No such luck at The Grotto.

Zintle sprayed the shag-pile rug in the en suite sitting room with carpet cleaner and started on the bathroom while it dried to powder. She sighed again, shaking her head as she removed a half-full wineglass rimmed with lipstick from near the bathtub. The bathroom smelled faintly of alcohol. Ms Greenwood was a good woman but she drank too much. It was an open secret among the staff. Management had turned a blind eye and tolerated it for years, but now the stakes were higher. The lodge had stepped up its game in the bid for three-star status, and if Ms Greenwood wasn't careful her job would be on the line. It would be terrible to lose her over something so shameful.

Zintle decided to leave the scrubbing of tiles, which she hated, for last, and moved on to stripping the bed. She yanked the corner of the duvet spilling down the side of the mattress. It didn't budge and she cursed, inching to the other end of the bed, pulling harder as she went. Finally it gave, rolling a heavy weight against her legs that made her buckle. She yelped, stumbled and fell against a side table near the window, overturning a lamp.

'Hhayi mhani. Jesus.' She pushed the lamp aside, knelt beside the bundle on the floor and yanked back the duvet. Underneath lay Rhonda Greenwood, face down and back turned, head barely visible beneath the rumpled folds.

Zintle heard a tiny whimper come out of her mouth. She reached her hand out, slowly, then jerked it back. 'Ma'am.' She put a hand on Rhonda's shoulder and shook gently. 'Ms Greenwood.' No answer. 'Ms Greenwood. Are you awake?'

She had no idea why she was whispering, only suddenly she felt scared. She shook harder, and watched Rhonda Greenwood's pudgy, prostrate body jiggle back and forth under her hand with no will of its own. Gulping, Zintle heaved, dragging the edges of the duvet and Greenwood closer. The body pitched and rolled, coming to rest on its side. Blonde strands of hair obscuring Greenwood's face fell away, revealing an ooze of thick, creamy-looking fluid inside and around her mouth. A dark red lump stood out behind her ear.

Zintle shrieked and scrambled on all fours for the door.

Sunshine slowly braised Vee's forehead in sweat. Eyes shielded, she estimated the peril of venturing out unprotected and shrank back indoors.

She dragged her tiny suitcase across the baked mud floor and looked around for her straw hat. Above her head, bouts of vigorous rustling emanated from the thatched roof. The mice usually did the rustling, especially at night, but she looked up to find a sizeable lizard languishing in a patch of sunlight on the wall. She made a half-hearted throw at it with a tissue box and missed. The lizard twitched a mere centimetre, turning its neck to eyeball her. Vee returned to searching for the hat. Dusty and squashed, she pulled it from under the rickety metal bedframe.

She paused, mid-creep out of the chalet, by the second bed. Spread-eagled in underwear and tangled in a sheet, Chlöe lay conked out. Her hair, a spill of rooibos tea brewed strong, had shrunk into a mangled halo of frizz. Her pale skin looked like blue-veined cheese, if there existed a kind with veins that throbbed in high heat. A few welts of a hateful indigo were blossoming in patches on her limbs. Paintball was a game unsympathetic to delicate skin, especially if one found oneself on a team that couldn't shoot worth a damn or even recognise its own teammates.

Vee, who'd been on the winning team, panged with guilt. Grotto's idea of boot camp came off more like a softened version of boarding school, but its rustic appeal was kicking Chlöe's pampered backside. Right out the gate, the cracks had turned into gaping fissures. After arriving early Friday morning, Chlöe realised she'd done the unthinkable: forgotten her bag of magical hair and skincare products. They hadn't even settled in properly when her whingeing had begun. The chalet was cramped and overrun with gleefully scampering critters; the mattress was too thin and lumpy; the shower spat freezing bullets. Vee didn't have the heart to point out they were supposedly under military conditions, especially after watching Chlöe stink at almost every activity. She'd fallen on her butt during rope-climbing and hadn't had the guts to tackle the swing bridge. Bishop the wildcat, picture perfect of a frontier woman unbridled on open prairies, had even flunked horse-riding. Who knew there existed any white girls who were scared of horses.

She ripped the top sheet off her own bed, wet it under the bathroom tap, and draped it over Chlöe, who was shifting and muttering in her sleep. *Don't worry, my lil' Vanilla Princess*, Vee thought, *we're out of here first thing tomorrow.*

And upon their return, Nico had better do a stellar job of explaining why they were marooned in hardship headquarters instead of, as she'd expected, lavishing in mod cons in the valley. Not that any explanation was needed. His point was loud and clear – stay in line, or I deploy my myriad ways of making you miserable. No way in hell had she agreed to a weekend of roughing it for the sake of a review, no way in all nine circles of Dante's Hell had Chlöe agreed. But they'd been assured by Grotto's management that their boss had insisted his journalists be "fully immersed in the true boot camp experience" in order to get an untainted taste of the lodge's facilities. Another Van Wyk blindside. *Well played, bossman*, Vee thought with a wry smile. She cast a longing eye away from the koppies and scrub downhill to utopia, her saliva thickening like drying cement. The colourful Cape Dutch estate, complete with twinkling pool, sprawled in laughable contrast to their camp. The luxury guesthouses were solely for those "who truly got away to get away". Their section, well... left a lot to be desired was putting it kindly.

Hat low, she sneaked past the makeshift kraal that was the cooking area, snatching a bottle of warm mineral water on the way. The morning regimen began at the crack of dawn and broke at seven thirty for breakfast and showers, lasting an hour and a half. Most of the team members were still lounging about after the meal, waiting for a camp instructor to kick the day's activities back into gear. If she ever ran into anyone from this lot in the city, Vee would've walked right past. The women were filling pots with water and loading them back onto glowing coals to soften the pap-caked interior before they were scrubbed. Laughing from a loose circle on the rocks circling the fire, the men rested near huge barrels, their labour complete. After every morning's workout, they walked over a kilometre off base to a water pump, filled the barrels, and hoisted them back on their shoulders, four men at a time.

She shook her head pityingly. White people were incredible. The toils others shouldered as a part of daily life they paid good money to get subjected to. Had anyone volunteered to spend a weekend in a real village with either of her grandmothers, the only thing they'd feel excited about was drowning themselves in the nearest river.

Outside the thatched fence, she hit the footpath and skirted the periphery, avoiding the main gate. None dared breach that iron curtain, and the security guards had superb radar for breakout guests. She scaled the fence at the lowest point, landing with a soft thump on the grass. Even the air felt cooler, lighter, on the other side. Popping open the mineral water, she splashed dust and grass off her feet, face and elbows before tucking the bottle underarm.

'Good morning, madam,' beamed the man at the front desk. 'How's been your day so far?'

'Oh excellent, thank you. I've just been to the spa…' Vee faltered. Presentable she was, true, but her face – parched and tense – and hands – clean enough, but brown moons of dirt glaring under her fingernails – were hardly spa-fresh products. 'Just for a massage. Can't sit up long enough to endure anything in this heat.'

The concierge returned a polite half-smile. "Trevor Davids" read his name tag. She broke eye contact and scanned the reception area, then looked through the glass double doors to the first, smaller, dining area. Even for a post-breakfast crush, the vibe was dead.

'Where's everybody gone?'

'They've reconvened for the final session of the conference. Today's the last day of seminars and discussions, tonight we host the closing festivities. Though some people bunked off early and went for this morning's tour of the churches in Oudtshoorn and the nearby ostrich farms.' He coughed. 'Aren't you part of the convention?'

'No I'm, uhh... It must've slipped my mind.' She plucked a pamphlet off the desk and fanned herself, forcing a smile. 'You know what, I wanted to order a drink at the bar, but maybe I'll do that from my room.'

'Which would be room number...?'

Maybe she could just walk off like she hadn't heard, and scurry like hell once she was out of sight. But the heat didn't encourage that kind of energy burst, and the concierge looked pretty damn fit. His eyes lasered her with open suspicion. One hand bunched into a fist, while the other glided involuntarily toward the reception phone.

She cleared her throat. 'Listen, Trevor. I'm with my boyfriend in a... um, private capacity. He'd hate for it to become widely known that we were here together, it's rather delicate.' She made a woeful face that hopefully screamed "kept woman in precarious position". 'Management is well acquainted with our intimate situation, I believe,' she closed wildly.

His stance loosened, arms dropping to his sides. 'Of course, madam. Room service will be glad to fill your order from your room.'

Vee muttered thanks and slunk off. The coast was clear as far in as the second dining room. Near the kitchen, a gaggle of female staff congregated. She lingered near the commotion, watching one of the younger girls wind her waist in tune to the local house music playing. The rest of the group peeped through a cubbyhole at the widescreen television in the adjacent room, cheering and loudly comparing the girl's gyrations to DJ Cleo's background dancers. Vee snickered and snuck past.

The kitchen yawned, mercifully deserted. The first huge, upright fridge concealed nothing impressive but swirling plumes of icy mist. The next was kinder, offering colourful pinwheels of fruit arranged on silver trays. She carefully lifted the clingfilm and swiped chunks of watermelon and kiwi on toothpicks, giving a throaty moan of joy when the cold, sweet juices burst in her mouth.

'Dammit,' she whispered. The walk-in fridge was locked, and getting past the mechanism would take professional skill, time and the right equipment. What she did have in the boot of her car was her "access pass" – a makeshift combo of tools for forcibly gaining entry where it had been denied – but the Chrysler was all the way in the guests' car park. She abandoned the walk-in for the chest freezer instead, examined the lock and brightened.

She rummaged through the drawers near the sink until she found a thin-bladed paring knife and a teaspoon. Kneeling, she slid the knife into the keyhole and jiggled. The metal hook of the latch lifted a hair's breadth. The freezer was new. She leaned a hip into it and the gap widened, enough to insert the teaspoon. She twisted the blade, gently leaning her weight into the teaspoon until the mechanism clacked loose. The lock undamaged - exhale in relief - she lifted the lid of the freezer and plucked out two fizzy drinks. Her mouth watered as she worked open the Coke.

'Yhuuuuuu! Kanindincedeni! Izani; ndincedeni!'

A girl, decked in the pink-with-grey-trim uniform of the maids, skidded in through the back entrance. She was somewhere in her early twenties, about Chlöe's age, fair-skinned and heavy-boned. And screaming the room crimson.

'Ndiyanicela bethuna, kanizondinceda!' Her arms flapped like two violent birds.

Vee scuttled away from the girl, sneaking the bottles behind her back. She stopped. Whatever this girl was pitching, it was definitely not a fit over a couple of pilfered soft drinks.

'Kukho isidumbhu kule room!'

'Hehn? I... uhhh...' Confusion gradually edged out frenzy from the girl's eyes. Vee put a hand over her ear, and then turned it palm up, adding an exaggerated shrug. She repeated the action a few times, hoping the mime got through: language barrier.

The maid looked incredulous. 'You can't hear Xhosa?'

'No,' Vee breathed in relief.

'Are you sure?'

Vee restrained an eye-roll. 'Very. What's wrong?'

Several things went on behind the girl's eyes as she seemed to take quick stock of this, accept it for what it was, and remember she'd been screaming over something more important. She clapped her hands like something hot was in them that she couldn't wait to dump, muttering and shaking her head as she clutched the front of her uniform. '*There's a dead body in the room.* Where I was cleaning!'

'*Whetin you say?*' Vee cried.

4

Aay my pipo, what kinda trouble dis now? Vee thought.

The person on the floor was unmistakably dead. It looked like a woman; she couldn't be sure yet. The barely-there dead smell punched a greeting up her nostrils right in the doorway, forcing her to make an about-turn as she fought her gag reflex. It was nowhere near an exact science, but all it took was one whiff of that imperceptibly rank odour and she had enough to make a strong guestimate on time of death. Fresh: half a day, maybe a few hours on that, but not much longer. She couldn't explain how she did it, but she could. The wondrously incalculable side effects of war… her mind could be tricked into forgetting, but her hypersensitive, stubborn nose was forever rewired.

'Whose room is this?' she asked.

'Ms Greenwood. Rhonda Greenwood. She's the deputy manager.'

The girl from housekeeping – Zintle, she'd whispered – kept herself wedged in the doorway linking the small lounge to the bedroom, intent on not moving an inch closer to the action. Mouth-breathing as much as possible, Vee knelt over the body. Rhonda's cheeks and nose sported a dull, ruddy hue. She examined the bruising behind her ear, near the back of her head, and shuddered.

'How long she been lying here?'

Met with silence, Vee turned. Zintle was staring back at her with a look of deep affront, galled by the suggestion that a dead person sprawled in a room under her charge was something she would keep quiet for any length of time. 'No, I mean how often are these rooms cleaned? When last did anybody see her? Last night?'

Zintle nodded. 'Yes. Most of the managers work late, especially now when it's busy. But sometimes… she comes to bed early. But not too many times. She works hard.'

Vee studied her, eyes narrowing when Zintle aimed a guilty look at the wall.

She turned back to the body. She licked her finger and brought it close to the woman's nose. No breath. Greenwood was definitely dead. She patted the pockets of her cargo pants for her phone. The screen registered four missed calls. She scrolled through the listing: three from Titus, one from Joshua. She cursed quietly, pressed exit and switched to camera mode.

'She staying here by herself?' She held her breath and snapped the first couple, one close-up and one wide shot, of the body propped on its side against the lower bed frame.

'Yes. All the senior guys have rooms but their partners don't stay here with them. It's not allowed. I mean, they stay the night sometimes but usually not during peak season.'

'Hhmm.' Vee snapped another close-up of Greenwood's face, lungs starting to ache as she leaned close to get the blotchy nose and raw lump behind her ear in the frame. Behind her, she heard Zintle's gasp at her audacity. *Trust me, I don't want to be doing this either.* Then why was she? She clicked on, capturing the protruding tongue and thick foam in and around the woman's mouth. When she finally had to inhale, the strong, gassy hit of booze made her gag.

'So you're telling me all the senior staff here got their own chalets?'

'No, no. They can have a room now and then if they want

it, especially if they work late. It's like that in the business.' The sound of Zintle's voice had shifted from the doorway to what sounded like a spot directly behind Vee. 'Only Ms Greenwood and Ms Motaung, the general manager, have chalets. They practically live here.' Over the click of the phone's electronic shutter, Vee heard a dull clink and thunk on the floor behind her, like glass against wood.

'They aren't married. I doubt they even have men,' Zintle said.

Vee ignored the girl's tone, staring at the body with sympathy. *Don't mind her, yah, she's young and naive.* She had enough experience with age to know when you got to Rhonda's, likely twice Zintle's, you weren't thrilled about blossoming into an overweight, unmarried, workaholic lush. *Bet you never imagined ending up here, either,* Vee thought, snapping the swipe of lumpy vomit on the carpet.

'Did you see her last night, before you went home?'

'I'm not doing nights this week. I went home at eight, when the new shift starts. There's a bus that takes us into Oudtshoorn, but it was running behind so I got a lift.'

Vee frowned, peering closely at Greenwood's hands. Shaking her head, she squatted, zoomed, snapped, and examined the shot at length. Something was off about the fingernails...

The silence behind her was creepy. She lowered the cell phone and peeped over the expanse of queen-sized mattress into the adjoining bathroom, in time to see Zintle working the neck of a bulging black rubbish bag into a knot. Gurgling came from the bathroom. Vee popped to her feet and dashed in.

'Nawww,' she groaned, watching water swirl down the bathtub's drain.

'Yintoni?' Zintle looked panicky. 'I only let the water out. I shouldn't do that?'

'No, I don't think you're supposed to do that. Maybe there was evidence in it.'

Zintle blinked in disgusted disbelief. 'Ngumphambano lowo,' she said. 'That's crazy. Like what, urine?'

Vee giggled into her hand. Zintle cracked a smile. 'Yeah, maybe urine. I don't know.' She patted Zintle's shoulder. 'I'm sure it doesn't matter.'

She took pictures of all angles of the bathroom and flicked through her efforts, Zintle craning her neck over her shoulder. When she reached the end, Zintle wrinkled her forehead and made a mouth-shrug. The gesture pretty much summed up the entire photo gallery: meaningless. Vee started to put the phone away.

'Must everything be correct?' Zintle asked. Vee frowned; Zintle continued: 'Do you want photos of the room exactly how it was? Before I found her?'

'Yes, but... you moved anything?'

'Lo glass.' Zintle pointed to a wineglass on a sidetable in the bedroom. 'Lo glass ibime pha ngasebhafini.' She clicked in irritation and repeated, 'That glass was by the bathtub.' Her face clouded. 'Ndiyicholile. I touched it. I picked it up with my fingers.'

Vee chewed her lip and considered. 'Okay, bring it back where it was. It's fine, you can pick it up, just do it carefully,' she coaxed Zintle over to her. 'Long as you're the only person who touched it.' Nothing suspicious about a maid's fingerprints all over a room she regularly cleaned. That's if anyone cared to check, like the police. If this was a police matter at all, come to think of it.

Pinching it by the stem, Zintle set the glass on the peach-and-cream tiles at the foot of the tub, twisting and turning it around several times. Satisfied at last, she nodded gravely, and Vee aimed the phone and snapped.

'That all? Did you move anything else?'

Zintle's immediate, involuntary nod quickly shifted into shaking her head. Vee narrowed her eyes. Zintle stuffed both lips into her mouth and covered it with a hand, still shaking her head and avoiding eye contact.

It was then Vee recalled how she had met Rhonda Greenwood, alive and well, a mere day ago.

————

'We've met before, haven't we?'

Vee had turned and looked down, quite a ways, into the bright brown irises of a plump woman, clipboard tamped against her chest by a pair of well-manicured hands. Her face was round, almost unnaturally spherical, and crowned with fine, artificially-lightened hair, teased – tortured, really – into a bun on top of her head. Her smile could've fracked the entire Karoo for free.

Vee smiled back politely. She and Chlöe were fresh off the highway, barely unpacked and sorely disappointed to find they weren't guests at the main lodge. Boot camp inmates reported at check-in to pick up "the drill", a list of gruelling weekend activities they were expected to jump right into once their bags hit the floor. She'd noticed the woman looking her over as she waited outside the camp's office, her mouth yawing the air in the way people did when they wanted to say something but weren't sure what.

'You don't remember me, do you?'

Vee shook her head.

'Hang on a minute…' The woman's face blanked out, her head taking up a curious bobbing motion, akin to a beach ball on a gentle tide. It went on for a while and just when Vee was about to interject, the woman's eyes lit up. 'Johnson,' she chirped. 'First name was a letter in the alphabet. Bee. Bea for Beatrice? No. Vee. Vee Johnson. You're a journalist.' Her smile cranked so high, there was practically an audible creak as her mouth accommodated it. Her head kept bobbing. 'Didn't comprehend our colonially obsessive tea-drinking, and shortbread meant something entirely different in your country. Hated PowerPoint presentations with needless animations. And loved the ocean. Loved it, loved it.'

Vee blinked. 'Whoa.'

The bobbing and jawbone-breaking kept going. 'People get such a jolt when I do that. I love it.' The woman's laugh was tinkly, yet full and broad-spirited, much like herself. 'I did this course a few years ago, you know, the ones that improve your memory by tapping into alpha waves to increase how much of your brain you use. *I know*,' she held up a hand, 'sounds like utter rubbish, but it actually worked. Well, for the most part anyway. When you're in hospitality, you can't afford to forget names and faces.'

Vee extended her hand, provoking the woman to bright, open laughter as she shook it. 'Oh, of course, I'm being silly, you don't know who *I* am! Rhonda Greenwood, deputy general manager. I know you from that thing last year…'

Please don't say the Paulsen trial.

'… the conference centre at Portswood. The Portswood Hotel at the V&A Waterfront. You were there for some journalism training group as was I, well, for a management refresher in my case. A couple of our tea breaks coincided and that's when we chatted. About shortbread, the silliest of things.'

'Oh, yeees!' Vee sighed into a grin. 'That was ages ago. You gave me your grandmother's recipe for genuine Scottish shortbread, and I gave you my mother's one for Liberian shortbread.'

Up and down went Rhonda's head, in agreement, and also because it now appeared to be a tic she had no control over. 'Which is more like a muffin isn't it, and truly scrumptious. How long are you staying with us?'

———

Vee blinked her way back into the room, all memory of

that effervescent Greenwood fading as she looked down at the crumple of human being near her feet. This woman had died with two – possibly more, who knew – great shortbread recipes in her head. This woman, whose alpha-enhanced brain was rotting away along with her everything else, was giving off more and more of That Dead Smell with every passing minute. She gagged, rushing for the door.

'What do we tell the police?' Zintle pressed, scurrying her short, plump legs to keep up. Vee didn't stop until she'd gulped her way back into the fresh, untainted air outside the chalet.

'Zintle, you can't tell the police I was in there with you. Please, okay, no… you really can't.' Zintle folded her arms. 'It won't be good for me, it won't be good for you either. I'm a guest. They'll ask why you told me about it.' *And there's the small matter of those pictures I took.*

'But I needed help. You were the only person around.'

'They won't see it that way.' Vee squeezed Zintle's arm. 'I beg you, don't. Tell your housekeeping manager or whoever that you just found her, which is true. And if they ask you about moving things, be truthful. You won't get into any trouble.'

'Where are you going?'

'Back.' Vee pointed in the direction of the wall and made a swooping motion with her hands. Zintle put her fists on her hips. 'You jumped from the other side? Yho, sisi, are you mad? You guys aren't supposed to come to the lodge.' She paused for a moment, then motioned Vee to wait before heading into the kitchen. She came back a few minutes later with two frosty, unopened soft drinks and sandwiches wrapped in foil. 'There's a party tonight because the conference is ending. There's a lot of food. They won't notice.' She smiled as she handed them over. 'Thank you.'

'And bless *you*,' Vee breathed in gratitude.

'Where the *bloody hell* have you been? I had to fake some serious period pains to get out of today's nightmare, and you just decide not to pitch up.' Chlöe plonked down on the grass. 'What's our Sunday afternoon viewing like?'

'*Sisterhood of the Travelling Skanks.* I was hoping to catch the rerun of *Jacob's Cross,* but clearly Porno Guy doesn't appreciate the finer things.' Vee handed her one of the sandwiches.

'Is this how pathetic our professional lives have become? Right now we could be chilling in a proper office, having a proper lunch and working on real assignments. But noooo. We're being team players, so nature is our office.' Chlöe said "nature" like it came dripping out of a toilet bowl. 'We get to eat tasteless sandwiches on top of a hill and watch racist porn through someone's window because we have no other entertainment.' She bit into the sandwich and grimaced. 'Thank you so much for bringing me here.'

Vee munched and took it in. The embankment overlooked a gorgeous expanse of open road, koppie formations and grassland that lay outside the lodge's enclosure. Within the grounds, though, the vantage point they'd chosen was purely strategic, affording an unobstructed view of a plasma TV in one guest's room. They had never seen and would probably never know who the occupant was, but the viewing content had certainly proved illuminating.

'Come on, crybaby, just suck it up a lil' bit longer and we'll be out.' Vee nudged Chlöe with her shoulder and Chlöe grunted, unsmiling. 'And look how much Porno Guy here cares about us. He keeps his TV on all day and his window open, and at least his choices are imaginative. He deserves *some* credit for that.'

'How do you know it's a he? Could be a very liberal, oversexed woman.' Chlöe stretched her legs and leaned back on the grass, rubbernecking to follow the exertions of the four nude actors on-screen. 'On second thought, definitely a man.

That's way too much admin for any woman to find it remotely sexy.'

Vee handed Chlöe the Fanta, her favourite, watching in mildly repulsed fascination as she guzzled it, mat of hair thrown back, a trickle of orange sliding down her chin and staining her frowzy T-shirt. Gone full feral, in a matter of days. 'Damn, Bishop. You have shamed your Afrikaner heritage.'

'Fuck that. This place is a dorp and it sucks ass. It's literally making my skin crawl.' Chlöe scratched her scalp furiously. 'I'm counting the hours till we hit the road. Please tell me we're leaving at the crack of dawn tomorrow, because for once I won't mind.' She squinted down the grassy verge, past the easternmost cluster of chalets nearest the kitchen. An animated group of staff were gathered, talking and pointing. Vee made out Zintle in their midst, looking quietly confused. 'What's up over there?' Chlöe asked.

"I'll fill you in later. Meanwhile, I just found out there's some plehjay and merrymaking going on tonight, some conference is ending. How you feel about being my date to a gatecrashing?"

Chlöe did a little jig of joy. 'Yaaay! Finally, something to break the bloody monotony. God, that's why I hate the boonies. Nothing *ever* happens.'

Vee watched a short man and stately woman, both civvies-clad and reeking of seniority, break from the uniformed gaggle and stride towards the chalet at the outermost fringe. A cluster of pink-with-grey-trimmers tiptoed behind them, Zintle in the rear, hem of her uniform's apron pressed over her mouth.

'Then stay tuned,' Vee mumbled.

5

'I look like wata-police.'

Chlöe blew an exaggerated breath. 'No, you do not look like a slut, young lady,' she wagged a finger. '*I* look like a slut, which is perfect. You look... moderately immoral. With great legs. Never bitch about that.'

'Oh, shut up. Over there looking shamelessly foxy in *my* dress.' Vee pulled at her top, trying to tug it down. For heaven's sake, she was wearing a shirt as a dress. She belted her purple silk scarf over her midriff and sighed. It was better than nothing. She glared at Chlöe, who made an apologetic grimace. 'Never again will I remind you to always pack a social outfit.'

'Sooorry, I forgot. But you weren't doing it justice. Perky you may be, but this dress needed my double-D bastards to really make it pop.' Vee gave mock gasp of shock as she covered her chest and Chlöe laughed. 'Meisie, if you leave them lying around, I *will* look. Can I have the dress?'

'Help yourself. The Dolly Partons crush The Pointer Sisters once again. At this rate you'll own half my closet.' She poked her nose around the hedge. There was just the one guard by the back entrance, looking thoroughly bored. 'You ready?'

Chlöe nodded.

Vee emerged from the bushes, trying to give the aura of a guest who had come outside for fresh air. Chlöe watched with bated breath and some amusement as Vee engaged the door's sentry. She twitched her hips and put on a winning smile. The man shook his head. She leaned in closer and murmured in his ear. He shook his head harder and straightened up, implacable. Vee slunk back.

'What the—'

'Let me try.'

Chlöe skipped round the hedge and up the stairs, innocence soldered onto her face. She tilted her chest to full voluptuous advantage as she toyed with curly wisps on the end of her French plait. She tossed in a joke and brushed her hand over his arm while he laughed. At last the guard nodded and she wolf-whistled Vee over.

'Black man's kryptonite,' Vee muttered, giving Chlöe a playful shove as they entered. 'You should be ashamed of yourself for manipulating the system.'

'Hey, don't hate the player, hate the game.'

————

'Well done, Grotto,' Vee murmured. The foyer was a space by leaps and bounds transformed. Dim lighting and fresh flowers disguised many an evil, but still, the place looked good. 'It hardly looks the same since I saw it this morning. These guys work fast.'

Chlöe handed her a glass of Chardonnay and took a sip of hers. 'I wouldn't know. *I'm* not a wall-jumper.' She popped a tiny cracker, stacked with colourful layers and sprinkled with parsley, into her mouth. 'More importantly, before we get made by someone who doesn't know us, or think we should be here...'

'True. Let's find out who's throwing this thing. I'm more worried about someone who *does* recognise us. Not exactly part of our assignment, this.'

'Chill. What're the chances—'

'I say, finegeh you nah easy o. Dah how you will jeh pass by yor friend dem without even speaking sef?'

As one, they whipped around in the direction of the male voice, Chlöe perplexed and Vee openly shocked. The lilt of Liberian pidgin in the middle of Oudtshoorn, or anywhere for that matter, was far from everyday.

'Whahappin so, we made palaver or uhn got no home training?' the man finished. The blonde woman on his arm looked bored, her only acknowledgement of their existence a blink in their direction before she turned away.

Vee scoffed, breaking into an immediate grin. 'Lovett Massaquoi.'

'How you been keepin', Ma, you awreh?'

'We tenkgawd o, what to do.'

The peroxide-blonde arm candy detached herself as if on cue and melted into the crowd without a backward glance, leaving the man with Vee. Chlöe watched their exchange with uncontained interest; the two quick pecks on each cheek, followed by the smooth handshake that ended with a brief wrestling of their middle fingers and snap against their palms. Vee had showed it to her, this famously cool snapshake, but she was still struggling to master it. As they stepped aside to let other guests filter in, the outdoor lighting streamed through the sliding glass and illuminated their corner.

Chlöe heard herself gasp before she could catch it. The man's face was... captivating. The landscape of his features was more hewn than crafted, like his maker had taken a machete to the bark of dark walnut, methodically yet somehow carelessly. His forehead, cheeks and nose appeared to rest on angular props that shifted in entrancing ways each time his expression changed. His laugh leapt past dark, almost wastefully full, lips, a laugh that seemed to emit from the bottom of a well, a sultry, disconcerting boom. At long last, the stream of jabber between him and Vee ended, and with a pat on her shoulder and a nod to Chlöe, he moved inside.

'Who was *that*?'

'Oh, Lovett Massaquoi, attorney-at-large. We've done some work together.'

'Lovett? What kind of name is that? Doesn't sound... indigenous.'

'His grandmother was one of those rare, olden-time feminists. She be damned her grandson was carrying her last name one way or the other.' Vee broke stride and threw a squinty side-eye. 'Come oooon... say it, I won't judge.'

Chlöe blushed. 'What?'

'Girl, please. I *know* you,' Vee teased. 'You were thinking he looks all menacing black male, like those tribal masks I got up on my living room wall.' She made an arc through the air as if lining up the array of miniature carvings of her country's sixteen tribes, a fascination for Chlöe every time she came over. 'Comes busting through the bush all junta rebel-like, his sweaty, rippling chest bared to the elements, ready to defile your cream with some chocolate...'

'You're an idiot. A disgusting, racist idiot.'

'I'm kidding, I know you're not a fan of penises. And since you're *not* asking, Lovett is and was no rebel. Lovett does not do guns or physical violence; Lovett does not do blood. Or swearing. I don't think dirt, sweat or morning breath have any feature in that hologram of perfection that pompous ass calls his life.'

'He seemed friendly enough.'

Vee shrugged. 'We...' She mish-mashed her fingers together to indicate it was complicated. 'We coexist. There's a working respect, but we still fuss with each other.'

'Is that all...'

'Hell yes.' Vee looked appalled. 'Lovett? Never. And long as

I'm not a skinny blonde called Tiffany, he ain't interested. Huge kryptonite junkie. Didn't you see who his date was?'

'Geez, calm down, I was just asking. How often do I get to see you in action with your kinfolk? Allow me my nosiness.'

'Hhmph. Well.' Vee passed a hand over her forehead. 'We're rare, I'll give you that. Everyone out here thinks Nigeria represents the whole west coast and speaks for all of us, you can imagine how problematic is. That's part of how I met him. You remember my birth certificate problem… it got annoying as hell every time I go to Home Affairs or have to apply for certain things.'

Chlöe nodded. It was hilarious enough that Voinjama went through life named after a trading city in northern Liberia, thanks to a clerical error on an identity document. She poked Vee in the ribs. 'Come on, why do you refuse to tell me what your parents meant to name you? It can't be that embarrassing. Was it Meredith?'

Vee smirked. 'I tell you, I kill you, you know how it is. But it wasn't done, that kinda thing is never top priority for kids. Then the war happened and… well. We did some hurry-hurry documents when I left Ghana for the States, that's what I use here.' She wolfed a sushi roll from the snacks tray. 'Anyway, Lovett finally saw to it. He's a consultant for firms and businesses, and also runs his own legal aid setup called Advocates for Refugees Abroad, ARA. He started it with a couple of his friends, and there's one in the US, one in Ghana, plus the one in Joburg. In fact, he's still pestering me to join his team as lead investigator. Convinced I'm wasting my talent at *City Chronicle*.'

'And that's how you met.'

'No,' said Vee. 'He had this case a few years ago. A Liberian couple living in some Joburg ghetto got reported to the police for abusing their daughter. Our embassy in Pretoria asked Lovett to get involved, to make sure they were protected and everything was above board with local authorities. The couple claimed they only spoke the Grebo dialect, which made everything difficult, especially translating court procedure and working on their defence. Lovett didn't buy it so while their team scouted around for a translator, he did his own hunting. I was visiting Joburg at the time, someone mentioned to him that I "investigated things" and he got in touch.'

'You're not Grebo. Or a detective.' Chlöe flapped her hand. 'Granted, you do have that knack for ingenious, moronic plans. What did you do?'

'Nothing crazy. Apart from elderly Liberians and people in remote rural areas, there's nobody who can't speak koloqua, or pidgin English. And if you know *that*, your English's good enough. I spent an afternoon tailing them and finally managed to video-record them having a full-blown discussion in a supermarket about the best type of rice to buy. Things turned around after that. Turns out the kid wasn't even theirs, they took her from her Ma who was the man's distant relative… it was a mess. In the end, they got deported to face the charges at home and the girl was eventually reunited with her mother.'

'And everyone lived happily ever after, thanks to Miss Cleverclogs.'

'Lovett did most of the work, but you know…' Vee batted her lashes.

'Seeing as you're such a bright spark, can you figure out what that means?'

———

'Legacy Entrepreneurial Advancement Deal. That's what it stands for.'

Eyes bright with zest and a head of light-brown hair so rowdy it looked like it was trying to escape, the towering man cut the caricature of bright-eyed and bushy-tailed. He knuckled his glasses up his nose with one hand, using the other to stab at each letter on the banner above the door. The banner read: "L.E.A.D... Into Our Innovative Present and Our Prosperous Tomorrow". 'That's us. Business owners who innovate,' he said.

Vee and Chlöe both opened their mouths.

'Expansion and diversification, is what it amounts to.' The woman who interrupted had an uptight, academic flounce about her, her short natural hair framing mousy features. 'It's a smarter way to do business, where big private financiers are the driving force behind up-and-comers. Lord knows our governments don't care enough to do it. Private investors are great at checks and balances. Our capacity to innovate, our fiscal probity and our chances of success... they make sure we've got it all before they back us.' She dragged in a long breath and exhaled into a gulp of wine. 'And in post-World Cup South Africa, there's good money to be made. Even with the global economic downturn.'

'Did she just, like, say "fiscal probity" at a party?' Chlöe whispered. Vee nodded slowly, alarmed.

A gnome of a man with a crown of shiny, beaver-black hair guffawed. 'Well, well, looks like somebody listens too closely during these boring seminars. There's no need to get so technical with our lovely guests. As kids these days would say, chill out dude.'

Several gathered round the circle tittered. The uptight woman turned to the wall, jaw flexing as she looked down into her glass.

'She means 2010 was South Africa's year and in 2011 we're still feeding off it, thanks to FIFA and other smart private investors,' Gnome-man continued. 'The LEAD incentive is a collaboration. Working with government, a group of these private fat cats intend to evaluate a group of small and medium-sized outfits, based on their performance in the economy so far. The companies that show the best proudly South African profile through their work get lovely goodie bags. A shitload of funding, a competitive edge in getting a lot of juicy tenders. Not to mention, a chosen few are nominated "national legacy enterprises".' He fashioned air quotes and whispered the last words like they were thick with intrigue, then laughed. His laugh was overly loud and he had a way of squeezing his eyes shut in the process, like life was a performance he gave with great pleasure. 'Basically you get a full purse and the prestige that goes along with it. That's some quality branding.'

'Hummph,' Chlöe snorted under her breath. 'Quality money laundering, more like. Jislaaik, when will the government realise the public can see these so-called upliftment ventures for what they really are? Cronyism, and more crony-benefitting ways of ripping us off.'

'This,' Gnome-man gestured at the room at large, 'is all part of the vetting process we've been undergoing since last year, the last leg of it actually. Every man for himself from here on out.'

Presenting the loudest pekin on the playground, Vee thought, watching him adjust his belt and puff his chest as approving nods went around the group at his summation.

'Yes, when there's pie on offer, you can bet we'd all like a slice of it,' said a plump Indian woman with a giggly voice and an enviable sheet of gloss tumbling past her shoulder blades. At her elbow stood a much younger, pretty Indian girl with a vaguely familiar face. Vee smiled; the girl shot back a rather strange look. 'But we'll be fighting like greedy children very soon, knives drawn to stab each other in the back. Pity we can't all have a share in it.'

The tall man with the wild hair sniffed and pulled himself up to his full, magnificent height. 'However the chips fall, some of us are pacifists and fully intend to be good losers. Sporting spirit and all that.'

'Of course *you'd* spout such rubbish! You're rolling already, you white oppressor,' joked a young dark-skinned woman with budding locks. 'Your company has the best chance of walking away from this looking rosy, whether you win or not. IT is the future, and the now, of everything.'

Tall-and-Lanky sighed dramatically. 'Good God, we aren't going to endure another lecture about black empowerment and the bloody rainbow nation, are we? Because we covered it in the sessions.' Beaming, he whirled on Vee and Chlöe. 'I don't believe anyone's introduced themselves. How churlish of us. I'm Ryan Walsh.'

'Akhona Moloi,' added Uptight, immediately re-pursing her lips onto the rim of her wineglass.

'Gavin Berman,' said the Gnome-man, massaging Vee with leery eyes.

'Aneshree Chowdri,' murmured the pretty and up-till-then silent Indian girl, her look sharp and meaningful in Vee's direction for reasons Vee could not fathom.

Another half a dozen names flew in from around the room, leaving Vee and Chlöe blinking like dazed deer.

'What're you guys doing here? Obviously you're not one of our lot,' someone asked.

'We're jo—'

'On a corporate retreat,' Vee interrupted Chlöe with an arm squeeze. 'We're under military rule on the other side.' She pointed in the boot camp's general direction. 'Thought we'd bust out for the night and have a little fun.'

'Ahhh,' breathed the room in unison.

'Party-crashers,' someone quipped cheerfully. 'What's it like over there? Must be exciting.'

'Talk about exciting over there, what about *right here*? Someone kicked the bucket in the lodge this very morning. We saw them moving the body when we came out of our first session. Talk about creepy. I thought they'd cancel the merrymaking.'

'And drive away paying clientele? Ag, you must never.'

'Yeeaaah... I heard it was the general manager.'

'I saw the general manager an hour ago. It was the head of housekeeping.'

'Head of housekeeping is male and black; the dead person was a white woman. It was the deputy GM. Apparently she drank herself to death. Sad, hey.'

Chlöe's neck snapped sideways, eyes agog. Vee shrugged, *I don't know what they're talking about.* Chlöe's gaze doubled back – *what do you mean you don't know, you're always the first to get the low-down* – then began to shrink with suspicion – *waaait a minute.*

'Hang on, this afternoon when—'

'I need the bathroom,' Vee said, shrugging off her arm.

'You should dance with me.' The Walsh man blocked her path. 'I can never find a properly statuesque woman in any gathering. Not that you're anywhere near tall enough,' his grin mocked as he eyed her up and down. 'But you'll do.'

Vee allowed herself to be whisked away, her back cutting off Chlöe's splutters.

6

Four hours later, Chlöe tottered over to a quiet patch of lawn at the back of the venue, near the last sprinkle of chalets across from the workmen's quarters.

'You *knew* about that woman who kakked it this morning!' She crouched over Vee, prostrate on the lawn. 'You always hide the juicy stuff from me. They're saying she drowned herself in a bathtub full of bleach!'

Vee emitted a gurgly groan from the back of her throat. 'Chlöe, please…'

'Are you drunk?' Chlöe waved a hand in front of her face.

'Not exactly. Circling the drain. Those animals are the business leaders of tomorrow?' Vee rolled onto her back. 'Hooo. Had to get some air. I swear, if one more person commented on my accent or how I "speak so well"…'

'It's no one's fault you sound like a Jamaican reading a dictionary.' Chlöe tossed Vee's handbag on the grass next to her head. 'Meanwhile, Cricket,' she curdled her mouth, 'you dumped a phone on me that won't stop ringing. And yes I answered it, it was driving me nuts. Clearly you wanted me to do your dirty work, so here's the message: you've been ordered by both your men to stop pretending you're so busy and call them.'

She watched Vee lazily extract the cell, flip through the call and message register, sigh and switch the device to vibrate. 'How long are you gonna keep this up? You can't avoid a resolution forever, hey. And why won't you tell me what this cricket story is about? Or the "my rib" thing? Which is kind of creepy, by the way.'

On her back, arms spread out across the grass, Vee chuckled at the sky. 'Ti jokes that I'm the Eve to his Adam, his rib. He said six months after we got together that I was the woman who turned his life from good to incredible.'

'You heterosexuals say the most repulsively cute things. You turned mine to shit within three months, so you're devolving. Next.'

Vee giggled. 'The cricket story *is* nasty. We – me and Joshua – went to Pringle Bay for a long weekend and I bought food from a roadside vendor on the way back. Disaster. There was nowhere to stop and the whole time I was hopping in the car like, well, a cricket. Eventually he had to pull over and,' her voice dropped to a whisper, 'I had to go village style, squat in the bush. There's no dignity in relieving yourself to the sound of someone laughing their ass off at you.'

'Haha. Two repulsive stories,' Chlöe laughed along, though it wasn't what she was in it for. She let it breathe, then poked Vee's thigh. 'Hey, don't pretend you didn't hear the first question. What're you gonna do? 'Cause your threesome's been stable for months now, but clearly it's hit a snag. Or you wouldn't have dragged us out here. This is classic you and your stubborn variety of avoidance strategy.'

'You're making me sober. Stop it.'

'You need to be, so you'll listen. As much as I admire your balls of steel, or tits rather, this is madness. You dared to say you couldn't choose, they went along with it, and now you're caught between a very sexy rock and a smouldering hard place. But it won't last, Voinjama. Women make lemonade and suck it up. Men can't.'

'I know.' Vee sat up. 'Don't call it a threesome, please.'

'Then? And that coloured girl with Joshua…' Chlöe clapped

a hand over her mouth. 'Eish, ja okay, I saw them together a couple of weeks ago. Didn't want to get involved, and I figured you'd find out one way or another.'

'Aria. Aria Burke,' Vee uttered the name like an evil spell. 'In America she's black by the way, but whatever.'

'And she is…'

'Ancient history. She and Joshua grew up in the same hood, their parents know each other, they've got a twisted backstory.' Vee yawned and put one arm back over her eyes. She was trying to appear nonchalant but Chlöe could tell she was annoyed. She kept swaying one leg back and forth on the grass. 'She's a professional dancer. I'm sure she's in town for some performance art thing, then she'll be gone. No big deal.'

'So you don't mind this ex-girlfriend swanning around on his arm? Still sleeping with him?'

'Nope. He's a grown man.'

'Mm-hmm.' *Tread carefully.* 'Look…' Chlöe drew her legs up and nestled her chin on her knees. 'Is this about Joshua lying to you about the Titus in Mozambique thing? 'Cause you insisted—'

'I *am* over it!' Vee snapped. 'These… goddamn, infuriating man-children, I swear…' Her fingers clenched into talons. 'Sometimes I could smack their empty heads together like coconuts.' She sat up, took one look at Chlöe's face and sagged. 'Chlöe, I don't see why I'm the one expected to clean up this mess. By myself, when I didn't make it. Year before last when I was falling apart and really needed Titus, he wasn't around. He left me. I had a miscarriage and he *left*.'

The words clung to the light dew in the air around them. Chlöe didn't move a muscle, in case the moment broke. Vee did not deal well with being left. Or feeling afraid. Vee did not deal well with the vulnerability of having to admit she counted on anyone enough to fashion their desertion into betrayal.

'On top of that, Joshua lied to me. I was desperate for answers, and he looked me in the face and lied that he didn't know Ti was posted in Mozambique all along. But he also knew that sometimes people really can't handle the truth. Me and Ti...' Vee's voice cracked. 'We messed up bad. We needed to run away from each other. Joshua was also the one who had to look at me every day and see how it was killing me. And then tell his boy about it, and hear how much it was killing him. But he couldn't own up because Ti swore him to secrecy, so he kept his word. He took care of a friend because another friend asked him to. I can't hate him for that. But I sure as hell can be vindictive for as long as I want.'

'Then... is this about being in love with him and not wanting to admit it? 'Cause that *never* ends well.'

Chlöe studied her friend's outline on the dim backlit lawn, watched her wordlessly slug through her dilemma. Vee's was a dirty beauty. Unkind, even, of the ilk of the unknowable Lovett Massaquoi and people who went through things. Real, brutal, life-altering things, that they then had to squirrel away in the name of normalcy and closure. The lines of her cheekbones and lips were angular yet soft, her eyes heavily tilted, the bridge of her nose surprisingly slender until the fleshy tip. It was a face to make men look, and look again. At certain angles it spelled trouble, and could suck you into wanting to find out how much.

Vee said nothing.

Chlöe licked her lips. 'Can I just say one thing?'

'God, not more *advice*.'

'No. It's... I don't like how you're letting this make you. You're letting *them* make you. Especially since you know who you want to be with. You're only prolonging this because you don't either of them to win.'

Vee let the night spin cobwebs over their silence. Finally she spoke: 'It's not about them, it's about me. I like being angry. Let me enjoy my shittiness till it stops making sense.'

'Well.' Chlöe plucked the grass, ripping up stubbly blades and stalks and rolling them between her fingers, letting the gentle wind sift them back to the ground. 'Okay,' she finished, nothing more to add.

She grunted to her feet and watched Vee resume her pose of languishing on her side, legs curved to her bum. 'Taking my drunk ass to bed and yours better follow soon. We've filed our piece, capped it off with a flippin' good time and I can't wait to leave this place in my dust tomorrow morning.' She stumbled as she tackled the incline of the grassy knoll. 'I'm serious, love,' she called over her shoulder. 'Don't fall asleep out here and get fondled by a security guard. You've got enough problems. If I don't see you in half an hour, I'm beeping you.'

'Urmmgghnff,' Vee mumbled.

———

Warm orange hit the back of her eyes.

Vee blinked from a doze and abruptly squeezed her lids shut again. Too bright. Where the hell was she? Grass and cool earth under her back. Outside… The lawn. Quiet. Opposite of inside. Noise, party, drunken louts. She patted the ground on either side of her. Empty. No Bishop. What the hell? That deserter, where was she?

Reluctantly, she bid her eyelids open. Adjusting to the glare of the security floodlights took a moment. She picked up scuttling, probably of one of the waiters or a maid, near the dark clutch of trees by the chalets. Other than that, no sign of humanity. She checked her watch: only ten minutes since Chlöe had left. It felt longer, but time felt slippery when you were between tipsy and a lost cause. She checked her phone: one new voicemail. From Titus: *Why you acting stank? You better holla back before I call one of my other women.*

Grinning, Vee propped up on elbows and lifted her face to the breeze. She imagined Titus's lips, trailing velvet down the verge behind her ear, fingers entangled with hers as he lowered his body to meet hers. Sometimes a memory of their lovemaking spooked her, so vivid she had to brace herself to keep her balance.

Then from nowhere, another image intruded: her lips in Joshua's curls, his mouth in the hollow of her neck as he stroked where the base of her spine curved into her bum.

Her eyes popped open.

Joshua Allen didn't have the good sense his Ma born him with. Messing around with his toxic ex-girlfriend, for real? Well, he needn't waste time waiting on her if his itches needed scratching. He was free to let Aria Burke wrap her well-muscled, modern-jazz-and-African-interpretive-dance legs around him any time, no problem. They'd look excellent together, their matching caramel limbs intertwined. They'd laugh over impossibly high-brow, insular American jokes that even she couldn't get and whisper shit to each other like 'Oh darling, this feels so irrevocably right.' Only they'd say it in Spanish, which they were both fluent in, because they shared that New York melting-pot backstory that she had no part of. The light-skinned, flowing-haired girls always won eventually.

Vee swallowed, the bolus of hurt wedged in her throat going down hard. No matter how many dam walls she shored up, somewhere else the walls were crumbling. But like hell was she going to wallow in drunken self-pity in a strange venue. Worry had rarely solved anything in the equation of life; regret, nothing at all.

She considered going back inside to the party; it was a shorter walk. Inside, where she didn't know anyone. Except Lovett, who always hobnobbed in tight, impenetrable cliques, doing his I'm-with-white-people laugh. No way. Even if it took all night, she would find her way back to the boot camp. Groaning with the effort, she wobbled to her feet and began the seemingly endless trek across the lawn.

A hand closed around her arm as her shoe hit the first step

at the end of the walkway. She tripped and nearly screamed.

'I'm so sorry. I called out but you didn't seem to hear me. You okay?'

'N— yes. I'm fine.' She pressed a hand to her chest. '*God*. I didn't think anybody else was out here.' She squinted against the security floodlights till she made out a face. It was the grandstanding loudmouth from the convention group. The one with black hair so stiff and glossy, it looked like the plastic bristles of a shoe brush pushing through his scalp.

'I believe this is yours.' He held out a length of purple material, whispery in the night breeze, and it took a moment before Vee recognised her scarf. She took it and muttered her thanks, draping it over her arm.

'It's Vai… Velajoma… Vanaijema?'

Here we go, she thought wearily. 'It's pronounced Vahn-jah-ma. Almost like "vine", as in "grapevine". Or Voi-een-jah-ma. Whichever.' She punctuated with a shrug, feigning nonchalance, but remained wary. This man wasn't out here in search of pronunciations. Dodginess was alight in his flickering gaze.

He chortled, flushing. 'You gave me your card.' He waved it under her nose. 'Been wondering how to say it. It's a lovely name. I'm Gavin Berman, if you remember.'

I did what? A vague recollection of doing the schmooze shuffle — polite laughter, strategic name-drops, business cards slipping with ease through her fingers — flashed in her mind. She pressed her eyes closed and caressed her forehead. How many had she had?

'So. Johnson.' He twiddled the card, flicking it under his fingers. 'Hhmm. Interesting. Are you coloured?'

God, this country. 'Do I look coloured?' Vee picked a twig off the scarf.

He laughed far too loudly. 'No, no, clearly not. It's rather curious, though. Why is your name Johnson, then?'

'Because my father's name is Johnson. Look, I'm really sorry, but—' She stopped herself. *Dammit woman, stop bloody apologising.*

'No, *I'm* sorry, for going about this the wrong way. It's obnoxious. I see you're a journalist.' He flicked her card against his thumb before slipping it into his pants pocket. 'You must be covering the event. Would you like to have a drink? I'm a mine of information at the witching hour.'

She relaxed. Slightly. 'Oh no, I'm actually not on this. Just visiting. Thank you for the offer, but no thanks. I have a very early start ahead of me tomorrow.'

'Mmm. Never underestimate the power of networking. Was that your colleague with the redhead, or are you guys... more? You both were quite intimate, the way you interacted.'

Vee bristled. 'We're...' She swallowed the rest, stopped short of saying 'just friends'. Friends were never a just, a throwaway, but romances in and of themselves. Often the truest kind. Who did this strange man think he was anyway, unabashedly prying? His gaze did another flick, a tiny smile on the corner of his lips, and without knowing how, she knew. He'd been watching them. As she and Chlöe reclined on the lawn, spinning their secrets, his eyes had been somewhere in the dark, sliming back and forth between them like okra. Smutting up their exchange.

That was all the answer she needed. She turned to leave and heard him bound up the stairs after her.

'One drink.' He barred her way. 'I'll walk you back to your room.'

His eyes roamed over and stuck to her body, wet and slimy. He stepped close enough for a blast of his breath to hit her in the face. Vee backpedalled, heart starting to thud. 'Wha—'

'Just think about it...' As his arm snaked around her waist, Vee saw her own arm shoot out with a will of its own. His eyes bulged as her fingers closed around his neck and shoved him against the nearest wall. A croaky gargle escaped his throat.

'Listen here, mister ass,' she whispered, appalled at her shaking voice. 'If dis dah you *not* being obnoxious, you best rethink it quick-quick.' She shoved him once more before releasing her grip, letting him sag against the wall. Bent double and coughing, surprise and outrage bubbled in his eyes as he looked up at her.

'Want start sumkana nonsense dis late night. You think dah brothel heah?' She sucked her teeth viciously and hustled across the stretch of lawn, looking behind her every so often.

'Ahem. Ma'am.'

The voice hailed from her far right. Vee swallowed a squeak of surprise and squinted into the night, trembling a little as she tried to attach a body to the voice. Darkness peeled itself back and the concierge from earlier that morning solidified, nib of his flicked cigarette bouncing sparks onto the stone steps. Tony was his name, if she remembered right. Timothy maybe. Tom?

'Are you all right?' Even as he asked his eyes filled with knowing, a little pity, a heavy touch of smugness. Uninvited guests were always uninvited guests.

'I'm fine.'

'I could escort you back to your room.' He nodded in the direction of the main building behind them. Through the glass doors, silhouettes crisscrossed the large dining area. The party was still in full swing.

Vee pursed her lips. *You know damn well my room's not on this side of the wall.* 'No, thank you,' she snapped, picking up the pace. Common sense slowed her down and brought her to a halt. 'Actually,' she turned back, 'I'd appreciate that, thank you.'

'No problem. I'll walk you as far as the gate. The security guard will see you safely through to the other side.'

He fell into step beside her. Vee hugged her handbag to her chest and hunched against the sudden chill.

On the steps of the concrete walkway several metres behind them, her forgotten scarf billowed and snaked.

Razor

7

'I can't believe this,' Lovett said.

'*You* can't believe this?!' Vee hissed.

Her pocket vibrated: another missed call from Nico Van Wyk. Five in total. She should've held off on letting Chlöe call him. She typed a quick text along the lines of getting back to him as soon as she had a free second and slipped it in her back pocket of her jeans. Silent mode could take the flak when he lost it.

She peeped across the room at Chlöe, tucked away in a corner of the small dining room next to Lovett's hyper-blonde, Slavic-boned companion. Chlöe's eyes zipped around in her head, one emotion swiping another off her face every few seconds: worry in Vee's direction and plaintive hope in Lovett's, awe at the blonde's impeccable attire at just gone seven in the morning, distaste every time she scratched her scalp and terror every time her phone beeped. Vee turned back to Lovett. He paced, calmly. A relay of soft sighs left his lips as he worked the wooden floorboards, stirring a warm draft of toothpaste and men's cologne every time he strode past.

'It's ridiculous. They're holding you on a very flimsy premise. They know it too, hence the time-wasting while they get their act together.'

'Lovett.' Vee stopped him with a hand on his shoulder. 'Lovett o-o-o. You boy, dah na play-play we on heah. A man is dead. Strangled with a piece of *my property*. They saw the marks round his neck where I choked him.' Her voice had thinned out to a child's whine. She drew in a long, shaky breath to steady it. 'Now, I don't know if you're trying to approach this as a lawyer or as a fr—' She stopped, baffled by the audacity of what she'd been about to say. Were they actually friends? Did Lovett even do friendship? She had no clue.

Lovett smiled wryly and patted her hand. 'It's taking longer than it needs to, is all. The police haven't laid charges because they barely have any evidence. The scarf is circumstantial, anybody could've used it. They've questioned you for an hour this morning, and you cooperated and stuck to your story. Because it's true. Nothing… untoward transpired between y'all, right?'

'Ehn? Meaning, did I sleep with him? With Papa Smurf? The garden gnome?'

Lovett pressed his mouth into a firm line. Vee sighed and shook her head no. 'So then. They just have to find this concierge fellow to settle everything.' He strolled back to the sliding doors, closing his eyes and inhaling deeply as the morning sun struck his face. Vee noticed that his shirt had not a single wrinkle in sight. She edged away from his suave aura, pressing her armpits to her sides to conceal half-dried circles of sweat on yesterday's rumpled T-shirt.

'But what if they don't find him? What if this killer got to him too last night? Two people dead already.'

'What? *Two people*? Which two people now?' He pivoted from the east-facing view to drill her with a look of deep concern, the kind given to addled unfortunates just before padded cells and calming drugs came into play. 'There's *one* dead body, Voinjama.' He held up a single finger. 'One victim. Just relax. And stop talking.'

Chlöe watched Vee slump into a chair on the other side of the room. Lovett, who did not seem like a sensitive man but did seem to have some type of rapport, clearly unromantic, with her, sighed into the next chair. Arms wrapped tight around her middle, Vee kept shaking her head and nervously jiggling the toes of her sneakers against the floor.

Lovett shook his head. 'Finegeh, jeh relax. Stop worryin' like dis.'

Chlöe smiled. Leaning towards the blonde, she half-whispered: 'This "finegeh", or "fine girl" if you're a stickler, it's such a major part of their slang, you know. I guess it's like "meisie" in Afrikaans. Only they say it *a lot* more often, right?'

'I guess so.' The blonde carried on texting for another second before looking up. 'You can understand that stuff they're saying?'

'I've got a pretty good hang of it,' Chlöe preened. 'The accent and the speed's the hard part. But you catch on. It's like pretending half your brain is dead and the other half is completely drunk.'

The blonde fired an as-if-I-give-a-shit look and went back to the war of thumbs with her iPhone. Alarmed, Chlöe saw she was tweeting. Nico's fuming on the phone earlier that morning had included his outrage that they and their incident were blowing up locally on Twitter, and he'd had to hear about it from an office underling. Chlöe looked back at Vee, who looked like she was trying to devour her bottom lip.

'Aay mah pipo,' Vee clapped her hands once, the corners of her mouth turned down. 'Wakana troubo I nah put mysef in again ooo?'

Chlöe closed her eyes, which somehow worked wonders in unjibbering the jabber coming from across the room. *You mean what kind of trouble has found you once again. And me, by extension.* Things were bad if Vee's facade of unfazed glitched for even a moment. Right now, it had a gaping hole in it.

'Aay you geh, man,' Lovett sighed impatiently. 'Ahn like de way you ackin' so. Ehn I na tell you, de pipo dem ain got nuttin to charge you wit.' *Come now, girl. I'm not at all impressed with how you're behaving. I keep telling you, these people haven't got a shred of evidence against you.*

'Da lie o! Dey got da scarf, da sumtin. And even sef, who say dey can't jeh hitch it behind me jeh because dey ain got nobody else to juke?' *How can you tell such lies! That scarf is a lot of something. Besides, who says they won't pin it on me just because they need a scapegoat?*

'Move from heah, man. You na nobody in dis town heah, nobody want hitch nuttin' on you. Da na nuttin hard to anythin' hard to sort dis out quick. So don't come chakla errytin wit dah yor mouf deh.' *Get real. You're a nobody in this town, so rest assured nobody's trying to pin anything on you. So don't mess this up by losing your cool.*

Vee chuckled. 'Well, you better be tokkin de truth. Because,' here she enunciated clearly, 'I will not fare well behind bars. People will die.'

At the sound of Vee's laughter, Chlöe blinked her eyes open. They'd started to water. Her throat felt dry and she was actually getting a headache. *Let's never go to West Africa,* she advised herself bitterly. Their pidgin could short-circuit the human brain. She wearily tuned back in when Lovett took off again.

'Ehn, you know you comin' pay plenty for my services, ehn? All dis one heah will be on my bill,' he joked. *Money.* He was either joking or serious about charging Vee for coming to their aid. Chlöe sighed. Lawyers: the rats of the working world.

'I beg you yah. You fini zwapping all my mah and only feecee news una give me so far.' *She's broke.* Chlöe knew that. But news about what?

'I say, I na fix de full report for you. I jes ain want tok plentay heah.' Lovett shifted uncomfortably in his chair, tilting his body towards Vee even more, as if that would create a soundproof wall between them and the rest of the room. His voice dropped to a whisper. 'We found him. But you won't like it...'

Chlöe's ears perked to the ceiling. There was a full report of some kind. That Lovett didn't want to discuss. Which meant it was private, and Vee definitely wouldn't want her knowing about it. And there was *another* "him"? Didn't she have enough problems of a phallic nature to juggle?

'Where is he? How... where's he been all this time? Lovett, look at me and tell me how my brother—'

Brother. Quentin. Vee's mysterious elder sibling. Chlöe exhaled shakily.

Lovett planted a quick squeeze on Vee's knee and her eyes flitted around until they slammed into Chlöe's. Their eyes held for what felt like an eternity until they both looked away.

'Finally, they're back,' Lovett interrupted, rising to his feet. Management was in the building, and it looked fighting furious.

———

Vee, Chlöe, Lovett and his companion threaded from the foyer into the dining room, led by the pinch-faced general manager. Clad in a cream blouse with a pussy-bow neckline and a snug black skirt, Samantha Motaung did not look like someone who'd been spearheading damage control since daybreak. Taking in the GM's neat cornrows snaking to curly tips over one shoulder, Vee felt another self-conscious pang as she passed a hand over her own scruffy hair. Motaung did a stellar job of masking her emotions, but her anxiety and shock at the morning's turn of events bled through. Above all, she looked damn well put out that they'd transpired on her turf.

'Well.' Motaung looked around at Sergeant Ncubane, Zintle and the concierge from the previous night, before nailing Vee with a frown. Vee held her gaze until at last she broke, only to turn and find Ncubane drilling her with a scowl of his own. Now that she knew his name and rank, and he'd finally succumbed and removed his ridiculous trench coat, the lead officer had lost his looming intensity.

'I've located Trevor Davids as you requested,' Motaung

darted her eyes between Vee and Ncubane, 'and he's happy to assist in any way. I'd love to have this cleared up as soon as possible.'

That's his name... Trevor. Vee exhaled, looking the concierge up and down. Minus the dark-blue blazer of his uniform he looked different, unkempt almost, and his curly dark-brown hair lacked the neatness of the previous day when she'd first met him. They'd likely rushed him away from his morning routine. His vibe was different, too, without the suspicious squint or a cigarette in his mouth. Right now, Vee couldn't tell if the lilt of his lips was a smile or a smirk. But he definitely remembered her. *Let's play nice now, Trevor,* she thought with a touch of desperation. Don't exaggerate our small fuss into a big palaver.

'Can you tell us...' Ms Motaung prompted, hands palms-up to indicate the floor was open.

Trevor launched into it, hesitant at first. Thankfully, he made no mention of Vee impersonating a guest to sneak into the hotel in the afternoon. He did, however, give a vividly accurate description of Gavin Berman approaching Vee as she crossed the lawn at about 12.40am. The group expelled a collective gasp as he gave extra colour to what he termed "a somewhat embarrassing altercation" between the two guests. Vee chewed her lip as Trevor's fingers stiffened into a vice, depicting the stranglehold she'd put on Berman. Motaung gaped; Ncubane clenched his jaw; Lovett threw her an indecipherable look lightly mixed with admiration; Zintle put a hand over her mouth.

'Did you actually see her off the grounds?' Ncubane pressed.

Trevor, please, Vee begged with her eyes.

There was a beat before Trevor replied, 'Yes, I did. I escorted her to the main gate myself. Sipho, one of the lodge's night guards, took her from there back to the boot camp where one of the other security guards saw her to her chalet from there.

He made very sure no one left that chalet all night. All of us at Grotto know it's highly frowned upon for boot campers to fraternise with lodge residents, and we wanted to prevent any more incidents of such. And yes,' he pressed on when Ncubane opened his mouth, 'I did see Mr Berman alive when I returned. He was still outside.'

'He was *alive?*'

'Yes. Definitely.'

'Are you *sure?*'

Trevor blinked. 'I'm confident I can recognise a living person when I see one, Sergeant.' Motaung cleared her throat and clipped her eyes at him in reproach. 'He was still lingering on the lawn where this lady herself had been sitting before he cornered her. I left him there and went back to the front desk,' Trevor added.

'And what was he doing there?'

'I can't say exactly.' Frowning, Trevor shrugged. 'Like, he was just standing there. Like he was looking at something in the distance.'

Ncubane sighed. 'At what exactly?'

Under the razor eye of his boss, Trevor did his best to bite back a retort. 'I really couldn't say. It was late and very dark; he was by the trees near the boys' quarters. It could've been anything, mind you, but allow me to remind you that the boys' quarters is where he was hanged. Perhaps he saw something that led to his death. Or maybe he was simply getting some fresh air and calming down after being…' he glanced at Vee with the tiniest of smiles, 'woman-handled.'

'Did you see this purple scarf she claims she left behind? On the lawn?'

Trevor thought for a moment, then shook his head. 'No, I didn't see a scarf anywhere nearby. But she didn't have it with her. I didn't notice anything like that on her when she left the gate.'

Motaung shared a quiet word with Trevor before dismissing him, and Ncubane moved over to Zintle. 'Sisi, now I'm going to ask you some questions, neh, and I want you to tell me the truth. Don't try to be clever and change your story nje and think I won't notice.' Zintle kept her eyes on the floor. Vee noticed tiny goosebumps had prickled up on the skin of her arms and collarbone. 'Do you hear what I'm saying?' Ncubane barked, making Zintle jump. 'Don't bullshit me, my girl, or there'll be serious consequences. You understand me?'

Lovett, silent and observant with no expression save his usual slight frown, exhaled loudly. Vee narrowed her eyes at Ncubane and put a hand on the girl's arm. Why did black people in authority still feel the need to treat each other like this, belittling another to flaunt how inflated their chests were? Trevor the Snide had breezed through his interview burn-free, but clearly he wasn't black enough to incite such nonsense. Even Motaung grimaced, pivoting on her heels to shoot Ncubane a frosty glare.

'Let's watch our tone, shall we, Sergeant,' she retorted. 'My staff have been very cooperative so far, and we'd like to keep the atmosphere as pleasant as we all can during this unfortunate event.'

'Hhmph,' came the policeman's reply. 'Do you know this woman?' He jabbed a finger at Vee so violently she took a step back.

Zintle looked confused. 'Yes.' She nodded furiously. 'Yes.'

'Eh-hehh. How do you know her?'

Zintle's confusion doubled. 'From the hotel. I met her here. I told you.'

'Nxc! Just answer me what I'm asking. Tell me again what happened this morning.'

Zintle cleared her throat. 'I came in for my shift this morning at five o'clock. After I changed into my clean uniform,

I dumped the dirty one into the laundry trolley and pushed it outside for the guys who load the laundry truck to find it. While I was outside, I saw Lwazi and Thomas talking between themselves like something was wrong.'

'Those are the two groundsmen?'

Zintle nodded. 'They said they found a dead body, a white guy, who was hanging by his neck outside their quarters. We went to look.' She swallowed hard at the memory. 'I didn't want to but we did. None of us recognised him, but we can't know all the guests. We started discussing what to do. I told them to go call the police and I would find someone who could help. So then I went across and called this lady, Ms Johnson, and she came with her friend. They waited with me until you guys came.'

'Oh-ho-o-o. So you don't know this lady from anywhere? Yet of *all the people* at this hotel, you went all the way across the fence to fetch her? Before you even told your manager?'

Zintle thought for a second before answering this one. As she dragged in a gigantic lungful of air, lips puckered, she resembled a desperate molecule, sucking in every drop of ambient energy to boost her own charge. Eyes closed, she said in one rushed breath, 'I met her outside last night when the guests were arriving for the party. I was admiring her dress and she was nice, she told me where she bought it. We talked a bit.'

'Oh? And did she also tell you she and her colleague were gatecrashing a private event?'

Zintle barely paused. 'I work here, I don't question the guests. What I remembered is she mentioned they were investigators. At first I thought she meant they came to check the hotel, like an audit, but she said they look into crimes. I thought she meant like private investigators or with the police somehow, that they would know what to do if there was a murder. That's why I went to her.'

Good girl, Vee exhaled along with her. *Well done.*

Ncubane snorted and flailed an arm. 'Hhayi mhani! They are investigative journalists! Those ones who look into stories and then write it for the newspaper. They are not private, and for sure they don't work for us. They don't open or close police investigations. Now our case will be spread all over the papers! You—' His face was a thundercloud; he looked on the brink of spewing a string of expletives. Ms Motaung raised her eyebrows again and he spluttered to a halt.

'She said investigation.' Zintle pulled a sullen face, crossing her arms tightly. 'All I heard was she could do investigations. So I called her.'

Lovett broke in with a low chuckle. 'I beg your pardon, Sergeant, but this sounds like a misunderstanding overblown. If we could just take this somewhere private and wrap it up...'

'My office,' Motaung crisped, striding toward the door.

———————

Chlöe cooled her heels for another twenty minutes before they emerged. Lovett's features remained inscrutable, but Voinjama's was a fountain gushing pure, sweet relief. Chlöe let herself breathe. Before they reached earshot, Lovett stalled Vee with a hand on her shoulder and a quick mutter. They both looked in Chlöe's direction before descending into discourse so rapid and guttural Chlöe could barely pick up any English in the mix. She sighed. They'd gone raw and she was out of the loop. Something was definitely up, but she'd have to follow that bunny down the rabbit hole to Vee's wonderland of secrets another time. They had bigger fish to fry.

'What're we telling Nico?'

'Nothing but good news.' Vee's tiredness cleared off with a smile. 'Thank the good Lord for Trevor, and now another security guard on patrol after I left the grounds came forward to report he saw Berman, too. My scarf may have got me into hot water, but that's not enough to charge me with murder.'

'Your scarf *and* your ability to go from zero to Hulk in

twenty seconds got you in hot water. I know you flip out when strange assholes feel you up because…'

Vee's face folded into a snarl.

'… of things of which we never speak, that happened in the not-war that we never mention. Whatever, I get it, but you have to work on that. Seriously, choking the guy?'

Vee's smile returned, sheepish. 'I know. Sorry.' She fished her cell phone from her back pocket and eyed it a long time before slipping it back. 'It can wait a minute. Food. There's a demon hollerin' in my stomach. Then,' she stuck her nose down the front of her T-shirt and grimaced, 'showers. You need to wash that hair. And change that T-shirt, it's holier than Jesus.'

'Then we can go *home*.' Chlöe frowned. No cheer of agreement. Instead, Vee had a faraway look, eyes lost in the distance as she chewed the inside of her cheek. 'We can go home, right? We're cleared to leave any time?' Chlöe pressed.

'Hhmmm…'

'What's "hhmmm"? Hhmmm is indeterminate and secretive. I need a firm answer.' Vee started walking and Chlöe scurried to keep up. 'Don't start. I hate that look.'

'Which look?'

'That one! The one where shit's brewing between your ears and you're not telling me shit!'

8

'What now?' Chlöe's eyes widened to blue planets inside her head. The phone call to Nico had not gone well. Far from. Disastrously far. But at least it was over.

'Now, nothing. That, as they say, is that.' Vee tossed her phone on the table and continued shovelling eggs and bacon into her mouth. She chewed thoughtfully. 'You were right; I should've called him earlier. He's been pickling in rage since daybreak.'

'*You think?* If he didn't have grounds for firing us before, he does now,' Chlöe replied. 'Which wasn't my point. That entire conversation was news to me. Why did you ask for more time so we could follow the story? What story? We're done here, and like he says, you can't write the story if you *are* the story. Remember that little gem called journalistic objectivity.'

'When I *might have been* the story, you mean. Shitty luck put me on the police's radar but now that I'm off it, no conflict.'

'It didn't sound like Nico agrees. Anyway, if there *is* a story it's for the crime beat, which we don't cover. We're here to write about the lodge and the retreat experience and *go home.*' Chlöe dug her fingers into her scalp and scraped hard enough to make Vee wince. 'I want to go home. Like, yesterday.'

'I know, and we will. But you gotta admit, something doesn't feel right. All these stuffed shirts gathered for an evaluation, which means they're competing against each other, right.' Vee's gaze skittered round the dining room at the breakfast crowd, half of whom had clinked glasses with them last night. 'An innocuous bunch. Yet, in the space of one weekend, two people turn up dead in an environment ripe with motive. How's that not suspicious?'

'Whyyyy...' Chlöe gave a long, pained groan, '*why* do you keep on about two murders? The other manager was a suicide, or death by misadventure or whatsit. It had *nothing* to do with Berman. Who is now officially the cops' problem.' She bit a pork sausage, glowering. 'This isn't some Agatha Christie whodunnit, where ten morons go on holiday in Egypt and only two come back alive.'

'Look.' Vee snatched the Samsung and switched to its photo gallery. 'Something's off about the entire scene where Rhonda Greenwood died. From the way the body was lying, to the bruises on her head—'

'Bloody hell, Vee! You took photos?!'

'Ssshhh! Dammit Bishop, pipe down.' Vee peered up from their huddle at the other diners, all either too sleepy or shell-shocked to be paying mind to their surroundings. The only person who seemed enthralled by their whisper fest was the young Indian woman from the party, who watched them with the same arrow-eyed interest from her own table across the dining room. The young woman caught Vee's eye and tossed her a toothy grin. Vee returned a puzzled smile and hunkered back down.

'Yeah, I took a few. Like I said, it didn't sit right. I thought...' Vee shrugged. 'If the cops came back with enough to point to a suspicious death, at least there'd be some documentation of the scene. I had to do *something*.'

'First, you took photos of a dead woman. Then, you nicked your business card out of the dead man's pocket this morning, which I witnessed you doing, by the way—'

'That was different! You saw those cops, foaming like a pack of rabid dogs. My scarf was bad enough, but *two* things linking me to Berman? Me, the kwerekwere with the unpronounceable name? Ha. Unless you were planning on leaving me here, behind bars.' Vee pushed the phone under Chlöe's nose. 'Girl, look at the photos of Berman. The dirt – look how it's sticking to the back of his shoes and smeared on the knees of his trousers. The sprinklers were on yesterday afternoon, so the ground was still moist last night. Assume the attacker jumps him from behind, scarf goes round his neck, squeezes till he falls to his knees and kpang! He's unconscious. Then whoever it was finishes him off and hauls him to the boys' quarters, the nearest and best hiding place. But we didn't check the surroundings. I'm sure if we'd looked, we'd have seen drag marks in the dirt from his shoes.'

Chlöe groaned. 'We're not people who look for *drag marks*. We're ladies. At least *I'm* a lady. One who's eating, and doesn't intend to hunt for drag marks when she's done.'

Vee wasn't listening. 'At least now we're free to move around. I'll get cleaned up, head into town—'

'Town?! And I'm sup—'

'Oh my *word*! Did they think you were a real suspect?'

Chlöe jumped a metre off her chair and Vee nearly choked on a mouthful of scone. Looming over them wide-eyed, the Indian girl immediately helped herself to a vacant chair before they had a chance to object. Vee edged her phone to her elbow and killed the screen.

'Aneshree Chowdri,' the girl said slowly, casting a wide net of weighted pause in Vee's direction, clearly expecting this would mean something. It didn't. A pregnant pause and several blinks later, Aneshree shifted in her seat. 'No matter. Anyway… I asked, did they really consider you a murder suspect?'

Her accent was poshly affected, a nice muddle of "larney" with the Asian lilt peculiar to South Africa. India by way of Durban most likely. The sultry droop of her sooty eyes and curve of jawline Vee found quite becoming, though her tone was sharp to an almost nasal vibration, at jarring odds with her looks. She looked like someone used to getting immediate compliance to a perpetual litany of demands.

'Um… we happened to be around when the groundsmen found the body, so the police questioned us, too. It was routine,' Chlöe said.

'Really? And how'd that happen? That you were around?' Aneshree's eyes probed. 'You're journalists, right?'

Vee opened her mouth, thought better of it and stuffed in the last bite of scone. She got to her feet. 'I'm heading out. You stay here and…' she eyed Chlöe over Aneshree's head, 'rub shoulders for a while.'

'But – should I – what if—'

'Won't take long.' She threaded out of the dining room before Chlöe could protest.

'She really didn't place me,' Aneshree muttered.

Chlöe barely heard her. Insides knotting up in distress, she watched Vee's retreating back as it hustled into the foyer. What the hell could one find in central Oudtshoorn, aside from more trouble and unwanted attention? What was she supposed to do in the meantime? Call Nico? He'd immediately order them back to town, a direct command Vee couldn't ignore. *Dare me and call Nico, see what happens,* Vee's voice threatened in her mind. Chlöe gulped and tucked her cell away.

Aneshree sighed dramatically and flicked her dark head in the foyer's direction. 'Your friend. She didn't make me out in the slightest.'

'Sorry, was she meant to?' Chlöe said, biting into toast. She had bigger problems; why was this girl still here?

'I thought so, but…' Aneshree shrugged and smirked. 'Considering she's the one keeping my brother's dick in her purse.'

Chlöe coughed toast into a napkin. 'Say *what* now?'

Aneshree giggled, preening. 'You two seemed pretty close. Or maybe you're not.'

'We *are.*'

'Then come on. *Chowdri.* As in…' Aneshree hiked her eyebrows and let them hover. 'Joshua Allen Chowdri. His sister.'

Chlöe gawped. 'Huh?' *Joshua Allen has another sister? Wait, Joshua's other surname is Chowdri?!* Vee talked about Joshua a lot, while pretending she didn't care to talk about Joshua, so Chlöe knew more than she needed to. There was a younger Allen sibling, his only sister, an overprotected model wannabe doing catalogue work somewhere in America. This person sitting in front of Chlöe was neither black, not even partly, nor American. 'Joshua has one sister. How do I know you're not lying? How do you know Vee? What are you doing here?' Squinting, Chlöe leaned closer, teeth bared. 'Are you *following* her?'

Aneshree laughed, more a snort than a laugh. 'Jeez, calm down. What are you, her pitbull? No one's following anyone. I don't know *know* her but I know *of* her – Cape Town's small enough. Besides,' her shoulder tugged in a semi-guilty, semi-proud way, 'I tend to follow my brother's antics with some interest. Depending on what they are.'

'So how…' Chlöe threw a quizzical look around the dining room.

'Oh, how am I part of this motley crew?' Aneshree popped a forkful of tiny orange wedges into her mouth. 'Work.'

'Work as in…'

'Software developer. Graphics here and there.'

'Ah, you're with…' Chlöe took a shovel to the terrain of last night's memory, already fallow under layers of hangover, scattered sleep and a healthy dash of morning trauma. The plump, older lady, waterfall hair, what had been her name? 'Mishra? Moodley? Moodley, mm-hmm. You were with her last night, you work with her. Thought she was in catering or something like that. Oh, I get it, you do their website.'

'She's in events management. And no, I don't work for her.

All Indians aren't in business together. She's my aunty's friend. And no, not all Indians are related either.'

'I didn't mean—'

'I'm here as an independent observer. Humouring my boss, you could say. So far…' Aneshree flip-flopped a hand.

'Not good, I'm guessing? Like, I don't know jack about any of this, but this new turn of events doesn't bode well for a smoothly running process,' Chlöe said.

'Well, let's just say I didn't expect it to be an easy ride from the beginning and it hasn't been one. Didn't expect a dead body served up with breakfast, that's for sure.'

'Can say that again.' Chlöe licked her yoghurt spoon absently. Vee was out there somewhere, stirring up plumes of drama. Chlöe scratched her scalp until she flinched. First things first – get cleaned up. Thoroughly, in the hottest bath or shower she could tolerate. Then she could think clearly, probably along the lines of an escape route, party of one, if it came to that. Vee could stay here and chase villains on her ace if she so pleased.

Aneshree shifted her chair closer. 'So. How long has she been frolicking with my so-called brother? Is she really from Libya? That's so hectic. What with this Arab Spring going on right now, and all the, like, Arab rage, how crazy is that. She must be worried sick about her family.'

'Uhhh… she's not…'

'Not that she looks Libyan. Maybe she's from one of those nomadic sects who look black. Hey, is it true my so-called brother got her knocked up and deserted her, then she had an abortion and a crazy meltdown?'

Chlöe slumped her head onto the table. 'Are you *kidding me* right now?'

9

Vee chewed a toffee and kept her eyes fixed on the sour-faced woman behind the reception desk. Every time the woman looked up, Vee rewarded her with a disarmingly slow grin that displayed all her teeth. Eventually, the receptionist-slash-security guard rolled her eyes and waved her over.

'Who did you say you want to see?'

'Dr Marielise Coetzee, the forensic pathologist,' Vee said for the fourth time in over 30 minutes.

'She's busy with cases, I told you. Don't you want to come back later?'

Vee's eyes popped. 'No. *Please.* I'll wait. I really can't leave and come back.'

The horrors of getting there in the first place! She had gone back to the boot camp and surrendered to the magic of a cool shower, toothbrush and comb. Her verve had faltered to ashes soon after. It took magical powers of persuasion to convince camp security that the circumstances of her stay had changed sufficiently to grant her freedom of movement in and out of the grounds. That accomplished, it took a hot, dusty trek to the nearest main road and a half-hour hitchhike before a driver finally stopped. Once in town, it was easy enough to find the brick building on Baron van Reede Street that was Oudtshoorn Police Station and the nearby coroner's office. Now she had to face this prickly reception.

'Sisi, you can't just stop here and speak to whoever, whenever.' The heavyset woman – Felicia Phiri, declared her name badge – scanned her up and down, distaste crinkling the skin around her nose and mouth. Vee sensed an acute infection of SGS coursing through her veins. Security guard syndrome: an intense, sadistic desire to exert power, however puny and fleeting, over all who had the misfortune of crossing their path. A disease of the chosen ones in uniform, behind desks and gates continent-wide. No wonder Felicia was so sour – her braids had been pulled so tight, tiny buds of follicular white peeped through the roots. *Your hairline won't thank you when you take those out*, Vee thought.

'You need to have an appointment or give a reason why you want to go inside, before I can help you. Or leave a message and I'll give it to Dr Coetzee.'

'I know, but—' The adjoining double doors burst open and suctioned shut. A harried-looking brunette in a white lab coat and heavy-duty galoshes, goggles round her neck, eyes down, glided past. 'Is that...?' Vee began. Felicia pursed her lips and crossed her arms. Vee took it as her answer and broke into a jog.

'Dr Coetzee?' The woman was a head shorter but had a hell of a stride. Vee was a little breathless when she caught up. She looked down into a pair of pale brown eyes with a faraway look that she suspected was somewhat permanent. 'I was wondering if I could bother you for a moment, if you have time.'

'Not *much* time.' Coetzee frowned. 'What's it about? Who are you?'

'Umm...' Vee scanned the long corridor. At one end was a uniformed officer and trio of lab coats, all striding towards them. She palpitated at the thought of running into Sgt Ncubane. 'It's hard to explain standing out here. And it's private. I swear, I'm not here to waste your time.'

'Well...' Coetzee motioned her to follow and stopped a

couple of doors down, unlocked and ushered her into a tiny office with walls of a nauseating green.

'Coffee? Sorry, instant's all I have,' she said, flipping the kettle on. Vee nodded, reminding herself that dead people were carved open in this building. Under the scent of potpourri, the office had a distant reek of uncooked meat, old fat, and a medicinal odour, all deeply marinated into the walls. Mug in hand, Vee dipped her lips in the liquid but didn't sip. Coetzee gave a questioning smile (was the coffee okay?) and Vee flipped a thumbs-up (perfect). The pathologist tugged an elastic tie out of her chestnut-brown hair, shook her head vigorously and promptly bundled it back up. Vee had a feeling she was sick of hearing how pretty her hair would look if she combed it. Coetzee had lively eyes, too, like she enjoyed talking but didn't often get the chance with the like-minded. *Better make this an interesting pitch, then,* Vee thought.

'I'm really pressed for time. It hasn't been a hectic morning, really I should be done by now, but I got another one coming in before I can wrap up. Young kid, fell out of a tree and broke his neck.'

Vee winced. 'Sweet Jesus.'

Coetzee nodded. 'Yeah. Terrible nature of the job.' She sipped her brew, throwing a perplexed look over the rim. 'Sorry, who did you say you were again?'

'I didn't say.' Vee took a breath and plunged on, 'Vee Johnson. I'm a journalist. In Cape Town. For *City Chronicle* newspaper.'

Coetzee put down her mug, leaned back in her chair and slowly ahhed.

'Before you start thinking anything, probably the wrong thing, let me explain. I'm in Oudtshoorn on a business trip, doing a travel piece on The Grotto Lodge. That's where I'm staying; it's about five, six kilometres from here. Very strangely, since I've been there…' Speaking succinctly and leaving no room for interruption, Vee gave a rundown of both deaths.

'Berman was brought in early this morning. That's an open police investigation.' Coetzee said. Her expression morphed from interest to one of serious affront. 'You can't possibly think—'

'I don't! I'm not here about that, believe me. Wouldn't be so stupid as to think the presiding pathologist would discuss a fresh murder case even if I wanted to. It's the other one. The woman who worked at the lodge.' Vee left a pause, adding, 'It felt off to me.'

Coetzee guarded a long silence, then followed it with a long sigh. 'Very unorthodox. I suppose since it's not a murder investigation... it depends on what capacity you're asking in. And *what* you ask as well. I can't supply confidential information. You're not a family member.'

'Asking as a concerned citizen who isn't officially investigating the matter.' Vee pulled out the Samsung and opened its photo gallery. 'Who also happened to be in the vicinity when these were taken.'

Coetzee leaned in, both eyebrows high. 'A concerned citizen has this on her phone?'

'The person who found her asked for my help. So I... please don't make me lie to you. This woman was long dead before I got anywhere near her.'

Coetzee closed her eyes and massaged her temples. 'I'm not liking this, but...' She dropped her hands. 'I myself didn't do the autopsy on Greenwood, but I went through the final report. What I can tell you, is there's not much I can tell you. Or can't tell you. Or can't *not* tell you.' Eyes still closed, she frowned, shook her head, and at last gave a dismissive wave. 'I mean the results were pretty definitive. But okay, ask. This isn't on the record, by the way.'

'There's no record for it to even be on,' Vee assured her, hoping throwaway promises wouldn't come back to bite her down the line.

'Fine. What didn't seem right to you?'

'First of all, was there anything to suggest someone else might've been involved?'

'It wasn't ruled murder or foul play, if that's where you're angling.'

'But was there a *suggestion* of foul play? Even a little bit?'

Coetzee funnelled her lips, pulling at an earlobe. She muttered a few noncommittal words and Vee plunged on, positioning the phone between them. 'All right, look at that. It's not a great picture but that's a large bruise behind her ear. Couldn't it be that she got hit on the head?'

The pathologist was shaking her head before she'd finished her sentence. 'Wrong. Look here. See the slight V-shape of the wound through the dried blood? That's more consistent with falling onto a hard, pointed surface than a blunt blow. The statement given by the maid that found her gave us a pretty clear description that allowed us to assess what could've happened. The working theory is she was thoroughly inebriated, which was confirmed by her blood work, fell asleep, rolled off the bed and hit her head on the side table, which caused the contusion. As far as I know, the evidence supports this.'

'She was drunk?' Vee said half-heartedly, remembering the wineglass by the bathtub and the cloud of stale booze surrounding the body. 'So drunk that she rolled off the bed, bashed her head, and couldn't move to the point where she died? Of what? Needing to pee?'

Coetzee pulled at her lower lip with her teeth. Either she wanted to disagree or still felt indecisive as to whether she could say more. Finally, she relented: 'Not just drunk. Thoroughly pissed. As in, blood alcohol in the stars. And she didn't die from the fall. She asphyxiated. The inebriated often fall semi-conscious into precarious positions from which they can't self-rescue. It's a form of positional asphyxiation and is more common than people think.'

'Uh-huh. What if I agreed, but had a slightly different theory? As in, she *was* drunk and died from suffocation, but it wasn't accidental. What if someone *made sure* she couldn't breathe?'

'A possibility, but...' Coetzee flip-flopped a hand, 'not likely. For instance, you see...' She took the phone away and scrolled to a shot that better satisfied. 'Great that you took this one, shows you what I mean. That dried foam around her mouth is likely vomit that got into her lungs. Imagine she's struggling for air, but immobile. She threw up, fluid filled her airways and she choked on it. She would've been well past it by the time she fell onto the dresser. If anything, the fall, or a blow, might've helped put her out of her misery faster.'

Vee nodded. 'Fine. But what's this bruising on her nose? Isn't that consistent with her airway being deliberately blocked, as if someone held a pillow over her face? Don't laugh, but I've seen forensic TV shows where they demonstrate how bruising like that happens due to deliberate suffocation.'

'It's not a stupid question.' Coetzee shrugged. 'But it's not one with a definitive answer. Look, for one thing, bruising like that is more helpful in determining cause of death in infants, for instance. They're much more delicate, not fully ambulatory, and fall into positions they can't move out of. For another, Caucasian skin displays bruising a lot easier than darker skin, so disruptions in the epidermis tend to stand out quite prominently without necessarily indicating an assault. If I remember correctly...' she paused, eyes on the ceiling, 'Dr Marais, who did the autopsy, concluded that the bruise was significant because that's how asphyxiation resulted. Greenwood, in a drunken pill-induced stupor—'

'Oh, God. Pills too?'

'Unfortunately. Anti-depressants and a sleeping aid; bad mix with alcohol. I gather she had a long history of substance abuse. So, she goes out face-down on a pillow. Like I said, not uncommon.'

'But…' Vee pressed the navigator button desperately. 'But… all right, look here, how she's wrapped up in the sheets. Drunk people pass out *on top* of sheets. She was wrapped like a cigar.' She tapped the LCD screen emphatically. 'That's significant. If somebody got her drunk, or she was already, then how easy would it be? She'd hardly put up a fight. It would look genuine.'

'I'm starting to worry,' Coetzee frowned. 'Should I be worried?'

Vee raised her hand in pledge. 'I promise, I'm an innocent bystander. I'm just concerned that maybe because it *looked* one way, it slipped under the radar. Not that I'm implying y'all don't know your jobs…'

'Huh. It does happen, believe me.' Exhaustion passed over Coetzee's face as she spoke. 'Oudtshoorn is practically a rural outpost compared to Cape Town, but we do get enough traffic through here for mistakes to get made. If I'm being honest with you, although you didn't hear this from me, this place is as challenged as any medical examiner's office. Half the time, understaffed and overbooked. You'd be surprised how often things get overlooked. Basic, laughable errors sometimes.' Coetzee drained her cup and walked it over to the small metal sink. Taking the cue, Vee rose to her feet.

'Now that you've got me mildly interested,' Coetzee said over her shoulder, rinsing the mug, 'any other clues?'

Vee brought up the last two close-ups. 'This isn't much, but… see her right hand? I snapped everything in the room and couldn't explain why it caught my attention. Look at her index and middle fingers, especially the index one. The nail is completely different from the rest. The others are all fake acrylic, but that one's her real nail. With a fresh scrape on it.'

'So what? Maybe she bumped it, the acrylic broke off and the finger got scratched.'

'How, is my question? It could've happened during a struggle. It would count as a defence wound.' Vee looked up from the phone and met Coetzee's concerned frown. 'You think I'm crazy, right?'

Coetzee shook her head with a laugh. 'I think my break is over, that's what I think. If—'

The sound of P-Square, belting *E No Easy* along to a jaunty hipco rhythm, reverberated around the tiny office. Chlöe's number flashed across the Samsung's screen. Vee interrupted her ringtone, mouthing an apology as she turned her back to Coetzee.

'What's up? Huh? You found what? Bishop, calm down, I can hardly hear you. All right, sorry I told you to calm down but you bustin' my eardrum. You found… *What?!* Girl, how the hell?! Okay, okay… you want me to get… mm-hhmm… Just breathe, I'm coming now-now. Don't touch any of my stuff, though.' Vee cut the call and made a disgusted sound in the back of her throat.

'Interesting day?' Coetzee asked.

'To say the least. Now, I'll take my leave. I know I threw a lot of conjecture at you, but thanks for listening. It helped to run it by a professional. Who could shoot me down properly.'

'No problem. Look, I was saying since you got my interest piqued, I'll go through Greenwood's report again. Feel Marais out if he had a notion of anything being off. Just to ease both our minds.'

Vee pocketed her phone. She felt something else in the cavity of her jeans, hesitated, thought it couldn't do any more harm, and brought out her business card. It felt weird handing it to another person so soon after… a person who was not only indirectly associated with Gavin Berman's death but might also be performing his autopsy… *That's it, I'm making new business cards,* she thought.

'Good luck with your investigation. Which isn't an

investigation,' Coetzee smiled wryly. 'You know, if you do travel writing for your paper, you ought to be transferred to the crime desk. Do more investigative stuff. You'd be great.'

'Ha,' Vee said. The irony. 'I'll look into it. By the way, you know where I can find a pharmacy around here? One that sells lice shampoo.'

10

'You!'

Vee backed into the door, away from Chlöe's wrath.

'I have lice and bruises and no clean clothes and people dropping dead all around me,' Chlöe ticked the offences off on her finger, 'because you dragged me to Hotel California to die. All of this is your fault!'

'That's not fair. We're working.'

'Fair?' Chlöe parted the curtain of wet hair over her face, and blue eyes lit to a high, slightly mad gleam peeped through. 'As your assistant, I'm condemned to suffer with you and you wanna talk fair?' She crumbled onto the bed. 'I haaaaate this plaaaaace.'

'All right, baby bird. Take a deep breath and relax...'

'I don't want a deep breath. I – WANT – TO – GO – HOME.'

'And we will. Soon. But for now, let's tie this bathrobe right up – there are things about you I'd rather not know. Whetin you drinkin'?' Vee sniffed a jug-full of cold, opaque liquid with floating gobs and wrinkled her nose. 'Seriously Bishop, it's barely midday. You look like a white trash episode of *Dynasty*.'

'It's actually almost one thirty, which you'd know if you hadn't gone gallivanting without me.' Chlöe drained the wineglass in her hand and smacked her lips. 'It's called a Cloud. Chenin Blanc, litchi juice. Crushed litchis. Grenadine. Vile shit, but it grows on you. The barman's concoction, he gave me a whole litre.'

'Among other things.' Vee frowned at the table laden with a tray of fruit, tiny sandwiches and other savoury morsels. 'How'd you get this? And this room? You better not tell me you stole another guest's room because the trauma of lice drove you to it.'

'Don't use that four-letter word, I beg of you! This never happened and we shall never mention it again.' Chlöe glared until Vee acquiesced with a meek nod, then her shoulders relaxed. 'After you left, I went back to our old room at boot camp to shower – yes, I said old room 'cause this is our new one. I started checking my hair to see if the itching was dandruff and discovered the unthinkably unspeakable instead. I marched right back here and raised all kinds of hell. As expected, they didn't want word of it spreading among the guests and ruining the hotel's reputation. Ms Motaung happily and hastily gave us use of this room while the other one is supposedly being fumigated. I've been taking boiling showers ever since.' Chlöe started to refill the glass. 'I also may have insinuated that our review carries quite a bit of weight to edging them towards a third star, sooo…'

'So nothing, because it doesn't. And we've filed it already, in case you forgot.'

'They don't know that.'

'And they don't have to. So bravo on hooking us up. But,' Vee prised Chlöe's fingers off the glass's stem, 'you've been on cloud nine for long enough. Let's get some lice shampoo in this hair before you spread it. I had that nonsense twice in boarding school and swore to behead the next person who gave it to me.'

'Again, I wouldn't be here catching vermin and sipping clouds and being harassed by Joshua's nosy sister if not for you, so it would serve you right,' Chlöe yelled from the bathroom over the gush of running water.

Vee swept in after her. 'Harassed by Joshua's *sister*? Here? As in, *my* Joshua?'

Foamy locks dripping into the sink, Chlöe gingerly lifted her head. 'Yeah, your sloe-eyed slut. Why didn't you tell me he was half *Indian* Indian?'

'I did.'

'No, you didn't. All this time I've been thinking *American* Indian, like riding on the plains hunting buffalo.'

'Hell no. Indian tandoori, not teepee. Cherishers of all things bovine, as is their custom.'

'Whatever. My jaw was on the floor at breakfast. That Indian chick—'

'*What?* The one that kept giving us juju eyeball last night?'

'None other. And she made sure to keep referring to him as her "so-called brother" to make sure I knew she's not chuffed they're related. Did you know he had a sister other than the one in the States?'

'Joshua's made of sisters. Four, besides Bianca. His father tried to compensate for the son he ran out on and he got all girls for his ejaculations. Karma is hilarious.' Vee caught Chlöe's one-eyed glare through the shampoo suds and laughed. 'What?'

'You never told me.'

''Cause I don't tell you everything. You have a big mouth.'

'Only sometimes. Never when it comes to your business, so give me credit for that. I don't pry any more, even when I have reason to. Case in point your tête-à-tête with Lovett this morning. I haven't asked a thing about it, nor will I. I know you, Stonewall.'

Vee left the doorway and went back into the bedroom. She sampled the nibbles and sank onto the bed. She listened to Chlöe rinse for what sounded like hours, after which she emerged with a shower cap and a sheepish smile.

'Egg-killing treatment phase,' Chlöe patted her head.

'I didn't say anything about earlier with Lovett because I'm not ready to talk about it yet.' Vee kept her eyes trained on the floor. 'But I will be. Eventually.' She looked up and smiled. 'Meantime, let me tell you what I found out in town.'

Minutes into the regaling, Chlöe interjected over a mouthful of strawberries. 'This sounds more like what you *didn't* find out. Let me remind you, as I have repeatedly, Berman's was the only murder committed here. Why're you stuck on bringing this woman in the mix? Do *not* give me that rubbish about gut feelings.'

'It's the gut feeling, sorry. And the photos. They mean something, I know it. Two murders at the same venue in twenty-four hours does not fall under meaningless.'

'They can if one was murder and one wasn't. It can mean absolutely nothing if you look at it that way, the way everyone else is. For what conceivable reason is someone at a random place in the bundus killing hotel managers and obnoxious businessmen? I'll bet you anything Greenwood and Berman didn't even know each other.'

'So what? That doesn't mean the perp—'

'The perp? We're saying the perp now?'

'—that *the perpetrator*,' Vee clipped Chlöe at the back of the head, 'didn't know both or either of them. The fact that Rhonda opened the door for this person is crucial. Her room wasn't broken into, so she had to have opened the door. That means she knew who it was. You with me?'

'Um-hmm. She opened the door for a mass murderer. The one still roaming around the lodge. Out for more blood. After offing both her and Berman. Yep, I'm with you.'

Vee shoved her. 'Fine, make your jokes. But I'm right.'

'Please. What you are is a consummate leaper, bosslady, and you're leaping right now. Even the pathologist doesn't agree with your incriminating evidence.'

'She said it wasn't impossible,' Vee muttered.

Chlöe patted her shoulder. 'Aww, shem. You can't stand being wrong. And,' she wagged a stern finger when Vee opened her mouth, 'even if you're right, which I'm not saying you are, I'll be damned if I'm sticking around playing detective and hoping the madman spares my life.' Chlöe folded an entire samosa into her mouth and crunched passionately. 'If anything, *you* should be worried. You're the black person in this equation. Don't you watch horror movies? Killers always start with the black people.'

'This one looks like an exception.'

'Then *I'm* worried!' Chlöe threw up her hands, then parked them on her hips. 'Honestly, the police have this under control. Remember how you always say investigation takes access? Well, how much can we accomplish right now? We can't go near the actual crime scene, and the cops have closed off Berman's room. And we can't wait around until someone "acts suspicious" so we can pounce. No guilty person's going to be idiotic enough to make a move now. It's either they've done it already and gone unnoticed, or they've talked sense into themselves. Either way, we're fresh out of luck, and therefore out of the picture.' She executed a sweeping, exaggerated bow, clapped for herself and tottered towards the bathroom. 'How much sense am I making?'

'Plenty. Which I hate.'

Vee plopped onto her back, spreading her arms across the bed. The sheets were crisp and smelled of peach fabric softener, reminding her of her own bed. Tambudzai, her maid who came in twice a week to clean, would've worked her magic by now. She imagined Tristan rubbing his miserly little mitts in glee at the thought of how much he'd make taking care of Monro for the weekend. 'You're right. We should go home.' She stretched her hand up, playing her fingers in the air as if running them over the intricate swirls of the ceiling's design.

The water shut off in the bathroom and Chlöe emerged, scrubbing a swathe of russet curls between the folds of a towel. 'Although…'

Vee sprang up on her elbows. 'I like although.'

11

'I don't like although when it comes with strings.'

'Those are my terms,' Chlöe insisted. They stepped out of the elevator. 'I can't take another minute here. If we do this and *I'm* right for once, we check out immediately. Hell, if we start driving now we should be home…' she counted hours off fingers, 'before 9pm. More than enough time to get our beauty sleep on familiar, lice-free mattresses and don our war faces to face Nico tomorrow.'

Vee nodded. 'Fine. You want out, let's bounce. But after your secret mission, I need to talk to Zintle one more time. Now tell me why we're skulking around reception.'

Chlöe poked her head around the corner of the long corridor, scanned the foyer and turtled her head back in. 'Our conversation upstairs got me thinking laterally. Hardly anyone's checked out since this morning because everyone wants to see the action. Human curiosity is gruesome, but it could be useful. It might sound counterintuitive, but the culprit is least likely to leave right away. And if they're still around, they're panicking. And trying not to look panicky.'

'Okaaaay. I'm kind of with you.'

'If you lose your shit right now, the police will pounce before you can say boo. They interviewed everyone important from the party, searched the rooms, stirred up gossip among the lodge staff. Everybody's on edge. Whoever has the most reason to be on edge is likely to do something stupid. What's the dumbest move the guilty party could make right about now?'

Vee turned it over in her mind, eyes starting to gleam. 'Hhmmm. They're likely to have something incriminating in their possession, in which case they'd definitely want to get rid of it.' She blinked. 'Bishop, we're not breaking into rooms to launch our own search. Not only do we not have the time or know what to look for, it's criminal and I bet you we'll get caught.'

Chlöe sighed. 'Not that. The room taking the most heat right now belongs to Gavin Berman. If he had a scrap of evidence on him that would put his killer in the limelight, that person would be looking to find it to either get rid of it, or smuggle it out. I'm being hopeful and assuming it hasn't been trashed, maybe it's too valuable. But how would you smuggle it out, if you only had time to think and act quickly, and you were worried your room and belongings would be searched, too? You'd blatantly clear it through customs, the last place anyone would look. And around here customs is...'

'Front desk,' Vee exhaled. 'If the killer found what they were looking for in Berman's room, they'd stash it somewhere safe until they could retrieve it when the heat died down. On the off-chance someone saw them taking an item out of that room, they wouldn't think much of it if it was handed over at the front desk. It diffuses a lot of suspicion.'

'The heavens opened and the angels chorused.'

'Chlöe Jasmine Bishop, you glorious wonder!'

'Don't get excited yet. I could be theorising out of my arse.' Chlöe poked her head around the wall again. 'Okay, stay here.'

'For what? I can't just linger in the hallway.'

'Because Trevor the concierge hates you. Remember last night? Vanilla trumps chocolate. Now stand back and watch the master work.'

Chlöe strolled across the expanse of wood panelling and carpet that constituted the foyer, coming to a casual halt before the front desk. Trevor looked up from his paperwork and barely refrained from rolling his eyes. Unperturbed, Chlöe plastered on a grin, one that went completely missed as the concierge dropped his head and casually returned to his duties. She cleared her throat, softly, then forcefully. At last he looked up, straightening his spine and interlacing his fingers. His face was a closed door. Chlöe beamed a silent prayer to the gods.

'Hi, Trevor. I was wondering…' she began.

'I imagine you were. Must be quite a lot of that in your profession.'

'Yes. Yes, there is. Curiosity is our business.' *Damn you, Johnson. This would be so much easier if you hadn't pissed this guy off.* She smiled harder. 'Pursuant to that, I imagine there's been a lot of foot traffic since the madness earlier. Has anything been left here by one of the guests attending the LEAD convention?'

'Something like what?'

'Like, uhh, a thing…' Chlöe fashioned meaningless motions in the air. 'Um, an item. Or a package. Maybe Mr Berman left one, meaning to pick it up later. Or someone left something for *him* to pick up later. Which obviously won't be happening now.' She tittered nervously. Trevor's deadpan face folded along more severe planes. 'I mean, considering this tragedy. Which we're all deeply saddened by.'

'That's private information, which I'm sure you know. Information only the police can enquire after. Which they have asked, and we've answered.'

'I understand. But could you tell me, if *anything* at all…'

The corners of Trevor's shoulders sharpened to dangerous angles. 'I can't answer that.'

Chlöe opened her mouth, closed it, thought for a second and then raised a "one moment" finger. She scurried back to

Vee and grabbed her by the wrist. 'Okay, this is where you come in.'

'Ugh, no,' Vee groaned. 'He just *stood by* and watched while—'

'Yes, yes. He let the bad man touch your special place.' Chlöe waved her quiet. 'But he also spoke up this morning and cleared your name, which could've gone a completely different, disastrous way. So let's just get this over with.'

They walked back to reception. Vee drew in a breath. 'Hello Trevor, I'm Voinjama Johnson,' she said, extending her hand and leaving it afloat until he had no choice but to shake it. 'We didn't meet properly and I apologise for that. I'm sorry too, for...' she exhaled, 'impersonating a guest and crashing the convention party. I'm sure y'all get all kinds of riffraff coming through here and pulling stunts, and it must get very old. It was unprofessional and again, I apologise.'

The pause ate up the air, till finally Trevor dipped a nod, relaxing a little. Vee looked to Chlöe and shared a flicker of triumph. 'Now can you *please* help us? We're only asking if anything's been overlooked. Berman left nothing here?' After the minutest shake of Trevor's head, she adjusted, 'Was something left here for him to pick up?'

'Everything belonging to Mr Berman, including his correspondence, has been turned over to the police.'

'That's that,' Vee said as they walked away.

'Yeah. It was a long shot.' Chlöe chewed her lip, slowing. Trevor couldn't have cooperated, anyway. Berman's belongings were his no more; they belonged to the investigation. Then, to his next-of-kin, if they bothered to claim it, whosoever they were. Everything else...

'Oh!' Her eyes widened. She turned and dashed back. 'What about something of his that wasn't really his property?' Trevor frowned and Chlöe flailed her hands in frustration. 'Uhh... like, it was in the room while he occupied it, but it belongs to the lodge.'

Trevor blew a weary, cigarette-tainted sigh in her face. He checked the relevant cubbyhole and came up empty-handed, then disappeared into the back room, emerging minutes later with a small, black plastic bag. Chlöe sucked in her breath. Vee skittered back to her side.

'I really shouldn't be doing this. We do not make a habit of compromising our guests' privacy.' Trevor's aura had altered. He looked unsure, an expression ill at ease on his otherwise placid face. A nudge from Vee and Chlöe placed on the desk, from her back pocket, an envelope. In it were five crisp R100 notes. Trevor peered within, barely twitching. 'But I suppose, seeing as you did make the valid point of that not being much of an issue at this juncture…'

Chlöe snatched the bag before he could change his mind, Vee right by her shoulder.

'Haaayy! Now we know who was entertaining us from the hilltop with these movies. *Ninja Nurses Reloaded*, *Weapons of Ass Eruption*,' Vee chuckled, scanning through the pile of DVDs with lurid covers. "I should thank God o. If this demonstrates the contents of the man's mind, I got off easy. Who left them here?"

'He probably did, seeing as he was supposed to check out this morning.'

'This is all from his room that belongs to the lodge?" Chlöe sagged. It was a nice tidbit, knowing their victim and porn fiend were one, but she'd been expecting more.

Trevor blanched. 'Those absolutely *do not* belong to The Grotto. They're from a video rental store in Oudtshoorn. We do at times procure…' he paused for delicacy, 'special materials of this kind if our guests make a specific request, but we certainly don't make a habit of it. All rented material is returned within a day or two, usually by one of our drivers or the laundry truck when we make a run into town.'

'No, I meant...' Chlöe squirmed away from Vee's finger poking into her side, and looked down at where Vee was pointing. Snuggled in one of the DVD cases was an extra disk, bright blue and unlabelled. Vee slid it out and put it on the table. They both looked at Trevor. Trevor looked back at them.

'This is not the hotel's property. So ...' said Vee.

Trevor plucked the DVD case from her fingers, hastily gathered up the others and stuffed them into the carrier bag, which he stashed out of sight behind the counter. 'These are our responsibility. *That*, I know nothing of. Finish and klaar.' He retrieved an A5 envelope, slipped the offending disk into it, placed it back onto the counter with a parting two taps of his fingers, and walked off to serve a gentleman at the far end of the desk. Chlöe shrugged, slid the envelope to her chest and turned on her heel.

Vee stopped short. 'We really gon' take this?'

Chlöe stared at her. Cold feet and backpedalling... this was new. Vee's style when it came to the questionable was a lot more arse-to-the-wind impulsive. 'After all of that, you're asking me?'

'We should. Shouldn't we? It's not like it's evidence.'

'We've been calling it evidence for the past twenty minutes. Now suddenly it's not?'

'What's defined as evidence? Any item the police are *specifically* looking for—'

'In the designated area where they expect to find it,' Chlöe jumped in. She bit her lip; they were on very shaky ground. 'Which isn't where we got this from.'

'Exactly. And it might have absolutely nothing to do with the murder.'

Chlöe waited, watching Vee chew at the insides of her cheeks, the furrow between her eyebrows ever-deepening. She held out her hand. Chlöe placed the envelope in it, and Vee slapped her palm on top of it with a decisive thwack.

'All right, here's what we do. We look this over, and if it has anything that's directly linked at all to the murder or murderer, we hand it over to the police.' Chlöe pursed her lips and Vee added, 'When we get to the bridge of explaining how and why we have it, we'll manoeuvre the crossing.' Vee looked at the envelope. 'We've intercepted something here. An exchange that was meant to happen or a link to something or someone important. Don't know. This lil' bone has a dog attached to it, so we hang onto it. Maybe wave it till someone comes barking. Who and why, we'll know soon enough.'

12

'Hhayi, sisi,' Zintle said, 'your hair is so nice. If you had told me before, I could have done a nice style for you. I do hair very well. That's what I used to do before I came here.'

'For true? Me too,' Vee enthused. 'Working in a salon was my first real job.'

'Ja, but you know, there's no money in it. That's why I started working here, to help pay for college.'

'Damelin, right?' Vee tossed a pair of jeans into her carry-on.

Zintle beamed, nodding enthusiastically. 'Business management and administration. This year I'm working full time so next year I can finish up and graduate.' When Vee straightened up, Zintle leaned closer and ran her fingers over her upsweep. 'Such nice texture. How do you keep it soft?'

'Plenty of moisture and coconut oil. No mineral oil or petroleum jelly. And I don't relax it often. It's bad for our hair.'

'I know, neh. We don't listen. We let our hairdressers dump relaxer on our heads and pull your hair like tcchweeee…' Zintle contorted her face and mimed a painful-looking stretching motion. They cackled and slapped palms.

'Hem-hem-hem,' Chlöe coughed, zipping up her small suitcase. She gave Vee a reproachful squint and helicoptered a finger in a "wrap it up" gesture behind Zintle's back.

Vee waved her away. 'You were telling me about Rhonda.'

'Ag. That one.' Zintle sighed onto the bed and shook her head, clearly defeated by the topic. 'I don't know. Sad sad sad story.'

'Sedsedsed', a snaky word tumbling over itself. Surreptitiously, Vee frowned in Chlöe's direction, lost. Chlöe turned her mouth down and rubbed a fist near an eye like a sobbing child. 'Oh, *sad*,' Vee murmured. She looked to Zintle again. 'Ehn? She seemed like a perky person to me. Not at all sad.'

'Ja man, of course. She had to be. Pretending was her job, you can't serve clients with a sour face. But ja. You think you can get to that point and not be bitter? Working somewhere for thirteen years and you're still second in command. No husband, no children. What rubbish. Sies.'

Vee closed her eyes, inhaled, took a second before unclenching her fists. 'She never married? I thought...'

'Divorced. They say he left her for a younger woman, now they have two kids.'

'Before or after she started working here?'

'After. Around...' Zintle lifted her eyes to the ceiling, 'eight years ago. I think he left her because she was never home long enough to be a wife.' She finally noticed the disdain on the faces of Vee and Chlöe and shrank, clipping her knees together and knitting her arms over her bosom. 'It's not *me*, that's what I heard people saying.' Her chin shot out. 'She was a workaholic. I've seen it myself over the seven months I've been here. She was *always* here. That's why she left her house in Oudtshoorn to move into the chalet at the back. And she was a drinker.' She eyed Vee up and down, and shot her a scornful click from the recesses of her throat. 'Kutheni ebehlala enxilile ukuba ebengonwabanga? Why was she a drunk if she wasn't unhappy?'

'How long had she been at the bottle, do you know?'

'For always. That's what alcoholics do, right.' Zintle's right foot bounced, picking up speed as her scowl intensified. 'Me,

I know about drunks. There are enough in my family, in my neighbourhood. So don't tell me. Don't look at me like I know nothing about it. Nxc.'

Over Zintle's head, Chlöe fired an "I told you so" glower. Vee replied with a mini eye-roll, sinking onto the mattress.

'Listen.' Vee slung a sisterly arm around Zintle's shoulders. She contemplated extolling the virtues of a single, career-focused life, saw little chance of success with her current audience and ploughed on. 'I know you liked Ms Greenwood. Everybody liked her. She was a nice woman, wasn't she?'

'Very nice lady,' Zintle echoed meekly.

'It hurts when good people die like that. It doesn't sit nicely on your conscience. That's why you threw her liquor bottle away, so it wouldn't make her look bad when they found her body.'

Spasms quivered through Zintle's shoulders, echoing under Vee's fingers.

'I… ehhmm…' Zintle opened her mouth, jawed the air for a few seconds, shut it. She looked at her hands, face pained. 'Did you…'

'I didn't see you. It only clicked later, that sound I heard. It was glass hitting against the bedpost, and I never saw or had any pictures of glass or anything solid enough to make that sound. There was only the wineglass; there had to be a bottle somewhere. No one else had been inside that room except you.'

'I thought if they found it… it would look like… I put it in the bin bag with the other rubbish. Are you going to…'

'No.' Vee gave her another squeeze. 'Don't worry about that. It's too late now and you didn't destroy anything the autopsy didn't point to already. But you have to tell me everything you remember.'

'But I've *told* you already.'

'Start again. Tell me about every time you had an interaction with Ms Greenwood the day she died, even just a few words in passing, *every time* you saw her.'

Zintle puffed a gust of warmth against Vee's cheek. 'Well, she and Ms Motaung handled the morning meeting for the day shift and then... nothing special after that. They had to get organised for the convention, so we were instructed to be on our toes throughout. This is a busy weekend, so they couldn't afford silly mistakes; we had to watch ourselves. Mr Gono, he's head of housekeeping, he had a brief meeting with some of the maids about getting across to the boot camp to clean up a bit, air out the empty bunks and bring in fresh linen. Ms Greenw—'

'Oh, meaning you guys actually clean up on the other side,' Chlöe arched.

Zintle shot waves of vitriol through her slatted eyes. 'Sies mhani, of course we clean. It's part of the lodge so it's part of our job. We handle the basics, clean when people are off the camp site, but no one waits on them like at the lodge. The boot camp's supposed to be like the rural areas, but even then it's been getting neglected.'

'I'll say. Frickin' lice haven...' Chlöe muttered under her breath.

Zintle, who couldn't make out what she said, just pursed her lips. 'Ja, anyway. Our workload's been stretched lately. Two of the maids left recently, so we're a bit short-handed. We've had to pull extra weight until new girls can start in two weeks.'

'People got laid off?' Vee asked.

'Not laid off like fired. They left... well, they didn't exactly leave us, they were asked to leave. Mssh. Okay, one was let go, and the other one got a severe warning and not long after she resigned on her own.' Zintle eyed Vee, scouring her face. 'Fine, you said everything. But this was long before. Things started going missing here and there and it became a problem. Small things. Mr Gono brought it up to Ms Greenwood and they decided not to bother Ms Motaung with it at first, they'd deal with it. Then it got worse – one time a guest forgot a lot of money and no one could find it when he came back to check. After that, they were proper pissed off, but Ms Greenwood insisted she would handle it quietly. She caught two of the housekeepers. Well, she announced that she caught them redhanded, "improper conduct" she called it, but we never knew how she did it and what they'd done exactly. We were relieved, until the extra work kicked in. I'll be glad when those girls start.'

Zintle caught her breath, waited for Vee's nod to continue, then streamed on. 'So, day before yesterday. Mr Gono had a chat to some of us about boot camp clean-up. Ms Greenwood was waiting to talk to him, so she hung around outside his office. After we left, I didn't speak to her again. I saw her rushing around a lot, very busy. One of the other maids saw her, maybe for five minutes, and she brushed her off. There was another debrief before the party started, but it was more for the kitchen staff—'

'Wait, wait, wait. You said another maid spoke to her and Rhonda blew her off.'

'Mm-hmm. Mamello. She wanted time off the next day because her son was sick, but Ms Greenwood said no. Actually, she was distracted; she said they would talk later and she would see. That made her hopeful she had a chance.'

'I'm confused. Who was distracted and who was hoping what?'

'Ms Greenwood…' Zintle huffed impatiently, 'look, this is what Mamello told me. She had been trying to corner Ms Greenwood all day to get time off, but she couldn't get her alone.'

'Why not ask Mr Gono? He's her direct boss.'

'Ja, but Mamello ….' Zintle's brows folded, disapproving. 'Since she got a new boyfriend, she's been missing work and making excuses. Like, she wants to be full time in cleaning the nice chalets, like how I do Ms Greenwood's, but she's not reliable. I keep saying she must watch herself. She's taking advantage, because since we're short-staffed she'll only get a warning. If she had gone to Mr Gono, he would have said no straightaway. But sometimes if you found someone willing to exchange shifts and asked Ms Greenwood nicely, she would talk to Mr Gono for you. But you had to corner her when she was alone. That's why Mamello persisted all day, and then she had to wait while she was having an argument with some lady before she got her chance.'

'What lady now?' Vee asked.

Zintle drew her shoulders to her ears in a "does it matter?" shrug. 'Ms Greenwood was talking to a lady. So Mamelo waited around for them to finish.'

'And they were having an argument?'

'I don't know. That's what Mamello said. She said when Ms Greenwood walked away she looked confused. That's why she didn't say no to what Mamello asked.'

Vee frowned, silent for a long time. 'Where's Mamello now? She on shift today, right now?'

'For sure. I can…' Fetching her cell phone from her apron's pocket, Zintle waved it with a questioning lift of her eyebrows. Vee nodded quickly.

Chlöe leapt from the faux leather lounger. 'Are you fucking kidding me? You can't seriously think this is important. It's not part of the deal!'

'The deal was to pursue every avenue, then we can go.'

'Yeah, every *worthy* avenue. How the hell is this relevant?'

'We won't find out standing here.' Vee trailed behind Zintle into the hallway, then threw a questioning glance as she held the door open. Grumbling, Chlöe stomped over the threshold after them. 'And stop fuckin' cussing, for shit's sake. Dirty ass mouth,' Vee clipped her at the back of her head.

———

'I didn't say they were fighting.'

'Ma-mel-lo,' Zintle drawled. She clapped her hands once and took a backward step, head shaking. 'Now you're changing your story.'

'Ah-ah! Me, I never said *fighting*. Ehh you, always adding extra spice and chakalaka to stories. She always does that.' Mamello tossed Vee a conspiratorial wink, tipped water into a spray bottle of what smelled like industrial-strength cleaning fluid and shook it vigorously.

'You know what you told me. Don't try and make me look bad.' Zintle cocked her chin, adamant. 'She *said* they were fighting.'

Vee blew a breath over her sweaty upper lip as she fanned the front of her T-shirt. The corridor suddenly felt too close, no air sifting in from any direction, the scent of cleaning agents and floor polish creeping up her nose. 'How were they – hey, hey, listen now, please – how were they talking to each other? They were yelling? Sort of yelling? Were they pissed off but trying to keep their voices low, like angry whispers?'

Mamello finished arranging a colourful plethora of cleaning containers on her push-trolley, pushed it to one side, peeped into the room she was meant to be servicing and quickly shut the door. 'No one looked angry. They were more like...' Deliberating, she massaged one ear, an arc of flesh stapled through to the uppermost curve with tiny silver hoops. Vee ogled, unconsciously massaging her own ear, pierced with three meagre holes, all threaded through with a fine gold chain. It must've been one helluva excruciating month if she did that all at once.

'Excited,' Mamello snapped her fingers. 'Ms Greenwood was excited. Maybe not *excited*, don't know how to explain it. Surprised, kind of. She stopped the lady and started talking, only this lady looked confused and kept shaking her head, and Ms Greenwood kept insisting. They talked a bit, then the lady started to go. Ms Greenwood stopped her again and asked something else, the woman shook her head and said something back, they laughed a bit and then she left.'

'Scintillating,' Chlöe groused.

'Who left first?' Vee persisted. 'Who walked away, the lady?'

'Ummm… yes. Yes, she left first. Then I took my chance to talk to Ms Greenwood.'

'And what was her expression? Greenwood, how did her face look?'

Mamello pursed her lips. 'It looked like her face, the one she always had.'

Vee pumped at her T-shirt, ignoring fumes of mounting impatience wafting from Chlöe's direction. Greenwood had been immersed in her job, thoroughly, and hands-on with clientele. With an excellent memory. It could have been nothing more than a genial conversation with a guest. Or a dangerous lot more.

'Maybe she looked a bit confused, too,' Mamello threw in, shrugging apologetically.

'You remember what the other woman looked like?'

'Errhhm… dreadlocks. The thin ones. And she was dark in complexion.'

'Like me?'

Mamello gave Vee a cursory once-over and shook her head immediately. 'No ways. You're normal dark, dark brown. She was dark dark, that foreigner darkness.' A moue of distaste funnelling her lips, Mamello caressed her tawny arms, as if afraid the darkness was infectious, would leap into her chromosomes and snatch away her God-given fairness. Vee gritted her teeth, but kept smiling. She knew all too well the increasing levels of disdain as one moved ever duskier down the precarious scale of black complexions.

'But I'm sure she was local; she sounded Mzansi. And she had big hips. Not biiiig, but...' Mamelo sized up the group, before dropping her eyes down at her own thighs with a defeated sigh. 'Okay, around my size. Somewhere around me and you,' she flicked a finger between herself and Vee. 'But definitely bigger, maybe by this much,' she indicated with outstretched arms. About a size 36, Vee estimated.

'We've cracked the case wide open! Let's call that gruffian Sergeant Ncubane and tell him we've got enough to make an arrest right now. A hippy black woman with dreadlocks is what, a viable lead? *Really?* That's a needle in a haystack.'

Vee hustled her down the hall by the elbow, throwing a wave to the two maids. 'Bishop, we can't know what's significant at this point. And it won't come with a label.' She shrugged. 'Fine, I'll admit I have no idea what any of this means. Maybe nothing. But maybe something.'

'How the f—'

Vee pinched Chlöe's mouth closed with two fingers. 'Maybe Greenwood saw someone she wasn't supposed to see. Maybe it sparked a memory or set her off on trying to remember something, and that's what got her killed.'

Chlöe slapped her hand away. 'That's a list of maybes, and you can't stand maybes. We have nothing, we know nothing. It's hot like hell. *Let's go home.*'

'Oh, we got better than nothing. We got leads,' Vee grinned. 'Let's go. We'll brainstorm on the road.'

The dance may have started out here in Oudtshoorn, but the full ballet awaited them back in the Mother City.

Chasing Rainbows

13

The Chrysler double-bounced and screeched against the force of the brakes. Folders slithered off the dashboard, contents ejecting onto Vee's lap and the adjoining car seat.

'Aay dammit, man.' She yanked up the handbrake, stole a quick glance in the rear-view mirror and slid out. The street was clear but the bumper jutted well off the end of her driveway into the street. She decided to risk it and dashed back inside the house.

Ten minutes later, a carton of fruit juice in hand, brown envelopes balanced under both arms and a plastic binder in her mouth, she struggled with the car door.

'Good morning, employer.'

Vee turned her head as best she could. Rows of teeth on flash, Tristan Heaney relieved her of the juice, pulled the car door open and bowed deeply.

'You know, young man,' she grunted as she got in, leaned past the steering wheel onto the passenger side and started restacking the folders, 'even when visitors can't see the clock, they must glean the hour from the look on the face of their host.'

'Huh?'

'It means you should develop a talent for knowing when to buzz off.' She slipped behind the wheel. 'It's a very insightful quote, from a great man called Ralph Waldo Emerson.'

'Well, this great man,' Tristan aimed a finger at his chest, 'is only eleven, so,' he shrugged wildly, 'whatever. I just came over to remind you—'

'Oh my Lord, you're the most mercenary child I've ever met. I haven't forgotten to pay you for taking care of Monro while I was away. We hit Cape Town later than I thought and I wasn't exactly going to walk over to your house at night to harass your mother. You'll get paid today, promise.'

Tristan raised his eyes heavenward and sighed in a disturbingly adult, disturbingly Joshua Allen, fashion. 'You always think the worst of me. I'm not here about *money*. It's something more important – DHLPP.'

Vee tuned him out. Her lips moved in time with her bobbing finger as she took stock of the haul on the front seat. Five files by her count, another two in the laptop bag. The rest, a stack she could easily visualise sitting plum in the middle of her hurricaned desk at the office. The current workload was in order. All of it she could put to bed quickly or leave to marinate awhile longer, leaving room for the new interest du jour—

'Envelope!'

'Dashboard,' quipped Tristan. She snatched it up, checking for the dozenth time that morning its contents were safe. This was everything they had to work with. A sinking feeling tunnelled through her breakfast as she eyed their "everything", an innocuous CD that barely made a bulge in a brown A5. Least it was something; it had better be. She stuffed it in a side pocket of the laptop pouch, then, thinking better of it, reassigned it to a pouch in her handbag. She zipped it up and gave it a final, satisfied pat.

She looked up again, to find Tristan studying her with a look of weariness undercut with endearment. Her eyes narrowed. 'Fineboy, don't eyeball me like that. Like this guy I used to date. In fact, like one I'm kinda still seeing, who thinks he can—'

'Ohhh my Gooood,' Tristan threw his head back. 'Please *do*

not make me listen to one of your boring love stories from 1964. Old people are always doing that. I,' he pressed a hand over his heart, 'have a life. I only came over to remind you about the shots.' She stared blankly and he stomped his foot. 'Shots. Vaccinations. Remember? You have to take Monro to the vet for the DHLPP and rabies. You keep forgetting and it's five weeks overdue.'

Vee grimaced, prickling with guilt. The number of reminders scrawled in red ink had overrun the calendar stuck to her fridge like army ants. 'Yeah, yeah. Damn. This weekend, I'm on it.'

'They never have weekend slots! That's why you keep rescheduling, 'cause you never have time during the week.' Tristan sighed. 'Let me take him. Before you let him die from kennel cough or something worse."

'All right, I hear you, but hell no. My baby, my responsibility.'

'Ag, man, he's three, he's not a baby.'

'Noted. But you're not gettin' my go-ahead to go walkabout all the way to the vet's. Forget it.' Vee pressed on the air conditioning and reversed, raising the window against Tristan's whines. 'I'll remember, I swear,' she called through the last inch of open glass. 'But I'm not changing my mind. Now get your butt to school right away.'

'It's school holidays!' Tristan watched the Chrysler's gold bumper swing off their street and cruise out of sight. He looked down at the icy box of mango juice still in his hand. 'Loser,' he cackled, piercing the carton with his pinkie.

———

Chlöe rushed over as Vee zoomed through the maze of cubicles with her arms loaded.

'Well hello, finegeh!' Vee said, dropping everything on her desk. 'Look at you.'

Chlöe skimmed a proud hand over her hair. Her naturally intense red now shone two to three shades paler, gelled back and cinched into a ponytail of wispy plaits. Vee lifted the braid and tickled Chlöe's nose with it, her eyebrows arched.

Chlöe gave her a playful shove. '*Yes*, it's completely lice-free.' She killed her smile, peering around the newsroom and craning her neck in every direction. Eavesdroppers and tongue-waggers abounded at *City Chronicle*. 'Okay, war faces. First of all, you got the disc?'

'Yeah, secret agent, I've got the disc. As agreed, I didn't try open it on my laptop, in case the message self-destructed and released nerve gas. I'll have it couriered to Richie's secret drop-box as soon as.'

'Ahhh… let me do it.' Chlöe bit her lip. 'You know how he can be. Bloody mood monster. Besides, I gotta call him anyway, make sure he understands our specific instructions.'

'More specific than what? We're not building a time machine. Tell us what's on it, period. A simple breakdown in plain English, if he can manage that. Not his usual… undecipherable Richard Fish language.' Vee crossed her arms. 'It's not fair how you keep hogging him from me. I've never met him, don't know what he looks like, only hear his voice on the phone now and again, and he's not exactly the kind of person you can Google and get reliable hits on. "The Guy" Richie might be *your* friend, but he's *our* contact.'

'Yeah, and he really loves that nickname, too,' Chlöe said sarcastically. 'Look, Richie's Richie. That idiot's playing cops and robbers with himself and I don't have the heart to spoil his fun.' The thought of her cyberphilic, underground rat of a friend losing both his cool and trust in them and withdrawing, all because they'd probed for more intimacy, caused her throat to dry. Vee pretended she didn't care, that she could return to life before there was a Richie to mine their paydirt, but Chlöe knew it would cut her to the quick, too. Richard Fish wasn't hugely conventional or prompt, but within their pool of "informed consultants" he was head and shoulders above the pack. 'It's easier when I handle him. He's the only one I'm in charge of, so allow me my meagre power.'

'All right, all right.' Vee plucked a tissue from her Kleenex box and dabbed her neck and chest. 'Hoo. The air-con ain't kicked in yet? And I've been salivating for my frozen juice all morning, had it right in my hand before that lil'—'

'We need to sync up our plan of action beforehand.'

'What plan of action?' Vee started threading out of the newsroom.

'I know you've brewed some masterplan. Spill it. I need to be prepared.'

Vee kicked in the door to the communal tearoom-kitchen and it suctioned shut behind them, dulling the office din to a buzz. Thank God the tearoom was empty. She squinted through the wide panel of frosted glass overlooking the sprawl of cubicles. The coast was clear. Vee then unbuttoned two notches on her blouse and yanked open the refrigerator's freezer compartment. The cold air brought goosebumps to her skin and she blew a happy sigh. 'There's no masterplan, o. We'll break it down to Nico as it happened and it shouldn't be a problem.'

'Since when are you the daft one? This man has it in for us. He gave us a clear directive and we disobeyed it. People tweeted and blogged and Facebooked all weekend about those murders and the journalists who were there. It's going to be a problem.'

'Why? Nico told us to follow a story, which we did. He—'

'He *never* said crash parties, drink and dance the night away with strangers, stumble on corpses and have the cops in our face.'

'We did...' Vee trailed off. 'We accomplished *a lot*, didn't we?'

'Stop it! Social whoring was not in the mandate. Walsh the computer geek, remember, the guy with the weird hair, he kept making eyes at you and dragging you to dance. I was completely sloshed. It looked bad. I don't get why you're not more worried.'

'Because you freak out enough for the both of us.' Vee squeezed her arm. 'Of course I've thought this through, and my conclusion is, don't worry. Nico might be bent outta shape, but this story is our leverage. We got this.'

'Portia's here.'

The fridge hummed, puffing chilly across the silence. Invoking the name of their old boss and all the memories she dredged up was a serious offence. Chlöe could tell Vee was debating whether or not to believe her.

'She's not here for us.' Vee slapped the freezer door closed. 'Of course not. Why would she be?' She buttoned her blouse. 'No.' She shook her head and undid the top button. 'Did you see her yourself? What was her hair like, up or down? Was she in jeans or normal pants? Jeans is bad, means she's trying too hard to seem casual.'

'Aha!' Chlöe said, but the victory was hollow. If Vee was rattled, then hope was lost. She added, injecting as much brightness and reason into her voice as she could, 'Who cares? She's not our boss any more so we can safely not give a shit what she's doing here, right?' Chlöe watched what she could have sworn was one drop of sweat bud like yeast into a glistening line of tiny beads on Vee's top lip. 'Right?'

There was a rap on the partition of the tearoom and they both jumped. A colleague motioned to them through the opaque pane of glass, then pointed down the hall. Eventually she walked round and cracked open the door. 'Nico wants to see you guys,' she said, closing it after her.

'Shit,' Vee mumbled. Chlöe deflated.

———

'Ah, if it isn't Pinky and the Brain.'

Portia Kruger stretched her endless legs - in a pair of skinny jeans - off an armchair and advanced. 'You ladies look great.'

She eyed them up and down. "You've clearly learned more about fashion than you've ever let on. I'm almost sorry I let you leave *Urban*.'

'You don't look too shabby yourself,' Vee replied. Portia looked incredible.

Portia flicked her a dismissive eye and brushed imaginary fluff off the sleeve of a sheer cream blouse. It was silk, the very same blouse Vee had recently turned her back on in a shop at the V&A Waterfront shopping mall, her eyes watering at the price.

Nico muttered a curse and exaggerated his sigh. 'Let's make this quick, we all have a lot to get back to.'

Vee flicked her eyes in Portia's direction and gave Nico a pointed, questioning look.

'Oh, I was just in the neighbourhood. Should I...?' Portia curved her manicured thumbs towards the door, eyebrows arched.

'No need. Stay. We're all friends here.' Nico settled his rump on the edge of his desk and brought his hands together in a dull clap. 'Let's hear exactly what happened out there.'

'Okay. I'm sure you've been through the rough draft of the story I sent you last night. We got something in in time for today's print run, but for Wednesday's we'll be going much deeper.'

'And the travel piece is completed and filed,' Chlöe piped up.

'Fully complete,' Vee echoed, nodding along.

'I'd like a face-to-face regaling of your adventures. Humour me,' Nico said.

'Um.' Vee cleared her throat. 'So... what had happened was...'

It didn't take long. She avoided the scenic route and kept to the highway, managing to get in as much detail as possible with neither obfuscation nor embellishment. It was a hard story to come out of looking like a champion. She couldn't read much on either Nico or Portia's face.

'Interesting,' said Nico.

'Hhmm!' said Portia.

'You can't write it,' he continued. 'Khaya and Andrew are stepping in to give us a really tight main. Hand your draft over to them, a copy of your police statement—'

'Wait, wait, wait.' Vee felt the hinge of her jaw slowly drop and pull itself back up. 'How – what do you mean I can't write it? This is my story – *our* story. We saw it go down, how can you take it away?'

'Use your inside voice in this office,' Nico snapped. He drew a calming breath. 'You're right, that's *why* I have to take it away. You guys are more than too close to this, you *are* it. You're right in the centre.'

'Exactly. For once, we were there as the news happened, not hustling for a scoop with a hundred other vultures. That's prime perspective.'

'A perspective that's not objective. Your involvement means you're part of an open investigation.'

'But it—'

Nico held up his hand. 'It may not be an issue any more. If the police believe you're perfectly in the clear, that's great. For all of us. But there's a possibility that it could change, and we need to consider that for legal reasons. From a journalistic standpoint, you know as well as I do you can't report on events that happened to you. Newspaper,' he jabbed his finger in the newsroom's direction, 'not tell-all publisher.'

A knot clogged Vee's breathing. Imagining the smugness radiating off the faces of Khaya and Andrew was almost too much to bear. 'This isn't fair,' she blustered.

'Fair isn't the issue. This is how it has to go. Hand over your notes and whatever else you have so far to the crime desk, so they can get a jump on a working layout. The word is out; the dailies have already run a dozen versions of this. They know two of our people were out there, and they know which ones. Some of them want an interview –' his hand shot up again over Vee and Chlöe's protests, '– a request that has been denied for now. Not until we get back on top of it. The sooner you both have a sit-down with one of our own while it's all still fresh in your minds, the better.' Nico absorbed their expressions. The points of his shoulders softened a touch. 'Look, this isn't even a lead story.'

'But it could be!' they chorused.

'*Possibly*. As it is, it's simply not enough. What's another murder in one of the most violent countries anywhere? Juicy would be stumbling across kickbacks and bribery in the LEAD investment ranks. Or the bidders stealthily bumping each other off for the edge. All we have so far is a dead business owner. And he's no Tokyo Sexwale."

'We're not even 48 hours in yet.'

'Still plenty of time to run stale in the news business.'

'That's why we're investigators. We dig. We'll find more, because there's more to find. This wasn't some random shindig. LEAD's hot right now. We can't afford to sleep on this.' Vee heard the childish quaver in her voice but couldn't control it.

'All true. But you're off this. Think about it. You know it makes sense.' He waited, scrutinising her face as it sunk in. 'You can get a crack at it later on, maybe hit it from a different angle. Insider's insight or something. But no to the lead.'

Vee's sandals ate up the floor in long strides, her shoulders tight, angry juts as she approached. Chlöe deflated. The debrief must have been a bitch of an ordeal, then. She could only imagine it: Vee fighting to keep her cool, reciting details through clenched teeth; Khaya nodding with overplayed gravitas as he rewound and nitpicked her statement as a beaming Andrew flicked his fat, hairy fingers through *their* write-up, *their* hard work.

'How'd it go?'

'Assholes.' Vee tossed her notebook across her desk. It skidded, sending pieces of stationery skittering off the tabletop to the floor. A few co-workers met her gaze and hunched back over their paperwork.

'Um, are we actual pissed or pretend pissed?'

'Dah so-so bullshit heah!'

'Okay, actual pissed it is.'

Vee sagged against the desk and dropped her head into her hands. Chlöe scooted a chair over, dropping her voice. 'Come on, you really didn't see this coming? You had to.'

Vee looked up. 'I know. Deep down of course I knew... it's just... I can't take this humdrum nonsense anymore. It's below me... us. We always get *this* close,' she held her fingers a pinch apart, 'then someone swoops in and shunts us into a dark corner.' She reared her head like a fearsome dragon's. 'No. This is ours. And we're sure as hell keeping it.'

'How?'

'You heard what he said in there. We can't do the angle about this weekend. Let those two dummies enjoy swinging their dicks around. Their piece will be a one-shot, one-off. But if it was an investigation...' Baffled, Chlöe nodded with enthusiasm, unsure what to say. 'Meaning if we turn this around, if we get something solid, then it's officially ours again, and of course we'll be taking the byline.'

'Ehhhh...' Chlöe narrowed her eyes, 'that's not *quite* what I heard Nico say.'

'Yes, it is. What we need is a game plan.'

'Isn't that what I—'

'First thing, let's get an edgier angle on the LEAD rigmarole. Nobody wants to read another dry regurgitation on how to fluff a promising start-up. They can grab a financial daily for that. They'll be in it for the murder – that's the angle we push. A participant was strangled at their conference – we can count on it being linked to them. Let's poke around Berman's personal life first, though. We've already put together a file on the easy stuff, so let's probe deeper. Who knows, maybe his ex-wife got shafted in the divorce or suffered a delayed psychotic break, drove all the way out there to get her own back. She could be spilling her guts to the cops right now. Though I think the venue and the viciousness combined makes this a non-domestic beef. This is personal to LEAD or someone linked to it. Start looking into the backgrounds of all the companies in depth. There's bound to be a red flag flapping around.' Vee looked up at Chlöe from the notepad she was scribbling on. 'Bishop. You with me?'

'Yeah. All the way,' Chlöe said, barely hiding a wince. In-depth anything meant mind-melting interviews. '*All* of them?'

'No, not all. The principals. The evaluation's in the final stages. How many finalists would you say attended?'

'About,' Chlöe wagged her head, 'a baker's dozen. Companies, I mean. Maybe more. As to total number of attendants, whew. People were in cliques, some companies were represented by more than one staff member… hard to tell. But remember, we already did prelim research on the ones who showed for the conference.'

'That's been handed over to Khaya and Andrew. If we're conducting our own interviews—'

'There's the list we got from the spokesperson and programme organiser, so it's a snap to get a head count.' *Please don't say we're going to interview each and every one on that list,* Chlöe prayed.

'Of course, we won't do a full body count. That would be crazy.'

Chlöe gulped down her relief.

'But with the top dogs, definitely. I know the best place to start.'

'About that. I've been trying Akhona Moloi since you went for your debrief, you know, for an exclusive. I figured she'd be sympathetic to *City Chronicle* journos above a couple of randoms, seeing as it's their debacle that's put us through the wringer. I've called Berman & Moloi Financial several times, no joy. I finally got hold of a personal assistant, who let me know it's not happening, least not today. Moloi's been tied up with the police since we left Oudtshoorn, going over her statement, possible motives, Gavin's state of affairs I imagine. Sounds like right now they're crawling up her ass. We can do our casual drop-by-and-push-in bit, but…'

'I figured as much. If we're to get anything out of her, we can't aggravate or she'll clam up. Nah, my head's in a different direction, for a different slant. Think less to lose, therefore less reticent and more verbal diarrhoea.' A tiny smile danced in Vee's eyes. She gave her thighs a determined pat, nodded and pushed off the edge of the desk. 'Your car or mine?' she called, threading to her cubicle. She glanced behind her. 'Bishop, let's hustle. There's a ton of ground to cover.'

Phone to ear, Chlöe quickly pressed hold when the line picked up and lowered the call to her neck. 'Sure, I'm right behind you. Lemme get that disk sent off and I'll meet you outside.'

'Why didn't you courier it immediately, like you said? Have you at least made copies?'

'Uh, yeah… I did, I did.' Chlöe realised she was nodding a tad too emphatically and willed herself to stop. 'Richie's been busy and absent-minded. And you know how paranoid he gets about strange packages showing up to his address; don't want him chucking it out. Let me make double sure he knows to watch out for it and confirm delivery. It's top priority, right.'

Vee frowned. Tucking a plastic binder under her arm, she said, 'I'm outside.'

'You know I hate being on hold, CC. I could be traced.' Richie sounded like he'd just woken up from sleep.

'Dude, go die. No one would bother tracing you, and even if they did, paranoia's only cute when you're actually important,' Chlöe snapped. 'Look, I need a favour. Ag man, shut it, you're doing it. And Vee had better not find out about it. No, I'm not hiding things from her… it's delicate, kind of… you'll get it once I explain…'

14

'You look good. Have I said how good you look?' Ryan Walsh flashed a wide, guileless grin. 'The city suits you as well as the country. Not many can say that.'

Vee gave a short laugh. 'You've switched it up too, I see. Whole other vibe.' His corporate ensemble – crisp suit, hair clipped and tame, pointy-toed shoes of blinding shine – were an unsettling overhaul. If not for the glasses, he'd be unrecognisable. 'More professional, less unbridled nerd.' She shifted her weight in the plush armchair. 'That being said, you need to elaborate on everything you just said, because I'm lost. We both are.'

'In the weeds,' Chlöe said, sipping her orange juice.

Walsh shrugged off his jacket with a murmured 'excuse me', lancing it with some disdain over the headrest of his leather lounger. 'What I meant when I said I'm done, is *I'm done*. Out. Pulling in the line, hitting the road. It's a factor of – is the temperature okay in here? I can switch off the air-con. Would you ladies like more refreshments?'

'We're fine,' they echoed.

His hands waved in defeat. 'Sorry, I'm flapping about like some old bat. We've recently redecorated. I'm used to more austere surroundings, but since we've got sharkish about attracting bigger business, my assistant's been on me to pull up my socks.' He looked around at his office's new aesthetic –

tastefully printed curtains, furniture of heavy varnished wood, thick moss-green carpet – as if himself in awe. He met Vee's eyes, smile tilting his lips. 'More classy, less unbridled nerd, I'd say.'

Lord, is he flirting? Vee thought. It was best to ignore it – unless, of course, it came in handy. 'You should be stoked at how well your company's doing,' she steered him back to business. 'Software developers aren't exactly thick on the ground on the continent. If The IT Factor pulls out of LEAD now, there goes your rep,' she said.

'Our rep will be fine. It's a thriving industry now, believe you me we'll find other contracts. Of course, business software and solutions, our core product, doesn't, and never will, have the rabid popularity of gaming technology and cell phone apps, but,' Walsh shrugged, 'for a pack of boring old fogies, we do all right.'

'Old fogey? At thirty-seven? And one of the country's wealthiest innovators? Tsk tsk. Your modesty is shameful.' Chlöe grinned wickedly. 'Might I recall SA's *Men's Health*, what, a few years ago. Eligible bachelors list. Shirtless edition.'

Walsh blushed so intensely that he looked like overripe tomatoes had exploded under the epidermis of both his cheeks. 'Ag, man. That was… I was younger. More deluded. Let my publicist at the time convince me I was more of a stud than I was,' he blustered. He clutched the top button of his shirt as if they'd requested he unbutton it, or worse, like he anticipated one of them leaping across the desk and ripping it open. 'Truly, I was dared by friends, it was only for a laugh.'

'And didn't hurt business or the image of a self-made man. Why would it? The guy who started as a solo consultant at twenty-five and built up his own tech company can do no wrong. You're a national success story. On your way to being the next Mark Shuttleworth,' Vee said.

'I'll say,' chimed Chlöe. 'Didn't The ITF do the records

interface for that cluster of private schools a couple of years ago? And got one of the government contracts for voter registration and national ID card systems?' Vee and Walsh lifted their eyebrows at her. 'What? I have a friend who's a complete tech head. He blabs on and on, regardless of whether I'm interested. It's handy information when you meet the people who matter.'

Vee rolled her eyes surreptitiously as Walsh fussed behind his computer monitor, about to rupture from flushed pleasure. He briefly got up to speak to an employee in the doorway, and she leaned over. 'Look, brown-noser, I know on the way here I said butter him up, but reel it in. You *just* researched the company,' she hissed. 'Lay it on any thicker and we'll be wading through bullshit.'

'I beg your pardon; my awe is genuine. I've always known a bit about him; how could I not? He's a UCT graduate, like, a famous one. He gets invited to speak at their IT and innovation courses, was part of the graduate recruitment seminars few years in a row. Walsh is one of the alumni they still make a big fuss over. One of those who *aren't* like me, if you get my meaning. And he gave us *posh biscuits*.'

'And I'd like to stay that way.' Walsh plopped back into his seat and swivelled the computer monitor to the wall, allotting them his full attention. 'A self-made man, I mean. Not self-*destructing*. I can only do that by not falling into the age-old trap of chasing fool's gold in the quest for instant and explosive success.'

Vee leaned closer. 'LEAD was promising that? I don't mean to sound rude, but from what I know and saw it didn't look like it had that level of clout.'

'Ah.' He sighed. 'They were definitely offering something too good to be true, certainly for this economy. And don't be fooled by a humble exterior. This is merely the beginning. The investment's government as well as privately funded, serving as a launch pad for small and medium-sized businesses. Had it worked, Lord only knows what a formidable force it could've become.'

A speech heavily reminiscent of Berman the inflated bullfrog's soliloquy on the night of his death. Vee shuddered. 'You're eulogising. Fine, you've pulled out, but surely this one little glitch doesn't mean everything's dead in the water?'

'*One little glitch?*' Walsh tilted his head, his expression that of a man wondering whether she might indeed be a mere pretty face. 'You clearly don't grasp the magnitude of this.'

She bristled and crossed her legs. 'That's why we're here. Explain it.'

'What's the date in three days?' He measured their blank stares. 'First of April. Kind of monumental, because come Thursday a new piece of legislation is poised to go into effect concerning the Codes of Good Practice. The laws governing varying aspects of black economic empowerment.' Another pause. 'It's the—'

'I know. No BEE workshop necessary.'

He chuckled. 'Good, I can skip the lecture. I'm sure, like most of the public, you've got a fair grasp of how our previously disadvantaged history has influenced the landscape to the point of no return.'

'You say that like it's a bad thing.' Vee shared a sidelong look with Chlöe.

'I say that like it has the potential to wreck the solid foundation that's been built so far, if we're not circumspect.' He used his chin to nod at a document atop his desk. 'Peruse at will. It's not confidential.'

'Pretty strongly worded,' she observed after flipping through the first two pages, passing it to Chlöe. 'Was it necessary to be so ....'

'Abrasively instructive?' He shrugged, then shook his head in disappointment. 'LEAD has essentially been a time-wasting exercise. This memo expresses my displeasure and outlines the steps I think the committee should take, should have taken, or at the very least what pre-emptive strike they should have *anticipated* in this eventuality. The committee works with government officials and should've been abreast of changes that would affect our eligibility. But everyone just let it coast, thinking it would resolve itself magically. What's left is a brewing mess. I mean, seriously.' His jaw worked as he rumpled the inch of hair he'd left unshorn. 'In three days, at least five of 14 companies will be out in the cold because of one simple amendment.'

'Can you break it down for us? Like you're talking to a five-year-old,' Chlöe said.

'The April 1 amendment is going to state that all BEE certificates used by local companies, from here on out, had to have been issued by a SANAS- or IRBA-accredited agency – that's the South African National Accreditation System and the Independent Regulatory Board for Auditors. The one little glitch that causes a tectonic shift. Any certificate from an unaccredited source becomes not only worthless, but illegal, putting that company at a huge disadvantage to enter any worthy bids. Therefore—'

'A third of the contenders won't be LEAD-eligible. Including…?' Chlöe said.

'No.' Walsh waved his hands emphatically. 'Not us. But five of the others don't hold up to that kind of scrutiny. To be fair, prior to this we weren't aware we strictly had to. But all the same, they'll be axed out of the running.'

Vee exchanged looks with Chlöe again. 'Isn't that good news for you?'

'Believe it or not, I prefer fair play. After scaling every hurdle to reach this stage, being knocked out now by a technicality is a damn shame. Myself, Berman & Moloi – that's Gavin and Akhona… well, it's essentially Moloi now – let's see, Moodley's

events management company… the TV production company…
all out. The majority, luckily, we're in the clear.'

'Moodley. The giggling Indian lady,' Vee muttered to Chlöe.

'But Kele – Kelebogile Letlaka—' Walsh said.

'Dreadlocks. The African crafts shop,' Vee said.

'She's a bloody recent graduate. Started up with a friend, two
honest young twenty-somethings, and look how well they've
done. Tourists loved their World Cup mementos. They've been
featured in *Top Billing Home* magazine; they were in *True Love*
two months ago. They're a grassroots operation finally coming
into their own. They can't afford to sit waiting to go through all
this again. It'd set them back aeons.'

'Aren't companies exempt from needing a BEE certificate if
their turnover qualifies them as a small operation?'

'They are. Less than five million per year revenue and all
they need is the EME – exempted micro enterprise certificate.
Which they already have, as do the other small start-ups. But
there's still the other four larger outfits who have to bear the
new cost of becoming fully and properly compliant, that's if
they even want to bother."

'Why can't LEAD just go ahead anyway, ironing things out
as it progresses? Sort it out later?'

'It won't be put on ice until this gets sorted, that's why it's a
setback for all of us. One of the driving points of the exercise
was that this was going to be, had to be, kosher from the start.
LEAD was meant to be a BEE facelift, to offset some of the
scandal around laundering, investment fraud and fronting. The
government can't afford another stink and private investors
have a significant stake that they can't bear to have tainted. So
here we are. The companies who pull out will cry foul if the
damn thing still goes ahead; if it doesn't, *everybody* cries foul
because we've essentially wasted months and months, and for
what?' Walsh scrubbed his palms over his face. 'It's a mess. A
typical rainbow nation cock-up.'

'The entire venture will get axed,' Chlöe said. 'How wasteful!'

Walsh reclined in his chair. 'Oh, they won't cancel it. They'll make shifts and changes, perhaps in record time, to get it back on track.' He shrugged lazily. 'Or you're right, they might scrap it, who knows, hey? I certainly don't give a damn now. I'm out. Dedicating myself to this was lost time, energy and revenue.'

'That's a damn shame,' Vee said, not sure what else to say.

'The nature of business is the nature of life. Some wins, some losses. I'll get back out there, find another toy to entertain me. I'm good at finding interesting toys with which to amuse.' He grinned, arrows of wolfish delight aimed straight at her. Vee muttered a curse under her breath and shook her head.

'For goodness sake.' Chlöe got to her feet. It was clear he was done pretending to take the interview seriously. 'I'll wait by the car.'

———————

'Alone at last,' Walsh said.

'Cut it out. This is work,' Vee said wearily.

'And the work part has ended. Moving forward… won't you accept my offer of dinner? Lunch? An innocent coffee?'

'Hmmph. Coffee with anything that has a penis is never innocent.'

His laugh was a surprise, an unfettered burst of mirth that blew his head back. She got a warm gust of chewing gum fruitiness to the face; saw a peep of dark, a filling, on his back tooth. Her mind leapt to Titus and his one sweet dimple, to Joshua and his lazy, laughing eyes. Perhaps this was how women lived dangerously, collecting suitors with cavalier ease, juggling them with disturbing dexterity. She'd tried it once, in her undergrad days in Legon. Back when it had just become acceptable for girls to talk about exploits and orgasms, to have a boyfriend each for tutoring, shoe-buying, restaurant-going, party time, and one for love, if one was disposed to such. She'd dabbled, and not very well. It had been no great disappointment to learn she couldn't let two different pairs of hands excite her – only to later find that the owner of one of those sets of hands hadn't had any such qualms about frolicking with other women, after which she'd dumped him, feeling foolish. And here she was today, living quite the scarlet life in another country. Vee sighed inwardly.

'Just to talk, nothing more. Two grown-ups enjoying each other's company.'

'Talk. About? More of this, professionally?'

He eyed her for a long moment, expression somewhere between amused and another thing she couldn't decipher. He opened his mouth, seemed to think better of it and drew it closed. 'Not so much. About… whatever you please. My schedule's wide open for banter.'

'For true? You just said you're done having your time wasted on pointless ventures. I'm tired of being hit on by bored businessmen.' She felt a stab of guilt when he winced. 'That was unfair, Ryan, I'm sorry,' she ran on. 'I can't, I'm seeing someone already. Two someones. I'll be damned straight to hell if I add one more.' His face twitched before he succumbed to more shoulder-shaking laughter. Vee crossed her arms, cheeks warming. Why had she said that?

'*Two* someones? I'm not terribly surprised.' His already bright eyes practically glowed as they bored into hers. 'You do have the air of a woman who knows how to handle herself with the fickle sex.'

'It's not like that. I'm not like that.' Vee uncrossed and recrossed her arms. 'Not that it's any of your business, but it's complicated. I don't need another person making it more complicated. But I'm flattered.'

'It's because I'm white, isn't it?'

'Whaaa – you really think…' The jovial bounce of his shoulders stopped her. She pursed her lips. 'You find yourself quite hilarious, I see.'

'Truth be told, I don't. Certainly not around women.' He cleared his throat, straightened his glasses, drew back with a squint to absorb her. 'You, I like. You're very unobvious.'

It was her turn to leave her mouth hanging open. Finally, she said, 'I don't know what that means,' and walked out of his office.

———

'Hey!' A hazy figure hailed Chlöe, flailing its arms in an exaggerated wave. 'Howzit?'

Chlöe squinted into the blinding sunlight outside The ITF's metal-and-glass building, one hand over her eyes as a visor. The arms and their owner advanced, weaving their way between cars in the company lot. Chlöe scuttled back under the protection of the entrance's awning, her arms stinging from a few moments' exposure. She could almost feel new freckles pinging to the surface of her epidermis every day, every night in her sleep. Soon, too soon if she didn't watch it, she'd resemble a chocolate chip cookie; aged, crumbly and speckled from irreparable damage.

Aneshree Chowdri wiped sweat off her forehead and the back of her neck, lifting a short ponytail. 'I saw you lurking over here and wondered if I should say hello. Then you saw me, and I couldn't walk away since I wasn't sure if you'd recognised me and it would be awkward if you had...' She popped a half shrug. 'Anyway. Howzit?'

'Cool,' Chlöe replied. 'And I was hardly lurking.'

Aneshree's mouth tilted at a sardonic angle, clearly indicating her thoughts on a journalist who didn't lurk. 'Be that as it may. Bit of a surprise to see you here.' Her dark brown eyes flicked skyward in thought. 'Then again, I suppose not really. You are probing murder and intrigue, aren't you. Where's your other half?'

'Inside.'

'Ah. With Ryan.' Aneshree amplified her sly smile. 'He's taken quite a shine to her, hasn't he.'

'Well, he'd better turn that shine off. She's *way* above his pay, and lay, grade.'

Aneshree sprayed giggles into her palm. 'Oh, wow! You're quite overprotective, aren't you. Are you paid extra for that?'

Chlöe squashed the urge to ask Aneshree if she knew the tenets of proper speech, how to inflect so that questions didn't resemble plain old sentences, how not to be so annoying. Instead, she turned away and stared down the sweltering stretch of concrete, fixing on where the drive out of the office park fed into the main road. From the corner of her eye, she couldn't miss the ripening of Aneshree's smugness.

'Ah, don't mind me, I like to tease. I'm just a little surprised your poking around led you here.'

'It has,' Chlöe replied stoutly. 'So it's more like fancy meeting *you* here.'

'Nothing fancy about that, either. I work here.'

Chlöe blinked. 'You never told me that. You never *once* said you worked for Walsh! In fact, you never mentioned working for anyone at the LEAD thingy.'

'You never asked me, did you.'

'Yes, I did. When I asked what you were doing at The Grotto.'

'No, you asked *what* I did. Which I answered truthfully. I specifically said – no, hang on – I said I was there on my own steam. Which I was. I wasn't meant to be at the convention or working that weekend, but my boss, Ryan Walsh, thought it would be very insightful if I was. And he was right.'

'So glad you find strangulations entertaining.'

'Wha—? I didn't say that. All I meant…' Aneshree frowned. She looked like she wanted to say something but was holding back. 'This isn't what you think. None of it is.'

'*What* isn't what I think?' Chlöe spat. If Vee were here she'd shoot her one of her trademark Vee looks, telling her to ease up, never batter information into yielding to you. This chick was very trying, though.

'As in underhand deals and dastardly deeds. It's a simple, unforeseen mess. The whole thing is a mess. Everyone's trying to get the best out of it that they can.'

Walsh's words… his echo, on the same premises, in a short space of time. Two people who, it now turned out, worked together. Chlöe frowned. 'What makes you say that?'

'What would make you *not* say that?' Aneshree folded her arms. 'Have you talked to Ryan? Of course you've talked to Ryan.' She muttered something, shaking her head. 'This stops us in our tracks. We can't—' She muttered again. 'We all have to start over. It's frustrating.'

'But how b—'

Aneshree stole a glance at her watch, caught sight of Vee approaching and, without warning, trotted towards the front entrance. 'Sorry, have to dash. A living to earn and all that. Nice seeing you again.' She bartered a smile and nod for Vee's look of puzzlement as they crossed paths at the threshold.

'And then?' Vee asked, tossing her chin in Aneshree's direction.

'She works here. At The ITF. For Walsh.' Chlöe gave a wild shrug.

Vee gave her head a shake. 'Huh. Well. Just don't sleep with her. We both know how you are about cuties you meet loitering around car parks. Case in point, Isabella during the Paúlsen case. That ended well.' Ignoring Chlöe's splutters, Vee pulled out her cell, checked for messages and dumped it back in her handbag. After a beat she retrieved it, idly fiddled with the screen, rolled it between her palms and stuck it in her breast pocket.

'So, the software king spill the beans on anything else? Besides lectures on corporate malfeasance and why he'll have fewer millions to fill his bathtub with.'

'No. We just talked.' Vee sighed. 'I feel bad for him, entitled brat or not. He really invested a lot in this. It's like Gavin's murder set off a tumbling row of dominoes.'

Chlöe eyed her for a beat. 'Wait. You like him.'

'*He* likes *me*.'

'Duh.' Chlöe giggled. 'The Vee Vibration. Say, what's the collective noun for a group of men thinking with the brain in the lower half of their body?"

Vee considered for a second. 'A suffering of fools.'

Chlöe threw her head back with a 'Ha!' Then, 'Just don't say no till you see his beach house in Llandudno. You'd be balling out.'

Vee cringed. 'Please. Granted, a little condescension doesn't put off some women, but I'll pass. He's a nerd with with hang-ups. I've got my own problems.' Her mind was elsewhere and her eyes kept drifting back to the gleaming three-storey rise behind them.

'What?'

'It's… That feeling just passed over me. Lizard zipping down my back. Something…' Vee stomped her foot, grappling to pin it down. 'Dammit, it's gone.'

'That creepy antenna of yours… Promise, if this was two hundred years ago, I wouldn't stop a village mob from throwing you on a braai for witchcraft.' Chlöe stepped out of the awning's shade and began walking as fast as she could, before she was scorched into biltong. 'We started here because you knew this guy was a soft spot that if we, *you*, massaged right, it'd be worthwhile. So now we rinse and repeat until…'

'Till something pops up,' Vee said.

15

Vee bit her lip and stared down at the doormat. "Welcome", it beckoned in cheery red letters. Was she welcome? Her hand inched towards the doorknob, then froze. She left it hanging, bunched it into a fist and then dropped it.

She leaned against the balcony's railing and stared out. On the horizon, white curls of brine crashed onto the stretch of shoreline that was Sea Point beach. Strolling couples dotted the picturesque backdrop. Couples everywhere. Hand in hand, jogging in tandem, throwing objects for a frisky dog. Kissing. In the distance, a man broke his embrace with his woman, hoisted her by the hips and flung her over his shoulder, mimicking falling to his knees under her incredible weight. Vee could swear she caught the delighted peal of the woman's laughter over the churn of ocean waves, over the dying throb of rush-hour traffic on Beach Road, over the cacophony of human life emanating from nearby apartments on the third floor of Joshua Allen's complex.

'You plan on loitering outside my apartment all evening?'

She turned, unsure of what her eyes would meet. They met his, onyx and implacable as ever. The beard was still groomed, though his hair had already begun to re-sprout, tiny licks of black hugging to his head. She smiled, chest throbbing. Joshua didn't smile back. Her face fell.

'Truce?' she said, angling the word between request and statement.

He said nothing. But at least he held the door open. Vee took a step, then hesitated. He left it open and disappeared down the short hallway. 'She's not here,' he yelled over his shoulder. Vee snapped her lips shut and stepped inside.

His apartment had undergone a facelift: cushions plumped and propped on sofas, books shelved, magazines fanned atop the glass coffee table, carpet fluffy and citrus-y with the smell of cleaner. His silver 12-speed bike, usually propped on the nearest wall, was out of sight. The black-and-white mural of American greats had changed address from over the fireplace nearer to the dining area: Nina Simone levelled an acrid stare through cigarette smoke; Miles Davis puffed his cheeks over his trumpet; in mink, Eartha Kitt levelled feline coyness over one shoulder. Vee went back into the kitchen. It gleamed spic and span, save for a counter littered with empty tins and vegetable scraps. Either Palesa, his housekeeper, had recently been in, or Aria had learnt to sing for her supper.

Joshua swept a small mound of chopped herbs off the chopping board into his palm and dumped it in a pot. He was still in his work clothes, resembling a page out of *GQ*: youthful, clean lines, svelte but approachable. 'Palesa says hi,' he spoke finally, looking at her through the steam as he stirred. Ginger, cumin and meatiness wafted their greetings up her nostrils. 'Aria's too busy to lift a finger around here. American women are way too progressive for stuff like that. Unlike some I could name.' He smirked.

'I didn't come to fight. I wanted to see if you're okay.' She let it soak. 'If we're okay.'

His shoulders curled up in a casual shrug; his eyes laughed, jeered, at her. He would wait her out, however long it took, till she came clean as to why she'd really come. 'Totally copacetic. Why wouldn't we be?'

She crisscrossed her arms so tightly over her chest that her breasts hurt. 'I also came to see for myself if your ex-piece of ass was really living here with you.' She shook her head like a sage admonishing a wayward child. 'That bitch ruined your life, did you forget that?'

'Aha. Finally we uncover your real motive behind this visit: to piss on your tree. How transparent.' He faked a look of severe affront. 'One, of course I didn't forget how Aria messed with my head, I was there for every second of it. Two, she's not *living with me*. She's in town for spell, had nowhere else to go—' Vee snorted, '—so I let her stay a couple of weeks. She's moving out on Thursday. And three, I didn't tell you because I didn't know how you'd take it. You always know how to stop me every time I try to move on, just like you know which strings to pull to make me stay.'

Vee locked her jaw to keep her face impassive but on the inside she crumbled. He'd turned her own words on her – *You manipulate me to stay every time I try to come to my senses and this time it won't work!* – the very arrow she'd shot through his heart in order make her escape back to Titus months ago. His assault was more like a poison dart than the character assassination she'd launched but still, poison was poison. She backed off a little way, eyes skittering to the wall, the floor, anywhere but on him.

'Voinjama,' he said, voice gruff with remorse. 'I'm an ass. That wasn't necessary.'

Her head bounced up and down. 'Yeah, cool, no problem. God knows I've said and done worse. What happened wasn't necessary, or right. If things had been different...' She dared to look up.

'Things are never different enough.' He muttered words somewhere between a prayer and a curse, then lifted the pot's lid and dipped a wooden spoon in. 'Taste this.' He swiped excess drip off the back of the spoon and swirled it around to

cool before holding it out. She didn't budge. She considered
reminding him how unhygienic and culturally reprehensible
she found putting a cooking spoon directly to one's mouth
then blithely continuing to use it. How American. But from the
look on his face it was clearly another test.

She stepped up and allowed herself to be fed. The stew was
rich, enticing her salivary glands. 'It's good. Very good.'

'Thank you.' He carefully balanced the spoon against the
pot, switched the gas off, and closed the gap between them with
a step. He planted his hands on the counter on either side of
her, boxing her in. The air between them warmed, thickened,
vibrated. He smelled of cedar, green grass and ocean air, of
creaking bedsprings and moans into each other's mouths, of
precious hours and days she often chided herself to never waste
on a man. Time that never felt wasted afterwards.

'Will you stop it, please, and let me pass.'

'What… this?' He leaned in and dipped his forehead to hers.
'I'm standing where I want to stand. Haven't laid a finger on
you.'

His hands, palms down on the edge of the countertop, drew
in, encircling her. He trailed his lips, barely brushing the skin,
but not quite, of her throat, jawline, earlobe. Her skin prickled
as his beard ghosted the pulse in her throat. 'Still not touching
you.'

Further down, with the barest of leans, fabric touched fabric;
Vee fluttered as the swell of his excitement brushed the crotch
of her skirt, then nestled in with confidence, edging her legs
apart.

'You're being a bully,' she said. Her voice sounded distorted
to her own ears.

'Whoa. Can't have that.' He pulled away immediately and
raised his hands in surrender. But his eyes… how they laughed,
filling her vision like black pools, tipping her back in until

finally she broke, linked her fingers behind his head and swept their mouths together.

'Touchdown,' Joshua grinned when they paused for air.

————

'Do you think I'm unobvious?' she asked.

Joshua guffawed. 'What?' He let the idea hover. 'You're not *obvious*, that's for sure. If those are the only options, then yes, you are.'

Vee lazily gave him the finger. Out of the speakers next to the bed, an indignant Rick James kept crooning for his baby to give it to him night and day. She tipped the volume down a tad, smiling at the irony of the lyrics. Joshua was the only man, only *person* she knew, with the gumption to loop a seventies funk mega-mix during afterglow.

She went back to her plate of food. 'You didn't make this,' she slurred.

'Woolies Foods. Though I take full credit for my own essential touches. And pork.' He pinched her nose. "I had a hunch you were coming, and I know your proclivity for protein that once had a face.'

He nabbed a bite off her spoon, wrinkling his nose when she offered up more. He went back to studying her, his head against the headboard as he tickled a trail down her neck and spine.

'You haven't answered my question,' she said.

'I just did.'

'My other question.' Vee clattered the plate onto the bedside dresser and pivoted as much as she could so as to pinion him with a squint. 'Did you...with Aria?'

He sighed. 'Weeell...'

'Unbelievable.'

'What?! Don't give me that look. How rude would it have been if I hadn't? She really puts it out there, the toned glutes and rippling deltoids all up in your face. I am but a man, weak of flesh and all that.' He tweaked her nose. 'Blame yourself. You wanted time apart to think about things, yet you know outside of my job I *detest* thinking about things. Had you stayed put and defended your turf—'

'Neither you, nor Titus, are turf I need to defend or pamper. Both of you were crowding me, dammit. I needed a break. And I definitely didn't suggest fucking your ex-girlfriends.'

'Stop. How crass.' He clicked his tongue. 'I didn't *fuck* her, we made sweet love. A far cry from our thing.' He made a face and Vee fought her facial muscles to keep from laughing.

'Asshole.'

'Love of my life.' He pulled her into his arms.

'Hhmmph. Anyway. In the interest of bygones and clean slates, I'll say no more. For now.' Vee snuggled onto his chest, smoothing his fine hairs, running her fingers over the stippled scar near his ribcage. 'Tell me, when – Oh! Before I get to that, did I mention I saw your sister? Your other sister. The one by your real father... I mean, the man who claims...'

He barely flickered a lash. 'My sister's in New York. My real dad's in New York.'

Vee kept silent. Joshua's biological father, the man who'd abandoned him and his mother, wasn't even a sore subject; he was no subject at all. Joshua could pretend nonchalance with expert ease all he liked, but he should've known it would play better with a different audience. She knew far too much. But, everyone had their demons.

Instead, she sidestepped into recap mode, sticking to the day's details since he was already up to speed on her weekend's escapades at The Grotto. 'We're covering our bases. After we left The ITF we ran around to four of the other participants, called another six, and found nothing extraordinary. They barely have time or want to talk to us, they're all too absorbed in a scramble to launch a damage control campaign that'll be effective.'

She sat up to better face him. 'I'm trying to piece it together in my mind. At first I thought this was about cold, hard cash. It's got that kind of rage behind it, only love and money cultivate this kind of crazy. You know… a competitor's in better shape than you, you axe the competition.' She scratched the bridge of her nose. 'That won't work. Of the three in the financials category, B&M Financial's in the best shape, but even so, the others on the shortlist still get a big enough boost to rise above the fray and make bank. Lord knows there are enough tenders flying around.'

'Exactly. Lose out on LEAD and there's still a smorgasbord of opportunities floating around to snap up. I don't see anybody strangling a guy to death.' He cocked an eyebrow. 'Nevertheless…'

'What?' Vee drew her knees under her chin.

'People kill for less. And their motives, while crazy to Average Joe, make perfect sense to them.'

'Too true.'

'Every system is corruptible and South Africa's is no exception. "Where two or more are gathered in my name, the spirit is present." Apply that saying to any group of investors or finance guys and there you have it. If there's money to be made, they're looking for a way to make it, legal or not. Just look at the Bernie Madoff scandal. That assclown and JPMorgan Chase's complicity made the public even more convinced we're the bloodsuckers they think we are.'

'Not all of you are vampires.' She rubbed his shoulder.

He gave a noncommittal grunt. 'Be that as it may. In a minefield of stinkers and stink, follow the money.' He got off the bed, picked a soft grey hoodie emblazoned with "Columbia University" off the back of a chair and wriggled it over his head, then pulled his pants over boxer shorts. 'There's your murdered guy—'

'Two. Two murders.'

'Fine, two. If they have anything to do with rotten deals, broken promises and pissed-off investors, that's open season in the motive department. Could be someone had a personal score to settle. Look at the fine print in that weird way you do. Your killer's in there.'

'To strangle a grown man like that and string him up like a side of beef...' Vee feigned a shudder. 'That's a middle finger to everything he stood for. You're right. It's *him* that's key, his life, his company, before we start widening the net. Because we only have one shot at this. Nico's itching for us to fall on our faces, while Miss Portia's on her broom cackling in the background. They're cookin' up something, two of them. A reason to sack me. Well, maybe not me so much, it's Chlöe he's gunning for.'

Joshua smiled indulgently. 'Why? He hired both of you, like, yesterday.'

'Won't matter. That small matter of her being untrained, it's never gone away. Things at the paper have got more strained, circulation's down, he's worried and hitting the bottle more often...' She quirked her eyebrows. 'He needs a slam dunk.'

Joshua shook his head and sat on the edge of the bed. 'Jeez. Your boss is an alcoholic. He's what, 42? Are you sure?'

'What's age got to do with it? Considering everything he's lost, who can blame him.'

It was common knowledge Nico had lost his wife and two-year-old son in a car crash five years previously. What Vee had had to dig to find was his connection to Portia Kruger. Turns out Portia had been an old friend of Lauren's, Nico's wife, and had even introduced the couple. The tragedy was like countless others in the traffic statistics files: young mother driving home from party with infant asleep in the back seat, neither had survived the collision with a lorry. Nico was still haunted by it and Portia, who'd waved her friend off as she drove home with no idea she'd never see her again, still blamed herself. One hell of a dark way to forge an alliance.

'He seems so *together*,' Joshua said.

'He is. Very. So was my mother in her dark days. Not everyone devolves into a loud, stumbling drunk.' Joshua opened his mouth to counter and she stopped him with a look. 'Finance may be your area, Mr Allen, but human frailty is mine. I've known a good number of traumatised drunks, so don't try to sanitise what it is,' she finished, putting a solid finality in her voice. She realised how much she sounded like Zintle in that moment.

'Okay. And don't let it get too far under *your* skin.' The look on his face said his mind had gone exactly where hers had – Rhonda Greenwood.

Vee laid back onto the pillows and pulled the sheets up. Joshua gave her his half-smile and left the room, leaving the bedroom door ajar.

16

Vee slept. She dreamt.

In her dream, she was collecting teeth. Not her own: other people's, that she would then sell; a professional collector, with her own market stall. Then her supply ran out and she travelled far and wide to find more. Dreamworld was in short supply, so she began to pull out her own teeth and keep them in a jar for a rainy – toothless – day. People began to approach her, then beg, then chase her for her jar of gems. She ran and ran and couldn't shake them off. Her thieving suitors went from a dark, faceless mob to a procession of people she recognised: Ryan Walsh a stringy giant; Akhona Moloi a mouse in huge glasses; Kele Letlaka with too many teeth and dreads like stringy seaweed; Moodley giggling so hard she could barely speak; Aneshree at her side with elbows sharp enough to cut Vee open. *Sell us your teeth,* they said. Vee looked around and saw she was back in the dining room of The Grotto Lodge. She edged away from them. Suddenly Gavin Berman appeared, a grey corpse hanging by nothing in mid-air. *You can take mine. Dead teeth are still good for something,* he grinned. Vee backed away till she fell, far, far, far down. She looked up and dirt was being scooped over her. She couldn't see who was doing the scooping but she knew, in the way people know things in dreams, that it wasn't anyone she knew. Dirt filled her mouth eyes nose ears she was choking her chest was caving in—

Vee opened her eyes and coughed. The inside of her mouth tasted like the earth after rain. She sat up, keeping her eyes closed. The thickness of the dream was still inside her, in her head. As was her grandmother's voice, her mother's mother, *Be careful, darling girl.* She flexed her neck and stretched her arms above her head, then opened her eyes. Through the bedroom curtains she could see it was dark out. Joshua was gone. Not just out of the apartment but farther; she could feel the emptiness he'd left. She looked on the bedside table till she saw his note: *Gone to get supplies. I took Cesaria. I'll be gentle, promise.* Vee released a long, slow breath. Typical. Joshua was forever concocting reasons to drive her car, even over short distances he could walk, not to mention bribing her with food to get her to stay.

She threw the covers back. A shower would rinse out her brain.

Ten minutes later, she'd finished microwaving her flesh on high in Joshua's powerful shower and was instant-messaging Chlöe about her dream. She picked her lacy boy-shorts off the floor and stepped into them. Her Samsung hummed with an incoming WhatsApp message.

Chlöe wrote: See, told you. Dreams abt teeth r bad! All the websites agree – anxiety dream. It means ur worried abt ur looks or aging. Or outliving ur usefulness if it's a job on ur mind. So you ARE worried about Nico and Portia and getting fired!

'Looks or *aging*?' Vee snorted, shaking her head. Dreams truly did mean different things in different cultures. Where she came from it usually meant: It's Death. Or danger, Vee typed back. It means watch your step cuz something's lurking. She added a number of emoticons: the knife, bomb with lit fuse, skull and crossbones, coffin. As her thumb hovered over "Send", she felt the lizard of foreboding skitter up and down her back. She deleted all of them and sent the text as is. No point tempting fate. I know you're not superstitious but… 'Neither am I. Strictly speaking,' she muttered defiantly to the empty room. Let's just be on our guard. Already I've got a bad feeling about this case.

I WASN'T SUPERSTITIOUS TILL I MET YOU, TITCHIBA!, Chlöe messaged. Now my world view's changed. If ur senses r tingling, then scareful we shall be. Nearly being murdered wasn't fun last time. Izzit ever in fact? If [poop emoticon] goes down I want it on record: UR ON UR OWN, MISSY!

Vee let out a hoot of laughter. Chlöe was a girl who refused to switch on her predictive text because typing out proper words was "super uncool"; how useful would she be when the revolution came? Vee *was* on her own, at least for the deeds calling for physical exertion and a clear head. 'And we weren't almost murdered, jeez.' Fine, they'd encountered some danger in the past but not mortal peril.

She turned back to the TV, playing low in the background. It was on CNN, live coverage of the Arab Spring. The replay showed frames of raw human emotion: people enraged in a public square, ducking and weaving through riot police missiles, tearful and jubilant as resignations and concessions were announced over loudspeakers. Egypt had declared itself free of a dictator, and now the entire North Africa wanted to dip their toes in the euphoria of revolution. A busty olive-skinned CNN reporter delivered commentary as it unravelled.

Are you watching this? she typed. A full minute elapsed with no answering ping from Chlöe before she gave up and tossed the phone on the bed. The world went beautifully mad every day and she doubted Chlöe paid much attention. Ah, the things she had to teach that young lady, all the while worrying whether the things she'd already taught her had sunk in.

She flicked through channels and soon was sucked in by another media phenomenon, the imminent nuptials of Prince William to Kate Middleton. A door somewhere in the apartment, possibly the front door, opened and closed. 'That was fast,' she called out, searching for her blouse. She gave up on it and headed to the kitchen. 'I thought I was gonna have to call the cops to bring you in. You – oh!' Vee flung her arms over her chest.

'Ohh!' Aria shrieked.

'Oh,' Vee said quietly.

'*Oh*. Uhhh…' Aria screwed up her mouth. 'Hmm. Maybe you'd like to…?' She waved a hand at Vee's state of undress with undisguised archness, head cocked, squinting her eyes. Vee couldn't tell if it was in distaste, surprise or just general discomfort.

Vee parried with a squint of her own. Pursed her lips and squared her shoulders. Dropped her arms. She moved out of the doorway that led to the bedrooms and spare bathroom and into the kitchen, stopping when she was just near enough to Aria to command a towering but not inappropriate proximity. 'I'm cool, thanks. Wasn't expecting anyone.'

'Clearly not.' Aria advanced until they were barely a pace apart. She stretched out an arm, and as Vee gritted her teeth, reached past Vee's head and flicked a switch. Floodlights bathed the kitchen. Aria lingered a second before retreating. Vee caught a warm waft of floral, vanilla and light woodiness from her nearness. She wanted to gag but couldn't; the combination was delightful.

Vee moved to the cabinets, studiously ignoring her semi-nude reflection bouncing off the toaster, the microwave door, the glossy countertops. She reached up into a cupboard and plucked a mug from its depths. She lifted the full coffee pot from its heating plate – *careful careful careful* – and held it out. 'It's fresh. Interested?'

'No.' Aria dropped her eyes to Vee's chest. 'Thank you. My appetite's gone for some reason.'

Vee poured, creamed, lightly sugared. Sipped. She wiggled onto a kitchen stool, drew her cup across the faux marble counter towards her. Heat and steam swirled over the rim, hitting the centre of her bare cleavage. She edged it away with a poke.

'So. Aria. How have things been with you?'

'Great. Yourself?'

'Brilliant.'

'Hhmm. Really? I heard a lot about a recent rocky patch… Was that, sorry I forget…' Aria knitted her brows. Whatever she was about to say next, Vee was certain it wasn't something she had to dredge her memory to recall. It had been festering on the tip of her fork-tipped cobra tongue for years, waiting for this moment. 'Was it before or after you lost your baby and Titus left you that you had that case that almost got you killed? The things you get up to!'

'Old news. Happens to the best of us. And I came out on top.' Sip. 'Have a brand-new job now, thanks to the great promotion I got. Misfortune can lead to wonderful things. I highly recommend it, that's if you can bear getting your hands dirty!'

They trilled merrily, Vee's teeth edging out of her jaw at the sound of their laughter blending together. Hers like thorns, Aria's like glass.

'What brings you to Cape Town?'

'Good fortune, actually. I seem to be blessed with it. Keeps me grateful.' Aria sighed and smiled. 'My studio in the States has ties with colleges all around the world. We run an interactive programme where teachers and students collaborate on jazz, interpretive dance, but focusing on new ways to incorporate tribal dance. African ceremonial moves especially.' A faraway mist filled her eyes. 'You know, dance is so physically *expressive*. So much like the act of love. It needs freshness and vitality injected into it every so often, or it stagnates and dies.'

'Doesn't it just.'

'I collaborated four years ago with the UCT School of

Dance and they invited me to be part of a programme they're running for six weeks. Can't believe I've already spent three.'

'Pity. I'm sure you'll miss it after you leave.'

'I won't have to. Not just yet, anyway. We've been invited to stay on another six months. How wonderful is that?'

Vee's smile threatened to snap, slicing her face in half. 'Absolutely…'

The front door slammed. Joshua strode in and stopped dead in his tracks.

'… phenomenal.'

Joshua edged, crept almost, from the mouth of the hallway into the kitchen, placed parcels with great care on the island countertop in the centre of the kitchen, his eyes volleying between them. Vee noted the tiniest twitch of his lips and the playful sheen brightening his irises. The urge to smack the smug off his face was replaced as quickly with overwhelming exhaustion. What the hell was she doing? Not just right here, right now, in the midst of this ridiculous tableau, but embroiled in this three-pronged – four, actually, if you counted Titus – mess.

'Don't mind me. Only made a quick stop to pick up a few of my things; wasn't planning on staying long.' Aria's voice faltered at the end of her lie and for the first time her gaze wavered in its assault; she likely hadn't come by for any reason other than stirring up trouble. .

'Ah. We agreed on Saturday, didn't we, to pick up the rest of your things. I wasn't expecting you.' Joshua's eyes darted to Vee, wordlessly ending his thoughts with, *As you can see, I have company.*

Aria's face flushed. 'Say no more. I'll get out of your hair.' She threaded an arm through the strap of her handbag and lifted it off the counter. 'Call me when this isn't a porn set any more, so I can get my shit,' she tossed at Joshua. And with that, she was gone.

Joshua turned to Vee. 'That – was – *awesome*.'

'No, that was pointless and demeaning.' Vee slid off the stool and walked her dirty mug over to the sink. When she turned around he was looking at her, expression serious yet tinged with mirth, like he wasn't sure how to gauge her mood.

'I'm not seeing her, Vee.'

'I know. I just....' she began, then let it hang. She just what? It felt like some fever had just broken. She remembered her conversation with Chlöe on the lawn of The Grotto the night of Berman's murder: *It's not about either of them and what they want. Just let me be angry till it stops making sense.* This was that moment, then. She realised she'd let go of the residual rage of the past two years without being aware she was letting it go, it had just slipped through her fingers. What she'd woven with Ti over three years would unmake itself its own way, had already unwound though they were good-naturedly pretending not to notice. And Joshua would always be here, would always be her Joshua. Their thing had never needed to be a performance. 'I need to go home. There's still a lot of work I have to prep for tomorrow.'

He sighed like he'd known it was coming. 'Fine. But then I went all that way for nothing.' He took a confectionery box out of the grocery bag and opened it up to her. 'It's not a bribe.'

'Of course not.' She rolled her eyes, pinched a doughnut frosted with lemon buttercream between two fingers and took a hefty bite. It was glorious. 'I'll stay *one* more hour and that's it.'

17

'It's not good news,' Vee said down the line to Chlöe, slamming and locking both the security gate and back door. 'Not that I expected Dr Coetzee to change her findings based on what I told her, but at the same time I *really* hoped she would.' Immediately she was inside the house, she grabbed a can of Ceres red grape from the fridge, popped the tab and poured half the contents down her throat. 'Accidental asphyxiation, they're sticking with it. Greenwood was apparently drunk enough to throw up in her own mouth and choke to death on it.'

'What a way to go,' Chlöe scoffed.

'You can say that again,' Vee replied. 'She's the expert, naturally, but – aaagggh Monro, shut up, stop making all that damn noise!'

'What's wrong with him? Have you taken him to the vet yet?'

'Not yet. He's not barking because of that. *Monro, baby, shut up, please!* It's these stupid teenagers in the neighbourhood. They go around at night throwing cans and firecrackers into people's yards and driving the dogs crazy. I just got back from Joshua's and haven't untied him yet, so he's losing it.' Vee waited for Chlöe's self-righteous sermon on coming home late after frolicking with lovers in Sea Point and irresponsibly leaving her dog tied up after Tristan went home for the day. Vee waited but Chlöe didn't bite. Vee frowned. Something was up. She herself was a liar of expediency: when a situation demanded, her tongue left quicksilver in the dust. Chlöe on the other hand, lied through her silences, which were rare and unwaveringly transparent. Vee knew she was hiding something and whatever it was had something to do with Richie, their hired geek. She made a mental note to twist Bishop's arm before tomorrow's morning meeting.

'Anyway,' she continued, 'I can't dismiss Coetzee's expertise. She's one of the medical examiners for the whole city of Oudtshoorn, she and that old papay she works with, Marais. But I feel they're missing something.'

'Of course you do. You're you,' Chlöe quipped. '*I* think they went to medical school, which you didn't. I can't say this enough times: Greenwood's death is a coincidence. There's no connection. And don't say—'

'There always is,' Vee cut in. 'I'm forwarding you her email. We'll talk about it tomorrow.'

She hung up and pulled up her Gmail account. *Wish I'd seen this sooner*, Vee thought, clicking on Dr Coetzee's email. She did an immediate mental retraction. Had she seen it earlier, it would have taken a dour dump on her evening with Joshua, and they'd both deserved an intermission. She went through what felt like the fiftieth re-read of Coetzee's replies, struck by disappointment once more:

From: Marielise Coetzee <mlcoetzee71@yahoo.com>
To: Voinjama Johnson <voinjama_j@gmail.com>
Cc: Kobus Marais <maraisk97@yahoo.com>
Sent: Monday 29 March 2011, 17:32
Subject: Autopsy concerns re: Greenwood, R

Dear Ms Johnson,
Hope I find you well. I'll cut right to the chase:
After discussions with my colleague Dr Marais (copied

here), we're convinced positional asphyxiation was indeed the cause for Rhonda Greenwood's death. In a nutshell, we found petechial haemorrhaging of conjunctiva (broken blood vessels in the eyes), oedematous lungs (fluid in the lungs), more haemorrhaging in the heart and lung surface, and congestion of her internal organs. Also, her stomach contents were approx. 160ml semi-digested material with a strong smell of alcohol, which was also present in the vomitus. All these findings, plus positioning of the body and high level of Zoloft in the bloodstream, lead us to accidental positional asphyxia (PA) due to intoxication as the justified cause of death.

Please be aware that in cases like these the death must satisfy certain criteria: 1. body discovered in a position that hindered normal breathing; 2. evidence that the victim placed themselves in that position without interference by another person; 3. sufficient reason they couldn't free themselves from that position due to intoxication/other drugs, unconsciousness, epilepsy etc.; and 4. there should be no other cause of death that could conflict with PA.

I hope this answers your questions and good luck with your article!

Best regards,
Marielise Coetzee
Senior Forensic Pathologist & Deputy Medical Examiner
Western Cape Forensic Pathology Services
South African Police Service (SAPS)
Baron van Reede Street, Oudtshoorn 6625
cell: 0837238999

Vee opened the next one and smiled at Coetzee's less formal banter:

From: **Marielise Coetzee** <mlcoetzee71@yahoo.com>
To: **Voinjama Johnson** <voinjama_j@gmail.com>
Sent: **Monday 29 March 2011, 17:49**
Subject: **Autopsy concerns re: Greenwood, R**

Hi Voinjama,

How's Cape Town, still as hectic as I remember? I keep thinking of moving out there one day… I really need a social life, haha!

RE previous email: sorry, had to copy Marais in so it's above board. I'm sure you got the gist that I had to tell him something. He thinks you're a medical reporter doing articles on interesting cases in the area. Just go with it if he follows up (he's been here for yonks, never follows up anything!). I still stand by our diagnosis, though unfortunately it isn't in line with your colourful theory. But it piqued my interest. Yes, a gash behind the ear could be caused by a fall, but the bruising on the nose, broken fingernails… it's not impossible. If you smell a rat and it stinks badly enough, contact me again if it's solid.

Cheers!
MC

Vee agitated her bottom lip until it throbbed. The ghost of an idea took shape in her mind. Standing in the darkness of the lounge, she quickly forwarded both emails to Chlöe, oblivious to the weight of her handbag and laptop case cutting into her shoulder. Then, she blitzed out a fresh email to Richie, trying to focus through her excitement and Monro's incessant barking as she outlined her request. It ought to be a cinch for a talented cyberstalker like Richie to accomplish. Wasn't he always carrying on about—

A chilly draft swept through the lounge and she rubbed her arms to warm them. The scorchers typical of March were receding and with April only days away, evenings had taken on a more hostile bite. Thumbs flying, she zipped through the rest of the email, attached two photographs she hoped met Richie's exacting standards, and pressed send. Then she put down the Samsung and rubbed her forearms. Where was that draft coming from? It couldn't be the sliding glass door with the metal security gate or one of the kitchen windows, but she double-checked anyway. Everything was secure.

The lizard was zipping through every muscle group on her back. Outside, Monro continued yapping up a racket.

She looked up towards the short flight of stairs. No, nothing was up there. She walked over to the guest toilet, pausing outside its door. She could see the streetlamps outside beaming clear through the raised window in the upper wall and she cursed under her breath. That blasted latch had been broken for nearly two months. She'd let too many things slide of late, the mound of errands on top of her piling and piling up, burying her under... *bad analogy*. She had to harass Mrs Konstantinou immediately to send workmen around, this very weekend, before it slipped her mind again.

Vee was turning away when a breeze sifted through the window, hitting her in the face, ruffling her hair. She cocked her head and stepped inside the toilet. The latch was broken but why was the window ajar? Her maid, Tambudzai, knew just how to arrange the metal lever in the lock position so the glass panel held fast. It was not in the lock position now. As if on cue, a dangling strip of white caulk broke off the ledge and smattered to crumbs on the floor.

'How the hell—'

The air behind her whooshed as the door swung inwards. The full weight of a human body, a hefty one, rammed into her back. Vee screamed. Her surprise faded to a gargle as her head met the wall with a crack. Lightning scratched hateful lines inside her skull. Her eyes swam. She buckled and clung to the wall, moaning, her bags sliding to the floor.

She kept her head pressed to the cool tiles for a microsecond more, then shook it to clear her vision. She was cornered. One exit, no way of reaching it, except to fling the door open and bolt. She sensed her assailant charging in on her before she had a chance to fully consider the option. She braced her forearms against the wall and pushed off with all her remaining strength, pulling up one leg. The heel of her boot connected with flesh; she twisted her leg to grind it in. An "uumpphh!" of surprise echoed off the tiles. Scratches and scrapes flew down her back as her attacker stumbled over her bags' tangle of straps and fell onto her.

Vee smelled cocoa butter and something flowery in the one breath she managed to steal before a fist of fingers scraped over her scalp, gripped a handful of hair and yanked. Howling, she dropped to a squat, wriggling until the hand lost its grip. She bounced to her feet and swung an elbow, missed, and pinwheeled. Slammed into a wall of flesh. *Cocoa butter and rose, that's what it is.* Hands smacked, grabbed and groped her. She grappled back, fighting the fingers trying to close around her throat. The attacker's other arm lightly bumped her head as it swung in to close the throttle, and Vee pulled her head back and swung it in a roundhouse arc. For a millisecond, the whites of her attacker's eyes filled her field of vision before it ducked. Fast, but not fast enough: Vee's vision imploded inside her skull as the side of her head connected with solid bone. Another yowl of anguish echoed through the tiles.

The jagged corner of what could only be a tooth scraped along her scalp. Vee shot out a fist that bounced off what felt like a neck. She stumbled, heard the crack and skid of her laptop case under her feet. She flailed desperately, groping for a handhold, finding none, freefalling, wrists issuing a distasteful pop as she landed on them. Agony bolted up her forearms. Her belly hit the toilet seat; she wheezed and bounced, legs flying up in the air.

Vee howled, positive if she opened her eyes she'd see a circle of cartoon stars spinning round her head. Near the opposite wall, coughs and rasps for breath drowned out hers. Good. She wasn't the only one losing steam.

Hands dragged her to her feet and rammed her chest-first into the honeysuckle-and-vine patterned linoleum. Vee lost her breath as her breasts went numb, then lit up her chest like two small solar flares erupting in her ribs. Slowly, carefully, her opponent's hands grasped hers and drew them, crossed in an X, behind her back. Grinding and popping, her shoulder blades moved, lifting the flesh of her upper back. Vee lost her breath in a soundless scream. One deft sweep of feet kicked her legs out from under her. Her knees hit the tile. Strong arms kept her pinioned, arms crisscrossed behind her back, as a heel stamped into her lower back. Her attacker heaved with exertion, puffing hot breath against the back of Vee's neck. Screams ripped from Vee's throat when the pointy arches of her shoulder blades threatened to meet.

A knee dug into her back one final time before the torture mercifully stopped. Vee gasped, sobbing, arms dead branches by her side. Cheek to lino, she watched the figure jump onto the toilet seat, mount the cistern, brace and grasp the ledge, and wriggle slowly through the window.

The toilet flushed as the toe of a dark sneaker cranked the handle, then it slipped into the darkness of outside.

Softly, Softly

18

Van Wyk scrubbed his hands over his face until his eyebrows looked like warring caterpillars when his arms dropped. 'How the fuck does this happen?!'

Vee and Chlöe shrank away from him.

'Um. This was an unforeseen attack, a home invasion. It therefore it can't be explained... necessarily...' Chlöe's voice tapered to a whisper, Nico's glare lasering her lips shut.

'I mean,' he loomed over Vee, 'how does someone break into your house and *wait*, undetected, in a secure neighbourhood? Don't you have an alarm system? Don't you realise, as a journalist, that disgruntled thugs may potentially moer you at the slightest provocation? Hasn't past experience taught you *anything*?!'

'I... it... it has. I have a dog, a big one. He was barking like crazy. But I was preoccupied so I didn't...'

The glare silenced her too. Vee massaged her throbbing scalp wound through the bandage covering half her forehead. Of all her aches, it hurt the worst. No, last night's monstrous headache had been worse, but that was on a leash now. Thank God her tetanus shot wasn't overdue. Now all she needed was to find out from her GP what else she could get from a stranger's repulsive saliva.

'Look, nobody feels more idiotic than I do. I'm pretty sure I interrupted the break-in and there was no way of sneaking past me. As to how, one panel of the sliding glass doors leading out to my porch got broken over a year ago. The guys had to disable the alarm to refit the glass. But then my landlady decided, why not repair the security bars all over the house before the comp—'

'Shut up. I don't care,' Nico snarled. 'This man could've killed you.'

Vee shook her head with care. Even after three painkillers, her cranium felt loaded with rocks. 'I keep telling you, definitely a woman. Unless it was a man on sex change hormones. Boobs and hips all over the place. She even smelled female. She wasn't fat but she was definitely no toothpick.' She flexed her shoulders, then wrists, grimacing at the nagging throb in them. 'And she fought dirty. Ghetto kinda dirty.'

'And she should know,' Chlöe gave a sage nod to Nico. 'She grew up on the streets.'

'I grew up in a two-parent household,' Vee snapped. 'But it was no joke o, I swear. This woman tried to tappay me without rope. Like this, she held me,' she flinched, shoulder blades protesting a re-enactment. 'That's a combat move. Rebels and combatants used it to subdue civilians. They'd, like, butterfly your arms behind you and cut off your circulation till your arms all but drop off. Only they'd tie your arms *to your legs*, so any tiny movement made the ropes tighter...'

She trailed off. Van Wyk and Bishop were both red-faced, shuffling their feet and avoiding eye contact. 'Oh, grow a pair, both of you,' Vee chided. The tacit office rule - never mention you've survived a civil war and we treat you like our de facto conflict correspondent - was a fragile creature, one she rarely threatened intentionally. She hissed her teeth quietly. 'She had skills, is all I meant. Even in the dark I could tell she was black. She had her hair tightly tied up. I'm positive it was Dreadlocks. And if she could kick *my* ass like that, she'd obliterate a man like Gavin Berman who had no muscle tone to speak of.'

Realisation slowly lit the darker flecks in Chlöe's eyes. 'Oh wow, you think she's *the woman*, the shadowy stranger Zintle and Mamello mentioned at the lodge. Of course!'

'Who's Zintle and Mamello?' Nico said. 'Never mind. Look.' He scrubbed his face again. 'Here's what's going to happen. We—'

'Wait! Before you render judgement.' Vee whirled over to his desk, reaching for her manila folder, uttering a low howl as her back glowed in pain.

'Maybe you should go home.'

'*No*.' Vee flashed him a raging glower of her own. 'That woman broke into my house and knocked me round like a village wife. Y'all know why? She thinks we're close to figuring out her identity. She's already got rid of one person who ID'ed her. Rhonda Greenwood—'

'*Oiii*,' Chlöe groaned into her palms.

'—was collateral damage, taken out of the equation because she knew something. Whatever it was, it was enough to make her killer nervous.'

'Her death was ruled accidental. Twice confirmed by two expert pathologists,' Nico said.

'How hard could it have been to fake? Given that her lifestyle was pretty common knowledge, not hard at all. Look at these.' Vee practically ripped the envelope trying to brandish the sheaf of colour printouts, brightened and resized onto standard A4 sheets. 'These are photos from the room on the day she died.'

'How did you get these?' The look on Nico's face as he examined them was a blend of awe and repulsion.

'Luck and circumstances.' Leavened by Nico's glimmer of interest, Vee rushed on. 'The bruises, the way she just lay there in her own vomit, the scratches on her hands that *could've been* defence wounds? She was a functional alcoholic; this is the demise of a dumb amateur.' Vee took a deep breath. If a hard sell was what it took to turn this thing around, then she was damn well going to give him one. 'Look, people are a sum of their habits. They can't help scattering them around like a trail of breadcrumbs. Everyone said Greenwood was two things: meticulous and very friendly. Precise, and never forgot a face. *Those are our clues.*'

Nico didn't respond. But he gave Vee an almost imperceptible nod to continue.

'Greenwood drank, but she had it on lock. Yeah, it stirred up whispers but she never let it screw with her performance. I think what happened...' She closed her eyes as she stroked the bridge of her nose, settling the scenario in her mind. 'There was an innocent exchange between her and this killer last week at The Grotto... for argument's sake, let's assume the same attacker from last night. At the time, Rhonda probably didn't get the significance of it because she barely had a free second with the conference going on; or maybe she did, who knows. But it didn't make her feel she was in danger, because that night she let the killer in without a second thought. Because she knew her.'

'How?'

'That I don't know yet. But we do know she died stone drunk and zonked out on anti-depressants. Maybe she took the pills herself, or was duped into taking more, I don't know.' Vee shook her head, making a mental note to stop saying "maybe" and "I don't know". Doubt cast a long shadow, and Nico hated that more than she did. 'However it happened, she has the liquor going, drugs going, and she conks out. On the bed, or she's moved there.

'And then the genius part. She's rolled up in the duvet, face down, arms pinned her sides so she can't move.' Vee stood ram-rod straight, arms flattened to her hips, did a couple of spins for effect. 'The duck-down duvet is used because it's heavy enough to lock her in. Otherwise why was it even on the bed? It's still summer, for God's sake, and the average temperature in Oudtshoorn was close to or over 30° every day. Now she's rolled up, passed out, can't move. All a killer does now is gently lift her head, bury her face in a pillow…' She spread her hands in finish. 'Watch the clock till it's over. That would explain the bruising on her nose, which was passed off as the position she asphyxiated in or the fall against the bedside table. Nothing else would be out of place.'

'What do the experts make of your wild theory?' Nico asked.

Vee waved a hand. 'That doesn't matter, because Greenwood isn't the case.' Vee upturned the envelope, emptying more papers, a flash drive, a USB cord, a Post-it pad and a pen onto the desk. And the CD, still intact, thanks to having the good sense to keep it in a security locker in the office. 'The break-in happened because of this.'

'And?' Nico arched his brows, looking back and forth between them as he turned it over and over in his hand.

'And what?' they chorused.

'What's on it?!' Nico roared like a man at sanity's end.

'Oh! Yeah. We… still don't really know. It's computer language. Gibberish. A code of some kind. Fragments of a code. The disk is kind of corrupted. Which wasn't our fault, we've handled it like an egg. But Guy Richie's still on it,' Vee chattered over Nico's ever-narrowing eyes. 'The best is on it and we'll have an update real soon. Without fail.' She flashed all her teeth.

'Where'd it come from? Am I right in suspecting it may or may not be evidence in the Berman investigation?'

Vee's grin collapsed. 'Errrr. We can't, shouldn't, disclose that till we know what's on it. In case it bites back at some point… you know, liability and all.'

Nico crossed the desk and sighed into his chair. He mulled for a long moment. 'Okay, here's my ruling. We're going to handle this gently, with kid gloves, because the potential for it to blow up in our faces and make us look like fools is massive. Here's what's going to happen…'

After an hour-long discussion, they left Nico's office, high-fiving once they were out of earshot. Chlöe moved in for a hug but Vee hissed and winced at the gentlest squeeze so she backed off.

'In your face, Khaya and Andrew. We get to keep our story *and* do the online version with the digital team.' Vee pumped a fist. '*Yes!*' Her phone rang and she slid out of her back pocket and frowned at the flashing screen. 'Hang on, I should take this. Third missed call from this number this morning.' Phone to ear, she punched her chin towards the newsroom, indicating they would meet in there afterwards, and threaded down the hallway in conversation.

Chlöe puffed her cheeks and let the air out in a long breath. That was one major slam-dunk out of the way for now. Now, if only she could see her way clear to coming clean with Vee about the other one…

Her iPhone beeped a message. She pressed a hand over her belly, quelling the flutters at Richie's text: Have you told her? Cuz I hav to call her about the other thing at some point.

Chlöe squeezed her eyes shut, muttering a curse. It had to be done eventually. *Today*, not eventually. But if she told Vee now and killed her high… Call her but don't mention anythn else. I'll do it, she texted Richie back.

She trudged through the newsroom chaos and slumped in front of her HP desktop. Moments later, Vee strode in, breathless. Chlöe cleared her mind with a shake of the head and tuned back in.

'God really loves us today. Guess who that was? Akhona Moloi. Madam uptight, Berman's business partner. She heard about my attack, no doubt from Walsh, she says she's got information—'

'Wait, how would *Walsh* know about it?'

'Ah, that was the real first call, before the meeting. He called this morning to ask me out again – stop making that face – and yes, I told him no. I can't date him during an investigation.'

Chlöe quirked her eyebrows ever so slightly.

Vee made an impatient sound. 'Before or after, I'm not interested. Pay attention. We're talking and I mentioned the attack. He was shocked, appalled, sympathetic. Then we went for the meeting, and voila, three missed calls from this strange number, turns out to be Moloi's private cell. Apparently she and Walsh still communicate, and he's lending her a hand during these trying times.' Vee paused for breath, then lowered her voice. 'She admits she hasn't been entirely truthful about events leading to her partner's murder.'

'Really? No shit.'

'I know right. Like, what does she take us for? *Suddenly*, overwhelmed by the spirit of honesty, she wants to run her mouth.' Vee threw her indigo blue handbag over her shoulder and grabbed her travel zip case, swollen with information dossiers on the convention. 'Well, we need every break so get your dry booty outta that chair, my ginger-haired comrade. Straight to B&M Financial, before she changes her mind.'

Chlöe sighed and started to pack up. Confession time would have to wait.

19

'You know what?' Vee popped the front of her dress to allow the air-con to circulate over her chest. She stretched her legs out in the reception lounge of Berman & Moloi Financial, a tidy outfit on the second floor of a red-brick building downtown. 'Sometimes good can come out of the worst situations. My laptop was crushed last night so I have nothing to even type a sentence on, much less a whole article. The screen's a mess. I can barely see with all that black inky stuff coming out the cracks. I doubt IT can fix it. You think Craig can fix it?'

'Nope. Even if they can, it's gonna cost so much to replace the screen you might as well get a new one.' Chlöe's fingers blurred over the touchpad of her iPhone. 'How's that a silver lining?'

'I won't be paying for it. Nico gave the order that if it can't be repaired, the IT staff should order me a new one. Of my choosing.'

Chlöe looked up, parted her lips to snipe something, then studied Vee's triumphant grin and decided against it. It was laughable really, how Vee was always going on about how they had to watch their step at work, how Nico was out to fillet them at the slightest provocation. In truth she was blind to how much he valued her. How she was the favoured one while Chlöe was, for lack of a better analogy, the red-headed stepchild. 'I hope all your work was backed up properly,' Chlöe muttered sourly.

Vee gave her a smirk that said "be serious". 'Then you should be worried about ramping up security at your house. One cock-up is enough,' Chlöe sniped. She hated how peevish she sounded but couldn't help it.

'Being taken care of as we speak. New window, new bars. The security company were notified of the break-in and they'll make extra patrols especially at night.'

'Mmmm,' was all Chlöe could manage. Feeling pressured to make a limp, half-hearted offer of a place to stay for a few days would've sucked, and Vee in turn would've hated finding a way to decline without hurting her feelings. In truth, she didn't want Vee crashing at hers. Though tiny, her place in a tidy complex of one-bedroom flats on Roeland Street in the centre of town was nice enough, but great flatmates she doubted the two of them would make.

Vee threw her a weird look, mouth ajar like something was tingling on the tip of her tongue, but she closed it. She fell to idly stroking her side, an area Chlöe assumed was one of her battle wounds. 'Should I invest in a tablet you think, or stick to laptops? Ooh, what about a touch screen?'

'Get whatever you want. Can I use your wireless?' Out of the corner of her eye, Chlöe saw Vee frown, then flick her gaze across to the reception desk when she realised it where Chlöe's question was directed. 'Your internal Wi-Fi,' Chlöe waved her cell at the receptionist, who countered with blank eyes. 'I'm trying to capture it on my phone and no joy.'

'It has a secure network key.'

'I realise that. That's what I'm after, if you don't mind.' Chlöe waved the phone again. 'Have to send an urgent email.'

Clad in a brown checked skirt suit of the Mr Price variety, the woman countered with the glower of a diamond drill. Messing about clearly stopped at the threshold of the establishment and was tolerated no further. 'We don't give it to visitors. You get it from Ms Moloi when you go in to see her.'

With that, the receptionist lifted the landline receiver near her elbow, murmured a few words into it, and tossed them each a curt nod as she put it down. 'Ms Moloi is ready.'

'Cheapskates,' Chlöe muttered fiercely as they left the lounge. 'How can you court new business if you skimp on amenities *at reception?* Like, excuse us.'

They traversed a long corridor with pale cream walls, slowing down as they passed two larger rooms with waiting areas, healthily populated with clients waiting to be attended to by consultants. Mostly black clients, Chlöe noted, of the ilk of honest middle-class graft and department store habitude. A healthy sprinkling of the new, polished aspirational class, garlanded in Jenni Button and Markham's. A smattering of coloured and white faces.

'Middle-class, family-style kind of operation,' Vee murmured.

'My thoughts exactly.' Chlöe squared her shoulders proudly.

Moloi's door stood open at the farthest end of the hall. The office mirrored its occupant: clean lines, practical to the point of severe, slightly depressing. One massive hardwood desk with an upholstered armchair, two standard wheelie chairs on the other side of it, a wall-mounted cabinet stacked with black binders and folders, a few books. The upheaval of Berman's death had made a dent, though: an extra, smaller desk strewn with more files and papers stuck out like a sore thumb in a far corner. The only thing nearing an indulgence was the carpet, which was clearly high-end. Chlöe bit back a laugh as Vee's lips moued a little in distaste. Brown, however richly blended with brighter colours, was not a colour her bosslady deemed acceptable in any form.

Chlöe brought her eyes around to Akhona Moloi's face and jolted in mild shock. Gone, or at least thoroughly wilted, was her starchy, exacting exterior. Moloi's eyes were puffy, but not red; eyedrops had effectively prissied that up, no doubt. Her short afro had reverted from the well-combed, shiny globe of curls she'd sported at The Grotto to a dry mat, knobbly and flecked in places with lint.

'Please excuse the mess.' Voice gravelly from a cold, or sobbing, Akhona flicked her chin towards the unkempt table, flinching in embarrassment. 'Since Gavin died...' She shook her head, eyes on the floor as she took several deep breaths. Chlöe and Vee jumped a little when her head popped up like an invisible string had yanked the back of her neck. '*Was killed*. I have to keep reminding myself of that, that he didn't just *die*.' She flapped her hands, dismissing unsavoury memories. 'We're trying to cope, all the staff. It's not easy reassuring our clients, but we're coming along. Please sit down. Oh, wait! Are you okay?'

They had a split second to trade bewildered gazes before Moloi sprang on tiptoe, leaned in and gathered Vee in a gentle, but awkward, embrace. Over her shoulder, Vee widened her eyes. Chlöe answered with exaggerated shrug.

'It must've been a horrible ordeal,' Moloi said, gazing at the bandage on Vee's forehead.

Vee recovered quickly. 'Oh! Yes, it was. Kind of. I've had worse.' She faked a laugh. 'Bumps and bruises always heal.'

'The internal damage is what no one really understands. The trauma of such an attack in your own house. I feel for you,' Moloi clucked. She crossed back over to her desk. They declined refreshments and patiently waited for her to launch.

Moloi took her time, sighing at length and flexing her fingers through her springy ruff of hair. 'I feel... foolish... negligent, for withholding this information. I say "withholding" because although I'm fully aware that the, um, shall we say prying and often predatory nature of your job means that full disclosure isn't wise, I'm a woman of good conscience. The police presence here yesterday reinforced my belief that we're all involved. And look what not being forthcoming led to. Darkness has followed us back to Cape Town. I don't know what the hell I thought it would accomplish… Well, saving this business is everything to me now. But this is bound to come out at some point. No one else should be put in danger.' Her eyes dripped sympathy all over Vee. 'You kind of remind me of her. Strong, clever, highly inquisitive, reckless even. Not that I'm saying you're reckless. As if I know you,' Moloi chuckled. Chlöe tossed Vee a sly smile (*maybe she does*); Vee slid her foot nearer, lightly crushing Chlöe's toes beneath her own (*focus*).

'Remind you of who exactly?' Vee urged.

'The reason I asked you here. Your *relentless* curiosity at the lodge so reminded me of her. We all noticed it, you two rabbiting around with your questions, while the rest of us were like deer in headlights. I suppose it's the natural way of journalists.'

Moloi noticed their polite impatience and cleared her throat. 'Sorry, I'm rambling.' She pivoted her desktop monitor to give them a better view and double-clicked the mouse to raise a digital photo. 'That there is Xoliswa Gaba.' She pointed, from among a cluster of people in professional wear, to a dark-skinned, full-eyed young woman with shiny nubs of dreadlocks eased against her scalp. Chlöe took quick note of Berman, inflated of chest and self-regard, and Moloi herself in a very ill-fitting pantsuit, both front row in a younger time. 'She used to work here about five years ago. She was very valuable to us.'

Vee began scribbling notes. 'And Xoliswa was—'

'Xoliswa,' Moloi corrected, emphasising the X with a sharp, resounding click against the roof of her mouth. She smiled, indulgent. 'It's fine. I'm aware you're not Xhosa. You were going to ask what she did, right? She wasn't one of the consultants. Not the financial consultants anyway, although she gained on-the-job expertise and became well versed in financial systems during her time here. She worked in our IT department, mainly programming and R&D type of thing. The job wasn't as clearly demarcated then as it is now, and she had a lot to do with that.'

'How old was she?'

'Hmm, let's say 29, 30 when she left. Started young. A fresh UCT graduate in computer science, and she stayed with us for eight years. She wasn't much younger than me when we parted ways; I was in my late thirties then. She was pretty, though, had that pull that pretty girls thrive on. She knew how to work it, too, none of that insincere, apologetic "Who, me? I didn't know I was hot" thing women do.' Her chuckle was rueful and showed surprise at herself. 'Sorry, *that* was bitchy. Guess we're all guilty of something. I'm constantly warned by my friends to stop underselling myself or behaving like I'm so ancient, or I'll end up dying earlier than I'm supposed to. I'm an old soul, though, can't help it.' She flapped the dismissive hand again. 'Xoli came in from temping at some dead-end job or other that had her frustrated because she wasn't challenged enough. I remember her interview, not very well of course, it was a while ago now. But I remember how fresh and switched on she was in comparison to a string of applicants who abused the word "challenge". "I like a challenge", "I always rise to a challenge". But Xoli had this energy, this push, that made me believe in her. She was raw, very much a kasi girl, rough around the edges you might say, but her education cleaned her up a bit.

'We took a chance on her, and she didn't disappoint. In three short years she went from technician, you know, handling basic data entry and client info, to running the IT department. The guy in charge, um, I forget his name now, became the boss in name only. She handled everything. We got results, better clients and turnaround because of her.'

Eyes closed, Moloi massaged her scalp, a furrow between her eyes as she tufted her hair. As if suddenly aware of the sorry picture she presented, her fingers feathered down to her lap. 'Xoliswa was restless. Restless and reckless. It was hard to please her, like, please her in a solid, final way. She'd push every issue further, finding a way to make it better or more. It was exhausting. Don't get me wrong, that's great to have in an employee, but know your limits. Know your employer's limits. We're after all a small company. Gavin tried with her. He...' She swallowed hard, exhaled. 'He was brilliant in this setup. It was his baby. He started it, he ran it, he loved it; groomed me as his partner. We had our share of mishaps, but he had a killer instinct for manoeuvring, for knowing the right fit for us. I learnt a lot from him, so much. In the beginning I thought I'd be just another BEE front, the black female partner who made it all look good on paper but didn't get to give much input. But it was *ours*, he made it *our* company...'

Vee held out a tissue from the packet in her bag and made sympathetic noises as Moloi pressed it to her eyes.

'I'm sorry. This isn't me at all,' she squeaked. 'I can't get over it, how he was strung and displayed like rotisserie chicken...' She swiped the Kleenex over her nose one last time, scrunched it into a ball and dropped it in the full wastebasket near her feet. 'It takes so much *anger* and *bitterness* to do that.'

'It does,' Vee agreed softly. Chlöe nodded.

'She was relentless. We had good equipment for our purposes, but she would angle for this upgrade or that. Wanted everything cutting edge, top notch overnight. To tell you the truth, I got bored with her. She performed, yes, but other than that I couldn't be bothered. But Gavin... got interested. He was a good man, but he was a man. Women were his weakness. And he had a thing... he had an appetite for black women.' She threw up her hands. 'There it was. He'd been divorced for several years and was free to be as stereotypical as he pleased. It wasn't my business but...' She tilted her mouth in a disappointed downturn that implied 'what could you do'.

You wanted *it to be your business,* Chlöe thought. She took in the painfully short, average-looking, flat-chested woman with a measure of pity. Everybody wanted love.

'Xoli had it, with extra spice. Gavin started sleeping with

her. He'd never been… appropriate with his choices. But it never jeopardised our work, never. I knew Xoli had an angle to play, but I didn't think too much of it and hoped it would blow over.'

'How long had she been here before they started shagging?' Chlöe piped up. Vee and Akhona gave her two different versions of purse-lipped censure and she gave a mini eye-roll. 'When did she start having a relationship with her boss?'

'Not straight away, which is what you may be thinking. She'd been around a good, what, five years, earned her stripes, got promoted, before I started noticing worrying behaviour. Xoli was focused, her work was practically her all. Gavin was professional in that respect, nothing of the kind had happened before, at least that I knew of. To be honest I didn't think they noticed each other in that way to begin with, other than playful flirtation.' When Chlöe opened her mouth again, Moloi rushed on: 'I'd say it lasted two years, maybe more.'

'I was going to say, so it didn't just fizzle out?'

Moloi shook her head. 'It kind of did, but not in the way I hoped. She wanted promotion right to the top, typical. But whatshisname, mmm, Frederick Louw it was, head of the division, I remember now. He'd been with us much longer, never mind she was sharper. We couldn't just fire him, and how does one wrangle two senior managers? Xoli became confrontational. My impression was behind closed doors the pillow talk went sour; the aggro was too much and Gavin got fed up. He ended it, thank God.

'I didn't know at the time we employed her that she had issues. Real problems. Once, during her time here, she took extended leave of absence for medical reasons, *psychiatric reasons.* Of course I'm not one to pry, but you do have to get a doctor's justification for things like that. She grew up in the township, in Gugulethu. Broken home, that kind of thing. Her father was absent and her mother not really…' Moloi circled a finger near her ear followed by a "if you know what I mean" nod. 'Her uncle supported her and her siblings, saw her through school and varsity. But that kind of background had to have left an imprint. Hey, she went to UCT, you know how those kids turn out. All that white stuff they do up the hill to fit in.'

'Ja, and where did you go?' Chlöe practically growled. Once again, Vee slid a foot over and tapped hers. *Cool it,* the tap warned.

'Wits,' Akhona quipped, lips tilted in a superior sneer. 'Yes, I did some postgrad courses in Cape Town, but nothing really... formative. All the same. From working with Xoliswa Gaba I got the feeling she was off somehow. Bipolar, schizophrenic, one of those disorders umlungus label you with when you lack self-control and common sense. That was only *my* feeling.' She pressed a hand to her heart. 'Maybe she simply struggled with her own demons, like we all do. It came to light, though, about the drug use. She'd come to work messed up, get in people's faces, not finish her assignments, rubbish after rubbish. Gavin and I had words over it. He was sorry the relationship had ever started, asked me to be patient until it calmed down naturally. It didn't and we had to fire her.'

'Why exactly? Did she flip out at work, hurt someone?' Vee asked.

Moloi answered with a lazy shrug. 'Not per se. Not that her rage wasn't a physical assault in and of itself. Besides the constant aggression, mishandling a major account. The exact details escape me. I can dig it up for you if you'd like. We've kept all our employee files over the years.' She took a breath. 'Her termination was all above board if that's your point. If not, Xoli would've had grounds to bring suit against us and she would've, given half the chance. But *she didn't*. We don't deal with millionaires here; we consult on family and individual portfolios. Larger business investments now and then, but for smaller outfits. You can't mess around when it's so personal. We'd given her written warnings, she kept begging for attention, so she was let go. We didn't hear from her again.'

Chlöe and Vee simultaneously leaned a tiny bit forward. It was about to get good.

'For years. Until recently. When we got involved with LEAD and the 2010 Legacy idea, it came with publicity and media attention. Nothing crazy, mostly local press. From absolutely nowhere, Xoli came crawling out of the woodwork like a viper. Talking rubbish, how she'd got her act together, we should forgive, she was the backbone of our success. First she wanted her job back. That was only happening over my actual dead body. Then she changed her tune – we at least owed her compensation because her ideas helped to elevate our status, we never would've got close to LEAD's nomination for the financial category if she hadn't sunk her genius into B&M.' Moloi rolled her eyes. 'I didn't entertain it, but Gavin felt sorry for her initially. He asked me to see what we could do.'

'What was she angling for?' said Chlöe.

'Money.' Moloi's voice shook, snagged on the word like the demand had driven a spear through her heart. 'What else? Crazy money. After we told her to go to hell, we needed every dime we had, it got worse. She sent threatening emails, she would call… all to Gavin. I guess because they had history.'

'Did you keep any of these emails?'

'They went to him personally. He let me read a few, naturally, since his problem had escalated into our problem. But no, I didn't, don't, have access to his email account. We told the police everything—'

'When? When did she resurface?' Vee asked.

'This past December. We informed her of our telling the cops, too, so she backed off again. For good so I thought; I mean it looked that way, but now he's dead. Now the cops are *slightly* more willing to look seriously, but they "don't feel such brutality can be the work of a woman".' Even Moloi's air-quotes dripped sarcasm. 'Oh, they're checking out his ex-wife, old girlfriends, but only to clear the law. Their main suspects are debtors and business partners, me even…' she flicked her eyes over to Vee. 'You've felt the force of her madness. Xoliswa Gaba should be locked up immediately. Since the murder I do know they've questioned her, but,' she gave a disappointed shrug, 'she's still walking around, so. I suspect she has a wonderful alibi, all her chommies from e'loxion will vouch for her. Meanwhile, their top suspects are the participants from the conference. Us! They think Gavin's murderer was amongst us. Are they crazy?'

'The police must be crazy to think that,' Chlöe quipped. Vee gave her another stern look. 'You've really been helpful. Do you happen to know where Gaba works, or where we can find her? Balanced perspective, you understand,' she said.

'Sure, sure. I wrote it all down before you arrived, and also have here her personnel file for the entire time she was with us. She'd better have something sensible to say for herself, although I doubt she'll talk to you. If she was responsible for this,' Moloi looked down at her desk, 'she'll rot in hell.' She pushed a stack of thin folders across the desk, including fresh business cards, at the back of which she scribbled her personal contacts.

20

'That's a lot to swallow,' Chlöe blurted once they were outside the building. The traffic in the city centre roared in their ears as they stepped onto the pavement into sunshine. '*A lot.*'

'Mm-hmm. You really helped ease things along, with your constant interjections.'

Chlöe snorted. 'You heard her up there! She's so… *eww.* Come on, wasting your life hoping a wanker like Gavin will notice you, seeing him parade his women in your face. She acted like she expected us to saunter down to Central Police Station,' she pointed in the general direction of CPS on Bill Bezuidenhout Avenue just three streets east of where they stood, 'and tell them the same story, which will naturally set off the manhunt for this Xoliswa person.' She looked at Vee. 'What're you doing?'

Vee had angled the Nikon, one of the office cameras, at the maroon-and-white crown of awning over the brickface's entrance, stepping off the sidewalk and into the street to get a better shot. She got off a one-click rapid-fire series before scuttling back onto the pavement as the light changed and traffic surged forward.

'Photos,' Vee replied. 'The web version of our piece has to be eye-catching and interactive.'

'Since you started this digi-techy stuff, you've been insufferable.'

'Print media is a ship sinking fast, Bishop, and I'm not romantic enough to stay on board. You looked at jobs lately? Some level of web or multiplatform writing skill is almost compulsory now. The ones that require *real* skill offer freedom as a columnist, they pay better, and are more exciting.'

'Akhona has no idea how right she is about you and a murder suspect having a lot in common.'

Vee chuckled, threw an arm around Chlöe's shoulders and squeezed. 'Stagnation is the enemy of progress, finegeh. I'm sure there's more you could do to ramp up your CV.'

Chlöe shrugged. 'Eh. I'm fine where I am, doing what I'm doing. Sjoe, half the time I'm reminded I practically just *got* this job. No need to start going crazy already.'

Vee opened her mouth to counter, then closed it. 'Well. You come from money, I only dream. Maybe that's the difference.'

Hurt and another expression Vee couldn't quite read flitted across Chlöe's face and made Vee drop her arm. The uncomfortable silence created a soundless vacuum against the drum of honking horns, shuffling feet and other human noise. 'What'd you think about that, though?' Chlöe spoke at last, jerking her thumb up at the building in front of them.

'Moloi?' Vee tipped her head from side to side. 'I believe she *is* scarred and scared, and the timeline of events at the lodge means she couldn't have killed anyone. But something's niggling at me, like there's a "more-ness" she omitted from her story. Who gets fired and pops up *five years later* raging hell like a Bruce Lee sequel? Blackmailing, strangling, housebreaking and beat-downs. Nah.'

'What, you think there's no Xoliswa Gaba?'

'Oh, she exists. Akhona's ass was on fire to hand these over,' Vee patted the files underarm. 'She can downplay how much any bad press would hurt them, but I'm pretty sure what she gave us on Gaba is way more comprehensive than what she's told the police. Because she wants us at the forefront, on her side. Yet she's holding out on us. But never mind for today. We shall allow her false sense of security to lull.' She twiddled her fingers like she was pushing magical waves up to Moloi's office.

'Do you think she and Berman ever…'

'No. She wanted him to, but I doubt he ever did. When he started chopping from another woman's bowl right under her nose, a subordinate at that, it pissed her off. Come on, all those years "making this beautiful thing *ours*", him mentoring her? She was smitten but I don't see her killing for love or anything else. Oh! That brings me to something else. Last night I had a hunch and put Richie on it.'

Chlöe's heart did a triple-thump.

'He's always bragging about that facial recognition software he's developing for some end-of-days counterattack.'

'I thought we agreed to stop entertaining Richie. Hackers feed off fantasy.'

'We did.' Vee pulled Chlöe to one side to allow a stream of hurrying pedestrians past. 'But it pays to listen occasionally. I sent him background and pics of Rhonda Greenwood from The Grotto's website, asked him to do a deep web search of her life, activities she was involved in, anything criminal if he could find it, and,' she made a fist, 'jackpot. Most of what he found wasn't hugely relevant or interesting, but some was. For quite a few years up until very recently, most of Rhonda's extracurricular activities revolved around getting clean. She was in AA, support groups, she took part in charities and sporting events all in aid of kicking the booze. She really wanted to stay clean, she *was* clean, and she surrounded herself with people with the same mindset.' Vee pierced Chlöe with her eyes, expecting a spark of clarity.

'I don't see…'

'*Addiction*, Bishop. She did things recovering addicts do. What did Moloi just tell us? *Xoliswa Gaba was a druggie.* Yes, the groups are specific to the problem, but sometimes their paths cross. The healing principles are similar. Richie the Wonderful found what connected Greenwood and Gaba: a group for professionals reclaiming their careers after addiction. There was an online attendance sheet that showed they had at least two meetings together, one at a conference hall and the other at a chapel. I'm guessing Gaba moved on, maybe it was boring or a waste of her time. Greenwood must've fallen off the wagon pretty recently. Job stress.'

'Greenwood lived in Oudtshoorn. Why the hell come all the way to Cape Town if she needs a support group?'

'Why not? Small towns are notorious for gossip, and Greenwood was the public face of a well-known establishment. She'd never risk anyone finding out about the darker side of her personal life. Plus, I now know she had a bad patch and moved here with her sister for a while. Took a leave of absence, "worked from home". Richie even dug up how and where *I* met Rhonda. Last year; The Portswood Hotel, Waterfront. I was attending a journo's workshop, she a course in hospitality management. Remember, I told you how shocked I was that she remembered me?'

'You've done a lot of digging into this woman's life. A *disturbing* lot,' Chlöe said under her breath. She was going to have to come clean soon – no, *now* – about what she and Richie had uncovered. And when she did, Vee, the most inquisitive person ever, would flip out. The same dedication to meddling Vee readily applied to much success in their investigations would go over far less swimmingly now that Chlöe had used it on her personal life. Chlöe swallowed, the slight tightening in her chest growing stronger.

'It makes sense. Rhonda remembered me, who she met on one occasion for what, two hours total, tea and lunch. And she had that mind trick of hers, for enhancing recall. Whether that nonsense works or not, she did have a kickass memory.' Vee's gaze got lost in the distance, surveying the traffic and bustle of bodies around them but not really there. 'Imagine she bumped into Gaba at Grotto, the evening before the party. Definitely Gaba was keeping a very low profile, she was there to snoop on Berman and Moloi, neither of whom expected her there. But bad luck, Rhonda booked her, said "hey, we've met before". That's what Mamelo from housekeeping saw and mistook for an argument, her boss insisting she knew this woman with dreads and that woman insisting just as firmly that she didn't. Rhonda probably walked away and forgot about it, but Gaba didn't.' Vee blinked back into reality. 'Murdering Gavin was premeditated. Gaba knew however she offed Berman, it had to be covert and squeaky clean. No link to her. There's no record of her checking in, she stayed incognito and didn't linger publicly. Rhonda messed with that. There was a chance she'd remember after Gavin's death the skulking guest, who would later turn out to be a resentful ex and ex-employee... Rhonda had to go.'

'Mamello saw them talking. Where's her comeuppance?'

Vee puffed. 'I have an idea why: Mamello didn't work that night. She finished day shift and left. If she hadn't, who knows. And anyone can tell in a heartbeat she's a dunce who's not worth bothering with. Chlöe, as unhinged as we're meant to assume this girl is, none of this has cold forethought, a "let's kill off any and everything that stands in my way" aura. It's more reactive and frenzied, like someone who had a targeted plan but kept tripping over nosy parkers.'

'*If* she offed Gavin, we still don't know *why*. How messed up is that, stalking your old bosses to an out-of-town conference, flipping out and killing two people? I mean,' Chlöe threw up her hands, 'come on. We *just* put a name and possible motive to this woman, and suddenly she's the one? Maybe she didn't kill him. Maybe *no one* killed Greenwood.'

'Gaba killed them both,' Vee replied, firmly, softly. 'We need the why.'

'Whatever. Everybody's telling fables, it's all upside down....'

To her own dismay, Chlöe shot her leg out and landed a vicious kick to a green City of Cape Town waste bin attached to a pole. Two women walking by squeaked in surprise and scampered ahead, looking back at her as they walked on like she was a mad person.

'Ah-ah! What's up with you? Usually we both love this part.'

Chlöe flailed a hand. 'It feels too easy. Either the story won't be worth jack interest-wise by the time we connect all the dots and motives, or we're missing something.'

'True. But something else is up. You've been evasive for days.' Vee crossed her arms.

'No, I haven't.' Chlöe shuffled her feet.

A man taking up most of the sidewalk as he talked on his cell phone bumped into Vee and, without stopping, raised one hand in apology. 'This is no place to talk. Let's go. Now.' Vee pointed at the cheerful green-and-white storefront of a Fruit & Veg City outlet across the street. 'Mixed fruit bowls with all the ice cream or blueberry yoghurt you want. In exchange, you get whatever this is off your chest. You're stinking up my high.'

'You won't like it.' Chlöe found she couldn't bring herself to look up. 'You'll feel the exact opposite of high.'

'Bishop.' Vee dropped her hand. 'What've you done?'

21

Vee pumped the handle of Joshua's front door up and down. The door came open on the second jiggle and nearly hit her in the face. The storm cloud hanging over her head pitched from slate grey to blood red and she let out a string of expletives. She'd wanted it to be locked, so she could have reason to kick it in. She sucked in a long breath, closed her eyes, thought through her strategy and approach... and realised she didn't give a damn about either. She was here to demand explanations, not dole them out.

Joshua was on the couch in the lounge, zoned out in front of a basketball game. He turned his head, saw it was her and threw his head back, groaning. He roughly massaged his eyelids and muscles of his face.

'I'm glad I found you home.' Her voice sounded stretched, like her vocal chords were walking a tightrope of barbed wire. *You don't know anything yet. Keep it together till you do.*

Joshua leaned his head back against the sofa's headrest. 'You asked... no, *ordered* me to be here. You made it expressly clear that I was to wait around after I got home from work because we need to talk. So... here I am.' He spread his arms wide. 'And, if this is a sting operation, to check if Aria's still here on the low, I guarantee...'

'Don't mess with me right now, Joshua Allen.'

He lifted his head a little then and looked at her like he was only now seeing her since she walked in, seeing the fury on her face, the hurt she was barely managing to contain. He sat up. Took in her expression and body language – her hands in fists, her entire upper body so rigid it seemed she was stomping on a geyser of rage to prevent it from obliterating them both. He involuntarily reached a hand out to her, then caught himself.

She cut him off before he spoke. 'How do you know Lovett Massaquoi?'

'Huh? Lovett? Lovett the lawyer? The guy with the rights advocacy setup for foreigners in Joburg? Of course I know him. You know I know him.' He shrugged. 'Haven't seen him in a while, though.'

She shook her head the entire time he was talking. 'Not *if* you know him. I said *how.*'

Self-preservation sounded a clarion of alarm bells through every cell in his body, she could tell in the little twitch that flickered his right eyelid and nothing else. She could practically see his brain through his skull as it zipped into the superdrive mode. *I know him through you,* nimble brain, ever the saviour, would say. *You worked that first gig with him, told me all about it. You introduced us. Remember, that Liberian doctor with the fancy house in Parklands threw a party and we all went, you, me and Titus? What was it, four years ago? Not that long. How could you forget? You must be trippin'.*

'Voinjama,' he said instead.

She deflated, all her stuffing leaking out. 'I was almost hoping you would lie to me. I *wanted* you to lie,' she jerked open her handbag, wrenched out a handful of creased papers and shoved them into his chest, 'so I could see the look on your lying face.'

'Vee… look. What could…' He scanned the printed pages, first quickly, in bafflement, then more thoroughly, his vision clearing, sharpening, with every line. '*What…* how… where'd you get this? Are you *crazy*? You *hacked* into my email and *printed* my correspondence?'

She barked a bitter laugh. 'Don't call me crazy,' she said softly.

A wrecking ball smashed his composure. 'Do you know who I work for? How much it values absolute confidentiality? Do you realise the gravity,' he shook the fistful of papers, 'of hacking the files of a JPMorgan Chase employee?!'

'I don't give a shit! You could be a goddamn secret agent for all I know or care! I wouldn't be surprised. And that's from your private email account, so calm down. It doesn't jeopardise your precious job.'

'It violates my privacy!'

'*Your* privacy?!' She reeled. 'Spare me the bullshit. What about mine, did you think about that?'

He screwed the printout into a ball with one hand, flung it. 'It's that, whatshisname, that Richie dickhead, your hacker buddy, he helped you do this. I told you to shut it down, Vee. This shit is illegal, it's dangerous, it's traceable. That guy can lead you into dark territory if you're not careful. You don't know who he's mixed up with, who he pisses off to get the kind of information he feeds you.'

'Leave Richie out of this. He's harmless. He feeds me what I ask him to feed me. The truth, when I ask him, *every time* I ask him. Can I say the same about you?'

'The truth?' Joshua scraped his hands over his head and down the back of his neck, then threw them to the skies. 'I hate to sound like the biggest cliché alive, but I don't think you can handle the truth as well as you think you can.'

'Try me, mister liar.'

'Stop it.' He grabbed her by the shoulders, gently but firmly turning her to face him, holding firm despite her squirming. 'You know damn well I wouldn't hide anything from you without a good reason.'

She twisted out of his grasp. 'Bullshit.'

He dropped his arms. She stepped away, nostrils quivering as her breath thundered in and out. 'Don't mess around, Vee. Tell me where and when and how you got this.'

'You tell me why and for how long you've known Lovett! Why y'all been exchanging emails about me since God knows when, especially since I had no idea y'all were even on speaking terms. Let's start there!'

He snatched the ball of paper off the floor, read through the first page again before tossing it onto the coffee table. 'Sit down,' he said, taking a seat himself. She stayed put. He pulled her in by the wrist. She tottered on her heels for a second and slumped onto the couch.

Joshua clasped his hands over his knees and looked sideways at her, waiting. She shifted in her seat and looked down at her lap, smoothing invisible wrinkles from her skirt. She spoke at last and all she said was, 'Chlöe.'

'Chlöe?' he scoffed.

'Yes. Well, Chlöe and Richie. She told Richie to…' Vee exhaled. 'Chlöe saw me with Lovett at The Grotto, overheard us talking about something that wasn't any of her damn business and decided to make it her damn business. In true Chlöe style, she went rooting around in my private life—'

'And mine.'

She flicked a sneer his way. 'Well, I don't care about yours. And I've dealt with her already.' She hit him on full beam with all the hurt and outrage she could muster. 'Half the time Chlöe's got no common sense in her head. But you ….'

'Are you going to hear me out?'

She crossed her arms.

Joshua exhaled and rubbed his eyes some more. Their rims were tinged pink like a handful of sand had been thrown into his face. 'All right. Guess the beginning's the best place to start. It's not as insidious as you think. Not any more, anyway. I truly didn't know Lovett from a jar of jam until four years ago, I swear to that. He contacted me out of the blue. Introduced himself, said the Liberian community here was small, he knew Titus, and the two of you had just moved down here from the States. He knew Ti from his work in Joburg with Deloitte, they had a common circle there. Therefore he, Lovett, knew you... and, by extension, me.' Joshua reclined in the couch. 'He only knew *of* you, but his interest was piqued beyond that. A, um, let's call them a group of interested parties, had approached him about your father.'

'My father?! What—' Vee whipped around to face him. Then, she straightened up, smoothed a hand over her hair and flexed her shoulders, sucking the torrent back in.

'Yes, your father,' Joshua continued. 'They were curious about his life. A little too curious about his activities during the civil war, the Charles Taylor regime, the security company he now owns and what it did back in the nineties...' A quiver of undistilled rage skittered through her cheek muscle at every word. 'The allegations of... shall we say goods and services, that people like him ran back and forth across the border during that period. They—'

'That was because—' She ground her teeth. 'Finish.'

'They claimed they were a forensic investigation NGO. Got most of their business from human rights groups and civil action firms, sometimes funding from big guns like legal teams working with The Hague. They'd been contracted to look into,' he rubbed the back of his neck, delicacy obviously failing him, 'small-time criminals, warmongers, even civilians who'd been implicated in various forms of violent unrest in unstable countries. Basically, they'd hook the small fry and twist their arms until they snitched on the big fish. They wanted to know about your dad... if he'd been involved... and how deeply, when, under whose directive. And they figured they'd get info about him from, well, you.' Joshua blew a breath. 'Lovett never went into details regarding what their information-extraction plan consisted of; he didn't know an awful lot himself. We knew they wouldn't dare drag you in, throw you in a dungeon and shine a searchlight in your face. You have an American green card. It was more undercover, gentle probing. They approached Lovett's firm, under the guise that as a fellow human and civil rights advocate he'd sympathise and comply. I'm sure they also thought he was a dumb, small-time African who'd be too impressed by their credentials and too meek to probe further.'

'They really didn't do their research, then,' Vee muttered. Morons were a food group for Lovett Massaquoi.

'Clearly not. Lovett smelled a rat. He dug, and found their company was a pure front. He never got conclusive proof, but he uncovered enough to know they actually *supported* war criminals. They were some kind of stealth organisation that worked with defence teams, ferreting out damaging evidence before it surfaced against their clients.'

She scooted about on her bum in order to draw nearer, eyes enlarged to huge globes. 'You keep saying "they" – didn't they have a name? And what was their plan of action, after they found their so-called damning evidence?'

'It doesn't matter now. Dig all you like but you'll find nothing under the name they approached us under. It was a shadow company put together for the purpose of information-gathering, because we sure as hell couldn't find anything substantial to link them to afterwards. They dissolved like a sugar cube once we put them in hot water. As to what their endgame was, I don't know, *we* don't know, we still don't. We speculated a lot, part of what the emailing was about, though we were careful what we wrote.' He reached out and stroked her arm. 'Once we started probing too deeply and asking too many follow-up questions they backed off. They knew we didn't trust them and they wouldn't get anything out of us. On our side, we'd hit a brick wall, so we let it go. We didn't forget about it, but we let it lie. It felt like the smartest thing to do, the only thing really. It's been, what, two and a half years since then. They never contacted either of us again.'

'Why did Lovett bring you into it? He asked you to... what?'

Joshua read the look on her face and chuckled. 'He didn't ask me to waterboard you, if that's what you're asking.' He read another flicker of her lashes and flinched. 'He didn't ask me to spy on you either, and even if he had, come on. He simply,' he spread his hands, searching for the right words, 'wanted to know if there was anything to it. Have a close friend ask you, delicately, if there was any chance of a smidgeon of truth behind their probe. So, on the off-chance there was, we'd be the first to step in to protect you. He's a really good lawyer, and not as cold and mercenary an ass as you think he is.'

'I don't think Lovett is cold or mercenary. I just think he's an ass.' She studied her knees. 'Why'd he ask you though?' The unsaid hung in the air – *Why not ask Titus?*

Joshua uttered a single, dry 'ha'. 'My feelings for you have never been much of a secret. Lovett took one look at me at that barbecue four years ago and knew if he ever needed to work an angle involving you, he had his sucker. Besides, Titus is a nice guy, and...' Joshua spread his arms, as if willing rest of the sentiment to fold into them, and then dropped them back to his sides as if that was it. And it was, really. Titus was a wholesome, sweet guy and there wasn't much else to him. You certainly didn't embroil him in anything darker than the mildest grey. Vee wanted her rancour to rise in his defence and couldn't summon so much as a peep.

She lifted her head. 'I don't ever remember you prying about my pa, either, no more than usual.'

'I couldn't do it. You've told me about your life and family, your own way, in your own time. It's not my story to retell. And I'm sure as hell not gonna let some shadowy group of fuckmongers twist your arm about it, or twist it through a second or third party.'

'But you know my father wasn't involved in any sick nonsense like that. He ran an honest security company, even during wartime, that's why—'

'I know what you tell me, Vee. And you know what *you've* pieced together. Fathers, parents, aren't obligated to tell their kids the worst of who they are. Much as you adore your dad, you're not naive.'

'Hehn?! So, what… then,' she blustered, head shaking, 'you think…'

'Why'd he spend all those months going back and forth between Sierra Leone and Guinea? Don't say he was looking for you,' Joshua stopped her rush of words. 'I know you got separated from the family when the fighting started, I know some of the horrible things you went through—'

'All,' she snarled.

'*Some.* You haven't told me everything, and your dad hasn't fully confided in you, either. After he found you, he kept making those trips. You said they were rescue missions, that he and other drivers went to remote towns and villages, wherever there were stranded refugees, and they smuggled them across the border or to ports where they'd be safe.'

'Those were the "goods and services" they traded in. Lives. They saved hundreds, and could never speak about it or take credit, because of the things they saw and dirt they themselves did to get people to safety.'

'That wasn't the only reason he made those trips, and I know you've questioned it more deeply over the years.' He made another gesture with his arm that stopped her from speaking. 'Whether you ever get the courage to ask him or not, that's none of my business. None of it will ever change anything between us.'

Elbows on knees, she buried her face in her hands. She

knew he was watching her, watching her shoulders move in time with her breathing. When she lifted her head, she let him see utter destruction on her face. 'Everything's so—' her breath hitched in her throat, 'it's you, it's Chlöe... Lovett, Richie... Why can't anybody just *talk* to me?'

'You don't know why?' His look was loaded. 'Chlöe *worships* you, misguided motives aside. Richie is your employee, and you're probably the most exciting thing he's got going on. You pay him to swoop in with the pay dirt, make your articles all crisp and edgy. Me, I'm just the guy who...' he shrugged. 'I look out for you. You don't need me to hover, but I do. Titus does. One way or the other we're all out here begging for scraps.'

Vee took a step back like the air had punched her, mouthing his words with an acrid look on her face. 'So I *made* all of you do this? I'm the one toxic spoke fucking up the wheel of paradise for everybody?'

Joshua cursed. 'It came out wrong, I didn't mean...'

Her face crumbled. 'You're the one person who knows me better than anyone else, Joshua Allen.'

'Then...' He squeezed the pads of his thumbs into his temples, hard. 'I can't believe the bitchass thing I'm about to say, but trust me with all of you.'

'Unless. Right? Or else. Everybody's got a bloody ultimatum,' Vee said, pain clogging her voice. She lurched to her feet, furiously wiping her face, and snatched up her handbag. 'Every time I'm finally clear on why I love you so much, that we're in this together, one more thing pops up to press chakla. *Nothing* is this hard. We don't want this enough.'

'Vee, come on...'

She wriggled out of his grasp.

Joshua was still staring at his feet when he heard the front door slam.

22

'How's it going?'

Vee looked up at Chlöe and faked a smile. 'Not bad.' She typed a few more edits and signalled to Darren Februarie across the room with an open-palmed "give me five minutes". 'Still incomplete but it looks good. It's not complete, but at least we've got something more substantial than our first pitch. I'm splicing in your segment on the companies' backgrounds – brief, we don't want it to read like a suspect list – and the bid setup.'

Craning over her shoulder, Chlöe scanned through the copy and layout. Not as polished as she was sure the final product would be, but Vee had sure picked up a trick or several on web editing. 'Me likey. A lot. I still can't believe Nico's giving us the run of page two for the Saturday print. We can squeeze in a lot about both the murder investigation and the current empowerment craze.'

'Right. Play both angles.' Vee tap-tapped and brought up another screen. 'Online is gonna look a little different. We put faces to success stories and give readers more insight into the companies. Comprehensive but straightforward, no jargon, no bullshit. Karl's helping with that. People can get interactive with it, post comments on the investigation and whatnot. And of course with every new development they can—'

'Follow it on Facebook and Twitter, of course,' Chlöe said.

'Which you'll handle.' Vee beamed up at her from her chair with genuine pride. 'I don't want to jinx it by crowing too early, but we did good on this one.'

'We so have. The screw-ups strike again,' Chlöe beamed back. The moment held until Vee's glow dimmed and she cleared her throat. Her face refolded along serious, guarded lines again.

'Let me dash this over to Darren, then we can go.'

'Cool,' Chlöe agreed. Vee rose from her cubicle with a Dell in hand, a loan from the IT crew until a permanent replacement for her laptop came through. Chlöe started to glide behind Vee's desk and kill time flipping through her assignments while she waited, but thought better of it just before her bum touched the swivel chair. Best not to push things right now. She deftly sidestepped the chair and rammed her hands into the pockets of her linen slacks.

'Ready.' Several minutes later, Vee reappeared and slid the powered-down laptop onto her desk. 'You're driving or should I?'

'I'll drive.' It was going to midday, the perfect time to cruise along an uncrowded N1 highway, but still. Chlöe needed something else commanding her focus on the drive down to the northern suburbs. Vee's silences could simmer louder than anyone's she knew.

'Good.' Vee slung her bag over her shoulder and headed for the door.

'Yup,' Chlöe muttered and followed her meekly.

———

'So… what've I dug up on Gaba?' Chlöe said, flipping through the stapled pages she'd taken from the plastic binder in her hand. 'More like excavated. Quite a riveting read for a slow afternoon. The woman reads like a regular Blanche DuBois with an extra side of crazy thrown in, if you get my meaning.'

Vee leaned against the top-floor railing of Parow Centre mall, opened the Checkers Hypermarket bag of fruit they'd bought downstairs and took out a plum. She willed herself to feel as relaxed as her posture suggested as she devoured it. She knew Chlöe thought she was giving her the silent treatment – which, just a little, she kind of was – but the truth was her surroundings made her edgy. She had just been chauffeured, *willingly driven* by her white assistant no less, outside the southern suburbs into the northern ones. Right across the Boerwors Curtain, Cape Town's imaginary fault line between the English and the Afrikaans. The secret to being black and foreign in South Africa was to stay, as much as was feasible, on the English-speaking side of the good old BC. White people behaved in predictable versions of vanilla everywhere in the world, but at least south of the N1 she spoke their language; literally and figuratively, and extremely well. Here – Parow, Durbanville, Bellville, Tygerberg – these were places she rarely ventured; she couldn't easily remember the last time either work or play had coaxed her out here. She could hack and decode human behaviour far better in the highly diverse office of *Urban*, or in Rondebosch for instance. Here it was different, the air *moved* differently, in an unnameable way...

'What does the file say?' Vee asked. She'd already skimmed the background Chlöe had compiled on Gaba, but she intended be graceful enough to let Chlöe do her show and tell. It was necessary, to cut through the fat of awkwardness going rancid between them since their confrontation two days ago. Vee swelled with weariness. In truth, all she felt was desensitised, over it. It was done. 'And tell it to me without fanfare.'

'No fanfare. Right. Ahem.' Fanfare was her forte but to her credit, Chlöe looked pained for only the briefest of moments before fixing her eyes on the pages in front of her. 'So. Xoliswa Gaba. Date of birth, 16 January 1976. My mum always said early-year babies were never quite sound. No one wants another gift they can't exchange so soon after Christmas, heh heh. And in this country, people who were born in 1976, yoh! Okay,

okay, sorry. Eldest of three, two younger brothers, born and raised in Gugs, father an electrician, mother a seamstress, blah blah blah, you don't care about all that.' Chlöe flipped the page. 'Now it gets good. It looks like a lot of Akhona's gossip checks out. Gaba's mother had a patchy history of "mental problems", no clear diagnosis or institutionalisation, just a hospital visit here and anecdotes there. She buggered off when the kids were young, doesn't say with whom or why, or where she landed. No trail. Kids were raised by a paternal uncle and his wife. Fast-forward a bit…' Chlöe flipped again, 'it perks up some more. In 1995 in her second year at varsity, Xoliswa had to take time off. Where was she during that period? Drumroll, please – she had a "holiday" at Valkenberg.'

Chlöe waited for a reaction, her eyebrows suspended for so long that Vee feared she'd wrinkle her forehead forever.

'*The* Valkenberg,' Chlöe stressed. 'The old psychiatric hospital in Observatory, of deeply creepy lore.'

'I know. I did a piece on it a few years ago, when I was new to Cape Town and freelancing.'

Chlöe shot her a look of admiration mixed with distaste. 'Anyway. The most I could dig up is she went in for exhaustion, erratic behaviour, having uncommon delusions…'

The words plucked at chords in Vee's chest. How erratic did one's behaviour have to be to rank as uncommon? She herself had had a full-blown… she still had no idea how to describe it. Mystical encounter of the third kind? Did she qualify as an outlier, oversensitive, doomed to a life of inexplicable happenstance because her wiring was too exposed to the surface? Or was there simply a dark current running through her, one that jumped to the surface if you prodded it just right? She shuddered a little at the memory of her fingers clenched around Gavin Berman's throat, and rubbed her hands briskly along her arms. If Berman had been more threatening, if she'd had more to drink, would she have…

'... spent about four months in the loony bin before she was released,' Chlöe rambled on. 'Gaba sat out the rest of that year, came back and finished without incident. Her UCT records state that her uncle voluntarily removed her because she wasn't coping well and petitioned that she be allowed back when she recovered. The extra info I got from admin files was he was concerned about the "lifestyle" she'd picked up on campus; I'm guessing drugs and shitty friends. So time passes, our girl graduates and moves on and up in the world. She took a job with B&M Financial and came to call it home. New life, new job, new boyfriend – the bossman. Somewhere in between her breakup with Berman and getting fired, she lost the plot again. Hence the short leave Akhona mentioned. She saw a private practitioner this time, a Dr Nhongo near N1 City, for "a tendency towards fixations and compulsive behaviours, with occasional bouts of paranoia". Nowhere on record was there a clear schizophrenia, bipolar, or even "hey, she's psycho" diagnosis. Maybe doctors record that somewhere else and lock it in a vault.'

'She's not a psycho, she's...' Vee rubbed her side, where a distant ache persisted. That brawl in her guest bathroom... she'd never felt so much rage in such a tight space. Not since she herself, a young girl at the time, had fought her way out of the Devil's belly, doing any and everything to stay alive. 'She's miscalculated,' she finished. It wasn't adequate canopy to cover what they were dealing with, but it would do until the negative developed fully. Until then, a strategist with ice water in her veins was not the picture Xoliswa Gaba painted.

Chlöe took a step backward. 'What, you're identifying with her now? She could've killed you.'

'Maybe. Could be all she wanted is what she's about to get – our attention.'

'*This* is how she gets it? Her methods are certainly unorthodox. And you almost sound like you approve.'

'Are there multiple means at her disposal? Did you take in

any of what you just read?' Vee said, slapping a hand against the printout with an exasperated "Whap!", making Chlöe jump a little. 'Look around you. The blacks in here are either cleaning or behind a counter. How many kids do you think climb out of Gugs or Mfuleni and up onto the pretty hills of a university? Gaba may be unorthodox and off-kilter but one thing I'm sure she feels, is justified. Maybe not murder, but Gavin should've seen *some* of this coming. You don't mess with a woman who's had your dick in her mouth – when she bites, it's lockjaw.'

Chlöe's eyes darkened to two glistening gems offset by the glow of her brightening cheeks. 'I know how badly race relations suck in my own country. I'm not privileged to the point of cluelessness. That doesn't make it right. Who are you right now?' Her voice was hoarse with emotion.

Vee deflated. 'Right isn't a binary. Do you have any idea what that's like, disgraced and forced to start from scratch?'

Chlöe cheeks reddened further. Her expression moved from outrage to contrition, like she knew the conversation had veered into choppy waters she didn't want to navigate. 'I'm sorry. I know I've said that a dozen times already without saying why—'

'It's over and done. Forget it. Let's focus on handling Gaba. Softly, softly is our approach…'

'No.' Chlöe drew a deep breath. 'I crossed a line by asking Richie to dig up information on Lovett Massaquoi. I knew he'd go the whole hog, and I didn't stop him. It wasn't some malicious thing I set out to do. It just got out of hand.'

Vee clenched her jaw and kept staring straight ahead. There it was, the Chlöe Jasmine Bishop catchcry – oh dear, how was I to know? I simply push a domino and stand around like a blue-eyed darling as a chain reaction is set off that I'm powerless to stop.

'I only wanted to know who Lovett was and what you guys were so embroiled in conversation about at the lodge. And yeah *I know okay*, I should've taken your explanation at face value and backed off. But once Richie hit me with all that other stuff, the correspondence with between Lovett and Joshua... I couldn't un-know it. You had a right to know, because no part of those emails felt like a conversation you'd been part of at any point. I felt terrible that you'd been lied to.'

'So you were looking out for me?' Vee parried, keeping her voice level. 'So I can thank you?' She gave a cool, lazy shrug. 'Okay. Thank you.'

'No! I mean...'

Vee plucked a small red apple from the bag in her hand. 'You know what these remind me of? Home. Of my grandmothers.' She bit and chewed.

'Huh?'

'When I was a child, for a while I lived with my Grammah. Paternal. Outside the capital, in a region called Bong County. Quite rural, hasn't developed much since the eighties. My Grammah used to come to town every now and then to buy and sell...'

'Because she was a trader.'

'Yes. She was. Well, *is*; she runs her own store now. But back then she was a market-woman, a mobile hustler, and sometimes she brought me with her to Monrovia. You know how children are, they come to fine-fine place and lose their country-ass minds. I was fascinated by the stores and the well-dressed people I saw going in. I thought only certain people were allowed and if we dared, we'd get stopped.' She gave a short laugh. 'Grammah laughed when I told her. One day we spent forever selling her market, and I got so hungry I wouldn't stop whining. Afterwards she took me to a supermarket on Randall Street, that's one of our major streets, and bought me apples. I'd been inside supermarkets before but that particular day stuck with me; how bright and huge it felt, the crunchy coldness of that apple. They were exotic almost, it cost real money to buy them.' She huffed. 'Now Monrovia has wheelbarrows full of apples on the streets. Apple garbage piling up in the city centre.'

'You said it reminded you of your grandmothers. Plural.'

Vee nodded. 'In a bittersweet way. My other grandmother was away at the time. By away I mean… sequestered. By the people in her village.'

'Your… wayward grandmother. The one you don't talk about,' Chlöe clarified.

Vee nodded again. 'The village had levelled witchcraft allegations against her for years, this one looked like it would stick. A young mother she'd given a herbal concoction to died; she used the mix improperly, and my grandmother was blamed. The chief and his council got involved… it was messy. It's the stuff of a 16th-century novel, but it still happens in this day and age.' Distress shrouded her gaze momentarily and she quickly collected herself. 'My mother already didn't want me spending too much time with her own mother, and in those days she was more eager to suck up to my father. So she allowed me to live with my paternal Grammah for nearly two years. Then she brought both of us both back to Monrovia, to live with her and my brother in the new house she'd built.'

Chlöe had a look in her eye, baffled and awed, like she was being handed privileged information and it was imperative to swirl it around in her mind and settle each piece in the correct conformation. Tentatively she said: 'So, is she? Your "special relationship" granny… is she a… you know…'

'A witch is a woman who knows something other people don't, Bishop. She's educated, she didn't have to be a spiritual *zo*, so that made her a bigger threat. The point I'm making is, mind how you go, prying in people's lives. Relationships are take it or leave it, all of it. You can't decide which things you like and which ones to throw out.' She crunched the last of the apple and spat the core into the second plastic bag she had for trash.

Chlöe's face dropped. 'All I wanted—'

Vee squeezed her arm hard and pointed. 'That's her, that's her, that's her!'

23

Chlöe squinted along the trajectory of Vee's finger. Across the way, past the expanse of store windows and the metal railing of Parow mall's upper foyer, walked a woman. The woman ambled along with post-lunch lethargy, clutching a brown paper bag adorned with a Nando's chicken emblem. Taller than average, gently muscled and hippy of build, a bun of dreadlocks coiled atop her head. 'You sure?' Chlöe said.

'Positive,' Vee breathed. A crackling rose under her skin. 'She's going into African Bank and we know she works there. And she stomped my face in for a good, violently long five minutes, at least. *That's her.*'

They wove through the thinning lunch crowd to the other side and stopped outside the bank's entrance. They paused to stare up at the bank's blue-and-white insignia, then at each other. Chlöe shrugged, shouldered past Vee and pushed the door open.

'Good afternoon. Can I help you?' A fair-skinned bank employee zeroed in instantly, hands clasped with schoolgirl poise over her uniform, her smile of rabid eagerness at full beam. Her name badge read "Cynthia Banda", below "Branch Manager". Vee looked around the premises. Tucked in the corner round the bend from Woolworths, the branch was small compared to the confident sprawl of First National Bank across the way. In terms of crowd catchment, this was not an optimal area. There didn't look to be much for Cynthia to manage.

Chlöe spoke before Vee had a chance. 'I hate to make a fuss, but…' Chlöe waved both hands as if warding off a horrid memory, '… customer service is so important to me.'

Cynthia Banda replied, 'As it is to all our staff. What—'

'Is it? *Is it really*? Because I came here last week, Tuesday, was it the Tuesday when we…?' She snapped her fingers repeatedly, eyeing Vee.

'Uhh… yes,' Vee nodded slowly, completely in the weeds. 'Tuesday. When it happened.'

'I was here last Tuesday. I don't remember you.' Cynthia squinted. 'Monday I wasn't.'

'Monday then. Yes, Monday! Didn't I take time off work to come here, based on all the incredible things I've heard about African Bank, only to get treated like rubbish? I wanted information about a loan for my friend here,' Chlöe squeezed Vee's arm, 'who's like a sister to me, a *sister*. Race might be our national obsession, but some of us can't afford to be racist.'

'No!' Cynthia's eyes nearly popped free of her expertly made-up face. 'We must never.'

'But the way I was treated, tjo! Esther here,' Chlöe pointed to Vee, 'her mother Mavis was our maid. Esther grew up with me, the same way as me,' Chlöe thumped her chest with pride, 'so when she needed a loan to open her hair salon in Khayelitsha, I offered to help. She didn't finish school and her reading isn't the best, so she can't fill the application. But when I came on Tuesday—'

'Monday,' Vee whispered.

'Sorry, Monday. The woman I dealt with *thoroughly* dealt with me. She barely gave advice, she wouldn't even *look* at the application, she said I must bring the person, bring valid ID and six months' bank statements, bring what-what, I mustn't waste her time.'

'Hhayi wena, who did that? *Who?*' Exorcised of managerial civility, Cynthia squared her shoulders around her ears like a general. She questioned Chlöe until she had a name, then walked off and disappeared behind a wall partition. She re-emerged moments later, stomping towards them with a flustered employee at heel.

'This is Xoliswa Gaba, one of our loan consultants. She's the one? Did you refuse to serve this lady?' Cynthia's scowl was ready to pulverise.

Mouth ajar, Gaba stared around the clutch of faces.

'That's her. Sorry, I… when I see her and remember our encounter,' Chlöe released a laboured breath and pressed her hand over her mouth. 'Is this the new South Africa?'

She whirled towards the exit and Cynthia quickly laid a hand on her arm, pleading for a second chance with a different consultant. Vee grabbed the moment to eyeball Gaba. She held her gaze in an iron grip and squeezed, noting with satisfaction as Gaba's facial muscles slackened, then tensed as the situation calibrated.

'Let me take care of them,' Gaba blurted. 'Please, I can handle it.'

'You better handle it very well,' Cynthia snapped. She strode off on crisp steps.

'Let's get some air, shall we,' Chlöe said brightly, threading towards the exit again before any objections arose.

Vee fell in step beside her. 'Hairdresser in Khayelitsha?' she murmured with a tiny smile.

'I learnt from the best,' Chlöe smiled back. 'It's working, isn't it?'

———

They settled in an alcove sandwiched between Woolworths, a home furnishing store and the escalators.

'What the *fuck*?' Gaba spat. 'You think you can take the piss where I work?'

'That's rich. You *broke into my house.*' Vee folded her arms.

Xoliswa Gaba was familiar with the fine art of falsehood and had been for a long time. Lies of the cruel, self-serving variety. Vee could tell from the way her expression changed, from outraged to calculating in milliseconds.

'Nonsense. If so, prove it.' Twin indents curved on either side of Gaba's mouth as she spoke, deep commas that twitched ever so slightly as she ran the gamut of whatever mental calculation she was doing. The rest of her face remained implacable.

A lightning aggressor, Vee thought with a little admiration. She nudged Chlöe aside and grabbed Gaba's upper arm. The surge of satisfaction she felt when Gaba's face contorted in pain and yelped was well worth it.

Chlöe pulled her away. 'Jissis, Vee! Don't—'

'Explain that, then. You take us for fools?' Vee leaned into Chlöe's restraining grasp, just enough to convey a threat but no more. 'You're wearing a full cardigan on a blazing hot day, for what? To cover your damn bruises. You're lucky I haven't gone to the cops.'

Gaba drew a derisive click across her palate. 'Nxxcc. Bitch. You think what—' She lunged. Vee sidestepped and smacked her hand away.

'Stop!' Chlöe ducked and shouldered her way between them, eyes wild like the referee for a jungle catfight. Her breath came fast and panic lit her eyes.

Vee took some of the wind out of her sails. 'Look, my friend. This,' she flicked a finger back and forth between Chlöe and herself, 'we're it. Your fifteen minutes of fame, the fair version. Which won't last long. How tough do you think it was to find you? We know the cops called you in, but that was for suspicion of Berman's murder, and they barely have anything to go on. They haven't run any *other* questions by you about the break-in, because I haven't breathed your name to them once. I didn't see my attacker clearly and as far as I know, it's another random crime. But I want the exclusive on your side of the B&M Financial story. In exchange, no cops ever come sniffing at your home or job with renewed interest.'

Gaba slowly, almost elegantly, raised her middle finger. 'Here's your exclusive.'

Vee smiled and waited.

Chlöe slowly lowered her arms but flicked her eyes between the two of them. 'Xoliswa, face it, there's no running away from this. Don't wait till the real tabloid cockroaches descend; be grateful we got here first.'

No one spoke.

'We know the full B&M saga. We interviewed Moloi. She told us a lot,' Chlöe said.

'A lot of lies.' Gaba glared, cheeks puckered, her mouth commas so aquiver Vee felt sure she was gathering reserves from the back of her throat to gob at their feet. 'Did she mention how…'

Vee leaned closer, as did Chlöe. The simultaneous adjustment was subtle. Vee barely noticed any more how they both perked up at incoming intel, like towers homing in on a distant radio station, but she caught the barest facial twitch as Xoliswa noticed. Noted the smug tilt of her chin and the flicker of her eyelids as she did so. *Volatile, a liar and perceptive,* Vee thought. *Mind how you move, Johnson.*

'So she told you how I made them and they fired me. For no reason.'

'She tells a different version,' Vee said.

Gaba waved her away. 'They drummed up some nonsense to smear my name so I would leave on my own. They kept undermining me until no one on my team could trust me or work with me. I busted my ass for them. They were ungrateful.'

'According to Akhona, you were far from a model employee. You were really good—'

'I was exceptional.'

'Fine. But unreliable and difficult. Polarising, instead of holding your team together. You dropped the ball with major accounts.' Vee shrugged. 'You got on drugs and lost it. You screwed your boss.'

Gaba's flinch took her back a step. 'She shouldn't have told you that. That was private. She promised—'

She barred her teeth and shook her head like an animal with a rag between its teeth, muttering in Xhosa, her face submerged in facial tics and twitches. After a moment she fixed them with the same glare, resolute this time. 'She told me to stop harassing them. All I did was ask for my due, and she made out like I was a stalker. She told me we would all discuss it, amicably, and come to a fair resolution. In the meantime my private record, my past history with them, wouldn't be open to anybody nosing around for gossip.'

'Come on. This is way beyond gossip. The police are hunting for a murderer.'

'What has that got to do with me?'

'You were at The Grotto. Don't lie. You were seen. You went there to—'

'To what? *Murder Gavin?*' Gaba snorted. 'Don't be bloody stupid, man. Why would I? For what reason? You think it's easy to kill a human being?' She widened her full eyes, sending her features into comic contrast, milky saucers against cocoa. 'Gavin tried to *help*. How would I profit with him out of the picture? If anyone needs to go, it's that bitch Moloi.'

'Then who killed him? Moloi?'

Xoliswa Gaba threw her head back and hooted long and hard. 'Please,' she snorted, 'I've laughed enough for today.' Her square manicured nails flicked lint off her cardigan's sleeve. 'Moloi's soft. Fucking town mouse. This would've been so easy to settle... no one had to die.'

Vee narrowed her eyes. 'What do you mean?'

'It's always something for something. What's in it for me?'

'The truth.' Chlöe looked incredulous. 'Don't you want—'

Gaba gave her a withering eye, like she was fast becoming a nonentity. 'No one gives a damn about the truth.' She lifted one of the loose locks draped over her shoulder and took her time winding it back into the fold of her bun. Then she drew her thighs together and clasped her hands in front of her, reminiscent of her bank manager's stance. Vee imagined those thighs crushing her spine into ice cold linoleum. The small of her back twanged at the memory.

'You don't even realise how far off base you are. But I'll give you credit for finding me and lead you back onto the path of righteousness. I'm not your story. Gavin's baby he allegedly built from scratch, Akhona, a lot of businesses around here, *those* are your gangsters, the fraudsters. Do you have any idea how filthy their hands are?'

'Surprise, surprise. Business is dirty,' Chlöe quipped.

'Shut up and don't interrupt me again.' Xoliswa Gaba looked straight at Vee as she spoke, and Vee stared straight back. An electricity shot between them, stretching across an invisible wire. 'Are you listening?' Gaba said.

'Intently,' Vee replied.

'Here's what I had on the now-unimpeachable Berman & Moloi that forced them to listen.' She took a pause; it lasted so long Vee feared they'd lost her. 'Once upon a time there was a girl who grew up knowing nothing but the hustle. Day in, day out, she saw people in her neighbourhood join that hustle to survive. Didn't matter what they did or how they did it, everyone was either part of it themselves or knew someone involved. Most times the wolf swallowed them, or they simply broke even and stayed above water. But sometimes,' she grinned, or more like bared both rows of her large, white teeth, 'they swallowed the wolf. They found a con to beat the system. Even if they waded through shit to do it, they came out the other side smelling of roses.'

'B&M were fake,' Vee said, carefully.

'The whole setup. That little girl didn't become a crook herself, but she knew how to spot a good hustle when she saw one. It involved working many, many late nights, browsing through company files. Hell, sometimes even breaking into encrypted files with restricted access. Listening at doors, recording privileged conversations. And yes, pillow talk.' She spread her hands with a coy smirk. 'But it was worth it. I even made quasi-friendships with a few of the big dogs who grease the pipeline for these deals, the guys who make sure things slip through untraced. One of them I'm still close friends with – uh-uh, no names,' she wagged a finger to shush Vee and Chlöe. 'Just like you, I won't betray my sources. All I can say is it's her side hustle and it pays more than her real job. In fact, the only reason she hasn't left her day job is because she doesn't want her company getting suspicious. She knows all the underhand companies that issue "certificates" for these businesses. The ones that award points on compliance elements that get you ahead. She knows the horror stories too: the cut-and-paste specials, shoddy work by unprofessionals that stick in your eye, they're so damn fishy.

'When I pieced it all together, I was *pissed off*. All the gloss, that empowerment bullshit, for it to be fake... They were using communities like mine to prop themselves up. I know it's impossible to turn a profit and still live up to all this philanthropic hype floating around, but to *use* us like that... I had to get hard evidence on how they were doing it.'

'Because by then you didn't want to go to them with self-righteous anger, or even to the financial council or the press. You wanted in.'

Gaba tipped her head in a small bow. 'Something for something. I'm how the other *other* half lives – or in this country, rather, the other eighty-five per cent. You work, you break even, you die. Meanwhile, the Gavin Bermans of the world...' Gaba shook her head. 'The man was not stupid. His family made "clean" money during apartheid and he channelled it into a new, rainbow nation company. He did what many small companies do – start small and safe. Build. *Then* start cutting corners, tiny unnoticeable ones, here and there. Hire a front that obliterates the competition on every major score – an educated black woman. She doesn't even need to be outstandingly qualified, just good enough. She trains, acquires more degrees, managerial courses and financial economics this and thats than you can fit up your rectum. She gets good enough. Now, the black face can stand as a qualified as a co-director and major shareholder. Berman Financial graduates to Berman & Moloi. If that's not the oldest front in the book I don't know what is.'

She eyed them, making sure they were keeping up. 'But if playing with the bigger boys is the ultimate lookout, you must aim even higher. Gavin was intelligent, but greed was his biggest problem. If he wanted it, he would grab it, forget asking. Just take, take, take.'

Something in her words and the tiny, almost apologetic smile on her lips, the way her dark irises pierced into Vee's, made Vee run cold. *She was there that night. She saw him attack me,* Vee realised.

'It's what got me into his bed and how I got *him* as pliable as you please. We both knew how to fake it to get what we wanted, but he thought I could be bought with trinkets and promises. So uninspired. And don't get me wrong, over time it got real… it felt real.' She glanced down with a shake of her head, then sucked in a deep breath and looked up. 'Point is, it's like he was tired of hiding; he wanted me to know he was a self-made man. That he hadn't got to this level with a rubbish BEE certificate, no self-assessments, a poor track record. Never. He'd earned, and *bought*, himself the image, wormed his way in with the right political friends and got their contracts, kept his ear to the ground.'

Vee exhaled at length and turned away, feigning boredom. Gaba grabbed her arm and Vee yanked herself free in one pull. Chlöe stepped between them again, eyes flitting back and forth.

'Consultant scam. That's how they were doing it,' Gaba said frantically. 'Since Moloi wants to spin tales about me, ask her about the kind of *business* they were running. If not for my loyalty, this would've blown up long ago.'

'That doesn't tell me why Berman wound up strangled, with *my* scarf mind you, landing me in a mess. You had dirt on him, *you* needed *him* alive. How come he's dead?'

'That's not the right question.' Eyes shut, Gaba tapped her fingers up and down the crease between her eyebrows. 'Ask me what you're really dying to know.'

'What the hell you were looking for in my house?'

'Viva!' Gaba applauded like a delighted child. 'Finally.' Her mouth commas twitched as her jaw muscles worked. The whites of her eyes reflected the mall's fluorescent lighting until they seemed to pulse like alien orbs against the backdrop of her skin. For the first time, Vee saw a mania that made her take a step back.

'One,' Gaba lifted the index finger of one hand, 'plus one,' she lifted the other, then brought the two together, 'will never make four. You've found me. Berman is lying on a slab somewhere with his organs in embalming fluid. Find your other two players.' She smiled. 'Good luck, ladies. A word of warning – you have no fucking idea what you've gotten yourselves into.'

She sauntered off in the direction of the bank.

Cocoa butter and rose, Vee thought, skin prickling as she watched Gaba's retreating back. That's what she'd smelled like.

24

The next day began with the kind of weather that had earned Cape Town's climate its capricious reputation. Vee sat in Cesaria with the driver's seat reclined, window halfway down while a heavy fog rolled in on a gentle southeasterly wind. She sat in mostly empty the parking lot behind B&M Financial's building, reading a printout of Richard Fish's overdue report on the CD. More like suffering through than reading. The masterful CD, the one that precipitated all this drama, the one that would make or break their entire investigation. The bombarding of the fog was proving far more fascinating – Vee watched a mass of wispy invaders swallow the parking lot foot by foot, until she could barely see passing cars and figures outside her windshield.

After a minute of inhaling tepid, briny soup into her lungs, she conceded a loss to Mother Nature. She rolled up the window, propped the report – could she even call it that? – against the steering wheel and found her spot again with a finger.

From what I could salvage after I overrode the encryption, this disk contains fragments of code, pieces of a software program written some time ago. It looks pretty elegant, not exactly genius or mind-blowingly original—

'You never think anyone's work but yours is genius,' Vee muttered.

It was designed for use in the financial or banking sector from the look of the data it was set up to capture. It has a client/server topology of the three-tiered kind, i.e. client – application server – database server. A Linux platform – which is an open source platform anyone can use – is the backbone, and it uses the Oracle database. It also has a Javascript front end: in "computers for dummies" language that refers to the user interface, in this case designed to host hundreds of concurrent users.

I tried to retrieve the data but was unsuccessful. Your best bet is to find the mother lode – who wrote the code or the source of the client data. I can't guess at how much code constituted the entire program or how much was lost but I can dig around for a digital fingerprint that looks like a match.

In summation: This disk is corrupted beyond salvation. Even if it worked, this is just a skeleton – it wouldn't provide more of than a snapshot. Who even stores valuable information on CDs any more? Amateurs.

'Here endeth the word according to Guy Richie. Let the church say amen.' Vee lowered two pages of wasted ink and rubbed her eyes hard. They had nothing. And Fish's services weren't cheap. When Nico saw the expenses they'd run up for his "consultation"…

She snapped the manila folder shut and papers slipped onto the floor of the car. She nearly missed her moment as she ducked to scoop them up. Walking up to the back entrance of the building, her movements – as usual – stiff as cardboard, was Akhona Moloi. She looked comically furtive, like a spy in a movie, with tinted aviator glasses, the collar of her camel-coloured jacket upturned against the murk and two heavy-looking tote bags underarm.

'Akhona!' Vee rapped the glass loud as she could. Moloi squinted in her general direction. Vee grabbed her handbag, locked the car and jogged up to her. 'Hoo!' she heaved when she caught up. 'Good morning.'

'Good… morning,' Moloi replied, more a question. 'Do we…'

'Oh no, we don't have an appointment. It's just, things

move so fast with these investigations. You get one piece there, another one yonder, you glue this and that.' Vee forced a laugh. 'I should've called, but you know how mornings can be. I figured with you shouldering all the responsibility now, since…' she gave a grim nod, 'you'd have a lot of early starts. Just wanted to knock this out of the way so I wouldn't clutter up your schedule later.'

'Ja, but it's just gone 7am. I don't—'

'You've been so helpful, and said if we had any more questions not to hesitate —'

'Ehhh…' Moloi had a wan smile on her lips as she tried to recall uttering those words. She blinked up at Vee through fogged-up glasses, suddenly evoking a laughably strong likeness to a children's storybook character. A mole or beaver; a perfect caricature of friendly, myopic bemusement. She muttered something, stuck a key in the door from a ring, and gave the hefty metal handle a couple of weak tugs. Vee relieved her of the tote bags, leaned a hip into the glass door and pushed a few time until it gave.

'I don't have time, though. You're right, it's an early start every day now. There's so much on my plate—'

'Completely understand. Deadlines, right? Ugh. I'll be brief. Should I take these upstairs for you?' Vee slipped inside before Akhona could protest, shouldering bags of what felt like rocks.

Moloi pushed the glass door until it suctioned shut, clacked the security gate closed after it and hustled to the stairs.

Vee bounded after her. 'I didn't know they gave out keys to these buildings.'

'Hhmmm? Mmm.' Moloi pulled herself out of some reverie. 'They don't, usually. But this is a small building. There's only the little shop down here,' she pointed down the flight of stairs to a kiosk, its window awash with cheap attire and trinkets, 'and one large room serving as a call centre above us. They're part of the job placement agency next door,' she popped a finger east of the green-glazed wall, 'who needed more space. B&M takes up the most space, the entire first floor. Gavin and I keep such strange hours that we managed to get our own keys.' She paused, one leg aloft on a stair, and shot a look over her shoulder at Vee. 'Gavin and I *kept* such strange hours. Well, Gavin *kept* and I *keep* strange...' She lifted her chin and blinked back tears.

'I'm sorry,' Vee said. Moloi nodded and waved the sentiment away, and kept climbing.

'Must be nice, though,' Vee switched subjects quickly, 'having offices in the CBD. This is prime catchment area.'

'Mm-hmm.'

'Compared to, where was it? The little place y'all started off at twelve years ago, off Main Road. Not bad for a start, but this is one helluva step up.'

They reached the top of the stairs and paused. Moloi's smile and patience were growing stale faster than milk left in the sun; Vee read it on her face. *Good*, Vee thought. If she had any chance of success with a surprise assault with nothing to back it up, she needed all the leverage she could get. She looked down at Akhona Moloi, a long way down, keeping her smile bright and guileless. Being tall was wonderful; the psychological advantage alone couldn't be beat. Sometimes, like now, she wore heels just to be cruel.

Again, Moloi mumbled something Vee didn't catch, and traversed the long hall to her office door. 'I see you've done your research. Yes, it's been quite a journey. We've come a long way, especially in our, shall we say *class* of clientele. We're both very proud of that. Oh. Not we, I mean *I'm...* ag shit, whatever.'

'You've been doing a lot of reading too, I see.' Vee peered at the books in the tote under her arm and ran a finger down a row of spines. *Marketing for the New Africa*; *Copyright and Patent Law in South Africa*; *Finance in the Digital Age*.

'Yes.' Moloi opened the door, hastily hoisted the bags' straps off Vee's shoulder and swung them onto the office floor. The office had deteriorated. Save for carpet space, which was being swallowed up fast, there was barely a surface uncluttered by books; stacked, open, strewn, or upended. 'I apologise for the mess. I'm up against it, as you can imagine.' She rushed to the windows and jerked the curtains apart, recoiled with an 'eugh' at the fog and dreary sky, and half-closed them. Then she wove behind her desk and hefted more junk – notepads, pens, dirty mugs – off the armchair, and sat.

Vee chose an empty upholstered chair, saw a sticky brown stain on its seat that her freshly laundered tan pants wouldn't survive, and took another. 'Like I said, I'll keep it short. Not so sweet, though.'

Moloi sat up straighter.

'Gaba. We tracked her down yesterday. Illuminating discussion ensued.'

Moloi tensed. Two ropes of muscle bulged through the skin on either side of neck. 'I don't know what you—'

'Consultant scam.' Vee smacked her thigh. "Akhona. Stop. If you level with me now, you can still direct how your part in this goes. I've been thinking about this a lot. Mainly, why would a skilled, talented black woman – I speak of Gaba now – why would she continue on here when she could've moved on in a heartbeat? In this economy, she's a black diamond – a head-hunter's wet dream. From the looks of her personnel records, you and Berman incentivised her nicely to stay. Nicely, but not handsomely. Yet still… she stayed. Why?'

'I told you, because of Gavin. They were lovers and she thought—'

Vee reached into her bag and brandished the disc, letting its reflective side catch the light before laying it on the table. 'What's this?'

Moloi's jaw slackened for a second before she clicked it closed.

'Don't think I'm bluffing with any old CD. Yes, it looks

different because I had to salvage the info and transfer it to a new disc. I've looked at it.' *Didn't make head or tail of it.* 'I had a computer expert look at it. Thoroughly.' *He didn't think much of it either.* 'Talk to me. Or you'll go down with a sinking ship after the captain's dead. Your funeral. Literally, perhaps. Gaba is quaking for revenge.'

Moloi shunted papers across her desk like a dealer at a cards table, fingers aflutter. She put one hand on top of the other and pressed both down to the desk, not before Vee saw how badly they were shaking. 'She was really quite talented. We didn't see it at first, but in time…' She rubbed one hand over the other gently, lullaby-soft, like she was consoling herself.

'She called herself brilliant.'

Moloi snorted. 'Of course she did. Gavin agreed; only in secret, though, as if she wasn't familiar with patting herself on the back.' Her expression curdled. 'The problem with brilliance, excellence, whatever you want to call it, is you have to control it. Make it work for you. Xoli's bright but ag, she's too out there. Resistant to the big picture. Instant gratification seeker.'

Vee crossed one leg over the other. Waited.

'Doing business the straight way is hard.'

'Integrity is impossible?'

Moloi grimaced. 'You kids these days. You know so much and still manage to sound ridiculous.' She clapped her hands once. 'It's possible, okay. But… impractical. It takes forever, and forever takes resolve. The players on the market now, they're not just hungry, they're ravenous. Do you even realise what hosting the 2010 World Cup here last year opened the door for? Madness. Pure madness. Just look at this cockup with the construction of the Gautrain express railway. Imagine, *imagine*, how much it cost to cobble that thing together for the World Cup?' Moloi's eyes were bright, stoked from within by an address she'd clearly given often. 'The initial estimate to build it skyrocketed nearly ten times by the time it was halfway built.

The government didn't deem the job fit to be handled by local contractors, so foreigners took over. It's up and running now, but the whispers have begun – how many billions did it cost? Why else would these foreign companies love investing here so much? It's a happy hunting ground! Leverage onto a major deal here, sweeten dirty officials there, slot as many bullshit clauses into their contracts as they can manage. Ways to extort public funds are endless, and once money leaves these shores, it's washed so clean abroad it's virtually untraceable. Reap, reap, reap, while the country weeps.'

'Mmm. You and Gavin sound like deeply concerned nationalists.'

'Don't be snide. You get the benefits of living here, none of the headache.'

Vee bit back her words. Moloi must have seen another type of fire altogether in Vee's eyes, one that made her hurriedly drop her own to the desk and begin shuffling papers around. 'I'm just saying. If the economy doesn't feed the dogs, the dogs will devour each other. Shortcuts and flat-out fraud are more the norm than the anomaly.' She glanced up, then looked away again. 'I'll spare you the rant.'

"Tell me how Gaba fits into all this'

Moloi collected the papers in one resolute sweep, knocked their edges straight and set them aside. 'Xoli started out as a data entry analyst, sometime programmer, and to be honest we didn't expect her to stay. Data people are essentially migrant labour. Fresh graduates. Pull extra shifts, don't mind mindless work till a better offer from Standard Bank or Old Mutual or wherever comes up, leave when it does. But she liked the fit, thought there was more autonomy and room to grow here, and we agreed.' She paused. 'She was eager to please. In fact, she was looking for a family, wanted to ditch as much of her township past as possible. Did we exploit that? Yes. Were we unfeeling opportunists? No.

'She was perceptive, creative, coloured outside the lines. Didn't swallow bullshit. She figured out the company was taking what Gavin called necessary risks.' Her mouth puckered in distaste. 'The scam didn't start with us. It's as old as time and government tenders. Which are the juiciest ones. Christmas all year if you landed one.'

Vee started to interrupt.

'Forget it. You want an exposé, you expose that part yourself.' Moloi shifted her swivel chair closer. Her gaze stayed down and off in the distance, scouring the wall like her lines were written on it. 'Government parastatals often threw out these bids; capital projects, tenders, what have you, for other smaller companies, usually BEE ones, to consult on. Tenders for any service – transport, procurement and goods supply, catering, you name it. The scam was pretty simple. If you'd done enough work for them, got known as a preferred supplier, you were conscripted to provide consulting services on tender. In our case, we were provided volumes of data to analyse, and naturally, hand in a quote for our service.'

'An overinflated quote.'

'Yes. We'd do the work for a fraction of that and get a nice cut for looking the other way while the fat cat on the other end pocketed his. Or, what happened more often, we'd quote to consult for say R2 000 an hour inclusive. Then we'd hire junior consultants to crunch the data for, say, R200 an hour. Not many, a few good ones. They'd churn the raw data into clean figures, run the analysis, log it into our system. We'd then send the lot to the aforementioned parastatal and our payment would be electronically released. It was well-oiled – you barely spoke to or saw the intermediary. No paper or electronic trail. All that had to happen was a split with the cronies on the other end who doled out orders or sent contracts our way. Of course, it couldn't be split with everyone. That would defeat the purpose of jacking up the quote and maintaining confidentiality.'

'So, this was a sweatshop?' Vee said. 'Y'all had the junior freelancers do the work, and either paid them a pittance or fired them.'

Cringing, Moloi nodded. 'Essentially. Sometimes we offered less from the get-go, having anticipated how much it would set us back. Other times there'd be some infraction after a few weeks to let them go and deny at least part of the salary.'

'Ah. That's how B&M cooked up grounds to fire Gaba.'

'*No, that's how she wound up staying.* She made herself an indispensable temp until she got on permanent payroll. There was nothing much to suspect back then and we were more careful. But working nights and extra hours to impress...'

'She found evidence of the shortcuts. That's how she made this disc, and others like it probably, and used it as leverage.'

Moloi primmed her lips, a strange, somewhat regretful look flickering across her face as she looked at the CD. 'We needed her kind of drive around here. Win-win.' She spread her hands. 'Look where we are now.'

Vee looked around, for no other reason than to avoid the look of imploring dejection on Moloi's face. If the office was a metaphor for where they'd landed, it was fitting. Uplifting it was not. The carpet desperately needed the suction of a vacuum cleaner. Vee couldn't bear to glance at the strew of papers, stationery, dirty cups on the table near the back wall. She looked back at Moloi, whose gaze had strayed off again, her thumb and index finger harassing her afro near her hairline. The patch of hair had been worn to a coin-sized area of stubble.

'You lied. Last time Chlöe and I were here, you swore the company never paid her off. How much does she want?'

'250K,' Moloi replied without missing a beat; the figure likely haunted her dreams. 'We gave her 50 last December.'

Vee sucked in her breath. That was about 20,000 US dollars. A lot of cash to splash locally, especially for a girl who'd never laid eyes on anything close. Vee realised it was *seven times* the bribe she'd allegedly pocketed for the Paulsen case. Was this all it took to get what you wanted – bide your time, turn the screws, watch the other side squirm until they rolled over? Fleetingly, she wished she had a more bloodthirsty instinct.

'That was just for starters,' Moloi read her face. 'After LEAD would come major exposure, new business. She made it clear she'd be recalculating her worth based on new developments.' She pulled out the tuft of hair and started on another. The faraway gaze lingered.

'You're terrified of her,' Vee said, treading lightly, afraid to break the lull.

'Gavin's gone. That leaves me… and her.' Moloi reeled her eyes back into the present and they locked with Vee's. 'If something happens to me… that will be that. Do you understand what I'm telling you?'

'I—'

'Write your story,' Moloi stopped fiddling with her scalp and waved dismissively, her hand moving in slow motion like she was shooing flies in her sleep. 'This place will survive it. I'll survive. But with her on the warpath, with this hanging over my head for God knows how long… I won't last.'

'Why won't the police—'

'Don't you think I keep asking that?!' Moloi jumped from her chair and Vee took a step back. 'I'm sorry. So sorry.' Moloi passed a hand over her face, fingers trembling. 'I'm freaking out. Please… I… Can we do this another time? I've given you a lot to digest in the meantime.'

Vee nodded. She walked to the door and dawdled, palm around the door handle. 'Look, you should take some time off. Don't let this swallow you up.'

Moloi managed a wan smile as she put her arms around her waist, giving herself a hug. Her mussed hair and clothes made her look diminished and a tad feral, like a schoolgirl who had barely survived her first fight. 'No hope now. New captain of the ship.' She gave a mock salute. 'Is there any hope of getting that disc back?'

'What, this?' Vee patted her handbag, CD safely tucked within. 'Perhaps. If you're willing to tell me what's on it. And how it ended up at The Grotto Lodge, waiting to be retrieved by…'

'I thought you already knew what was on it." Moloi's lips thinned into a tight line.

Vee smiled. 'See you Monday, Akhona. Stay out of trouble.'

She shut the door behind her and hurried to the exit. It was exhilarating to have hit the bullseye with her suspicions, but also a relief to be leaving the building. Moloi's agitation had a disarmingly infectious quality to it. It was an eager beast eating away at her, and the beast wasn't happy to feast on one victim. It wanted a taste of anyone else in the vicinity. Vee was glad to be well away; the intensity of Gaba and Moloi back to back in the space of two days was too rich for her blood.

She couldn't shake a vague sense of unease. It goaded her all the way down the long passageway, breathing down her neck like a sullen bully. The quiet was almost cloying, sticking to her skin as she trudged past endless, pale walls, feeling like a dirty bolus moving through a bleached gastric canal. Akhona Moloi must have had the final say on the décor – the place was painfully bland. Vee checked the time on a wall clock, then walked around the whole floor. Vacant offices and an empty reception area yawned in her face. She retraced her steps to Moloi's office.

She knocked and re-entered the office in one swoop, unsurprised to find Akhona still standing and self-hugging in the same spot. 'Sorry, one last thing. You know this woman?' She held out her cell phone.

Moloi squinted at the picture on the screen, neck bobbing like a pecking hen's as she peered closer and pulled back repeatedly. At last, she gave an exasperated grunt, grabbed her glasses off her desk and scraped them back over her eyes. She held the phone aloft at an appreciable distance, pouted and shook her head. 'Noooo... no, can't say I do. She seems familiar, though. Who is she?'

Vee studied her long and hard before answering: 'Rhonda Greenwood. The deputy GM from the lodge?' The photo was a respectable one, off The Grotto's website. 'You sure you don't remember her?'

Moloi handed the phone back with a shrug. 'Uh-uh. No, wait. You mean the one that died during our stay?' She frowned. 'Why would I know her?'

'No reason. Just background.' Vee slipped the Samsung away. 'Where's your staff? It's almost nine.'

'Ah, I let them off today. They deserved it, what with how crazy it's been lately. We all need a personal day to clear our heads.'

———

By the time Vee stepped outside again the fog had dissipated like a midsummer's dream, beads of dew glistening on handrails, poles and windshields, burning off under the sun. The morning sun had made a feeble appearance but Vee wasn't fooled: in a half hour, by the time she got back to the office, the city would be an oven.

She crossed the parking lot to Cesaria, and just as she reached for the door of the Chrysler she saw a figure walking up to the same entrance she'd gone through with Akhona Moloi. Not walking up, as a matter of fact, *scurrying*. The person – a woman obviously, from the way she moved – threw off her coat and tried, unsuccessfully, to stuff it into her oversized handbag. She did manage to retrieve a cell phone, which she talked into briefly.

She hung up and paced, clearly waiting for someone, occasionally glancing around. Vee knew she couldn't be seen from where she was, but she crouched behind her car anyway. The young woman's movements looked familiar, and when she drew a little closer, Vee saw it was Aneshree Chowdri.

'No way,' Vee frowned.

Moments later, the door opened and Moloi poked her head around the security gate. Aneshree ran up with obvious relief. They spoke for a second – from this distance, there was nothing to make out but mutters and murmurs – and Aneshree stepped inside.

Vee rose to full height after they disappeared from view. 'You na insah, you na know…' she whispered. Know she did not, but, especially now, she most certainly had her inklings. She quickly got into the car and called Nico Van Wyk.

25

The next morning, Vee was in the tearoom tipping semi-frozen pineapple Liqui Fruit juice into her mouth, straight from the carton, when she saw Chlöe zipping towards her through the frosted glass partition. She cursed; the sound came out muffled by the carton and a few drops of liquid gold dribbled onto her blouse. Chlöe wasn't high on the list of people she wanted to see right now. She'd just divided her morning up between working with Darren and his magicians in the cyber hub, and shooting off emails to Nico, occasionally popping into his office. The hub always left her feeling wired and daunted, all those nerds spouting terminology that was still beyond her and pouring boiling coffee down their throats at an alarming rate. To be honest, since a hasty text yesterday morning she hadn't communicated with or thought about Chlöe at all. She knew what the first words out of her mouth would be.

Chlöe pushed the door open and said, 'Where were you this morning?'

'Working from home. There was so much to write up...'

'That was yesterday.' Chlöe stretched out an arm behind her to indicate the past. 'Where were you,' she brought both arms in front of her, '*today?* Saskia Sourface decided to herd all the interns off on some training exercise and it draaaagged. I kept waiting for you to come save me! You never even said where you were yesterday. Just buggered off and sent a lousy text.'

'I was at Berman & Moloi yesterday.' She tried to look apologetic but knew she was failing miserably. 'I had a hunch and acted on it. There wasn't time to rope you in.'

'Oh.' Chlöe's eyebrows plummeted. Her lips began to funnel, millimetre by millimetre, into a small, pink-glossed pout until she resembled a colicky baby. The two other occupants of the tearoom picked up their drinks and snacks and shouldered past them.

'You ever notice how people treat us like plague sufferers around here? We don't even need to ask for privacy, they just throw it at us.'

'What hunch?' Chlöe insisted. 'Since when have you started having hunches and running off without me?'

Vee grabbed another carton of juice, mixed fruit, from the freezer compartment, popped the tab and poured down a gulp that made her teeth vibrate. 'Since always. The beginning of time as we both know it.'

'Let me rephrase. How can I stress *how much I hate it* to get you to stop?'

Vee opened a cabinet and took out a glass, glugged in some juice and held it out. After a lengthy, mutinous squint, Chlöe took it.

'Sorry, it had to be done. And it was worth it. Gaba wasn't telling us the whole truth, for one thing. Each time we threw a punch, she hit us with another one, or some half-cocked theory.'

'Duh. Frickin' artful dodger, that one. She kept swinging the conversation back to Akhona, like there was something she didn't want to rat about.'

'Exactly. Making such a meal of being "fired for insubordination" without mentioning what she wanted in return for her pain and suffering. Turns out her silence is pretty golden, because she'll be getting *a lot* for it. If I hadn't barged over there with a bluff to make Moloi talk...' Vee recounted what had occurred the morning before; by the time she'd

233

explained the scam and extortion portion, Chlöe's jaw had
flopped open like a puppet's.

'Gaba wants *how much*?'

'Imagine if we'd been offered even half of that. Not that
we'd ever take—'

'No, never. *Never.*'

'But goddamn it. Imagine for a second we had...' Silently,
they did. Vee had to shake her head free of the reveries when
they tipped into ridiculous: yacht-owning, jewellery-splurging,
Camps Bay-mansion-buying. 'Anyway, that's not the best part.
Moloi's selling the place.'

'What? Why? Who told you?'

'A little brown birdie that keeps popping up all over the
place told me,' said Vee, and finished off by describing the
furtive encounter between Aneshree and Moloi in the parking
lot. 'Why skulk around there, *now* of all times? Because The IT
Factor is buying out B&M, that's why.'

'Whoa,' Chlöe said, eyes wide. 'Are you sure? Would the
great Ryan Walsh use an underling like Aneshree to broker a
deal this big? You didn't actually hear...'

'That's the thing, I don't think Aneshree's an underling.
Bishop, what else makes sense? Akhona's great in a team but
there's no way she can run that place. Not without Gavin. But
if she sells up, the monkey's off her back.'

'If she sells to The IT Factor, she's in the clear with a *profit*.
The reputation of B&M will fetch a very tidy sum.' Chlöe spoke
slowly; Vee could practically hear her cogs whirring. 'Moloi can
even start afresh. Oh my word.' She turned to Vee. 'It won't
even matter if the scam is exposed. Her dead partner will take
most of the heat, she'll be portrayed as a reluctant sidekick.
When it blows over, she'll be that much richer. No wonder
she's got no problem handing us the exclusive on a platter.'

'Yes!' Vee pumped her fist. 'You should've seen her hustle
around that office. It's both a mess and a graveyard. Like when

you're packing up a house to move. What, her staff suddenly have a day off? Please. After I ran into Aneshree outside, it clicked – she's putting her affairs in order. Once the deal's done, she's out. On top of that, going public means—'

'Gaba's leverage turns to dirt. Gaba can either take what she's been offered so far, or walk with nothing. If she even dreams of dragging Moloi down, everything goes poof.'

Chlöe made her "I'm thinking" face: pushed her mouth into a snout and wiggled it around, a crease furrowing her brow.

Vee smacked her lightly on the shoulder. 'Come on, this works and you know it. Akhona's only holding out until she's sure her ass is covered, but this scoop is ours. You should read what I've put together for the Saturday print, *incredible*. Go take a look at it.' She tipped a finger. 'I'm telling you, we've scored big time.'

Chlöe didn't take her eyes off the ground. 'That's not my issue. It's… the way you talk. *You* got the scoop. Have a look at the story *you've* written up already. Are we still a team on this or are you making all the decisions while I carry your hem?'

'Bishop, what's your gripe? I had to ambush Akhona without you but now we're that much closer because of it. It wasn't a deliberate attempt to cut you out.' She made a fist and thrust it out. 'We're still a "we" in this, I promise.'

Chlöe dithered for several seconds before she bumped Vee's fist with hers. 'Okay. But "bosslady" is only a figure of speech, bosslady. No more…'

She stopped. Vee followed her gaze through the glass to the newsroom below. Nico was on the prowl, rubbing a hand over his bald dome as he scanned the floor, stopping at desks and barking inquiries.

'Think he's looking for us?' Chlöe asked. Almost as if he'd heard her over the distance, he looked up, spotted them, hit a purposeful stride and in no time flung the tearoom door open.

'Ebony and Ivory, status meeting, now,' he ordered.

'Actually, we have an update on—'

'Save it. Nothing beats this. Akhona Moloi was attacked in her office late last night. It doesn't look random; it's tied to your investigation.' He searched their stunned faces. 'We don't know what shape she's in, so I need you down there fast. Spin that magic of yours into gold, before anyone else does. Because if she dies, we've got nothing but a shitheap of conjecture.'

Blink

26

'We've tried everything. Don't you think we should—'

'What. Give up and go home?'

Chlöe's resigned shrug was more of a 'hell, yes!' than a 'why not?' The undersides of her eyelids were bruised a very pale shade of grape, and Vee had never seen her look so mutinous. Murderous, in fact.

'Look I know, this has been the longest day in the history of our lives, it still isn't over and things aren't shaping up as planned.'

'You think?' Chlöe snapped. 'This,' she jabbed a finger at the Mediclinic building in front of her, 'is a private outfit. They're made of way sterner stuff, and you can't sift in and out of wards through randomly looking for patients like at a public hospital. Hell, those nurses are like *actual bouncers*, if you failed to register the size of them.'

Vee exhaled. 'No, I didn't. But we had to try something.'

'Which didn't work.. It was pathetic, in fact.'

Vee was only half-listening. Chlöe ground her teeth and followed her gaze. They were standing in yet another parking lot: fenced in, spotted with hibiscus shrubs and adjacent to the beige-and-blue multi-storeyed hospital occupying most of the lot. The lot was about half-full; sedans and family SUVs mostly. She made out the press vans of two other rival newspapers; one of them had even been audacious enough to camouflage between two ambulances. They'd catch a ton of flak for that when the hospital caught wind of it. The other van was parked nearer a back wall, displaying a *Mail & Guardian* logo across one of its doors. Now, the caustic smile on Vee's lips made sense. If the good old *M&G* were sniffing around, *City Chronicle* was really up against it. *M&G* possessed the resources and clout to drum up a piece hard-hitting enough to make theirs as electrifying as a shopping list.

'What do you suggest we do?' Vee quietly asked, as much to Chlöe as to herself.

Give up and go home. It's after five, Chlöe thought. This, naturally, was the furthest from what Vee wanted to hear. She wanted sparkle and spit-shine, and Chlöe felt fried. Figuratively and literally. Thankfully, Vee had had the presence of mind to park close to one of the high shrubs, so at least her side of the Chrysler wasn't cooking in the sun. 'I don't have any bright ideas,' she said, yanking open the passenger door and climbing into Cesaria in a sullen huff. 'I do know if you'd parked in the shade, we wouldn't be baking in our skins like human potatoes right now. We're not all blessed with natural SPF.'

Vee slid into the driver's side. 'Looord. I'm sorry, okay. Sorry I parked us in a frying pan and refuse to run the air-con because it burns too much gas. Sorry we've had to work flat-out all day and didn't get a proper lunch.'

'Add sorry we didn't take that bribe. Or stayed working at *Urban.* We wouldn't be doing this,' Chlöe flapped a hand wildly, to indicate "whatever the hell we're doing now", 'to keep our rep alive at a place that doesn't appreciate us.'

Chlöe regretted the words as soon as they left her mouth. News of the attack on Akhona Moloi put them and the paper in priority mode: LEAD and everything tied to it was now a main course. They'd been grinding at it since noon, employing every resource and calling in every favour at their disposal to stay ahead of the pack. First stop was the hospital, but they left soon after – in the news business, everyone's first idea tended to be a bad one. Moloi was in surgery with a ruptured spleen and other injuries, and getting her to speak to the press afterwards would have to be carefully managed. If it happened at all. The next best, and far trickier, manoeuvre was nailing down Xoliswa Gaba. They drove to the northern suburbs, starting at her flat in Parow: none of the other tenants had seen her since the previous morning. Next, a trip to her family home in Gugulethu: they had stood outside the gate while members of her family and neighbours loudly instructed them to piss off and stick objects where the sun didn't shine. Finally, they stopped at African Bank: head-shakes, shrugs and cold replies. No one wanted to be associated with Gaba, but the upside was no one seemed to be helping her either.

Vee turned her head slowly, and for a microsecond Chlöe felt an actual sting against her cheek where Vee's dark eyes landed on her face. Chlöe shrank in her seat. It hadn't helped at all to hear that, every time they'd made a visit, the police had been there first, searching for Gaba. She'd gone from a person of interest they hadn't been too interested in, to prime suspect. Vee's cell phone had been sutured to her ear all afternoon; fielding calls from the office, getting updates on Moloi's condition, using Richie to retrieve Gaba's cell number and leaving message after message in her voicemail. No luck – the cell had been switched off and likely discarded.

You had to look closely to see it, but Vee was exhausted. She was coasting on fumes, and yet she would remain at the coalface, ever digging. For a flicker of a second, the air in the car took on a shimmer, a thickness. Chlöe found herself looking at Vee through it, but not at the real Vee – a Vee in the middle of a thunderstorm, head thrown back, mouth open to the rain and flying debris and churning winds.

Suddenly, the mirage dissipated. Chlöe shook her head side to side and blinked at Vee. The same, everyday, infuriating Vee, only the clench of aggravation on her face had loosened and she looked bright with inspiration. 'Give me your phone,' she said.

'Why…' started Chlöe. The image of thunderstorm Vee skittered across an alley in her mind, and she quickly handed over her iPhone. 'She won't answer. I don't know why you're banging your head against rocks if she won't answer.'

'She will.' Vee reached into the back seat for her handbag.

'*You serious?* This woman was severely beaten last night in her own office, by none other than our mutual acquaintance and reigning psychopath. She wants this day to be over, not to have us climbing down her throat the second she wakes up.' Chlöe snorted. 'If I were her, I'd give anyone connected to this case the middle finger. That includes us.' She glanced over and saw Vee had pulled out a business card. 'What's that?'

'Moloi's personal number, oh faithless one. Remember? The card she gave us at our first interview.' Chlöe leaned closer, the scribbles in black ink on the back of the card jogging her memory. 'Family, friends, the press and assorted harassers won't get any joy on her usual numbers, but I'm certain only a select few have this one.'

Defeated, Chlöe grumbled incoherently, leaned back against the headrest and closed her eyes. For a moment, another absurd one, she willed herself to sleep, or at least to doze. She wanted to forget the day. She wanted to ignore the writhing nest of snakes in her chest, goading her to snap. From behind her eyelids, she sensed rather than saw Vee pacing outside, phone to ear, a vertical dash between her eyebrows as she spoke. Chlöe recognised the voice she'd switched to was the buttery, mollifying, even somewhat cunning tone she used as a drill bit to extract information. Within moments, far too quickly to indicate success, Chlöe felt the car depress as Vee got back behind the wheel.

'Dammit. She hung up on me.'

241

'Least she picked up. Meaning your theory's correct,' Chlöe mumbled, parting her eyelids slightly.

'Moloi's sister picked up. She barely let me finish before she hung up, and now it's going straight to voicemail. Buuuuut…' Vee completed a text, pressed send and rested the cell on her knee.

Less than a minute later, it rang.

'Speaker, speaker, and record it,' Chlöe hissed. Vee fumbled for a second and tossed the phone back to her. She deftly clicked the touchscreen and brought up what she needed.

'… heard it was you and thought, hawu, this one will never show respect for the dead, so I shouldn't be surprised she's calling.' The voice emanating from the microphone sounded painfully thick and hoarse, like rubble tumbling down a long, deep pipe. It didn't resemble Akhona Moloi's voice at all, nor any woman's, nor even a man's, but Chlöe could tell it was her. 'My sister's being overprotective but ah, thank God for her, because for sure I can't keep fielding calls. We were both shocked to hear this phone ringing. I brought it along for emergency calls from clients. Once she read me your text,' Moloi laughed, and the laugh immediately mutated into a frightening cough that took time to die down, 'I knew I'd better answer, or you'd keep calling. Tenacious as ever.'

Chlöe tilted the phone towards Vee; Moloi hadn't called for her anyway. She was just the lackey who worked the equipment. 'Your word was reckless as a matter of fact,' Vee replied with a chuckle, then flipped back to her drill bit voice. 'It's horrible what's happened to you, horrible and horrifying. I can't imagine what that must have felt like. Mssh, what am I saying? I have first-hand experience.' She allowed for a polite pause. 'I know you've been through hell, you're exhausted and not up for a long conversation, but if you could just go over what happened last night.'

Voices came down the line, raised in debate: one clear and

plaintive, fraught with emotion, the other Moloi's dry, scary rasp.

Vee frowned pointedly at Chlöe, urging her to translate. Chlöe covered the phone's microphone with a hand and said, 'My Tswana's not that great, hey. Besides, I can barely hear what they're saying.'

'My sister is highly unamused right now,' Akhona croaked at last. 'She's insisting I rest and let you guys stick your interview where the sun don't shine.'

'That venue is full up right now, believe me. But I get how impersonal this is, I really do. If you'd prefer we come up—'

'No. That won't fly.' Another fit of coughing blasted down the line. Vee moved the phone away from her ear until the firing came under control. 'Sorry,' Moloi's gasps were followed by the wet sound of something liquid, 'they've given me this disgusting solution to calm my vocal cords. It'll be a while before I sound human again. And stuff for pain and sleep. I'm drowsy... so tired.'

The line went and stayed quiet. They looked at each other.

'I was working late yesterday evening. At the office,' Moloi finally spoke. They both sat up straighter.

'How late?' Vee asked.

'I can't be sure. After eleven, thereabouts. I needed distractions and interactions at an absolute minimum yesterday, that's why I gave my staff the day off. You showed up unannounced in the morning but that only took up a half hour. I didn't want my entire day eaten out from under me, so I'd cancelled all meetings and calls the day before.'

'So no one else dropped in after I left?'

'Mmm. A client or two, nothing hectic.'

Pointedly vague, Vee noted, but let it slide for the moment.

'By lunchtime I was in the zone and can't even tell you where the time went. When I looked up, it was dark outside. I thought I could push through till midnight, I was prepared to, but then...' Fear and anger changed the timbre of her voice. 'Xoli barged in.'

'She what? How did she get in? Unless you...'

'*What?* Don't insult me by suggesting that I'd be insane enough to *invite* that her anywhere near me. I – I've been going over my actions, how I must've been careless. I was starving; all I'd eaten all day was a large packet of crisps. By half-eight in the evening I was about to swallow myself, so I went down the road for a Steers burger. I'm fastidious about it – going in, lock; going out, lock – but I... I must've forgotten. I look back on it now and can clearly see how I only closed the glass door and but didn't shut the gate completely when I got back from Steers. I was distracted.' Her voice cracked some more. 'Hunger nearly drove me to sign my own death warrant.'

'If you'd—' Vee began.

Chlöe cut her off. 'Why? If she wanted to confront you or *make* you hand over what you owed, why come to your office in the middle of the night?'

'I – I... Look, it wasn't my intention to provoke her to madness... I didn't think – she's so... '

Chlöe cursed quietly and began to speak again, but Vee raised a finger and shook her head. Chlöe sank back, seething. 'So last night, Gaba went to confront you, then,' Vee prodded. 'She's tired of waiting for y'all to honour the rest of the payment, and with Gavin gone, it sank in that it's not going to happen. Not unless she forced it out of you. Last night she snapped.'

'She didn't get tired of waiting. *I confronted her. I* got tired.' Moloi was on the verge of sobbing. 'So flippin' tired! Who can live like this? I'm not Gavin!' She hauled in several deep breaths. 'After you left the office yesterday, as you left you said get some rest. It... I... it really hit me. I wouldn't, *couldn't*, get any rest while she was terrorising me. I thought about it long and hard, and then I called her. Gave her a piece of my bloody mind. Told her there was no money coming, not today, not tomorrow, not ever. I told her about telling my story to the papers since the cops intend to drag their feet. Either till kingdom comes or until I'm dead. But once I blew the whistle on myself, who would disbelieve it? She'd be blown out of the water and I'd be free.'

'You mean, after you sold the company and cut her off at the knees, then you'd be free. Is that what you've been hiding, that you're selling the company to The IT Factor?'

'What? *Selling?* Selling B&M? Are you mad?' Moloi's voice rose to a screech higher than a sound system's feedback. Chlöe and Vee both winced and held the iPhone farther away from their ears. 'My girl, you can't just *sell* a company. It's not like selling sweets. There are steps, many, *many* things to consider before a leap like that. And putting a convincingly positive spin on our portfolio right after the CEO and managing partner dies? Not to mention finding a buyer in this climate? God, as if I don't have enough on my plate already. Nothing's being sold, my dear, nothing. Our future is up in the air. Me and uh... Ryan, Ryan Walsh, we've been... talking, considering. About forming our own consortium, us, the jilted group from LEAD. Show everyone the private sector has balls of our own and doesn't need handouts. But honestly, I can't think about all that right now. Xoliswa is my only focus.'

Chlöe coloured the air purple with a string of expletives. Vee laid her head back onto the headrest and repeatedly thumped a fist against her forehead. 'You realise what you've ignited, by threatening her?' she said through gritted teeth.

'I didn't threaten her! And *I* put my *own* life in danger, to save it! Who else could I depend on? I got bloody fed up, I called her and spoke my mind, and got back to work. It was stupid, but there it is.'

'So she came up to the office?'

'Fuming like a bull. Was I shocked? Yes – I expected a scheme-up that would take days, not an immediate reaction –

but also not, at the same time. She started screaming, smashing things. Saying how she needed that money to start a new life, start her own business, maybe even leave South Africa. Her friends were counting on her to produce start-up capital and she had investors itching to sign up her talent. Hela! Talent where? Pure comedy – I laughed and laughed. So very talented that at 35 she's still slaving in the northern suburbs as a glorified bank teller. I told her she could continue deluding herself, but as for me, it was over. Nothing, *nothing*, that Gavin and I built together was leaving B&M. That's when… she lost it and went for me.'

'I hit back however I could but I'm not a fighter. I was nearly unconscious when she fled and left me there. Had to crawl to my phone and call my sister, get her to call an ambulance. Dead of night. That was the longest wait of my life, let me tell you. But now everyone knows. They see her for the psychotic bitch she is.'

Chlöe buried her face in her hands; Vee bowed hers over the phone. Chlöe imagined they were both thinking the same thing: considering the extent of her injuries – broken shoulder, dislocated hip, multiple bruises in addition to the banged up spleen, prostrated in hospital – had the gamble been worth it? Weighed against the murder of an indispensable business partner and quite possibly the man she loved, Akhona Moloi – triumphant – seemed to think it was.

27

They climbed out of the car. It felt imperative to breathe open air immediately, to know a sunny, predictable world still existed outside its doors, different from the one they had immersed themselves in.

'Did it record?' Vee asked anxiously.

Chlöe grunted in the affirmative as she fiddled with her iPhone. She sneaked a glance at its clock: 17:12. She couldn't for the life of her give a comprehensive account of the events that had transpired since she'd stepped out of her flat at 8 a.m. that morning. The day was bunched up in her head, a coiled, gnarled string of highway rides, stops, snarls, slammed doors, and now this. Her stomach growled; she didn't feel hungry in the least. Most likely her gastritis, which she'd activated years ago stressing and cramming for exams at university, was playing up. 'Now what?'

'Damn, Bishop, give me a minute to process.'

'We can't jol out in a parking lot as we *process*.'

Vee flapped her hands in a 'calm down' gesture, and took a minute in silence. 'All right. Here's what's doable for the rest of today. We—'

'I need to go home. Not feeling too well.' Chlöe touched her tummy.

'Um, sure. You all right?' Vee gave her arm a light squeeze. She smiled. 'I wasn't about to suggest we stake out the hospital if that's what you're afraid of. We won't get much more out of Akhona for today. Gaba is in the wind as we speak, we won't be getting an update on *that* anytime soon. My thoughts are we go home and start on this while it's all very fresh. I'm tired, but I can whip out a first draft tonight and send it for your thoughts. Tomo—'

'Why do you get the first draft? You wrote up the last piece. And my phone's got the recording, don't forget.'

Vee blinked, then narrowed her eyes. 'I wrote it up because I always do. I lay the foundation and we both build it up from there. Anyway, doesn't matter who has what, Chlöe, your name still appears, under my byline. But hey, if you'd rather, get your own rough draft started. We'll compare and edit before we merge documents. Happy?'

'Whatever.' Chlöe caressed her tummy some more. One side of her didn't feel like arguing, but the other with the writhing snakes...

She opened her mouth and was cut off by Vee's new ringtone, another discordant Afropop atrocity that set her teeth on edge. Vee peeped at her phone on the car seat, frowned at the unfamiliar number and answered, cradling the cell in the crook of her neck and shoulder. She was rummaging through her handbag again, saying, 'Hello... hello... can you speak up please, the line's bad...' when her face changed. She straightened up so fast she nearly dropped the phone and banged her head on the roof of the car.

'What?' Chlöe hissed, catching her eye. 'What?!'

Vee tipped the cell away a fraction and mouthed 'Xoliswa', mouth contorting dramatically over each syllable to render it as clear but soundless as possible. She got out and trotted over to the shade of an acacia tree near the wall close to where they were parked, beckoning frantically. Chlöe skidded over to her and pressed her ear in close.

'Where are you? How did you get my private number?' Vee breathed. She smelled like the butterscotch candy she'd been sucking on.

Chlöe stomped her foot and rolled her eyes, in a "she's not going to *tell* us, *is* she" sort of way. Richard Fish hadn't been able to track Gaba because she'd had the common sense to ditch her phone and acquire a new one.

'Baby, baby, baaaaby, you can have my private number!' Gaba crooned. 'Tjo! My parents used to *love* that song. We used to have this record player, those old ones that cost an arm and a leg now, and they would play that song and dance around the house like mad people. Reminded them of how they met. My mum worked for the phone company during good old apartheid and my dad saw her one day on the bus to work.' There was a smile in her voice. 'You're not too young for that track, are you? No, you're an eighties baby. Doesn't matter where you were in the world, black people were all nuts about Motown music. So you remember those good old days. In fact,' steel rimmed her voice now, 'I think you and I have more in common than I gave you credit for. I think we both remember a time when our lives were made of sugar and nice things, then one day, *bang!*, everything was shot to hell. The little girl in us had to die.'

'What do you want?' Vee asked. Chlöe could only stare at her profile in admiration. She looked shaken, but her voice stood ground like a boss.

Gaba's laugh was haughty and bitter. 'For you to know you're not the only one with resources. And you're not that hard to find, at home or at work. Speaking of, where's your white maid?'

'She's not...' Vee clamped her hand over Chlöe's mouth, then waved an apology when Chlöe shoved it away, glaring. Vee put a finger to her own lips, then continued, 'She's not here. Not right now.'

'Ah. Too bad. But never mind. That's neither here nor there.'

'What - do - you - want? You've crushed Gavin; I'm not sure how Rhonda Greenwood got in your way, but she did; Akhona is pretty much out of commission; what's next? Full extermination – if you can't have it all, no one else should.'

'Only fools want it all. I want what's owed to me.'

'*Owed*? How's that?'

'Figure it out. You have everything at your fingertips, but you're stubborn.'

'Shut up and listen to me.' Vee exhaled shakily. Huddled close, Chlöe used her shoulder to give Vee's a nudge of solidarity. 'Stop messing with us. My job isn't forcing connections between non-existent dots. Or to providing her majesty with the audience she craves. Our only agenda is the story. Sit down with us, tell us your side of it, *all of it,* and you can still get in front of this.'

'How? So you can print more lies, making those thieves look like heroes? You don't want my story, *you want to keep printing lies!*'

'You've lost control, my dear. Control is all you want here. And the more you lose, the harder you make it on yourself. Look what you did to Akhona. Take back the reins.'

'Fuck you and control. Look – now you listen to me. If you don't back off, I can bring hell to you. I can do it. Stop messing around.'

Vee laughed a loud 'Ha!'. '*You* listen. This isn't a movie, *this is real.* You're a wanted woman. You talk a good game about intelligence, but you're nothing but hot air.'

Chlöe started to speak and Vee yanked the cell and backed away, eyes firing razors. Chlöe stomped her feet, mouthing animatedly and not quite soundlessly, 'Are you mad? Stop making it worse!' Vee moved off, turning her back.

'Don't talk to me like that.' Gaba sounded dangerously quiet and close to tears.

Vee lifted her face skyward. Chlöe knew well the look on her face – ironclad resolve tinged with fury – and knew she was beyond reasoning with. 'That's exactly who you are. Just another angry black woman, blaming everybody for her shitty choices. Call me if you want to salvage what's left of your life. Otherwise, don't waste my time.'

She hung up, switched the phone off and turned around.

Chlöe stared at her, mouth hanging open.

28

The drive to town was uncharacteristically placid. On the surface, at least.

Vee braved the unnervingly icy force field radiating from Chlöe as she negotiated traffic along Adderley Street. They had cooled their heels in the Mediclinic car park in a kind of mildly shocked lull after Gaba's call. There was a vague hope, too, that Moloi would feel revived enough to go over her story once more, but she'd sounded exhausted when they did get through a second time.

Now, they were penned up in the cringeworthy midst of evening traffic. Vee flipped the indicator, swung into Strand Street and nosed towards the Castle and the Grand Parade, intending to take a shortcut to Chlöe's complex on Roeland Street. She glanced sideways at Chlöe, who had leaned her head against the passenger window. She sighed. Time to turn on the charm. 'You don't agree with what I did back there, clearly. But we don't negotiate with terrorists, am I right or am I right? It was necessary.'

'Necessary? Irresponsible, more like!' Chlöe erupted. She smacked her hand against the partly wound window so hard the glass vibrated. 'Stupid, egotistical heroics. Call Akhona again, if you've forgotten how it panned out for her.' Her breathing was jagged, her face scarlet.

'This isn't about heroics, I'm just... I'm trying to save our asses, Bishop. Get our credibility and prestige back. I know it sounds like the same thing but it's really not. Remember, when we were hot shit around the office? We dumped *Urban* and walked into *City Chronicle* with swagger. Had colleagues hitting on us for advice, because we were that... magic duo. I *miss* that. Now we get run around town for scraps.' Vee waggled her shoulders and sat up straighter. 'Let's turn scraps into lightning. Nico may actually wet himself with joy if we close this piece with a bang... which is the opposite of what he'll do if we screw it up.' She gave Chlöe a grave, loaded look. 'Tear us a new asshole. Just one. And then force both of us to shit through the new one at the same time.'

'How are you saving us? By staring her down to see who blinks first? Thoughtless and reckless is what you're being.'

'What?' Vee spluttered. 'I only moved back home on Monday, when I was positive it was safe. The neighbourhood watch are on special alert with regard to my house. The busted glass door and window have been fixed, so have all the security bars. The armed response company's on speed dial. I'm not taking any chances.'

'Right. Because you're the only one she'll target.'

Vee gave an exasperated scoff. 'She doesn't care about you. Nor would I let her touch a hair on your Disney princess head.' She cast a weak, sidelong grin.

'Naturally. Because I'm not the important one.'

'Do you *want* to be important enough to murder?'

'I don't know. Maybe,' said Chlöe, gesticulating wildly. 'I don't want to feel like... I dunno, a vestigial object. Like the sunglasses protecting *your* precious eyes from the glare of your own wonderment.'

'Glare of my own...' Vee mumbled, completely floored. What were they even talking about?

'It's like something's infested you.' Chlöe spewed the word "infested" in a way that made Vee's skin shrink against her bones. 'We've been fine, covering the stories we're used to and staying out of the line of fire. But since you smelled blood in Oudtshoorn you've been on a crusade to...' Chlöe shrugged. 'Prove something to yourself. Or to Nico and Portia. Like if we nail this, Nico's going to hand over the entire crime desk to us on a silver platter.' She shook her head, a short laugh catching at the back of her throat. 'That's not going to happen, I hope you know that.'

Vee's shoulders tensed. *Maybe I'm not fine riding my desk while my career passes me by*, she wanted to say. Instead, she swallowed the jab. 'Be that as it may, I want this to be over, as much as you do. If we can come out shining too, the better.' The half-apologetic, half-goofy face she pulled didn't elicit a sea change, but Chlöe softened a touch all the same. She flicked a chin nod, temporarily appeased, and wiggled deeper into her seat, eyes trained outside the window and arms crossed. The pout stayed put.

'Got to give Gaba credit, though,' Vee said, almost to herself after minutes of silence. 'This wasn't the heist of the decade, but if she'd pulled it off... whoa.'

It pulled the pin out of the grenade.

'Wow. Let's hand out blue ribbons to the lawless. Why am I not surprised that's your takeaway?' Chlöe sneered.

'You tell me.' Vee heard a dangerous softness creep into her voice.

'For a second, it sounded like you two were bonding. Getting all chummy over a dark past.'

The silence grew fangs. Vee changed gears too gruffly. The mechanism ground and whined, out of sync, until she whacked the shift in place with the heel of her hand. She jerked the steering wheel left and swung out of traffic, cars behind her honking up a storm. She inched past the overhead walk of Golden Acre Mall, turned right off Strand Street into Lower Plein, which bypassed the taxi ranks and nosed Cesaria to the zinc-roofed stalls fringing the Parade. She pulled in tight to the blue Toyota Tazz in front, drew up the handbrake and turned in her seat. 'Whatever's going on here,' she flicked a finger back and forth between them, 'stop it or spit it out. You've been peevish all damn day and I've had it. If you're feeling left out—'

'*Left out?*' Chlöe flinched like a bad taste had flooded her mouth. 'You think this is about feeling *left out?* My cool black friend refuses to sit with me at break so I'm acting out? Get over yourself.' She glared outside, then whipped her neck around so fast her French plait made a "whumph" against the window. 'If you want to know the truth, yes, there's an infuriating, and might I add *suspicious*, element of exclusion to recent developments. And no, I don't mean going to B&M without me yesterday; that's a symptom. I mean *everything.*' She shaped her hands into a globe signifying a world of slights. 'Never getting elbow room to work on my own. Having to follow you on assignment, whether I want to or not. When was the last time I got to shadow another journalist? That piece in January, about Parliament and the by-elections and ANC Youth League? I couldn't go. I'm sick of it.' Chlöe thumped her thigh.

A nearby fruit vendor dipped his head to Vee's window and pointed at the spot she'd filled, wagging his finger and shaking his head. Vee got out, slammed the door and saw his point: she was parked on a yellow line. She ignored the cautionary stream of words he poured at her in a language she couldn't understand, perhaps Setswana, she couldn't tell. If a traffic cop dared try to clamp her car, she riled enough to cuss him out.

'Where the fuck is this coming from?' she shouted.

Chlöe slammed the passenger door and stormed towards her. 'Try the place where I constantly defend you while you swan around in your "I'm not local, I don't understand this horrifying country" bubble, like you shit diamonds. Try the part where I'm gatvol of wondering if I deserve to be nicknamed *puppy* by the entire office.' Her voice cracked on the end of the sentence. The splotches in her cheeks grew.

'God...' Vee dragged out a breath, playing for time. Damn Nico Van Wyk. Damn all of them; herself, Nico, Chlöe, even Portia. This had been mounting from the get-go. She should have been the only one hired, but she trundled in with Chlöe – "baggage", Nico called her. *It's both of us or nothing,* she told him, but never told Chlöe. It would be buried and forgotten, she stupidly thought. Now, she looked across the sidewalk at the worst judgement call she'd made yet. *Don't you see me fight for you? Don't you realise every time I "kept you at heel" I was protecting you? That Nico offering you a "solo project" is his way of throwing you a bone, isolating you and watching as you fail?* She gulped it down and said instead, 'You want autonomy, act hungry. Fight your own battles.' She threw her arms open in challenge. '*Pick* some battles, for heaven's sake. Otherwise standing behind me can't be misconstrued – you're being spoon-fed until you grow some balls. You could've stayed at *Urban* and made fashion editor in a few years. But no, you *chose* to stick with me.'

Chlöe reeled. 'Really? How can your lackey fill in gaps *and* find time to shine? How can I, to my full cowardly ability, *get from behind you,*' Vee took a step back from Chlöe's clench of sneering teeth, 'when I'm being used left and right?'

Vee smoothed shaky hands over her hair. 'Doggit,' she awed. 'Now I'm *using* you?'

Chlöe shifted from one foot to the other. Her blush leaked down from her neck to her clavicles and cleavage, like an invisible, overzealous makeup artist was shading her in. She looked odd standing there, soundlessly yapping the air, hair flaming in the setting sun like angel Gabriel's sword. She glanced around and Vee followed her eyes. Behind them, a small crowd buying apples, naartjies and sweets had decided to linger and watch them. The vendor shot Vee a toothy grin and surreptitious thumbs-up in appreciation.

'I – I… if it sounds… then… yes. Yes.' Chlöe set her jaw and nodded firmly. 'I feel used at times, and I have a right to my feelings. Let's not pretend we have the most typical relationship in the world. We're not just friends who happen to work together, or colleagues who hang out occasionally. It's confusing. Let's pick a lane and stick to it.'

Vee gave a tight, harsh laugh. 'You want boundaries? *You?* After you disrespected mine five minutes ago?'

'You said you were over the Richie hacking incident! I never would've done that if you'd simply trusted me to begin with.'

'I would've when I was ready. But no, not fast enough for you. By your logic, I *forced* you stick your nose into my private life—'

'I take responsibility for my shit, okay?' Chlöe placed a hand over her heart as if taking a pledge. 'But… I – I'm saying… we're always walking a tightrope. One day I'm in, next, blackout. Call me a needy brat if it floats your boat! But I'm your friend. I'm on *your side*. I'm not the assholes who've screwed you over in the past, to the point where you're always in defence mode. Or the guy who runs out on you after a miscarriage…'

Vee cut her eyes to slits.

'… or the "love" who lies about his ex-girlfriend being in town, or – or – or…' Chlöe flailed her arms, '… the dodgy lawyer you know nothing about. I'm not Portia or Nico,' she yelled at the fruit-buying onlookers, whose expressions were a milieu of shock and amusement, 'and for bloody sure I'm not a raging rebel leader pointing an AK-47 in your f—'

Vee slapped her.

The blow registered as sharp needles radiating across her palm; Chlöe's head thudded against the Chrysler's roof and bounced. As one, the crowd yelped 'Yuwi!' and shrank back. Every eye turned to marvel at Vee, the breaker of barriers, the slapper of white girls in the street.

Vee froze, then rushed forward. Chlöe blinked for several

seconds and wobbled to rights, bracing against the side mirror. 'Chlöe,' Vee whispered. Her handprint, a cartoonishly stark outline, flared across the side of Chlöe's face.

Chlöe took another step and swayed. 'You… Did you just…?' She touched her cheek, looked at her palm, touched her cheek and looked at her open palm again, as if trying to capture the bizarreness of the act in her hand.

'I'm sorry.' Vee reached out. Chlöe shoved her away and stalked around the car, yanking the passenger door open with such force Vee feared it might come off in her hand. 'Bishop, stop,' she pleaded, as Chlöe dragged out her belongings. 'I'll take you home. I didn't mean to… I'm sorry.' Chlöe slammed the door and Vee's heart crumpled when she saw the glimmer of tears. Chlöe said something in a quavering sob, something Vee didn't catch over traffic noise. She jogged off, struggling with the strap of her laptop case. Vee stood, rooted, as her friend ran across the road and disappeared down the next street.

A hand dropped onto her shoulder and she started. A woman in a headscarf and bright floral-print top scanned her face with deep earnestness as she spoke, a meaningless jabber that made Vee feel strangely tired. *Chlöe's right. I should learn the language, any one of them. I'm a selfish turd living in a bubble.* The back of her eyes began to prickle.

'Ah-ah. Sisi, ko chii? Muri right? Anozviona saani angataura newe kudaro? Pachena pane vanhu kudai,' the woman said. The language was definitely Shona, she had enough Zimbabwean friends to spot it. Or Venda. Lips pursed, the woman straightened Vee's clothes as if the encounter had left her disgracefully dishevelled. 'Nxc. They still think they can do as they please. White people, neh,' the woman spat.

29

Vee's hands shook as she slumped behind the steering wheel. She turned the key over and over; the ignition coughed in response. She shook her hands like limp rags for a minute, then held them straight and level with her face. The tremor persisted. She shook them some more; turned the key again. The engine growled. She dropped her head with a thud onto the headrest and squeezed her eyes shut. The prickling behind them had morphed into throbbing.

A distant chime resonated around the car, faint but incessant. She opened her eyes reluctantly and flicked them to the radio. It was still off. The sound continued in the back seat. P Square ringtone. Vee lunged for her handbag, turning it upside down. Chlöe...

It wasn't Chlöe. She frowned at the unidentified number. Her spine snapped straighter. Gaba. Had to be.

The number looked different, though. The first call had been on Vodacom; this was MTN. She stared hard at the Samsung in its smash-proof purple case, willing it to cease and desist, silently begging it for an early night off. She could swing by Eastern Food Bazaar on Longmarket Street for some tandoori chicken, lentil curry and butter naan bread, haul it back to the car and trough out in the back seat. Or drive straight home, kick up her feet with a big bowl of bitterleaf, maybe a beer, and episodes of Sam and Dean Winchester serially killing monsters on *Supernatural*. Or just lie in bed, starving, marvelling at the utter elegance of her bitchiness. It was deserved.

The phone fell silent. She exhaled. The phone wailed again. She took a big gulp of air and answered.

'M-m-miss Vee. Miss Vee. It's m-me.'

Vee exhaled in a long stream. It was Tristan Heaney. 'Twinkie? What's up? Oh Lord.' She massaged the knot between her eyebrows. 'Chill out, you lil' boy. You've become a stalker. I remembered about Monro, all right. I took him to the vet for the shots and paid for him to sleep over at the kennels until I got settled back at my house. That's why you haven't seen him. But don't worry. I'm picking him up at…' She flipped her watch and mouthed 'dammit'. It was 5.57pm; the vet's office and kennels closed at 6pm. Only fairy dust could magic her from central town to Kenilworth in three minutes. 'We'll do pickup tomorrow. Meantime—'

'I have him already. I picked him up.' Tristan's voice sounded uneven.

'You *what*? How did you manage…' Then she remembered. Tristan had nagged and guilted her so much she'd made him co-guardian of her husky, just to make him feel grown up and involved. The vet had her permission to release Monro into his care, if ever she was unavailable or indisposed. It was all for show; he was never to *act* on it. 'You went outside our grid, all the way to Kenilworth—'

'I took a taxi.'

'Tristan Heaney! How many times have I said—'

'Miss Vee! I need your help.' Long pause. 'Please.' The scolding dissolved on her tongue. The quaver in Tristan's voice was accompanied by erratic breathing. Tearful hyperventilating, in fact. Why was he whispering?

'Twinkie,' she cajoled. Jesus, had Monro dashed into traffic and been run over? Was her dog… 'Talk to me.'

'There's a lady here. She... has me. Us.' Tristan's gulp was audible. 'She says she knows you.'

'What lady?' Instantly, she knew the question was ridiculous. Ice formed a cage around her heart. 'Describe her.'

'She...' Tristan choked on a sob. 'A black lady. Oh, sorry. Um...'

Vee imagined him closing his eyes and blushing in that way he did, when he felt she'd be disappointed in something he'd done or said. Immediately, she felt angry with herself for over-diligently teaching him to mind society's niceties – don't describe people by their race, accent or weight – instead of how to defend himself against nefarious strangers. 'It's okay, sweetie. Tell me exactly what she looks like.'

'She has dreadlocks. In a ponytail. She's tallish, but shorter than you. H-her bum is a bit big.'

Vee could've sworn she heard a muffled chuckle in the background. Her flesh went cold. Xoliswa Gaba was right there, listening. *Amused.* Vee could see those indents on the edges of her lips twitching with mirth. 'What happened?'

"She – I think she followed me. She was outside your house. When I came to check if you were home yet, if you'd picked up Monro. She was sitting in her car, with the door open, just waiting and staring at your house. Weird look on her face. When I went through the gate she started staring at me... for a long time. Then she waved. I... I... waved back.' His voice cracked on the last word.

'Sssh. You did nothing wrong,' Vee cooed over his sobs. She imagined him, huddled God knows where, hands shaking as he held the phone to his ear, face red and streaked with tears, blond hair falling in his eyes while an impassive stranger sat by his elbow, monitoring their conversation. Was she on speaker? She couldn't pick up any distinguishing sounds in the background. 'What time was it and what kind of car was she in? Did you see a licence plate?'

'It was around five. I don't know, about the car. I'm not into cars like that.' Seriously? Another thing she'd have to coach him on. 'It was white with four doors. And… and…' he was definitely pulling on his right earlobe as he tried to come up with something, 'uh… I don't know!'

'All right, take it easy. Finish telling me what happened.'

'Um. I went to the front door, knocked, no answer; I checked the back for Monro and peeped through your windows. No one answered so I left your yard, closed the gate and she was still there. I wanted to call you but I knew you were busy. I knew you were so busy you'd forgotten about Monro. So I decided to go get him. I was going tell Dr Neilson you sent me to get him. I – I'm sorry.' The line fell silent. Vee knew he was thinking of a more heartfelt way to relay how sorry he was. A rush of pride went through her for this 11-year-old who was scared witless, but still possessed the decency of spirit to feel bad for betraying her trust. The silence hung, and he rushed on: 'I know I should've paid more attention to my surroundings like you're always on about. Diligent observer. But all I was thinking about was seeing Monro and practising a convincing story for Dr Neilson.'

'You didn't notice her trailing you or anything?'

Tristan didn't answer but his regret was climbing through the phone at this point. 'I'm sorry,' he quailed. 'She was definitely there afterwards. Before the vet's, I stopped at a BP filling station to buy a Magnum ice cream.' Vee forgot herself for a second, smiled and rolled her eyes. Sugar might literally be the death of this kid. 'I noticed she was outside, standing by her car. She even waved and tried to call me over. It was kind of creepy but, you know… And I was, like, focused on Monro. When we came outside and she was still there… then I was really creeped out.'

'Why didn't you call me? Why didn't you tell someone at the vet?' Vee barked.

'I wasn't *scared*! I'm not a fricking baby!' He wheezed. 'And I ran out of airtime. She took the battery and SIM out and chucked the phone anyway.'

Another vital lesson: keep modes of communication active at all times.

'I got out of Dr Neilson's building and she was still there, smiling and waving at me... the look in her eyes freaked me out. I thought if I went back to your house she'd... follow. So I went and sat down in the waiting room and pretended I was waiting for you to come get us. Every now and then I checked, and she hadn't left. I had to wait until the receptionist left the front desk to go to the loo and I sneaked inside an empty room with Monro. I thought we'd wait until it was dark, and sneak out. But everyone locked up and left, no one knew we were in here. And she found us.

'She made me... I – I had to...' Panic ripped at the edges of Tristan's voice. Vee's throat closed. *Monro is an exceptional dog, practically a wolf. Monro could eat a stranger. Monro would keep them safe,* she chanted. The husky would fall back at Tristan's command though, if it sensed they were in danger. If either of them made a wrong move... if Gaba was armed...

'She made me tie him up downstairs. She said if I forced him to attack she'd call her friends, her bad friends. They would take him to the township and – and,' another gulp, 'tie him to the back of a bakkie and drag him until he died. Or they'd put him in a barrel and p-p-pour petrol on him and braai him alive.'

It was almost impossible to hear him through the sobbing. Vee gripped the phone and noticed the hand that held it was trembling, so badly it bounced a little against her cheek. *When I was a child, I thought as a child...* There was no point castigating Tristan for his plan now. All she needed was to find out... 'Where are you?'

'The vet's. We're inside.'

'What, in the *building*?' Vee said pointlessly.

'Yes! Near—'

Tristan's voice cut out. There was rustling and muttering in the background; Vee held her breath. He whimpered and cried out. She shouted his name.

'I hope you kids enjoyed storytime for today,' Xoliswa Gaba drawled in her ear.

Her voice brought every thought spinning in Vee's head to a standstill. 'You better not lay a hand on that boy.'

'Relax. Your little English muffin is fine. For the most part. A bit... dishevelled, but he'll live. Since I drove you to such boredom last we spoke, I decided to use a different tack to kick your investigative juices back into gear. Bring the gravitas of the situation to your doorstep. Though I wonder... roaming about alone, no one looking out for him?' Her laugh was chillingly friendly in its lightness. 'Ah, I'm being silly. He's valuable. Maybe he'll make more of an impact than Gavin did.'

'He's a child. You make one wrong move and I'll have the police taking your world to pieces before you can blink,' Vee said. Why did she sound so pathetically clichéd? Why didn't she believe herself?

'How?' Gaba laughed. 'Ask yourself, my dear, if cops will bother to come to his aid in the township. If they do, do they know it the way I know it? Some of them can find their way to Mzoli's for braaied meat and fuck-all past that. Perhaps they'll get lucky.' Gaba snorted. 'Eventually. But your friend, eish. I'll pass him on to *my friends*, and I'm sure even you know how dangerous our local townships can be. You follow the news. What happened to that Anni Dewani just a few months ago... that poor woman, so out of place in Gugs, brutalised on her own honeymoon. Such a disturbing case.' She paused. 'I can organise a special treatment for him in a snap, and by the time the cops get their asses in gear, you won't want him back in the condition they'll find him in. His own mother won't want him back.'

Vee leaned her head back and closed her eyes. 'What do you want?'

'An audience, of course.'

The line went dead.

30

Vee didn't bother to lock the car. She crossed the street and strode into Golden Acre Mall, searching for the nearest ATM. She took no notice of how people streaming by on either side of her took one look at her face and quickly stepped out of her way. Finally, she found a First National Bank cash machine and withdrew fifteen grand, her daily limit to the hilt. Then she slipped into a nearby Coca-Cola kiosk, bought a Coke and downed it in two long gulps. Then she made five phone calls in rapid succession, sitting in Cesaria with her feet hanging out of the driver's door.

The first was to Chlöe.

It rang and rang and rang, then cut to voicemail. 'This is Chlöe Bishop. If you know me, then you know I suck at returning calls. But I'll do my best. Leave a message. Cheers.' Vee closed her eyes as it played. She typed a text, rendered horridly senseless in context and punctuation by infuriating input from autocorrect, then deleted it just as quickly. Technology did not deserve to be messenger of some sentiments. She would make it out of whatever awaited her tonight; she would see Bishop again. She had to.

Second to Kara Heaney, Tristan's mother.

'Hi, Kara. It's me, Voinjama… Vee, your neighbour. From the house across… haha, yeah, owner of the wolf. Guess you still haven't saved my number. It's a good idea if you do, in case... true, exactly. Listen, I'm sure you're wondering about Tristan seeing as it's kinda late, but just calling to let you know he's with me. Yeah, not to worry. If you tried calling him... ah, you didn't, okay. His phone got stolen today and... oh no, nothing like that! He's fine. Just some kids in the neighbourhood messing around with him. He had a rough day, so he came over after I got home from work. Been missing his father, feeling anxious about school starting next week. Ah, you know boys, can't always tell. Anyway, we played video games and came out for pizza at St Elmo's in Rondebosch to cheer him up. Please forgive me, I didn't even realise the time. You know us childless women, we don't think. I know, right! Okay... not too late, absolutely. I'll bring him home soon as he picks his lip off the floor. Mm-hmm... yes. Good. Later then.' Vee hung up and looked at the cell phone for a long time. *She didn't sound worried.* Kara Heaney's voice had picked up a slight edge of concern, but she hadn't been worried to begin with. Her son was running the streets after dark and she hadn't noticed. Vee wondered how much grief counselling, if any, the Heaney household had undergone.

The third call went to a dodgy beer-and-puke-encrusted side street in Salt River, to a bar called Uzochi Eze's establishment. As the phone burred steadily in her ear, she imagined the place: tucked between Queenspark, China shops and the factory store enclave, it served as a rough demarcation between the industrial and business districts. "Finetime Bar & Restaurant, The Best in African Entertainment & Cuisine" announced a blue hand-painted sign made from plywood. The name was painted in careful cursive, next to a drawing of a man in a boubou and woman in a colourful ankara dress, dancing. She wouldn't need to talk long – Uzo knew he owed her a favour three years overdue and that one day, or night, he would get this call – so when he answered, she kept it brief. The main thrust of her request she kept *between* her words, where only two foreigners who knew how to procure and secure and fix broken things in desperate times would find it. She could hear him taking notes but knew not a single detail was being written. 'Last time was deeply personal to you, and I came through. This is personal to me, so don't let me down.' Uzo grunted and hung up.

The fourth call to Richie was even shorter. How much did he know about hacking into and remotely disabling an alarm system? She had no idea which type of system and which company had installed it; that part was left with him. She sent off the address for Dr O.T. Neilson and Partners, Veterinarians and Surgery, in Kenilworth.

The last one was hardly a call at all. This time, she prayed for the recorded message on Joshua Allen's voicemail; she wouldn't have been able to bear hearing his actual voice. She wouldn't be able to lie, and Tristan needed her right now. Her prayers were answered, yet still she left several seconds of dead air on the recorded message. This was Joshua – what could she even say? 'I miss you. Let's talk… later. Okay?' was all she managed. A tender, somewhat fearful promise, but more than enough. If anyone knew how to find her between her words, it was Joshua.

At that moment, she had deeper considerations. She simply sat for a few minutes, her body slack and gaze afloat ahead of her, unaware of time slipping past. Tension built and released within her, like a charge crackling between poles. She started the engine, revved it a few times and gave a nod at the answering growl. Slammed into gear, shot through a yellow light and did an illegal U-turn at the top of the road, headed for the N2 on-ramp.

Game on.

———

Chlöe was never more relieved than when she jumped off the minibus taxi. She wished she'd worn a hoodie, to pull up over her head. There were few things than fighting tears unsuccessfully in public transport. As the minibus pulled away, she turned away from all the staring, pitying eyes.

Fresh tears welled up and she wiped her face on her forearms. They kept coming. She lifted her halterneck top and used it as a tissue, sobbing into the fabric, then scrubbing her face until her skin felt raw. She kept the top pressed to her face, feeling a soft breeze graze her bare tummy and knowing her bra was partly exposed, but not caring. It was calming. She dragged her breath in and out through the cotton until gradually it calmed. She dropped her arms and straightened the top over her jeans; it was sodden, like someone had thrown a glass of water at her. She sniffed and carried on walking.

The latticework of streets in front of the office was deserted and dark, permeated by the eerie, buzzing quiet that so defined the centre of town after dusk. Their building looked deserted but there had to be a few diehards still upstairs, burning the midnight oil for tomorrow's print. Nico was still there, she was sure of it, along with a few brown-nosers panting for a gold star and a pat on the head. *To hell with that,* Chlöe thought bitterly. She'd had enough of this place for one day.

She rounded the corner and started down the ramp to the basement car park, throwing one last look over her shoulder to make sure the night security guard was aware of her presence. She stopped. A man, crisply dressed in dark slacks and a white shirt, got out of his car, an Audi, and looked up at the *City Chronicle* building. Holding a large brown envelope, he looked undecided about coming up. Chlöe frowned; there was something familiar about the man's crispness and briskness. As if he felt her eyes, he slowly looked across the road at her. A car or three zipped by before he finally moved to cross the street.

'Hi,' Lovett Massaquoi said.

'She's not here,' Chlöe answered.

'Yes, I guessed as much. I called her today. She sounded very caught up and couldn't talk. So I left a message. She didn't get back to me.' Chlöe watched his eyes drift down her body – she tensed when she thought he was staring at her breasts, then realised he was looking at the damp stain on her top. He looked up into her waterlogged eyes, parted his lips a little, and then closed them. 'In any case,' he ended the pause, 'I've got a package for her. I'm leaving early tomorrow and it's urgent. I would've had it couriered but I'm staying close by. At the... um...' he snapped his fingers and pointed up the road.

'Arabella Sheraton,' Chlöe finished for him. Where else would he be staying? No Cresta Lodge for this one, that much was sure. 'Give it here.'

He clutched the package closer to his chest. 'It's highly sensitive, personal material.' He spoke slowly and studied her for a disconcertingly long time, as if speaking to a mentally addled child that couldn't be trusted to follow things through. She didn't know what to make of the look... on another day it would have frightened her a little.

'Do you think I can't handle confidential material?' she challenged. Maybe he *did* know that she'd been the one behind the hacking of he and Joshua's personal emails. She held her hand out and, when he hesitated again, flicked her fingers in a "come on, let's have it" gesture. He relented.

'Are all of you like her?' she blurted.

His eyebrows curved up and eyes widened. The first real reaction. 'How?'

'Like...' She screwed her mouth around over clenched teeth and still no words came. 'Fucked up,' she choked, her voice cracking. 'Broken and–and–and–and clueless as to how other functional human beings *do* life.'

He crossed his arms. 'Depends. How fucked up people are is a function of how much they've lived through. How they weave it into their normal lives. The tough part is not letting one overtake the other.'

Chlöe looked away. 'Humph. You're not as clever as you look.'

She'd forgotten the booming quality of his laugh, which made her start. He had a huge laugh for a man his size. 'Sorry to disappoint.' He put his hands in his pockets. He softened a little, but only a little. She doubted he was someone who wasted much time nursing others through their vulnerabilities. 'Vee is a great person,' he added.

'Really? Pity she doesn't say the same about you,' she spat. Heat erupted under her skin.

He chuckled, nonplussed. 'I'd be worried if she did.' He laid a hand on her shoulder. Not a comforting pat or squeeze; just laid it there for a few seconds and then removed it. 'It's important she gets that. Please.' He gave a final half-smile, teeth very even and white against his complexion, and made his way back across the street.

Minutes later, in the basement-level parking bay, Chlöe sat clenching the steering wheel of her VW Polo until her knuckles went white. She eyed the brown envelope, lying on top of her laptop bag on the passenger seat. She grabbed it and tore it open.

31

Tristan sat stone-still in the dark, valiantly trying to make out how dirty his trainers were by way of the stream of orange light emanating through the window from the streetlamps outside. Every time he moved – scratched, swung his feet, lifted his bum to peel the sticky plastic of the chair he sat on off his skin – the woman gave him a burning, terrifying look. She sat right next to him on the row of chairs in the hall outside the waiting room, her right hand gripping his wrist in a vice. He'd tried to run once already and she had peeled his wrist so far back Tristan was sure it would snap. He was grateful she hadn't used the knife on him. Now he knew two things: she could seriously hurt or kill him with no qualms, and no one would hear his screams. The practice, the street outside, were deserted.

The scary chick had tension rolling off her in waves. She sat with her legs taut, knees slightly raised so only her tiptoes touched the ground, like a diver poised to jump off the board. Her hair smelled waxy and perfumed, like a scented candle. Her smell was light, girly, a mix of deodorant and perfumed lotion. The way his mother smelled on the days she tried to make an effort, but not as nice as she had when his father was alive. Nothing like what she'd become right after he died... Staying in bed for days, dragging herself up in spurts to use the loo and force food down her throat. His aunt and grandmother watched over her while she did everything, and once Tristan had heard them say "suicide" when they thought he was out of earshot. His mother's smell had surrounded her like a cartoon cloud. It followed wherever she went and would always remind him of sadness, the soul-destroying kind no one could fix.

'Sit still, or I'll cut you open,' Scary Chick leaned in and hissed close to his face. Her breath smelled like the ocean, clean and kind of salty. Tristan wasn't a fan of body odour. Every scent carried a memory, usually one he could link to his dad. More recently, to Miss Vee. One time, out of the blue, after a month working for her, she presented him with a gift: a new T-shirt, baseball cap and a stick of Nivea for Men deodorant. The present had really been about the deo, he knew; he owned a ton of cool T-shirts and caps. He felt bad and amused at her attempt to explain puberty and bodily changes to him.

Tristan obeyed and stopped fidgeting. She meant every word. If he tried anything dodgy she'd hurt him again; if he got away she'd find him. She did it easily enough the first time he tried. The last two people to leave the practice, a pair of gossipy ladies, were too caught up in their loud conversation to give the ground floor a proper search before locking up. He was alone now, he thought after they left. Until footfalls cut through the quiet…

He shouldn't have tied Monro up *before* attempting to hide. That was a mistake. He pricked his ears, hoping for any sound from the dog: snuffling, whimpering, a low howl. Nothing. One thing he did know, was the husky was still alive. If his instinct was right, his captor was terrified of dogs. As long as Monro was unharmed and Vee was out there, Tristan knew they had a chance.

Minutes that felt like hours ticked by. Tristan kept his eyes trained on the window, watching night settle in, hearing sounds of life on the streets outside lessen and fade. Scary Chick's grip on his wrist was torture. He wanted to flex it but pretty much knew the next time he even twitched, she'd punch him. Or worse, bring out the blade from a pocket in her cargo pants. Her eyes kept darting and flickering over every object and at every sound. With a jolt, he realised Miss Vee couldn't get in. The practice was locked. How would she find him? Was she even coming? She didn't care what happened to him. She pretended to care while he was crying in her ear like a stupid little girl. The second he hung up, she rolled her eyes and went back to work… writing a story about real criminals, while this one took him to the township and had his limbs chopped off.

Dread took over Tristan's chest, crowding out the oxygen until he choked up. He blinked rapidly.

'Aw. Are you crying?' Scary Chick looked down at him in a way that made Tristan want to moer her. 'You better save your energy for prayer. Pray that she's coming.'

'She's coming,' he warbled.

Scary Chick eyed her phone. 'You better hope so,' she replied softly.

———

Adrenaline munched through Vee's fatigue and spat out the kernel, leaving behind a clear head and embers of fury. She dug under the back seat and retrieved a pair of Adidas, flung off her heels and wriggled into them. She checked the contents of the sturdy zip case she kept in the boot next to the toolbox – the remains of an old metal hanger, a thin-bladed pocketknife and portable bolt cutters. Her "access pass", tools to break into just about anywhere.

Her cell beeped: new text. Richie. The alarm system was disarmed; he could hold it open for about an hour and pass it off as a technical glitch if it was flagged, but not much longer. An hour was more than they needed.

She got out of the car, did a satisfactory sweep of the street, and started to move, forcing herself to walk. Never before had she paid such minute attention to the surrounds of the vet's office. She noted one security guard outside a gated complex across the street, half asleep already. If they triggered an alarm, there was a strong chance he wouldn't hear it, or react if he did. She slowed going past the vet's parking area, scouring it for weak spots, thankful for a handful of lucky breaks. For one, it was an open lot bordered by a very low wall – no barbed wire, no injuries. Two double-storey structures shared the plot, one was the vet practice. She had no clue what went on in the other, but tonight it appeared dark and dead. For another, Neilson didn't run a 24-hour emergency and the practice was small – highly individualised care, they called it – with staff that clocked out daily. Way less interference.

She came to the end of the street, squinted left and right. Dark outlines, both male, tall and burly, stepped from behind a row of parked cars and moved towards her in the gloom. Vee ran towards them.

'Hey,' she breathed. The two men, the third behind the wheel of a dark blue Mazda, acknowledged her with nods. She laid out the plan to them and three pairs of alert eyes stared back at her. 'Is that all?' the burliest one rumbled. By the light of a streetlamp, it was hard to tell if he was sneering or sporting the rabid grin of a man who found it amusing he had been summoned onto a dark street for so little.

Vee glared. 'Yes. Nothing more, nothing less.' She leaned in through the passenger window and said to the driver, 'Don't park here. Drive around this block and keep doing it until you see me, or one of us, come out. If you hear an alarm go off, drive to the side road straightaway and wait two, three minutes. If you don't see any of us, leave.' The stretch of Main Road traversing Claremont and Kenilworth was tricky – you never knew when a cop car or armed security van could drive by. She slapped the windscreen of the Mazda twice and the driver fired the engine and backed out immediately.

She typed a quick text, pressed send and trotted up the street, clutching the zip case to her chest.

Scary Chick heard a sound outside and jumped a little in her chair. 'Let's go.' She leapt to her feet.

'Wha—' Tristan tried to hang on to the chair, gripping it one-handed. She twisted his wrist again and he howled, releasing it. She grabbed his face, forcing the heel of her hand into his mouth and prising his jaws apart until his fight subsided. She wrapped the other arm around his torso and dragged him, sobbing, towards the staircase.

Vee thought she heard a scream emanate from the depths of the building. She listened closely; the night did not answer back.

She threw a signal to her two shadows in the rear. 'Like we talked about. You go one way, you go the other. Both of y'all keep a look out. Do *not* come in unless it's do or die. One way or the other we're coming out.' They melted into the shadows.

Vee ducked around the corner to the service entrance doors, praying there wasn't barred by a padlock or deadbolt from the inside. She examined it. The double doors were oft-used thoroughfares, and if she knew anything about people, it was their love of convenience. Bolting both top and bottom latches of a door like this, every single time... no. Too much hassle. Most likely ones at the bottom were not in place. The lock was a simple one; the work of less than a minute's zealous jimmying to click open. She slipped in, leaving the door ajar.

She went through a crowded supply room. A tower of heavy-looking boxes; sample containers, bottles and jars with labels she couldn't read; a huge, unused refrigerator for samples and specimens. Vee opened a door and stepped out into a corridor; dark, deserted, as eerie as it was bereft. A row of green plastic chairs, seating overflow from the main waiting area, lined the wall.

A strong sensation stung her between the shoulder blades, where her inklings and precognitions sometimes arose: Tristan had been here, mere minutes ago. Even before she came through the door, she envisaged him sitting in the fifth green chair, eyes wide with hope, waiting. Just him, without the bitch. She stared at the chairs a beat longer and dismissed the notion. He wasn't here now. They wouldn't sit pretty, waiting for her.

Her eyes were drawn to the stairs. She took a step, then reconsidered. Monro. She patrolled, whistling softly, until she heard his characteristic snuffling and rustling, and followed the sound. She pushed open the door into what looked like a vet's exam room, and found straining at the leash. He barked at the sight of her.

'Ssshh, baby.' She joyfully buried her face in fur, undoing the complex cluster of knots that tethered him to the leg of the table. One down, one to go.

She climbed the first flight of stairs, dread drumming its thunder in her ribcage. Her adrenaline seemed to have crested, ebbed and was surging once more. Bravado had deserted her, though. She scanned the corridor at the top of the next flight, tiptoed to a door and peeped through the pane of glass at the top. Of course; more examination and surgical rooms. Tristan could be up here somewhere, tied to an animal's operating table like a sacrificial offering. Doped up or completely passed out, Gaba grinning as she brandished some type of evisceration tool over his prostrate body. Or… already dead. Vee closed her eyes. *Stop it.*

She kept walking and felt a nudge on the back of her hand. Monro pushed his snout into her palm and padded away, coming to a halt on the landing at the top of the stairs.

'What, up there?' she whispered. She got closer and saw the stairs rounded up another flight. Its access was cordoned off by a rusting security gate that stood ajar, its handlebar pulled out of the notch.

The roof. Of course. Vee swore under her breath and kept moving. Monro nosed through the gate and bounded up, and Vee marvelled that such a large animal could move so stealthily, blend in so effortlessly. He lived for these moments – the hunt. The staircase ended in a wide landing, bare except for more dusty, empty boxes and broken, rusted office furniture. Monro sat on his haunches in front of the door. Dull orange light filtered through its pane of glass onto Vee's face. The release bar of the door's handle was down in the open position, and someone had dragged the battered remains of a swivel chair in the door frame to hold it open.

Vee knelt and rubbed the dog's fur. 'You're not scared, so there's comfort in that,' she muttered. 'I truly have no clue what's going to happen here. But Tristan is out there,' Monro gave a soft whimper at the boy's name, 'and we have to get him. That's all.' Monro rubbed his muzzle over her cheek. 'I'm serious. No Cujo shit. No one dies tonight. You come only when I call or we're in trouble. You got me? Stay.'

He stared resolutely ahead, right through her, right through the door almost, like he had a bloodlust for one person only, and she lay on the other side. His lake-blue irises glinted spookily.

Vee scraped the rusty chair on its side to hold the door open and stepped through.

32

The roof was a sprawl of poured concrete with a shallow sunken pit of stone and gravel in the middle, rimmed by a waist-high brick wall. The brick wall was spliced in the middle by rust-flecked metal railing. There was no fire escape or exit leading down: you either left the easy way, via the stairs, or the hard way – a drop. Vee hurriedly calculated the survival odds of undertaking either option with ease and swallowed. *No one dies*, she'd said. No one gets hurt was another story.

'Tristan!' she cried, relief choking her.

He looked like hell, but he was intact. His complexion had gone an odd combination of ashen splattered with beet-rouge. His hair shot out in a riot of directions, and she noticed streaks of dirt and whitewash paint on his face, arms and bright-green T-shirt. He fought as he was dragged up those stairs and through the doors. Pride swelled in Vee's chest. She could tell he was mining the deepest reserves of his bravery and she rewarded him a steely, encouraging eye. His face crumpled and he tented his T-shirt at the neckline and dropped his head down into it.

Gaba stood behind him, one arm draped across his chest in a casual chokehold. In her other hand she gripped a knife with a chillingly sharp, thin blade. The knife hand was dead steady; she knew how to use it. 'Glad you could make it.' Gaba looked relaxed but her skittish eyes betrayed her. In the soft artificial lighting bouncing up from the street, her features made a strange spectacle, a mask of hollows and greys afloat in darkness. 'Give me your phone.'

Vee didn't protest. She pinched the Samsung out of her back pocket and tossed it. It landed amongst the gravel and rubble in the centre. Gaba grabbed Tristan's wrist and hauled him along as she walked. She pulled them both down to a crouch, picked up a heavy stone and smashed and smashed until the phone was a mass of brittle plastic and powdered glass. Vee winced. At least she was fastidious about backing up her data, especially the contacts list.

'Why am I here?' Vee said. 'Can't you self-destruct without an audience?'

Gaba advanced, snarling, the knife extended, her other arm clutching the front of Tristan's T-shirt. She wrung it into a knot in her fist, Tristan struggling in her grip. She gave an annoyed grunt as she snapped her arm down to her side, causing him to stumble. The sound of Tristan's jeans scraping along the cement as Gaba dragged him was one Vee would never forget; it was so reminiscent of the rasp of Gavin Berman's pants as his corpse swung outside a doorway. Tristan thrashed and shrieked. Gaba kept coming. The fabric of the shirt ripped.

'Stop!' Vee screamed. 'Please.'

Miraculously, Gaba complied. Tristan stayed down, keening. 'Oh, now you're listening. When there's nothing left. *Nothing*. Do you understand?' Gaba turned her head to profile and stared into the night with a disarming serenity. A few dreads had fallen free of her ponytail and dangled over her cheek. A breeze ruffled them back and forth against her skin in a caress, like a part of her was consoling her. She was a woman who had set sail in search of glory and strayed too far off course. 'I handed everything to them on a plate, my ideas, my creation, and they didn't have the decency...' Gaba shook her head. 'Assholes played me for a fool. Right under my own nose, and I didn't see it. Same as you. Had you—'

'Shut up! I don't care! You've got a knife on somebody's baby!' Vee felt her vocal cords tear a little.

'I'm not a baby,' Tristan sniffed from the ground.

'You lost me the second you did this. Tristan,' her voice dropped to a growl, 'get behind me.'

'No.' Gaba grabbed Tristan's shirt and hovered the blade near his neck.

Vee took a few steps closer. 'You won't.' She squinted at Tristan and issued a tiny nod. Gaba caught it and yanked him upright, but Tristan was faster. He wriggled out of the shirt and slithered bare-chested onto the concrete. Vee had but a split second to follow the pale blur of his skinny chest, her heart lifting as it dashed towards the stairs. A split second before Gaba held up a fistful of empty green shirt, flung it aside with a roar and charged.

Dammit. Vee braced herself. *I haven't done this shit since boarding school. And we didn't use knives.*

She ducked, knowing attackers instinctively threw all their weight behind their swing. Gaba plunged into empty air and staggered, nearly losing her balance. She jumped with fleet feet and swung again, barely missing Vee's upper arm. The knife made a "whzzzz!" as it sliced the night, advertising the extent of damage it would do if it hit flesh. Vee tottered and jabbed Gaba hard in the throat. It didn't do a world of damage but it left her gagging, her eyes watering. Vee had a few seconds to retreat and recalibrate.

The odds tallied against her, knife notwithstanding. She had the height, but the weight advantage swung the other way. To top it off, Gaba was inspiring in her agility, although she didn't cut the figure of a woman built for speed. Vee knew she was faster, but only by a small margin. Savvy was her only shot – creating a distraction, grabbing a makeshift weapon, a miracle from above. Gaba expertly edged her across the gravel square, away from the exit. Running for it was a rapidly shrinking opportunity.

Vee faked to the left and pretended to duck. Gaba swung hard, her jab nicking Vee's elbow and drawing a thin line of blood on the inside of her arm. Pain barely had a chance to register before Gaba barrelled towards her. She kicked Gaba in her stomach in the same instant Gaba swung her knife hand. This time it made contact, sinking into Vee's foot. Vee clenched her teeth in preparation for the exquisite pain of the blade gashing her foot open, but none came. She looked down in awe – they both did – and saw the blade sunk into the thick treads of her sneakers.

They looked up at each other, snorting hot air through their noses. Gaba launched herself once more, screaming and cursing. Vee dropped to a squat and shot out her fists like armed missiles. Gaba's face melted in surprise a split second before impact, but she couldn't slow down. As they collided, Vee gagged as Gaba's warm breast tissue enveloped her hands up to the wrists. Gaba let out a howl of anguish and flailed blindly, nearly bringing them both down. Vee shoved and Gaba slammed into the metal railing. The old metal fixture creaked and groaned as it loosened, a few rusty screws popping out of the crumbling brickwork.

Vee's shock morphed into cold horror as both Xoliswa Gaba, pinwheeling her arms, and the railing fell over the side.

Vee screamed and shot her arm into air, knowing it was pointless. She scrambled to the edge on knees and elbows. One end of the railing had detached, but the screws of the other side were holding fast. It grated and clanged as it lost momentum. By some miracle, Gaba's fingers were still wrapped around it. Vee crawled on her stomach and stretched out her arm. Gaba wasted no time grabbing on and digging her fingers into Vee's forearms. The railing gave a sickening groan under their combined weight.

'Fuuuck! Tristan! Monro! Tris— ugggh aarrrggghh!' Vee

cried. It felt like her arms were being yanked out at the shoulder joint.

'Miss Vee!' Footsteps pounded onto the balcony. Tristan surveyed the chaos, eyes huge as he raked his fingers through his hair. The railing gave another ominous groan. Tristan quickly climbed onto Vee's back, affording her traction by nailing her to the ground. He began hauling her in by her jeans.

A streak of black shot past and Vee nearly wept at the sight of her dog. Monro advanced to the edge, teeth bared, eyes lit with ferocity, his huge shoulders hunched in attack mode. A single bark and Gaba's expression dissolved in pure terror. Between the ground below and the dog she was clearly willing to take the former. Grunting in bursts, she kicked her legs, rattling the metal. Vee roared in pain, arms aching.

'Monro!'

The husky snarled and sniped at Gaba, muscles rippling as if he wanted to jump on the railing to reach her. At last, he tuned in to Vee's pleas and turned to study her. He stepped closer and gently closed his mouth around the soft flesh of her upper arm. Vee howled, more in shock than pain. Monro was forcing her to let go.

A series of low but audible calls and whistles floated up from the safety of the ground. The tag team had finally located them.

'Miss Vee! Just let her drop!' Tristan shouted.

'It's... too... far down,' she stammered, peering over. Was it? The longer she held on, the closer it looked. Her arms were logs ablaze with pain.

'There's two guys waiting underneath. She won't die! Let her go,' he sobbed.

Vee pulled Gaba off and yanked her arms back over the side, rust and gravel scraping her midsection. Gaba's fingers flailed and lost purchase on the railing.

A flash of gratification erupted in Vee's chest as Gaba's horrified eyes tumbled into darkness.

33

Takeoff was executed in a seamless, practically dream-like sequence, compared to takedown.

Tristan scraped the pulverised remains of her cell phone into his torn T-shirt and they raced downstairs. Vee was forced to stop a couple of times, once to yank the knife out of her sneaker before she tripped over her own feet and again to take a breather against the wall, rotating her shoulder blades and wincing. They retraced her steps, scooped up the access pass which she tossed the knife into, and shut the service entrance behind them. Neilson and his bewildered staff would deal with the unlocked door the next morning, as well as the busted railing on the roof if at all they ever ventured up there. The Mazda idled at the end of the lot. The two shadows made sure to show Gaba, alive and clearly in full-blown shock, bundled and shut in its boot.

The shadows exchanged frightened looks at Monro's presence. 'The dog,' protested the driver simply, surprising Vee by possessing a perfectly normal baritone. She did not want to think of these hulking shadows as real men, with voices and lives or wives, waiting for them to return home unscathed.

'He's with us. Drive,' she shut him down.

They swerved onto Main Road. She checked her watch, breathed a grateful prayer and leaned back. Fifty-two minutes.

Guy Richie pulled it off. Not once did an alarm or siren wail as they sped down the road.

They dropped her off right in front of her car. Vee tucked Tristan and Monro into the back seat of the Chrysler. She crossed the road again over to the other car and leaned in through the front passenger window of the Mazda. 'Remember what I said?' She looked hard into each of their faces in turn. 'She stays alive, no matter what.' Not-John nodded slowly. She handed him the envelope of cash and tapped the windscreen. Without another word, the engine gunned and they cut into the night. A short while later, Vee and her charges were let out in front of her car.

The car was a graveyard the rest of the short drive home to Leicester Street in Harfield. She took the 2nd Avenue entrance to her house, avoiding driving past Tristan's house. She parked in the garage, got out, let Monro out. The dog pattered into the yard and slumped onto his favourite spot on the lawn.

'I tried to get him to attack when you guys were fighting, but he just sat behind the door and wouldn't move. I tried to drag him—'

'He's my dog. He answers to me,' Vee replied flatly.

'Are you pissed?' Tristan whispered, dropping his eyes.

'*Am I pissed?*' Vee barked, banging the side gate. 'Let's review every warning I've *ever* given you, up against what just happened, and you decide!'

'I-I-I thought if...' Tristan backed away.

'You don't think!' Vee grabbed him by the shoulders. His bare skin burned her fingers. 'You act. You don't trust nobody, you don't stop to listen, *you act*. And you *never*, ever, give in to threats, no matter how serious.'

'I didn't know what else to do!'

'So you—'

'She knew where you worked! The street and building and everything.' Tears trailed a fresh route through the smudges on his cheeks. 'She described inside your house. She said she was gonna come back here wi—' his chest pumped up and down with laboured breaths, 'wi-wi-with her friends and *kill us*.' He swiped his eyes with a forearm and kept it up over his face. 'I thought if I did what she said, she wouldn't hurt you.'

The knot in her throat threatened to strangle her. 'Still. You stick to the rules. Run, scream, draw attention to yourself. A real sicko could've...' She hyperventilated. 'You don't protect me. I protect me, Monro protects me. I protect *you*. You can't go runnin' wild and actin' grown, tryna fix messes and fight villains. That's *my* job, and believe it or not, it stinks. You're not Nancy Drew's sidekick. You're 11, you're nobody's saviour!'

'You're not a saviour, either!' Tristan shouted back. Sobs shook him and Vee melted, wrapping her arms around his frail body. She felt a storm of her own gathering, but she flared her nostrils and blinked it back. She held him and let him sob it out, his head in her neck as she knelt on the lawn.

He pulled away when the tank was empty, his breath coming in ragged bursts. He grabbed near his navel as if to lift his shirt to wipe his face, then remembered he didn't have one on and used his palms. They blinked at each other, the silence of the garden enveloping them, and Vee realised if anyone happened by and saw a black woman hugging a half-naked white kid on a dark night, she'd rot in jail for three lifetimes. She smiled weakly, and Tristan smiled back. A look wavered in his iron-grey eyes like he was holding something back.

'What?' She shrugged. 'Jeh tell me. I nah vex any more.'

He sniffled. 'Who's Nancy Drew? Does she live on our street? Is she the coloured lady with the Rottweiler we hate?'

Vee slowly closed her eyes. 'Jesus wept,' she murmured, pulling him in for another hug.

She forced him into her bathroom to get cleaned up. While he showered, she dressed the gash on her arm, swallowed a couple of Panados, then unzipped the access pass, careful not to touch Gaba's knife. She stared at it, not sure what to do next. Finally, she fished it out with her hand inside a Ziploc bag and turned it inside out, then stashed it in a shoebox behind a stack of old clothes at the back of her closet. A problem for another day. Tristan emerged in his jeans and sneakers, and she practically had to sit on him to blow-dry his hair. She threw one of her smallest T-shirts at him.

'This?' he scoffed, holding it aloft like a diseased rag. 'No ways. It's for girls.'

'Put it on. You're going home, not entering a beauty contest.'

He read her face and eased it over his head, looking sour. 'This sucks. It's pink.'

She eyed the look. It was no collage of superheroes like his had been, but it would do. 'Stop whining. You know who your Ma named you after?'

'Ag man, how many times do I have to hear this...'

'Hush up. Tristan Ludlow, *Legends of the Fall*. One of the finest roles ever played by one of the sexiest, most talented actors ever. You think Brad Pitt would stand around yapping about wardrobe or he'd step up like a hero?'

'Brad Pitt is old. Bet he couldn't do his own stunts like I did tonight,' Tristan muttered.

Vee pushed his head out the door.

———

'Thank you. So, so much,' Kara Heaney murmured, pressing Vee's hand between hers. The woman's eyes even misted a little with gratitude.

Vee felt like a fraud and held her smile long as she could. She looked away at the front yard. It looked clean enough, but too many odds and ends were littered about; unused bricks likely fallen off a wall somewhere, empty paint cans, a battered wooden crate and the skeleton of a bicycle. Perhaps someone had tried to de-clutter a garage and lost heart. Several stones were missing off the cobbled walk. The lawn was broken up into islands of dying grass, like patches of disgruntled, yellowing pubes. *This ruffian needs to stay home more and help his mother,* Vee mused with feeling. Gardening and caretaking – new addition to the list of valuable skills for young miscreants. 'Ah, well. What are neighbours for?'

Kara nodded, blinking back the mist. 'I haven't been much of a neighbour, have I?'

Vee shook her head emphatically. 'There's a lot on your plate. And it's never easy after… It's not easy. Especially with boys.'

'They're a terrible lot, aren't they?'

'The worst,' Vee laughed, then sobered. 'It takes time.'

Kara nodded. 'I should talk to him about the incident with the neighbourhood kids.' She jerked a thumb behind her at the front door, through which Tristan had instantly ducked when they arrived.

'No!' Vee jumped a little at her voice in the quiet street. 'Nah, let him sleep. He'll talk about it when he's ready. His wrist will be sore. He stood up for himself when those kids tried to take his phone. He fought bravely.'

'I can imagine.' Kara cast a glance back at the house, as if imagining her warrior child within. 'He's a fighter. Like his dad was.'

Vee trudged home. A hot upwelling of tears pushed up her throat as she latched the gate behind her. She sank onto the first step of the veranda, pulled her knees up to her face and broke down. Monro trotted over, nudging her and whimpering. She wrapped her arms around his neck and sobbed.

A Suffering

34

Xoliswa Gaba was dead. Suicide.

'In all honesty, I'm not that shocked, really,' Akhona Moloi remarked hoarsely. Her vocal projection had marginally improved over the weekend. 'This could only have gone one way, down a path to complete destruction. What else lay ahead after all the havoc she caused? Did she have the backbone to face prison, if she couldn't create a law-abiding life on the outside?' She sniffed. 'May Jehovah not strike me down, but perhaps it's better this way. Hell has finally ended for all of us.'

'Did she reach out to you? Before she...'

'To *me*? What – why? I didn't even know where or when it happened.'

A sour taste coated the back of Vee's throat as she said the words out loud for the first time: 'Yesterday, Sunday. When it happened, I mean. The body was only discovered today at daybreak, at her aunt's house. She must have gone to hide out there after...' *After our encounter. Where I threw her off a roof.* Guilt had set up residence in her chest, started logging serious hours and she couldn't shake it off. One thing she did know for certain, neither she nor Uzo nor his hired muscle were responsible for Gaba's death. Uzo's men had deposited Gaba in one piece somewhere in the township with nothing more than a stern warning: messing with Voinjama Johnson is messing with us, and you don't want that. Go home, get your head right, move on. It seemed Xoliswa Gaba had decided to go home on a permanent basis.

She pinched the bridge of her nose. All weekend, a headache had set up cosy digs between her eyes, and she knew it would remain there until… She would have to call her grandmother, and find out the cleansing and realignment rites she needed to perform. 'Did she at any point give you any clue to what she was planning?'

'I don't know what you're getting at.'

A weird trickle rode the length of Vee's spine. 'Nothing. It's just surprising she gave up without a last-ditch effort. She had you on the hook for a nice sum, why not take it and walk? Actually… there was this lingering impression she had more up her sleeve than she let on.' She gave an empty chuckle. 'Like she was waiting for the perfect moment to play a trump card. I don't know. Guess there wasn't one after all.'

'She overestimated herself, that one. In life, you pick your battles.'

Vee sat up straighter. The damage to her throat made her sound different, true, but Moloi also sounded… icier.

'Anyway. Never speak ill of the dead,' Moloi said, instantly breezier. 'I only wish she'd accepted we did everything we could do for her instead of… taking this route.'

'True. It's so terrible and final.'

'Ja, hey. But don't feel like it's your fault! Don't blame yourself.'

'I—'

'You, me, Gavin, we all did, *tried to do*, what was in our power. It's all one can ever do. These things play out as they will.' The connection muffled. Conversations floated around in the background, Moloi's gravelly whine threaded with two other excited voices. 'I'm sorry, Voinjama, I really must go. There's a lot to catch up on. I'm allowing myself a few more days' bed rest then it's back on the horse. Holiday's over, I'm afraid.'

After she hung up, Vee sat tapping a pen against her desk for a long time, thinking.

———

The next day, Tuesday, she had all but forgotten about it.

'I can't say, Darren. Chlöe didn't come to work yesterday. I don't expect to see her today either.' Vee nodded through the stream of complaints Darren poured into her ear. 'Yes, I do get it. But I'm not comfortable putting it up without her seeing her drafts. Give it till this evening. Yeah fine, do that updated version on the reactions to the suicide and new developments that I wrote yesterday, it should do for now. Understood. I'll…'

She leaned down, the Dell propped on her dining table in the lounge. An email from Richie, with the subject line "Intrigue and subterfuge", popped into her inbox. She opened the attachment. It was an article, or snippet of one, from a web magazine. Vee read the first few lines, lost interest and minimised the browser window. Despite the relatively well-oiled success of four nights ago, she didn't have a palate for Guy Richie at present. How many times had she told him that, beyond the latest smartphone or laptop, she and Chlöe didn't give a rat's ass about advances in geekdom?

A minute later, her spine snapped straight. She maximised the attachment again.

'… could be our best option. They play off each other much better that way,' Darren was saying.

'Mm-hhm. Febs, let me call you back. In fact, I'll be in the office in a couple of hours.'

The piece she read was short and concise, a mere informational highlight in the breaking news shorts. 'What does it *mean*?' she asked the empty room. She re-read, mouthing it out loud line by line, tilted her head back to frown at the ceiling, then her eyes widened. After the third time, she flopped back down in the chair. 'Well, I'll be a horse's ass backwards…' she whispered.

The security door was smashed in. Vee walked through it several times, into the building and then back outside onto the street, studying it from every angle. She ran her fingers over the metal frame and conchoidal ring of fractured glass, wishing she had the Nikon or any of the office cameras on her. She glared at the Motorola flip phone in her hand, a loan from her friend Connie, in disgust. The damned thing worked well enough, but it was a model that didn't exist any more, a mascot of a bygone era before phones had cameras and dinosaurs evolved into birds.

'Sisi, if you explain to me what you are looking for, maybe I can help you,' the security guard offered.

She glanced up at the awning of B&M Financial. What were her other options? What did any of it matter now? It was all too bloody late. 'Erm, is Ms Moloi here?'

He shook his head. 'She will be back maybe next week. Terrible thing happened to her on the premises. That's why this here,' he touched the hole in the glass door, 'is damaged like this. She was attacked in her office. Violence, too much violence these days.'

'So there was a break-in?' She knew the answer already.

'What?! Ai, ai, sisi, no. No one can break into this building just like that. There's this door, and also the security gate. Once you enter and close, you'll be safe inside as long as you want.'

'But someone can get inside if you forget to lock it.'

He shook his head again. 'The security company installed the proper stuff. You can never be too safe in town. Even if you forget to close this gate,' he rattled the iron cage that was drawn aside, 'this door,' he tapped the heavy glass, 'will automatically close behind you. That's why we leave it open during the day, so people can just walk in.' The door was held open by a heavy cement block. 'You can't open it from the outside. This handle can only lift and open from inside.' He lifted and lowered the metal bar across the door's breadth to demonstrate how it served as both handle and release lever. Up, open; down, locked.

'Then who smashed the glass?'

'The paramedics. Ms Moloi managed to make an emergency call, but they couldn't get upstairs. They tried to smash the door. Someone had to alert the security office and they quickly sent someone with special tools to unblock the mechanism. Then they went upstairs to help Ms Moloi. We heard she couldn't even move. It was terrible.'

'Why wasn't one of you around?'

The guard shrugged. 'She cancelled the security last Wednesday. She was thinking about closing the account. Now look, something like this happens to teach you a lesson. I can tell you, she'll renew it and get this door replaced chop-chop.'

Vee wasn't listening. It felt like she'd been punched in the stomach.

———

Vee plucked the copy of *Brainstorm* off the array of magazines fanned atop the reception area's table at The IT Factor's office. She had driven around for an hour looking for one, and also to cool down. And here it was, in print. It was always the last place you looked. Every road led back to this office from the outset, and she hadn't seen it.

The receptionist perked up. 'Ooh, that's a hugely popular IT and software magazine. And it's locally owned and features local companies like ours. They actually did a small feature on us this month.'

'You don't say,' Vee said, closing the magazine over her index finger as a placeholder. 'I need to see Ryan Walsh immediately. Don't mind me, I know the way.'

'Um, I don't think…' the receptionist began, rising halfway from her chair.

'He's not in.' Aneshree Chowdri stood in the mouth of the

corridor, blocking it. One look at her face and Vee knew that she knew that she knew. Right then, any resemblance Aneshree bore to Joshua scattered like ash. Why had she thought that? This girl didn't have his long-bridged nose with a talent for flaring when he was being sarcastic, or his kind, teasing eyes. Hers was a mask of deceit.

Vee walked up to her and leaned in close. 'Tell you what. You step aside, and help keep this process as civil as possible.'

Aneshree flattened herself against the wall. She jawed the air, her heavy lashes eating up her face the wider her eyes got, like spiders attempting to climb her forehead. 'We're not forced to talk to you.'

'Ah. But it's a sound idea if you do.'

'I… we never thought… This wasn't meant to happen. I couldn't… wasn't really involved. I knew as much as I was told.' She wrapped her arms around herself. 'This is my job. I just did my job.'

We all did our jobs. Never stopping to ask the right questions. Spinning cogs in flawless machinery. Vee brushed past, leaving Aneshree staring after her as she went down the hall. She got to the door of Walsh's office and took a deep breath. As she reached for the handle, a passing employee called out to stop her. He caught the expression on her face, clamped his lips together and kept walking.

Walsh looked different. It wasn't just the switch from a suit back to jeans and T-shirt, the uniform his entire hive seemed hellbent on adhering to, one he was clearly more comfortable in. He looked settled somehow, calm. Mellow. He stood at the window, hovering over a refreshments tray. She clicked the door shut behind her and he turned. For all of one second, a surprised grin lit his face. Vee gave nothing in return. His smile crumbled like a bulldozer striking a high-rise. He collected himself, reset his jaw in stone, brought his lips together in a tight line. He set a steaming mug on the tray, eyes never wavering from hers.

'It's good to see you again. How have you been?'

Her pulse thumped in her ears. 'How *have* I been?' She dropped her chin to her chest and laughed at the floor. 'I can't rightly say, Ryan. This past, almost two weeks is it...' she did the maths in her head in terms of fact-checks and edits and copy edits, '... to call it a rollercoaster would be unjust. Do you think "gobsmacked" is too theatrical?'

'Voinjama...'

'Stick to Vee, asshole,' Vee snarled.

His cheeks ripened. 'I can understand how you'd be upset.'

'*Upset,* ehn? That's too bland, try again.'

He simply stared.

'I'm being inconsiderate. Because as exciting as it's been for me, you'd probably call this past two weeks nothing short of epic.' She waved the *Brainstorm.* 'I bet everyone in the office got a free copy today. You guys must be super excited. Should I read it out loud or is that overkill?' She didn't wait for his answer and read:

"Digital hype often seems to centre around PCs, mobile devices and their apps. That's about to change – enter financial and auditing software. The ugly duckling of tech could soon outshine its prettier, more popular sister. A new and positively ground-breaking technology that takes the nightmare out of empowerment compliance may soon be available to the business community. The aptly named BEE Scalpel touts itself as a sharp, diverse and user-friendly platform that will span all BEE services. It is also no small chest-pounding moment that the proud parents behind the genesis of this brainchild are local outfits, in the form of Berman & Moloi Financial and local whiz kid The IT Factor.

"Both companies have received some eyebrow-raising press of late due to their involvement in LEAD, which is heading in the direction of another investment scandal. In the wake of the tragic death of B&M's director Gavin Berman, it's a ray of hope that the business landscape still respects and recognises independent innovation. It's not yet clear how widely the software will be marketed. There's a good feeling, though, considering the buzz around empowerment hasn't always smelled of roses. Looks like the potential for expansion here could add some much-needed shine to a fading rainbow."

'Sit down and hear me out.' His voice was fragile.

'You…' Vee twisted her mouth but couldn't dredge up an insult scathing enough. 'Murderer. All of you. You conspired to kill that woman.'

Walsh's expression changed from hurt to thunderstruck. 'I've never hurt a fly in my life! Insult me all you want, but hear me out. We both know you won't leave until you have.'

She slipped her hands, shaky, into her pockets, but didn't move towards a chair. She didn't leave either.

35

'I asked how you were feeling, because I truly am concerned,' Walsh said.

'What, are you worried you might have another emotionally unstable woman on your hands?' Vee replied. She slowly raised her head, trying to stay calm. Her hands wouldn't stop shaking. 'I didn't come here to flip out on you. I need to know how you let this happen, how much you knew. Because I just realised how *stupid* I've been.' Appalled by a sting of tears, she half-turned and squeezed her eyes shut. Walsh moved towards her and she glared him to a standstill. 'Gaba *killed herself* over this. I saw her, before she…'

He looked away, turning back to the window. A dry chuckle shook her shoulders. Of course he knew about her final encounter with Xoliswa Gaba. Moloi knew. Vee saw it on his face, right then, the same way she'd heard it in Moloi's voice. They'd known from the beginning. How could she not have seen?

'Gaba wanted to tell me, tried to, but as usual her M.O. left a lot to be desired. I'm only filling in blanks now.' Vee took a deep breath. 'Once upon a time there was a very bright girl. Kind of messed up, but fine is the line between brilliant and insane. Girl cons her way into a sweet job, perks, advancement, the works. Most of all, into a makeshift family. But Girl, like all of us, is a creature of habit. She's a fighter and a taker. Maybe she knew she was being used, but she thought she had the upper hand. She didn't. She was up against two, or should I say three, masterminds on the other team.'

His expression shifted a minute degree. 'I left out all the good parts for you to colour in. Call me a coward, but I don't have the energy to confront Moloi. She won't subject herself to this. Not when she's in the clear, and clearly has no conscience.' she concluded.

He nodded, silent for so long she wondered if he intended to respond. There was nothing compelling him to; he could order her off his premises. He lifted his head and had the audacity to look haunted. Vee wanted to break his nose. 'Off the record?' he asked softly.

She laughed. 'Yes. Why not?'

Walsh ran a hand through his hair. His haircut was overgrown; in a few days he'd be as bushy as when they first met at the lodge. He pushed aside a stack of paperwork and perched on the edge of the desk. 'Firstly, I'm sorry. You may not trust where that's coming from, but it's sincere.'

'Don't you dare,' she said, jaw working.

He trained his eyes on his hands, intertwining fingers and scratching a thumb over his palm as if trying to scrape off debris or dead skin. 'We didn't *mastermind* this, at least I didn't. That suggests a deplorably malevolent level of premeditation, and I'd never be a part of something like that.' The role of mastermind was already taken, said the look he shot her. Vee felt a chill down her back, the memory rising in her mind of Moloi blinking behind glasses like a befuddled nocturnal creature rising in her mind. 'That much I can say for myself, though it won't alleviate my conscience, which, believe me, I do possess. All of this started from an idea. One idea that started as a light-hearted conversation over a boring business lunch, and sprouted into a product.

'Naturally, LEAD threw us into the same sphere,' he continued. 'Berman immediately struck me as a gambler with a sharp mind and an ear to the streets. Whether he knew LEAD would come to nought or not, who can say. He had enough BEE crooks as golf buddies to know where the money was and how to tease it out. He was fed up with lengthy rigmarole and wanted to walk out of there with more than he'd come in with. Akhona followed wherever Gavin went, they were a package deal. We got chatting sometime early last year, during the World Cup, about projects we'd poured our resources into over our careers. The fruitless endeavours and what-ifs. Gavin let on about a tool that his IT guys had developed but he'd never run with; time, capital, R&D being what it is. He asked me to take a look, see if it had wings. Moloi was uncomfortable with the idea but at the time I didn't read much into it. He gave me one of the most incredible developments I'd seen in a while. Simple, cross-cutting, very now. Once it was in front of me I almost kicked myself for not having thought of it myself.'

'The Scalpel.'

'Yes. Gavin christened it that.' Walsh's smile curdled, as if the irony of a man who met a murderous end coming up with a name steeped in violence didn't escape him. 'A program that needed work, but made us business partners. In a nutshell, the software is a BEE evaluation tool. Not every company has the time or resources to fork out for a full evaluation, not knowing beforehand their readiness for the market. Scalpel's a turnkey system that does an all-in-one job. Computing raw data on a company's current status, summing up potential, verifying portfolios and paperwork for a scorecard, finding ways to bolster an existing scorecard. You name it. With fine-tuning, the proper backing and recognition from the accreditation boards, it'll be the first of its kind to do it all.'

'And private businesses and auditors could lease the software and use it on site for their own evaluations, meaning endless knock-on profits for you,' Vee added. 'Hell, even the government could pimp it as a standard platform. Of course, a system like that eats raw brainpower. You'd need personnel for everything, from data input on up. Trained personnel, the kind B&M's consultancy provides. They needed you as much as you did them. All bases covered, all backs scratched.'

'Yes.' Walsh blinked at her, delight and *attraction* in his eyes. Vee felt sick. 'Long story short, I'd handle the nerdy component, they'd provide the financial expertise. It was all set to run smoothly.'

'Until a pesky oversight in the shape of Xoliswa Gaba, the actual creator, reared its ugly head.'

Walsh clenched his jaw. 'She was their best programmer, and she'd learnt to work way outside her scope. She was a rare thing – in effect, a systems developer. System software starts with a prototype, a blueprint if you will. Lines of code; which command performs what function, push here to start. A lot of research goes into the early stages: system architecture, logical design, data modelling. Then finally there's the physical implementation. After PI comes beta testing, checking what you've done is functioning.' He eyed her and she nodded that she was following. 'In a company setup, like here, these steps are a team effort. But Gaba did it, with very little outside help. When she was confident enough with what she had, she launched a beta test, the first raw version of the software. As her superiors, Gavin and Akhona oversaw the process.'

'And not long after they relieved her of it, and of her job too.' Now Vee understood the seat of Gaba's outrage, her inability to let sleeping dogs lie. They'd excised a piece of her soul and gone running. 'She completed it—'

'No, she did not complete it,' Walsh parried emphatically. 'I'd never have looked at it if it were that advanced.'

'That would've been stealing. You wouldn't feed off a worker bee's glory, would you.'

He showed the first flash of anger. 'You clearly don't have a grasp on how this works. We had to do a gap analysis, assess limitations, overhaul the original formatting. We customised it. Trained analysts in how to use it... a ton of extra work before it went live! The IT Factor put the heart and soul into what was essentially a skeleton.'

'You're just saying words. I bet Gavin and Akhona made all the right noises too. Patted her on the head and said B&M didn't have the resources to see it through. Next thing she knew, she was out on her ass,' Vee said, glad to have got a rise out of him. 'Companies have an ironclad clause in their contracts: intellectual property remains theirs if an idea or product is developed during the course of employment. Maybe she could've fought it, but she slunk off, defeated. Years later you breeze in with the likes of Aneshree up your sleeve and take it to the finish line. And I'm supposed to believe you were completely in the dark.'

'Look, I swear to you, I had no idea how badly they treated her.' He saw her expression and ducked his eyes. 'Maybe... I could've probed. It did feel too good to be true and... I didn't want to rock the boat with too many questions. Berman wanted more money, and I wanted to make a beautiful product. I saw nothing wrong with that. Until Berman started hemming and hawing about its genesis. I nipped it in the bud asap. He knew from the get-go – I don't do subpar work with shoddy tools or shifty partners. He had to come clean about Gaba. She was an issue firmly in their camp and they had to handle it. I didn't want any blurry ethical boundaries.'

'Oh, they handled it. After she got wind they were raising her brainchild from the dead, she be damned she wasn't getting played. The first bribe was meant to fill her eyeball and get rid of her, but no chance. She wanted a fight.'

'I wasn't in the loop about blackmail and bribes till it was too late. I tried to stay out of it. *They* advised me to stay out of it. Meddling would drive the situation to critical mass that much more quickly.'

'It went to critical mass anyway! You didn't stay out of it to *help*. Covering your ass fell in line with protecting your sanctified name.'

'That's not true.' He stood and rammed his hands into the pockets of his jeans.

'Bullshit. Why didn't you pull the plug, or wait? Wasn't Berman's murder enough of a red flag, or have you talked yourself past that too?' Vee didn't realise she was shouting until the door creaked open a few inches and half of a colleague's frowning face poked in, murmuring, 'What's going on? Is everything—'

'Piss off!'Walsh barked, and the door banged shut immediately.

'Did you even suspect it, when Moloi started playing the puppeteer?'

'This isn't…' He shut his eyes and inhaled deeply. 'It's not how you're making it sound.'

'My bad. I have a flair for the dramatic when dead bodies keep dropping around me,' she said. She walked towards him, and felt no small measure of triumph when he shuffled away, a tint of fear in his eyes. 'There are no wealthy morons, Ryan. My yearly income's probably your monthly toilet paper budget, so sell that shit somewhere else. I get it, I should've connected the dots. Akhona strung me along, *strung me up*, yet I didn't see it. She made me before I made her, smelled my desperate journalist vibe and fed it. Sat back while I built a half-assed story around a mysterious disc full of gibberish. She was probably laughing the whole time, knowing what was on it was like looking through a keyhole and trying to describe the room on the other side. I didn't see who was really laying down the breadcrumbs for me to follow. Hell, why should I complain? I got the scoop. She just made sure it was after everything was in the bag.'

'We all hedged our bets, far too heavily, I see that now.' He looked distant, like he was talking to himself.

'But you had your doubts, didn't you, soon after the murder,' Vee pressed. 'And my attack. It didn't add up. Besides Berman, who was dead, the only people at that lodge who knew of the disc's existence were you, Akhona and Aneshree. You had Aneshree sniffing around like your pet bloodhound, I'm guessing because the disc was work product for her anyway. So who had Gaba on a leash? Who put blood in the water? Moloi. I know it knocked around that big brain of yours. You knew Gaba was being manipulated... but why would she allow it, why didn't she fight back? Why didn't she ever come after *you*? She had it in her. The answer is crystal clear. Gaba was being kept in check with either a threat or a promise, by someone who spoke her language. With Gavin out of the picture, nobody *but* Akhona wielded that kind of power.'

'No.' Walsh shook his head slowly, like a man coming out of a reverie, then faster, eyes hardening to cold stones. He pushed off the edge of the desk and strutted behind it. He didn't sit; all he needed was a method of forging distance. 'No. Don't you dare insinuate that I, we, colluded to remove Berman and foist blame on that troubled woman. That's beyond low and ludicrous.'

'Moloi did the heavy lifting, Ryan. Granted, she cared about Gavin too much to go as far as executing him herself. But she hadn't gauged how disturbed Gaba truly was, and once it clicked, she saw her advantage. Controlling Xoli must've been like riding a tsunami, but she had to try.' Vee eyed him long and hard. 'What's she told you? Akhona? That it was a coincidence Gaba came to The Grotto? Bet she said Gaba heard it through the grapevine, or that Gavin let it slip that y'all were working on a major contract up there that would effectively cut her out. But I bet my life Akhona was the one who told her, threw it in her face what was happening. She knew what Gaba's stressors were. "Your ex-lover's trying to screw you one last time." It would've been her one chance to get back at Gavin for mixing business with pleasure, not to mention ignoring her feelings for him. All she had to do was goad Gaba, and the drama began.'

'That's ridiculous. How on earth could she have twisted her into doing all this?'

'Because she's that good. And Gaba was that broken,' Vee answered simply. 'I can't prove it, but Moloi has hard proof that Gaba killed Berman. All she had to do was blackmail her to stay in line and keep her mouth shut. Maybe threw in more promises of money. Dangle, dangle.' Vee heaved a leaden sigh. 'Even if Gaba wanted to back out, she couldn't. She tried leading me to water, but I wouldn't drink. Moloi... who'd believe *her* capable of this?'

'Exactly. You're wrong. Akhona Moloi behind some Machiavellian plot? Jerking us all, *me*, around? Yeah right.' He laughed but it rang hollow. His face darkened again. 'She couldn't possibly...'

'Come on! Ask your new business partner how she really got her injuries. I learnt a lot about security doors and spindle-lock mechanisms today. Ask her, how an intruder managed to *break into her office* without actually breaking in. How Gaba got around an alarm system and two security doors... or if Moloi simply let her up herself. The whole attack was staged. But Moloi forgot the door, and to be honest it's a detail no one's bothered to check. We're all too busy feeling sorry for her.'

Walsh was ashen. He leaned on his desk, weight propped on white knuckles, emotions rioting across his face. He whirled to the window again. When he turned around, his expression made Vee feel a tiny bit sorry for him. 'Why... I don't... *Why?*' he said.

'Why *not?* The whale of her career is under her nose, jeopardised by one rogue element. She needed Gaba shut down. Well, Gaba's been shut down.'

Walsh massaged his temples, making his hair stand on end even more. 'I told them to send her to me. We could've incorporated her into my team, hired her as a private consultant. I was willing to prepare a package to smooth any ruffled feathers—'

'"Send her to me". The grand summons from the IT king.' Vee jerked a shoulder in a bitter shrug. 'They didn't. You were *willing* and they weren't.'

'How dare you stand here flinging smug accusations?' The mask slipped completely, revealing a man battling fury, shame, apprehension and, behind it all, fear. 'Did you have a different ending in mind? Perhaps I should've been so blinded by the urge to fuck you that I'd run to you to spill my guts? And then what? Your self-serving union of muckrakers get their scoop and to hell with the deal, my reputation, potentially my company?' This time he was the one who advanced, pushing away from the desk, his legs eating up the carpet in two strides till he loomed over her. His lip curled. 'I guess that makes us both mercenary. We'd both trade afterglow for our own ends. Good thing we never acted on it.'

'Wow.' Vee smiled bitterly. 'May I remind you of your words to me not long ago, how you're great at finding toys with which to amuse,' she said. Petty satisfaction swelled in her again when he flushed with embarrassment. 'Amusement come at a price. Watch your back, maestro. Gavin and Gaba left theirs to the breeze.' She tossed the magazine onto his desk, gratified when it skidded and knocked over his mug, splashing coffee onto the cream carpet.

Outside in the canopied parking of the office park, his Audi Z4 crouched like a smug bluebottle fly in one of the reserved slots. Vee shot furtive glances around the lot before digging her car keys deep into the paint job. 'Fuckwit,' she muttered, sprinting to her car as the alarm screamed to life.

36

'Hey.'

'Hey,' Vee replied reflexively, not looking up. She jerked a little when she did.

'So I heard a joke this week,' Chlöe said, giving the awkward silence no room to breathe. 'A white guy, another white guy, a black woman, *another* black woman, and an Indian chick all walk into a police station to report a murder. The cop on duty looks at them and shakes his head, like "Seerias? Ag nee, man! If you want to report a true rainbow nation crime at this station, you need to involve a cripple or the president."'

Vee didn't laugh but her smile was genuine. 'That's a terrible joke. I think it'll be a long while before any disabled people go around committing high-profile murders. What, like Oscar Pistorius is suddenly going to flip out and run someone over with his bionic legs? I think not.'

'Anything can happen. We're Mzansi, for sure.' Chlöe flicked a finger, indicating she wanted to enter. At Vee's nod she inched in, scanning the space. Compact, but nice. Definitely cleaner. The desk and chair were fresh additions. The metal sink was scrubbed clean and there was even a shiny electric kettle. Van Wyk wasn't going to like any of this.

'Nico's gonna flip out.'

'Not on us. The newest members of the online team, who just cracked the biggest fraud case *City Chronicle* has ever handled. We even got a raise, *I* got a new office,' Vee spread her arms around at the cramped splendour, 'we're sailing. For now, at least.'

'For now. Guess that's more than we can hope for. At least you finally located his funny bone today. Major cool points on the lunch idea, I must say.'

Vee had circulated an office email, detailing her full awareness of the rumours that she took an "incentive" during the Paulsen case. Being magnanimous of spirit, she was willing to share her ill-gotten gains with all and sundry. Economic downturn and rand value being what it was, though, the full extent of her muster was toasted sarmies and fizzy drinks, delivered to the office at lunchtime. The staff had found it hugely amusing. For the first time ever, they looked her in the eye, and with respect.

They fell silent, letting the room soak in it. Chlöe pretended to admire the decor, letting her gaze roam to the framed photographs and news clippings mounted on the wall. Vee had put up her favourite personal photos, her greatest hits, in understated frames. Pride of place was her first major assignment on xenophobic violence and an opinion piece from her early freelancer days which featured in a major editorial in New York. There were a couple of group snapshots of workshops Vee had attended, with eager young minds huddled around Elizabeth Blunt in the first, who Chlöe knew was a major deal for her coverage of civil unrest, and Christiane Amanpour in the second. Chlöe had seen all the photos many times before, but she pored over them. She knew her face was being examined, that Vee was wondering why she, a beast with a makeup brush, had barely made an effort to disguise the fading bruise on her jawline. Chlöe wanted her to feel guilty. She turned around suddenly and was gratified to catch a flash of remorse in Vee's eyes, before she looked away.

'I didn't expect you back today. Thought you'd ride out the

week till next Monday,' Vee cleared her throat, breaking the spell.

'Oh, I wanted to. Being a couch potato is dead boring. Gave me a taste of what I'd be facing if I *did* quit in a fit of pique.' A muddle of expressions flickered over Vee's face at the concept, but she said nothing. 'Anyway. I had to deliver this personally. I took a blood oath.'

Vee took the package. Her brows arched ever so slightly when she lifted the ripped flap of the envelope, which Chlöe hadn't bothered to replace. Their eyes met for a heartbeat, then Vee pressed on, lifting out its contents. She shuffled through the stack, not poring over any particular one, her face a wall throughout. She set them aside and walked around the desk, a single one in hand. When they were standing side by side, Chlöe saw it was an 8×6 cm photograph.

'That's my brother,' Vee said, tapping a corner. A man hunched on a stoop in what could barely be called a courtyard of a dilapidated building. The shot wasn't clear, but it looked like he was washing clothes in a large metal basin. Other people in attire just as bedraggled milled about in the corners.

I know, Chlöe wanted to say, but stopped herself. Something on Vee's face, or the nothing on Vee's face, shut her up. She let the stillness roll on and over, feeling it slicing the belly of some nameless thing open.

'This guy,' Vee tapped again, 'he's a helluva person. There was this time,' she settled onto the desk and Chlöe slid up beside her, 'right after the war, when we finally got reunited. We were in the refugee camp in Ghana – Buduburam. It was no vacation spot, let me tell you. Terrible in those days, not an ideal place for kids. My mother sent us to live with relatives, someplace better and safer, while she stayed in a hostel for refugees. The relatives had a nice house, they fed us well, never mistreated us, but...'

'They weren't your mother.' Chlöe understood. For all

her maternal hang-ups, she wouldn't trade her mother for the world.

Vee nodded. 'Not even close. We hadn't always lived together, all three of us in the same house, grandmother included. Those last years of the eighties when we had that, man, they were the best. We understood things had to be different in exile, but not *that* different. So we took a bus, several buses, by ourselves with the few bags of clothes we had, and set out to find our mother. My brother made sure no one stole from us or hassled me all the way there. And he got us there intact. I didn't think for a second I had anything to worry about, but I look back and realise he was no more than a child himself at the time. Seventeen, looking out for a twelve-year-old. Quentin could always find me, protect me.'

Vee took a long pause, so long Chlöe thought the story was over.

'The only time he couldn't... no one could have. The civil war came down hot on everybody, people saw it coming but they didn't at the same time. It got crazy so fast, I was separated from my family. One day I was a kid with honour roll and schoolroom dramas rattling round my juvenile brain, a yard to play in after school, fresh food daily. And the next...'

Chlöe swallowed. 'Did you kill someone? When you tried to escape the rebels. Is that why you never talk about any of it? I understand if...'

'Do you?' Vee gave her a confused look, tinged with kindness. 'I still don't. I never will. You're not meant to have words to explain everything life throws at you. Leftover human beings. Souls tossed by the roadside or rotting in swamps, piled up like meat. Being in a dark room for days, not knowing if you'll ever get out.' Her voice dropped so low it was nearly inaudible. 'Having unimaginable things said and done to you.'

Her eyes carried a weight Chlöe had never seen. 'No, I

wasn't... violated. Not physically...not really. But I was married. Ha! Believe that if you will.' Vee stared ahead, her face pulled in an indescribable arrangement. 'A war wife. They grabbed girls from all over and herded us together. Cook, clean, wash, service them. The ones they had no use for, they killed. The lucky ones died of their own volition. Like those ancestors on the ships, you know, who couldn't bear the thought of slavery, brutality, separation...so they jumped overboard to release themselves. The rest of us who lived, if some boy hopped up on drugs took a shine to you, that was it. My "husband" was only 14. Had crazy eyes for me on the first day. I tried escaping... nearly made it. Nearly. Nearly killed him trying to.' A horrified squeak came from inside the office and it took several seconds for Chlöe to realise it came from her mouth. Vee hardly seemed to notice. 'He kept razor eyes on me after that,' she continued. 'Used to take me into a room and lie on top of me. Just lie there, erect and everything, with no idea what to do. We were children. That time... it's like a fucked-up fever dream that happened to somebody else.'

She held up the photograph again. 'This Quincy is my brother, and not my brother at the same time. He's recovering his old self, too.' Vee caressed it with delicate fingers and soft eyes. 'He has a four-year-old,' she spread out the stack and plucked out another shot, 'my niece. Guinean mother. I need to find them. This is why I need Lovett.' She indicated the entire spread of snapshots. 'Lovett can root up a whole graveyard if need be, damn the consequences.'

'Yes. Okay.' Chlöe nodded, trying to understand, but really she didn't. This was fathoms out of her depth. She liked her own brother only sometimes and her sister, well, that bordered on bloody never.

'My life is a spider story, Bishop. A winding tale of never-ending happenstance. Things you can't unhear once they're out there.' She gave Chlöe a last, long look, then pushed off the desk. 'I'm just saying.'

'I hear you.' Chlöe hopped off, too. 'Gladys.' She gave a slow, evil grin.

Vee fought a smile. "Oh, you sneaky wench. See, this is why I don't tell you anything. My parents were huge Motown fans, okay. Quincy Jones and Gladys Knight, that was their inspiration for naming their children.'

'Jesus. There *are* things I'd rather not know about you,' Chlöe said.

Epilogue

Trevor Davids impatiently stabbed the fast-forward button on the remote, casting a wary glance at Zintle Msengwana. 'Don't worry, it'll start up soon. It just takes… one moment…' He hit the side of the video monitor repeatedly, as if that would clear the screen of the squiggly lines jumping across it.

Zintle fidgeted in her seat. This place had gone beyond getting on her nerves, it was under her skin. It would've been simple to blame it on the gloom that had hung over The Grotto since the murder happened, but she couldn't lie. Months beforehand something had been following her around, building in her chest, eating into her slowly. A sadness, a dissatisfaction. She was better than this.

15 more days. Just 15 more days…

'Aha. There we are.' The monitor came on. Trevor brightened, then quickly rearranged his face, as if he'd remembered their meeting was of a very grave nature. 'This footage might be disturbing, okay? But it's important you see it. Watch the screen, please,' he ordered, making the two-finger "eyes over here" point at her then aiming it at the television.

Zintle fought a swell of irritation, the feeling tightening into unease. Why had she been called away from her work in such an underhand manner, and not by Mr Gono, who was the only one who ever had a word to say to her, but by this stuck-up Trevor of all people? And why were they alone in the security team's room, with the door closed, surrounded by equipment for the CCTV camera system that the entire staff knew didn't even work? Did they have something on her? Like hell; she hadn't put a foot wrong since she started. They did this kind of thing. Just before Caroline had handed in her notice last year,

The Grotto had suddenly pulled a stunt about her not being full-time staff, and hadn't paid her in full when she left. Was this entrapment? Zintle swallowed hard. She'd been watching a lot of crime series lately. The world was a lot shadier than she'd been aware.

Trevor unpaused the tape. The feed captured inside one of the rooms, in which nothing appeared to be happening. She blinked. The room looked very familiar. When Ms Greenwood passed in front of the camera, Zintle jumped and uttered a tiny yelp of shock. Trevor remained unfazed. Rhonda went about several tasks, then disappeared from line of sight briefly. When she returned, she had in hand a vodka bottle, from which she poured herself a stout drink. She downed with in slow gulps, contemplative as she stared out of her bedroom window.

'There's a lot of that. Here… and here again… yeah, again.' Trevor fast-forwarded and paused to several drinking episodes, only allowing it to run for a few seconds. 'It goes on for days. Evenings were heavier. Then there's this.'

The next bit of taping made no sense at first. The camera switched on when Rhonda was freshly dressed for the day but still fiddling with her fine strands of hair in the mirror. Timestamp: 6.47am. Another stretch of nothing, fast-forwarded. Around noon Rhonda bustled in and searched the room. She found it - a folder and day planner - and bustled out. She swallowed a pill from a container on her dresser, changed shoes to a more modest heel and left. More nothing. Trevor jumped the tape several hours. Through the parting in the curtains, one could see night had fallen. Rhonda, exhausted. Opens the top two buttons of her blouse. Swallows another pill. Disappears into bathroom. Glass of wine poured. Rhonda stares at it long and hard. Shakes head, walks back to bathroom. Comes out quickly, frowning towards the en suite lounge where the door was. Hurries past. Over a minute passes. The tape stopped.

Trevor swapped it with another. 'This is the feed from the angle in the lounge.'

Rhonda walks back in, laughing and trailed by another woman. Dark jeans, black top. Dreadlocks.

'You recognise that woman?' Trevor asked. Without thinking, Zintle automatically shook her head, Trevor's voice a dull echo emanating from far away. True, she didn't really know the woman. But she'd seen her photo in the papers. She was big news lately.

The tape showed their chat, polite laughter. Zintle asked for sound and Trevor shook his head; there was none. Another glass of wine poured; Rhonda sips hers with reserve. Time spools; the conversation grows animated and the laughter genuine. Wine flows freely. Rhonda leaves the room, giggling. Dreadlocks cranes her neck round the door after her, then quickly tips the contents of a nearly empty water bottle into her wine, stirs with her finger. Rhonda returns. More chitchat. Rhonda's eyes droop. She wobbles to her feet. Dreadlocks steadies her by elbow. Giggling, Rhonda waves her away, stumbling to the bedroom.

'You get where this is going,' Trevor said, low and sombre, switching tapes again.

Bedroom again. Rhonda curled up on the bed, fully clothed. The room seems empty. After several minutes, Dreadlocks steps in sight, duvet in hand. Throws it over Rhonda, pokes her gently, then very slowly but clumsily rolls her up, feet and head sticking out. Dreadlocks leaves her face down; Rhonda doesn't stir. More minutes pass. Dreadlocks picks up two pillows, gingerly lifts Rhonda's head, sandwiches it in between, gently presses the pillows together. Rhonda thrashes, feebly, then spiritedly. Dreadlocks, looking terrified, keeps pressing. Rhonda wriggles and tries to kick out; Dreadlocks jumps away. Rhonda twitches, precariously near the edge of the bed. Falls, banging against the dresser. Rolls onto the floor.

'Not much else happens. The intruder, Gaba, tried to finish her off on the floor, and got scratched by Rhonda.'

Zintle had both hands over her mouth. She lowered them and saw they were wet. She wiped the tears properly with her sleeve.

'I'm not showing you this to upset you, or frighten you. We cleaned the personal effects from Greenwood's room before giving them to her family but we double-checked for anything… untoward. I had no idea she had nanny cams in her chalet. She obviously put them up around the time the thefts started, to catch our in-house thief. Do you know what a nanny cam is, Zinzi?'

Battling another flash of irritation, Zintle nodded, sniffling.

'Well, the others didn't, which is why I'm glad I'm the one who caught it. She had two in there, glass figurines, looked like ordinary decorations. They carried lots of footage. I think she reused some of the tape, but yeah, that's some of what's on it.' He looked extremely uncomfortable. 'I know she was really close to you, Zinzi…'

'Zintle,' Zintle said firmly.

'Yes, yes, Zintle, sorry. You cared about her. She wasn't perfect but she was good to all of us. This is proof that the Gaba woman killed her like she did the other guest, but what good will that do? You've read the papers; she committed suicide. Why bring all this up, why drag Greenwood's family into an investigation that didn't even include her from the beginning, y'know? That would be cruel.'

He paused. 'That's… well, that's not all. Those tapes also show Mamello getting up to no good. Pinching things from her room, small trinkets; using her perfume; sneaking her boyfriend in when it was a quiet afternoon and they… had a jol on her bed. Unforgiveable. I can only guess that Rhonda hadn't yet watched it before her demise, or there would've been serious consequences. It also… shows *you*. Not anything bad,' he rushed on when her face changed. 'But after Rhonda died, you brought that journalist into her room, to see the body…'

'*She helped me!* She never did anything, *I* never did anything,' she sobbed.

'No, no, no! It's nothing bad, I promise. If anyone else found out, though, you could be in serious trouble, love. That's why I showed you this, so we could work together.' He squeezed her shoulder. 'You're so responsible, one of our finest housekeepers. But we could use this. If we put these spy cameras in other spots and caught the other staff up to no good, we could tell Motaung. She'd clear out the rubbish and it would help The Grotto. She would know we were good people that she could trust. Team players. It would work in favour of everyone.'

Zintle got it then. Now this secret meeting made sense. The deputy GM post was back up for grabs, soon to be advertised once the media storm mellowed out, and head concierge Trevor Davids had his eye on it. This mampara didn't care how watching that video affected her. He didn't mind shoving her friend Mamello's betrayal in her face. The ladder was there, and he was scrambling up the rungs already.

She carefully moved his hand off her shoulder. The air in the room had disappeared. She rose and walked to the door. 'I never liked sports, Mr Davids. So I'm not a team player,' she said quietly. 'Ms Motaung takes running this place very seriously. So did Ms Greenwood. Maybe those cameras you found weren't the only ones she installed. Maybe she, they, have more evidence about some other people, who knows what, and were biding their time.'

The triumph on Trevor's face crumbled. Zintle walked into the hall and turned back to him. 'I've handed in my notice. Come month-end I don't work here any more.'

———

Before he knocked off that day, Trevor ran his fingers over the tapes and figurines, stashed away in his locker. It was over.

No one else need ever know about them. He thought about the pile of waste the lodge amassed daily, which was collected and dutifully carted off to the incinerator. He rejected the idea as soon as it popped in his head. There was no way he was going to burn this lot. With one vicious sweep of his hand, he dragged it all into his rucksack and zipped it up.

Never discard leverage; never discount a rainy day.

Acknowledgements

Putting a novel together is as fulfilling a task as it is gruelling. Editing that novel again years later is a special brand of punishment, one that ultimately pays off. I'm hugely grateful to everyone who allowed me to impose upon their lives A SECOND TIME in order to push this manuscript through various draft stages.

My special mentions go to:

Angela Voges of Typographica Manuscript (South Africa), who proofread, edited and scoured the manuscript for unsightly lumps and bumps.

D. J. Cockburn, James Murua and Zukiswa Wanner for scouring the early drafts with eagle eyes, punching holes in my story, giving sound feedback and occasionally saving the beast from falling over its feet.

Karl Smith and Stan Peabody, for their much-needed technical insight into software programming and hotel management, respectively. Thank you for allowing me to torture you for hours with my endless questions, and kindly correcting me when it was clear I had no idea what I was talking about.

Samantha N. Ngcolomba, Paidamoyo H. Maenzanise, Siyamthanda Skota, Jite Efuamuaye and Jumoke Verissimo for their help with translations and tweaking scenes.

The Botswana Police Service and the team of forensic pathologists at Princess Marina Hospital in Gaborone, for facilitating a glorious summer of post-mortems. Especial gratitude goes to Dr Kaone Panzirah-Mabaka, who joked that I should spin a mystery around an interesting case of 'suspicious demise' that we worked on. Well, I now have! Thank you for immersing me in the language of the dead and listening to my hare-brained theories.

Lastly and most importantly, many thanks and heaps of blessings to the amazing women of Cassava Republic Press: Bibi Bakare-Yusuf, Emma Shercliff, Layla Mohamed and the entire CRP team. I am grateful for your continued commitment to telling stories that feature flawed, badass women from different regions of this continent. But most of all, for the kindness, patience and support you've shown throughout our professional relationship. Yor tenkyu plentay o!

CASSAVA CRIME

THE LAZARUS EFFECT

H. J. Golakai

ISBN: 978-1911115083

Voinjama Johnson is an investigative journalist for the Cape Town magazine Urban. Her life is a mess and Vee's been seeing things: a teenage girl in a red hat that goes hand-in-hand with the debilitating episodes she is loath to call 'panic attacks'.

When Vee spots a photo of the girl from her hallucinations at a local hospital, she launches an investigation, under the pretext of writing an article about missing children. With the help of her oddball assistant Chlöe Bishop, she's soon delving into the secrets of the fractured Fourie and Paulsen families. What happened to Jacqui Paulsen, who left home two years ago and hasn't been seen since?

The Lazarus Effect is a gripping new addition to the African crime genre from a talented debut author.

CASSAVA CRIME

EASY MOTION TOURIST

Leye Adenle

ISBN: 978-1911115069

Easy Motion Tourist is a compelling crime novel set in contemporary Lagos, featuring Guy Collins, a British hack who stumbles into the murky underworld of the city. A woman's mutilated body is discarded outside a club near one of the main hotels in Victoria Island. Collins, a bystander, is picked up by the police as a potential suspect. After experiencing the unpleasant realities of a Nigerian police cell, he is rescued by Amaka, a guardian angel of Lagos working girls. As Collins discovers more of the darker aspects of what makes Lagos tick—including the clandestine trade in organs—he also slowly falls for Amaka. The novel features a motley cast of supporting characters, including a memorable duo of low-level Lagos gangsters: Knockout and Go-Slow.

Easy Motion Tourist pulsates with the rhythms of Lagos and entertains from beginning to end. A modern thriller featuring a strong female protagonist, prepared to take on the Nigerian criminal world on her own.

CASSAVA CRIME

WHEN TROUBLE SLEEPS

Leye Adenle

ISBN: 978-1911115632

Amaka returns in this gripping sequel to the award-winning *Easy Motion Tourist*, and trouble isn't far behind her.

The self-appointed saviour of Lagos's sex workers, Amaka may have bitten off more than she can chew this time as she finds herself embroiled in a political scandal. When a plane crash kills the state gubernatorial candidate, the party picks a replacement who is assured of winning the election: Chief Ojo. But Amaka knows the skeletons that lurk in Chief Ojo's closet, including what took place at The Harem, the secret sex club on the outskirts of Lagos.

Amaka is the only person standing between Chief Ojo and election victory, and he sends hired guns Malik and Shehu after her. Chief Balogun, his powerful father-in-law also hires a gang of thugs for the job. Caught in a game of survival, against a backdrop of corruption, violence, sex and sleaze, Amaka must outwit them all to survive.

CASSAVA CRIME

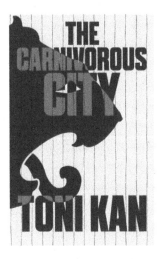

THE CARNIVOROUS CITY

Toni Kan

ISBN: 978-1911115243

Rabato Sabato aka Soni Dike is a Lagos big boy; a criminal turned grandee, with a beautiful wife, a sea-side mansion and a questionable fortune. Then one day he disappears and his car is found in a ditch, music blaring from the speakers.

Soni's older brother, Abel Dike, a teacher, arrives in Lagos to look for his missing brother. Abel is rapidly sucked into the unforgiving Lagos maelstrom where he has to navigate encounters with a motley cast of common criminals, deal with policemen intent on getting a piece of the pie, and contend with his growing attraction to his brother's wife.

The Carnivorous City is a story about love, family and just deserts but it is above all a tale about Lagos and the people who make the city by the lagoon what it is.

Support *The Score*

We hope you enjoyed reading this book. It was brought to you by Cassava Republic Press, an award-winning independent publisher based in Abuja and London. If you think more people should read this book, here's how you can make sure this happens:

1. **Recommend it.** Don't keep the enjoyment of this book to yourself; tell everyone you know. Spread the word to your friends and family.
2. **Review, review review.** Your opinion is powerful and a positive review from you can generate new sales. Spare a minute to leave a short review on Amazon, GoodReads, Wordery, our website and other book buying sites.
3. **Join the conversation.** Hearing somebody you trust talk about a book with passion and excitement is one of the most powerful ways to get people to engage with it. If you like this book, talk about it, Facebook it, Tweet it, Blog it, Instagram it. Take pictures of the book and quote or highlight from your favourite passage. You could even add a link so others know where to purchase the book from.
4. **Buy the book as gifts for others.** Buying a gift is a regular activity for most of us – birthdays, anniversaries, holidays, special days or just a nice present for a loved one for no reason... If you love this book and you think it might resonate with others, then please buy extra copies!
5. **Get your local bookshop or library to stock it.** Sometimes bookshops and libraries only order books that they have heard about. If you loved this book, why not ask your librarian or bookshop to order it in. If enough people request a title, the bookshop or library will take note and will order a few copies for their shelves.
6. **Recommend this book to your book club.** Persuade your book club to read this book and discuss what you enjoy about the book in the company of others. This is a wonderful way to share what you like and help to boost the sales and popularity of this book. You can also join our online book club on Facebook at Afri-Lit Club to discuss books by other African writers.
7. **Attend a book reading.** There are lots of opportunities to hear writers talk about their work. Support them by attending their book events. Get your friends, colleagues and families to a reading and show an author your support.

Thank you!

Stay up to date with the latest books, special offers and exclusive content with our monthly newsletter.

Sign up on our website:
www.cassavarepublic.biz

Twitter: @cassavarepublic #TheScore #ReadCassava #ReadingAfrica
Instagram: @cassavarepublicpress
Facebook: facebook.com/CassavaRepublic

Transforming a manuscript into the book you are now reading is a team effort. Cassava Republic Press would like to thank everyone who helped in the production of *The Score:*

Editorial
Angela Voges
Layla Mohamed

Design & Production
Michael Salu
AI's Fingers